The Homes
We Build
On Ashes

D1519619

We gratefully acknowledge the support of the Canada Council for the Arts and the Ontario Arts Council for our publishing program. We also acknowledge the financial support of the Government of Canada through the Canada Book Fund

Cover design: Val Fullard

Library and Archives Canada Cataloguing in Publication

Park, Christina, 1970-, author
    The homes we build on ashes : a novel / by Christina Park.

(Inanna poetry & fiction series)
Issued in print and electronic formats.
ISBN 978-1-77133-233-0 (paperback). – ISBN 978-1-77133-234-7 (epub).
– ISBN 978-1-77133-236-1 (pdf)

    I. Title. II. Series: Inanna poetry and fiction series

PS8631.A74794H64 2015   C813'.6   C2015-904995-4
                                                 C2015-904996-2

Printed and bound in Canada

Inanna Publications and Education Inc.
210 Founders College, York University
4700 Keele Street, Toronto, Ontario, Canada M3J 1P3
Telephone: (416) 736-5356 Fax: (416) 736-5765
Email: inanna.publications@inanna.ca   Website: www.inanna.ca

MIX
Paper from
responsible sources
FSC® C004071

The Homes
We Build
On Ashes

a novel by
Christina Park

inanna poetry & fiction series

INANNA PUBLICATIONS AND EDUCATION INC.
TORONTO, CANADA

For my family,
JB and Ti

❧1❧

BUSAN FIRE

N<small>O TIME IS A GOOD TIME</small> for a city to burn down, but at around seven o'clock that November evening, it seemed to be as good a time as any. The streets were spectral and an indistinct twilight descended from the sky, like a low and suspicious apparition. Out of nowhere, as if blared out like an official announcement over the curfew loudspeakers, a blood-curdling shriek could be heard across the neighbourhood. It was so loud it rang like a siren and was followed by the clamorous howls of frightened folks running in all directions.

Startled, Nara and the group gathered in her home that evening, spilled out onto the streets, as did neighbours and surrounding villagers. Confused at first, they looked at each other wondering what all the commotion was about, hastily ascribing it to drunken soldiers or a group of mischievous children playing a prank. Suddenly someone pointed to the top of the hill, and then the world stopped, choking on its own folly.

Sun-hi could hear her mother rustling in her room. "*Oma,*" called Sun-hi. "*Oma!* Lunch is ready. Young-min, come and have some lunch!"

Sun-hi had already been up for hours having prepared breakfast for her younger sister, Young-min, and her mother, Nara, long before the abundant rays of the sun had cracked through the broken diorama of the city. But her mother had not joined them. Throughout the morning, the two sisters had played together and pretended to be at school as the sun inched its way overhead with no help from the usual morning winds. When lunchtime approached and her mother had not yet emerged from her sleep, Sun-hi proceeded to prepare the meal without a second thought. Like the eldest child of any Korean family, even at the tender age of thirteen, she was the head of the household in the absence of parents, which did not happen frequently, but maybe more than it should have. *Oma must be exhausted*, thought Sun-hi, and like a good daughter, she had left her mother to rest while she went about the daily chores of cooking and cleaning. Young-min, only five years old at the time, came to the lunch table yawning and rubbing her eyes, already yearning for her early afternoon nap.

Young-min was deaf in one ear and nearly entirely deaf in the other. During an air assault a year earlier, when the sky fell black with the menacing screech of bombers overhead, she ran for cover with the rest of her family, but being so young, her legs were more ambitious than her little feet allowed and she lost her footing. As the Allied bombers flew past, an explosive landed too close to her, detonating with the expected vigour and grand display of spewing dirt and accompanying *boom* that caused her ears to bleed out. As Young-min fell back from the potent force, she looked up and saw a formation of dragons, fierce against the red sky, fly onward. Then, sound faded with the slow thump of her heart as it returned to her chest. Still alive and relieved she was not actually seeing demons, she teetered back to her feet and ran to her mother's arms in a nearby ditch. But as she leapt into Nara's arms, she grew quickly confused at how the world had become so suddenly still and quiet. Though she was not completely deaf — thank God — from then on, she could no longer hear the chirping of the birds that flew the very same sky that would eventually reassume its customary blushful haze. And she was left to wonder what had happened to the clear sound of laughter and the muffled sound of desperate sobs, starting with her mother's.

An aromatic stew bubbled on the stove and the savoury smell of cabbage, soybeans, and chillies wafted through the newly built house, filling it with the comfort and flavour of a family secure. Sun-hi brought the stew, cooking pot and all, to the low dining table, set it carefully down, then headed back to the kitchen to scoop up some rice.

It was then that Nara finally woke. She could see it was already close to midday. It was extremely unusual for her to rise so late in the day, but perhaps not unexpected. She finally had a home and a proper pillow upon which to rest her head. The pillow was very much like the traditional rolled one she had when she was a child, only this one was not embroidered in silk with large fuchsia flowers, but it was similarly hard-packed with raw rice and delivered a restful night's sleep, which was more than enough for her. She did not miss the embellishments. When she had laid her head on the pillow the night before, the dreams she had pushed away for years had rushed back, like the flood gates to a secret land flung open wide, and these dreams had obviously kept her in the place between heaven and earth a little longer.

She stretched her arms first and then her torso, a sweet lingering extension of her body, and joy, even surprise, struck her at how refreshing a simple thing could be. A profound smile must have painted itself openly across her face, for she recognized the stark contrast to the strange mix of sadness and remonstrance that would descend on her only a moment later. She got up to pull back the curtains of her room and paused, grasping at the curtain as a baby wraps its fist around a mother's finger. She still could not believe she had windows in her home, and curtains to match. Even to hope for a piece of clean, untattered cloth seemed forbidden to her not so long ago. She heaved a deep breath, closed her eyes, and quaked gently at recognizing the irony. Years earlier, as a forced labourer, she had never been able to own any of the fabric she wove, only able to touch the silk as it slipped through her fingers, moment after moment, day after appalling day. Those years in the factory, in a land so very close but an eternity away, had stolen part of her soul, made her bitter and angry, and left her to look for God when He could not be found. There, she had often been beaten, nearly starved, and left in dirty, unlit quarters shared by dozens like her in small cramped rooms. Later, she'd heard God was in short supply at that time, absent as much in Asia as He was in Europe, and deaf to the wails of millions lifted up to Him, those pleas ostensibly cast aside to fall upon nothing but ashes.

Nara's brow darkened and her frown was so heavy that it cast a shadow in her eyes as she uttered beneath her breath words of bitter remonstration. But, by the same breath, if one heard her in that brief moment, one might be moved to think that this passionate reaction to a memory gave her an unusual sensibility, for in her spasm of anger, she was still not vicious or fanatical as she had often witnessed or experienced herself. She simply knew she had been wronged. She was born in the year of the March First Movement, also known as Sam-il Movement of 1919, when "occupation" was a dirty word, but "assimilation" was criminal. When she was still very young, Nara's father had explained to her that she was born the year that brave nationalists spoke up against the repressive and brutal colonial occupation under the military rule of the Mikado.

"It was a bloody independence movement," her father had explained. "The nationalists wanted to declare their grievances, marching peacefully..." he paused, "and then were put down." He had not said more than that. His dewy eyes and sombre tone were enough for a young Nara to want to caress her father's cheek and try to understand what all of that meant.

It was not until years later, when Nara was old enough to hear the stories of brutality and violence, beatings and floggings, executions and massacres, that she could fully comprehend the significance of that movement. While the declarations for independence were important, it was the militant reaction to them that showed the true face of the annexation.

She had returned to Busan some eight years earlier, leaving behind a culture that had been entirely unfamiliar to Nara. Indeed, the Japanese culture was in stark contrast to her own. Hers was a complex intertwining of social obligation, familial honour, and community commingled with sharp emotion and boisterous expression. This apparent incongruity forced people to internalize and mediate, to be staunch, steadfast, and unwavering (what Koreans call "*Han*"), but, most of all, to live in harmony with their neighbours, near and far."

Her thoughts meandered and led her to Min-joo, a friend as close to her as a sister — no closer still — for Nara knew she would cling to Min-joo not merely in this life but in the next as well. However, Nara refused to dwell on that part of the past any further. She pushed the memories out of her mind as hard as she could, unable to bear the guilt.

Nara let go of the sliver of the curtain still in her grasp as she pulled it back to let the light into her room. The sky was pale blue, streaked with strips of clouds that frayed at the edges as the gentle wind blew upon them.

On most ordinary days, the sea breeze blew gently across the harbour onward to the heart of the port city, occasionally kicking up in bursts typical of the local microclimate here in the south. Due to the city's topography and influence from the prevailing East Sea winds, the weather conditions changed from one hour to the next, and even from one square mile to the next. But, on this random Friday, beneath a clear sky, the wind lay sluggish for most of the day. November was here and after weeks of cold and rain came a short reprieve and a string of sunny days that warmed up the cardboard boxes, wood frames, and thatched roofs that when summed up together sprung forth houses built on the rubble of former bomb sites. The ramshackle homes had been erected over the ashes not to hide the devastation of the bombs, but simply because there was no other land upon which to build.

Most of the homes were fully constructed stand-alone structures while others were barely remnants of houses clinging to their former selves. These had been built a couple of years earlier by the UN troops. They were *hakobang* houses made out of cardboard boxes so that they could be assembled quickly, easily, and of course, cost effectively for refugees and displaced villagers just as the Communists were descending from the North. Most of the makeshift houses still standing were battered and broken by now, teetering on collapse if not held up by the gasps and hopes of the residents inside. People living in this area hung homemade lanterns and wind chimes that tinkled melodically in the breeze to guide lost ones home, but these were a poor replacement for the light and lost songs of better times.

Though the land was abundant in limestone, which could be used for mortar when ground into powder, these homes were instead sealed together with mud and clay and often an oily sealant made partly from ox dung — highly flammable, but of course, they did not know it at the time. The homes were built huddled together like starving, shivering children for much the same reason: to retain heat, share misery, create community, and survive.

If it were not for the autumn winds, a smell of swamp and sea would have hung in the air of this ocean-side city. The waters had receded earlier than usual that day, so far withdrawn in fact, they left bare several rows of sand banks, sadly none of which would be high enough to save the city from a tsunami should one suddenly hap upon its shores.

Unlike Seoul, which despite the war was already a sprawling vibrant capital by the end of the Korean War, Busan was considered the poor cousin of the south. But Busan had once been a beautiful metropolis, abundant in colour and fine regalia. You could almost still see streams of brightly-coloured ribbon from women's *hanbok* knots rising in the wind, fluttering like a wild and magnificent display of kites. The streets too had been filled with beautiful women, both noble and common, in deep blues, bright reds, fuchsia, lemon yellows, and emerald greens, accompanied by men wearing pure white baggy garments and wide-brimmed black horse-hair hats. Commingled together, it was a remarkable blend of jubilant resplendence and sublime simplicity mimicked only in nature by the exotic birds of the Amazon. The air would have had the pure smell of sea and sand, of salt and abundant fish, unpolluted by visiting ships and greed lubricated by oil and corruption. The activity from the shores had delighted even the most delicate and obstinate, whether snub-nosed or cosmopolitan. The scenes in the city had once been the sight of fishermen, servants, and sophisticated society, living there or vacationing, allowing themselves to be swayed by the elements of the sea, to stand at the edge of precarious abandonment. It had thrived as a fishing town, thanks to commerce and good repute.

Over the centuries, like any port city, Busan saw its share of sailors and adventurers, would-be conquerors and curious onlookers, and it welcomed or turned back all manner of wizardry, concoctions, potions, notions, garments, coloured stones, and fierce dragon-like weapons. Marvels and terrors of the manifold earth attempted many a time to land on the shores of the city, introducing themselves as ideas, kindling fantasy, kindling tyranny. Busan refused most of those grossly unwelcome advances for millennia, but at one point, when it was weary and thoughtful, fatigued by the continual tide of wooers and at once distracted with its back turned against the sea, Busan was seized upon and ravaged. Enemies smelling disenchantment stole upon Busan again and again until it turned from strong heroic keeper of the gateway to tattered victim, sadly succumbing to persecution.

Now, after decades of reproachful abuse and downtrodden first by the shadowy swords of samurai ghosts lonely for purpose, and then the treads of a legion of ten thousand boots, there was a sorrowful ambience in the narrow streets and shanties.

Now, if one walked in the narrow dirt lanes, the dystopian crowds would feel oppressive, and the longer one walked, the more one was in torment. The noise of the city — the constant hum of military trucks, the loud shouts in unfamiliar languages that boomed across the encampments, and the eerie groans of its melancholy inhabitants — could both agitate and enervate even the most serene or disengaged to seek justice, regardless of hidden and obvious obstacles. The city was inimical to good health with roads slippery as mucous, fever-breeding vapours rising with the heady steam from the streets, the gloomy skeletal faces of its populace, and its clusters of dilapidated homes.

In Nara's home, however, the stew continued to bubble a little in the middle of the table and lifted its savoury scent as she finally brightened the doorway — a sliding wood frame covered with rice paper. Though the paper was thin, it was a mighty barrier to the bright dining room, vacant as it was of any furniture except for a low bamboo rectangular table and three new embroidered cushions given as house warming gifts when the home was completed.

Young-min was already at the table but upon seeing her mother, she immediately stood up. Sun-hi was scurrying back to the dining area with three bowls of rice finely balanced in her hands. The first two bowls were comfortably seated in one hand while the third perched precariously between the one full hand and the edge of the other, which had been left partly free in the event a sliding door needed to be opened.

Nara sat down with a carefully cultivated air of indifference. That indifference was not only the expected attitude of the eldest in the group, but an earned right, while the two daughters gave her a respectful bow and salute, and Sun-hi observed the right and proper form of entering the room despite the teetering bowls and sweat upon her brow. The two daughters had thus made this simple act of sitting down together for lunch ceremonious and filled with such respect and sense of duty, that one would be left with no doubt that their culture was steeped in ancestor worship and Confucian order, no matter the barbaric conditions of the outside world. One did not have to subscribe to the old Confucian religion of centuries past, in fact, by then, most did not. Yet the teachings were so embedded within the culture and hierarchy that it permeated every aspect of everyday life and that had been genetically encoded into the Korean psyche over a thousand years. It ran deeper and stuck harder than the thick sticky air from the sea on hot summer days and neither a blow to the head nor a rewriting of the history or the attempt to render the language obsolete would be able to change that.

Refreshed and alert, Nara looked upon this simple meal and quietly pondered the notions of faith and believing, God and unanswered prayers. These were lofty considerations during a simple lunch, yet important to Nara, for this evening it was her turn to host the monthly committee meeting that rotated from one church member's home to another's. The meetings were held to go over the administration of the church as well as to socialize outside of the rigid religious setting. But, it was not so banal as that, as this was also the first time Nara would host members of the church in her new home, this home for which she had long struggled. She would take this opportunity to express her gratitude to the very people who saved her family years ago by giving them refuge in the basement of that church when they were emancipated at the end of the Occupation and returned to their homeland.

The church itself was founded by Irish and American missionaries who had probably been Presbyterian. But it was, in part completed by American GIs who had instead most likely been Catholic. At the time, there seemed to be a large Catholic contingency among the solider population, evidenced by the way they crossed themselves at the sight of death. And there was a lot of death and so there was also a lot of crossing.

Busan was a rolling landscape of hills and shallow valleys that together surrounded a harbour. The church could have been constructed anywhere, but it was ultimately built at the summit of the highest visible hill in the city, so the steeple could be seen from almost any vantage point for miles around. It was eventually turned over to the local Koreans, a large number of whom converted to the "the religion of the east" (east in relation to Korea, of course) in the late 1800s and early 1900s when there was a concerted campaign to convert and christen a wide swath of Asia. Though the campaign failed utterly in certain countries where the notion of "saviour" was so wholly foreign and culturally discordant that it never had a chance, the doctrine of saviour and resurrection was desperately needed in Korea and thus the religion thrived.

Nara's new home was the manifestation of this religious fervour as it had been miraculously built by her, and members of the church, in only a few weeks. It was as if the home was born out of one breath. Yet everyone who knew Nara knew it was sheer endurance and tenacity of purpose that were the tools that built her new home. And if endurance and tenacity were her tools, then her heartache and tears were the bricks and mortar.

As the three ate, there was an unfamiliar serenity at the table. "We'll go to the market today," Nara stated bluntly, without a hint of emotion but loudly and clearly enough so Young-min could hear.

The girls sat up excited. They did not often go shopping, particularly for special food, but they knew tonight was a special occasion. Nara had been planning the meal for some time, and had prepared many of the key dishes in advance, having for several weeks socked away small sums for this very purpose. The *kimchi* had been fermenting for days already, and the homemade bean paste from the best soybeans she could source had been in jars for nearly a month. Today, they would splurge on some fresh vegetables and whatever good meat they could find. And, if they were lucky, they might be able to find an *ajumma* in town who might have some sweets for sale made from boiled, pulled rice, a rare and glorious treat. The girls could not hold back their anticipation, and Sun-hi almost let out a tiny squeal, but was quick to observe her mother and limited her response submissively. Still, it was clear all three shook with animated liveliness and looked as if they wished to flee haphazardly from their usual composure, but of course, they carried on with as much indifference as they could muster, finishing lunch, removing the plates, and washing the dishes, first.

The streets were bustling and crowded, particularly as the sun was out for the first time in days and people were anxious to be reacquainted with it. The long familiar streets were a coalescence of uniform, yet uniquely divined homes, gables, and turrets. The town arcade was in disrepair, though still housing the covered market, but it was better to shop in the open-air market where there was a mild current of air wafting pungent aromas of food in-between faint intervals of sweet flowers and fragrant incense.

The three dodged through the melee, starting at the point where the cacophony of clucking birds and insistent peddlers began. It was obvious that all three would have liked very much to take their time strolling past the different vendors, chatting with the weavers and bloody-handed butchers hanging out their wares, and catching up on town gossip. But time was waning and the sun high in the sky looked heavy and ready to drop below the horizon with only a moment's notice.

Clutching the skirts of their dresses to move faster and more nimbly, they fluttered from one vegetable stall to another, from one merchant to another, and puffed hastily past interesting but extraneous distractions. Then, all of a sudden, Nara stopped cold. As she halted, the girls trailing behind slammed into her back unable to stop quickly enough as there was no itinerant warning.

Nara stood frozen for a moment, but only a moment, regaining her composure almost immediately. She thought she saw a woman who looked familiar to her. Or, more correctly, she thought she saw earthenware that was familiar to her, made with the same sure hand and distinctive craftsmanship she had seen many years earlier. But, when a man at the table coaxed her close, and she was able to have a good look at the woman sitting behind him, she realized it was not the same artisan and she carried on as if it was merely an unnecessary break in an intimate dream.

The girls still tucked in behind Nara, confused for a moment, recovering as soon as they saw their mother scurrying forward in double-time, as if to compensate for having stopped so abruptly.

Having found what they needed, the girls and Nara scampered along the harbour and up the steep and windy dirt road to their home with its ivory walls with black rounded shingles, standing close to their neighbours' houses. Shaped like a perfect square, it was reminiscent of one of the quadrants of Nara's childhood home.

In those days, in an odd inversion, it had been the poor who lived on the hills and had grand views of the city and the harbour below. Why the destitute had been relegated to the higher climbs of a city was not clear, but nevertheless, her new home, despite the similarity in shape, was still in stark contrast to the home in which she grew up, which was a large, sprawling, old ancestral home, possibly the finest house in all the town. Each time she climbed up the dirt road to her new home, Nara felt a little worn and was ever so slightly worse for wear, more so from the memories that came back during the ascent than the walk itself. But she always found a lightness in her step when she came upon the threshold of her house for this was not an inheritance; this was the house she had built with her own hands.

It was already around three o'clock by the time they deposited their treasures and trophies from their hunt onto the stone slab on the floor in the kitchen. Nara and the girls set off to work right away, peeling and chopping vegetables, carefully removing the fat and chewy portions off the beef and chicken before cooking them, cleaning the rooms, setting out plates, washing and making the rice and preparing their garments.

As is always the case, the guests were not coming for dinner. They were coming to meet and discuss church operations and administration and catch up on the membership. However, it was absolutely expected (and not expected at all) to offer and serve food to all guests, enough for a meal plus a second or even a third helping. It was customary, but in an odd distortion, not customary at all. This part of the social order was exceedingly confusing, but unequivocally clear: serve lots of food, always.

A group of people in one's home can be bewildering at first sight. As people arrived, there were the customary bows and praise, compliments and flattery, all part of the tribal dance and cadences of any well-bred social order careful not to tread too far into puffery or sycophancy, but far enough to meet the required amount of social and hierarchal obligations.

They gathered in what would be a drawing or living room and started the evening with sepulchral prayer. Though the meetings always started off somewhat sedated, it never took long for familiar friends to warm to each other, and quickly, the lively group found itself again.

What was unusual about this group was that it was a mixture of the traditional Korean hierarchy of landowners, scholars, peasants, and servants, from the highly intelligent and articulate to the uneducated and simple. It was unusual for such a wide swath of society to mingle together like this as if all were equal. Perhaps this was in large part to the fact that this was a church group, which by nature promulgates the underlying conceit that everyone has an equal chance at salvation. But more likely, it was because the Korean War had managed to eradicate centuries-old hierarchies and societal barriers making for a more level playing field for all individuals, no matter the ancestral bloodline, sort of.

"Obviously, Stalin was wrong," said Mr. Poom, an educated elder and new guildsman who helped others find funding or loans. "It was his veto at first that was the major deterrent and then Kim Il-sung, the slug, persuaded the Soviets and the Chinese into a war that they didn't seem to want. He must have convinced them somehow."

"Yes, it's reported he promised a swift campaign. Stalin probably saw big strategic gain and small risk," the Pastor chimed in. Nara was surprised to hear the Pastor talk about politics so readily.

"But," Mr. Poom explained, "this inextricably grotesque outcome resulted in the split of our country, it seems both Kim Il-sung and Rhee Syngman had failed in their designs to see the Peninsula unified. Ach, it was doomed from the start. It was all for nothing."

"Nothing more than to consolidate their own party's hegemony and remove each other as a threat," said the Pastor.

"The Soviets and Chinese didn't know what they were doing," Mr. Poom declared, dejected.

"Hopefully, history will tell the right tale after all of this," said Nara. The others nodded.

"Speaking of that," said Mrs. Noh. "I saw that teachers are still using some of the textbooks from the Occupation in the schools, most being unable to replace them with our earlier versions, or at least, not yet. It seems no one has had sufficient time to rewrite the textbooks properly to the original narration," she said sadly. Mrs. Noh's former occupation as a dancer was not well representative of the fine pedigree standing she had as an educated professor. Female entertainers were brandished as being similar in occupation to prostitutes, but no one in the room dared think that or felt this way about Mrs. Noh. Mrs. Noh had danced in a ballet in London at the turn of the century, and she had done this despite having no formal training. It was not clear how it happened, and hers was evidently a small part in the production, but there were newspaper clippings to prop up whatever version should surface one day. This small feat alone made all the difference in the world to her social standing. Indeed, she was a bit of a celebrity, and it gave the group a sliver of pride to know her. This mix of charm and cultivation made for a refreshingly sprightly element in what would otherwise be a rather boring group of grey pantaloons and dowdy dresses.

Except for Mrs. Pyon, of course, who by her nature brightened even the most dour of places.

"Yes, those books are as pitiable as the sight of artful propaganda misleading reasonable faculties," replied Mrs. Pyon with a little acrimony. "Those responsible for this should remove them immediately. The tender minds of our young must be nurtured carefully," she added wistfully. Mrs. Pyon delighted this small society with her wit and chirpy appeal that bordered on flirtation but never went far enough to cause any harm. A daughter of a nobleman, she had been properly educated like Nara.

"What's that?" replied Mr. Suh, a rather low-minded, highly practical Machiavellian. He feigned to be hard of hearing sometimes so he could buy a little time to think about what to say next. He was a businessman, not always shady, but not always straight either.

"Misleading versions," Mrs. Pyon spoke up.

"Ah, what a corruption," stated Mr. Suh rather dogmatically.

"I was not saying that, Mr. Suh. Creativity is not corruption," corrected Mrs. Pyon. "Bastardizing it is. Propaganda, Mr. Suh. Propaganda."

The other dozen or so in the group nodded their heads again.

"Ach! What good is art and literature if it can't take up arms?" declared Mr. Suh trying to comment on the subject but instead only managing to confuse it. "The whole sickly aristocracy with their art and their letters," he mumbled, then caught himself as he remembered that many in the room were from well-bred *yangban* families.

He has a lamentable lack of logic, thought Nara, scrunching her face in disapproval of Mr. Suh.

"I don't think you can blame any of our own ruling class," asserted Mrs. Noh. "Stripped of title and tithe during those difficult times, I may be deluded, but much of our nobility probably had nothing to do with the reinterpretation of our history." A few in the room squirmed uncomfortably, for the truth was unclear. Indeed, how much of the insurgence, of the annexation, and of the subsequent Occupation was helped and propped up from the inside? No matter what, there were always cowards and panderers and profiteers at every turn.

"I might hesitate to say, Mr. Suh, but I believe you do not intend to disorient things like this. You're talking about art? Whatever is original, including our stories, our art, our history, and so on, ought to be carefully restored and preserved, not washed away like yesterday's dish water," Nara said. "And, if there was any wrong-doing by our own ruling class, this will be rooted out. The truth will surface and shame will fall on them."

"Yes, yes, of course," agreed Mr. Suh, correcting himself with a grumble and shrinking with an inkling of cowardice and stupidity.

"Let's read from Exodus, shall we? Chapter 15: "The enemy said, I will pursue, I will overtake, I will divide the spoil; my lust shall be satisfied upon them; I will draw my sword, my hand shall destroy them. Thou didst blow with thy wind, the sea covered them: they sank as lead in the mighty waters," read the Pastor.

The Pastor was new. He was the assistant minister to the reverend emeritus who had occupied the pulpit for many years until just last year. The previous reverend, the one who had given Nara's family shelter and helped her bury her husband, was older now and had decided to retire, feeling he was not as agile, both in body and in mind. The new reverend was a benevolent shepherd of this eclectic and intelligent congregation. There was no doubt of his faith and his good intentions, but to Nara, he was disappointingly bourgeois, like one more tied to the earth than one dangling from heaven.

The evening meandered over a variety of lively discussions and in-between the friends feasted on the sumptuous meal Nara and her girls had lain out before them, which was of course, *not* dinner. One could not deny, though, that all of this was just the pretext to having a convivial gathering, while remembering occasionally that they were there to praise God and thank God and ask God or blame God.

As the evening continued within the walls of Nara's home, in the rest of the city, there was an eerie, unearthly stillness. The streets took on a ghostly pallor and then without warning, as sudden as a nightmare stealing upon night's rest, an immense commotion rustled in the neighbourhood accompanied by high-pitched screams and shrieks.

Struck, Nara and the group ran out onto the street and looked up to the heavens. If hell had not already landed on their shores earlier, then surely, it had arrived now. From a distance, a bright tangerine hue rose up vertically and trailing behind it was an immense billowing black cloud of smoke and heaving breath. The fire looked like it was very far away, surreal and dreamlike with a conspicuous nightmarish residue.

At once, several of Nara's guests and church members abruptly started running madly in the direction of the fire. Their homes were in that direction. They ran as swiftly as they could with neither breeze nor angels to help them, screaming the names of their husbands or wives or children who had been left there.

Others scattered in various directions unable to cope with the sight of the rising flames and the red anger that lay below, fearful they would be consumed. Nara realized the homes of her friends were under threat by the ominous, glowing dragon. Taken aback by this cruel iniquity, she despaired for her dear friends who had helped her so. In shock, she stood frozen for what seemed an infinity. She was lost in a cumbersome daze, so heavy it took severe tugs on her arm to bring her alight.

Looking down, she blinked slowly at a pleading Sun-hi who had a distinct cold fear reflected in her eyes. But Nara was anxious to do something to help her friends and pay a debt she felt she owed.

Nara could not judge how far the rising smoke was. And even though the billowing black cloak was directly in front of her eyes, it still seemed very far away. When she lifted her arm to the heavens in the direction of the flames, the fire seemed untouchable. By this, she estimated, it was likely too far away to touch her own home.

She could not fathom with what trickery a fire could move, like evil entering a soul, unpredictable and raging. It could seep in without being noticed and spread like a disease, wreaking havoc and hell in one fell swoop. But because the demon flickered between sight, sound, and smell, using distance to hide and deceive, Nara felt calm and unthreatened for her own home. She did not perceive danger.

"Stay put, Sun-hi. Don't go near the fire. Stay home and take care of your sister. I will be back soon."

"*Oma, Oma*! Where are you going? Where are you going?" sobbed Sun-hi.

"Stop! Sun-hi, you must be strong. You're the eldest daughter. Show some courage," scolded Nara. "Stay here and watch your sister. You will be safe."

"Don't leave us, *Oma!*" Sun-hi cried.

"Look," Nara scolded again and lifted her arm towards the direction of the fire, "the fire is far. It will not come here. Now stay with your sister. I must go help our friends. They need my help. Stay here!"

"But..." Sun-hi sobbed. It was too late. Nara rushed off in the direction of the homes of her friends and disappeared in the cloud of kicked-up dirt and dust.

"I'm afraid," Sun-hi finished saying.

Sun-hi ran inside and waited for Nara to return. Some time passed, perhaps two or three hours, and the initial chaos outside lulled into sombre reflection. People were no longer running and scrambling in all directions but instead assumed the role of curious observer of the raging mammoth in the distance. Some looked up, some looked down, some looked inside themselves.

A quiet blanket descended over Sun-hi's neighbourhood and everyone seemed to retreat into their homes as the darkness of night thickened with only a night-light glow coming from the distance. Some neighbours continued to wander aimlessly. But it was as if the dust had settled and a ghostly calm had been restored.

Even more hours passed and both Sun-hi and Young-min had fallen asleep.

They were woken by shouts. "FIRE! Run, Gi-young! RUN!" a mother yelled at her child. Sun-hi jumped up and ran to look outside. Men and women and children were running wildly down the street immediately in front of Sun-hi's home. There were women screaming, men and children howling, and a shrill fear filled the air. It was a tumultuous chaos that seemed to swallow the outside whole.

Sun-hi's face lost all colour, and in a pale daze, an expression of absolute terror drew across her tiny face. The fire that was once a distant nightmare in the sky was now rapidly approaching the house. It was not far away. It was here. It was monstrous and ugly like a giant goblin. It was only a few houses away and was about to land with fury upon Nara's doorstep. Sun-hi started to shake uncontrollably. With adrenalin rushing through her body, she ran to sleeping Young-min.

"Wake-up!" Sun-hi shook her younger sister who, fast asleep, was unaware of the fierce, and violent demon outside. "Wake up, Young-min!"

Young-min roused and though she could barely hear the raucous outside, she clearly heard the desperate screams of her sister. She rubbed her eyes, groggily rising up out of her slumber. "What?" she asked with a mix of muffled speech and motion of hands. "What's going on?"

Sun-hi yelled, "Fire! Young-min!"

Young-min heard. She grabbed the blanket that was covering her and ran with her sister as fast as her legs would carry her, faster this time, in fact, than during the air raid when she lost most of her hearing.

As they crossed the warming slab of the stone floor of the kitchen, Sun-hi suddenly felt an urge to grab something from her home. She wanted to salvage something, anything, and save it from the wrath of the approaching fire. Greyish-black smoke was already starting to permeate the house. In her delirium, coughing and with distorted vision, she could not think straight. When passing Nara's room, she did not grab the cash that was hidden under Nara's rolled pillow or the lacquered jewellery box on the vanity. The box did not really have any jewellery in it, only a few trinkets and photos, except for one precious piece: Nara's wedding ring.

Instead, as the girls dashed, Sun-hi focused on the cooking pot she had used earlier that day to make lunch and because of the chaos and adrenalin pulsating through her body, she randomly and completely without thought, grabbed it and only just in time. Flames had licked their way to the roof and already started to eat away at it. The shingles and then the beams started to fall in on themselves and within a minute or two, the entire house collapsed, just as Sun-hi and Young-min spilled out onto the street in front, almost trampled upon by stampeding neighbours.

Homes all along the street were scorched and turned to cinders almost instantaneously.

In great gulps, Sun-hi and a sobbing Young-min could see the fire devouring everything in its path and ebbing like a brilliant orange-and-red tide. The fire poured over the roofs and eaves, systematically bulldozing down each street while the smoke billowed higher, accentuating the darkness of the sky.

As villagers ran, they too grabbed anything they could find — blankets, old clothes, sacks to smother the flames — trying, in vain, to save some of their belongings before they were quickly engulfed in flames. One woman tried to hold onto some small traditional metal boxes but she was forced to drop them when they became too hot to hold. Others reached for treasured embroidered blankets, lovingly handmade, yet others grabbed small wooden masks carved by ancestors. Finally, they simply reached for anything that was not already smouldering.

Sun-hi and Young-min limped as quickly as they could to an open area where they collapsed and dropped like sacks heavy to the ground, panting, sweating, covered in soot. There, they waited for the dawn to come.

Not far away, Nara sank down amongst the flames, which were as angry as the fire in her eyes. She was not aware at this time that the fire had devoured her own home as well. She wept for all her friends, and everyone she knew in the neighbourhood who had lost everything.

It was only as the fire continued to consume that the fear seeping through the nooks and cracks in the neighbourhood became chaos unleashed. A madness descended on some parts of the city while those who had lost their homes earlier in the evening crept along the streets like zombies. They hobbled back and forth entirely off balance, lost and hopeless and no longer fully conscious amongst the living.

The wind, which had been sluggish earlier in the day, was now energized by the frenzy lifted in the air like a sacrifice. It was the wind that carried the fire feverishly through the city like a raging succubus seeking revenge, tearing wildly through the streets of the city.

Then, finally, perhaps as a result of God's wrath or regret, near the dawn, the wind suddenly changed direction, as if to set a grievous error right. It poured back over the ashes and eventually extinguished itself as if full of remorse. The way

the wind changed direction was an about-face of destiny —
incredible and garish as any nightmare turned sweet dream.

A solemn stillness reigned when the morning arrived. Thousands
of houses were now reduced to mere dust. Nara had a severe
distaste in the mouth, likely from the poisoning ash and smoke,
along with an unbearable pressure on her temples. She had
heavy hands, a beaten body, and a broken heart. Her spirit was
worn down to the nub, raw and calloused, with nothing left to
keep her from feeling the blindingly painful sting of her tears
as they streamed down her cheeks. As her empty eyes gazed
across the wasteland, she pondered the mysterious incongruity
that must come to subsist between the individual human being
and universal law. Her waking senses proved worthless to her
and all of the world seemed insubstantial and irrelevant. Why
did it all exist? For what purpose?

Smoke hung low in the air and the dawn's pink sky was the
only view left.

When the morning light broke through the blurry ink of twilight, the girls returned back to where their house once stood
and waited. As Nara staggered back, she saw the crumbled
remains all along the streets in her neighbourhood recognizing everything and yet seeing nothing. And so, even before
reaching her home, she already knew there would be nothing
left. There was not even the hope that hers would be the only
one left standing, and she was right. In the quiet dawn, Nara
took short stumbling steps towards her waiting daughters as
if drunk and blind and mad. She bent over mechanically to
pick up the cooking pot Sun-hi had dropped by her side, her
hands open in despair.

The cooking pot was the only thing salvaged from the fire.
The only thing left from her years of toil and hard work. The
three flew into each others' arms and clung to each other for
dear life. There it was. Everything and nothing. The immense
injustice, heartache and pain were palpable. How could this

happen? After all they had gone through, after all they had survived, only to be knocked down again and again by a merciless and vengeful God. He had taken everything from them: their home, their dignity, their chance at a life.

Holding each other, the three wept tears so bitter and pain so raw, their hearts felt like they were being squeezed from the outside and punched out through their bodies. The salt from their tears seemed to crystallize and drop like diamonds on to the dirt and ash below. After a long, silent pause, they opened their eyes and blinked from the still bellowing wafts of smoke. Sun-hi let out a little cough. Young-min stumbled, and grasped tightly on to her mother's skirt so as not to fall.

Nara looked up, took in a deep breath and let it out slowly, resigning herself to the moment. She held up her chin. She held out the pot to Sun-hi who took it back, then Nara searched and grasped for the hand of each daughter. She held their hands tight, knowing that what she held in her hands was all she had in the world. The three of them, solitary and alone, walked away from the ashes where their home once stood, bereft of everything. They walked several metres, so the home now gone was far away enough that they could not hear it calling out for them. Sun-hi and Young-min could not bear to look back, but Nara looked back to stare at the spot where only a few hours earlier stood the first home she had built with her own hands. Unable to bear the weight of the great incongruity of fortune and loss sitting low on the backs of the already destitute and poor, she collapsed and let out a great wail — so heart wrenching, the angels themselves would have shivered and wept. It was the only vociferous scream she would let out in her life, lifting her agony to a deaf and heartless God. She scratched at her chest and tore at her hair and pounded the ground with her fists so hard it was as if she was filled with the intent to rip open the abyss so it would swallow her whole. All the while, hot tears continued to wash down her face leaving long streaks of misery on her cheeks and a permanent stain on her heart.

Her loss was great, but her grief was immeasurable, and she fell to the ground dishevelled, exhausted, and sobbing into the dirt. She could scarcely let out any words, but between her heavy whimpers, she whispered at the ground, into the very bosom of Mother Earth, "Why?" And this "why" was a "why" for *so many* unanswered questions, for so much suffering. It was a culmination of all those years of pain for her father and mother, for her husband, for Min-joo. But, though she directed the *"why"* as a sincere prayer, beseeching both heaven and Mother Earth for any sense of a reason for all of this, no one answered, and nothing but a quiet void hung in the air.

Her daughters, exhausted, dropped to their knees and stared blankly forward, in shock and fear, struck for the first time by the sheer cruelty of the night. It would be generations before victim would turn victor, and it would be like the wind that night: the tide would turn as quickly and as inexplicably as it had come.

The entire hillside of the city was blackened by fire. That night, the Busan Fire of 1953 raged on for more than twelve hours, leaving 28,000 people homeless and even tens of thousands more by some accounts.

While local villagers, already resilient and vigorous from decades of abuse, started to clean-up, a whole city looked up and saw a church at the top of the hill still standing. The steeple could be seen for miles around, giving many of them hope. Some say that not even a single window was blown out nor one wall blackened by soot or smoke. Some witnesses even claimed that the fire looked like it had literally leapt over the building, as if *it* was fearful of the very wrath of heaven. Many people called it a miracle that the church was left untouched, while skeletal remains of a few standing structures, once called "homes," revealed to the passerby nothing more than a still emptiness inside.

Ꮆ2Ꮆ
SCHOOL DAYS

THERE WERE TENTS AS FAR as the eye could see. The tents were the best they could do, but they were not homes. Still, amongst the destitute and forlorn, there was a force that unified them in their adversity. The hardship they suffered and now universally shared overrode any desire to spiral into depravity and inhumanity. The tents quickly created a community in which its own version of the law could run rampant. Though tent cities can set the bar of human dignity low, and it would seem only natural that this kind of living arrangement would give people reason to defuse responsibility and civility, and succumb to the temptation to victimize each other further, the population would not be dictated to or controlled by what amounted to an unfortunate circumstance. Their collective memory raw, they remembered well the way they were dictated to by a more sinister will a few short years earlier when the Japanese occupied their lands and minds. Through a collective wisdom the nation earned through grievous experience, they knew clearly that Nature had not executed a malign plot against them and this made it easy for them to rise above the catastrophe rather than cower in defeat.

It was true there was constant exposure to the elements: the winds blew harsher, the sun beat hotter, the winters were colder, and the nights were darker. The tent dwellers' skin became wrinkled and tough like leather, their eyes watery and red, their hair crumpled, and their bodies sometimes covered in inexplicable sores, perhaps from frostbite, perhaps from rat bites, perhaps from cockroaches, from disease, from the lack of sanitation, or perhaps from the toxic ash upon which their homes were built.

Yet although there was indeed fear and danger, it could not be otherwise in the aftermath of the fire, the population tried to maintain civility and social contracts. While it was true health deteriorated and water distribution was difficult, the victims of the fire united under the banner of the communion of survivors, the forgiveness of sins, the resurrection of the body, and the reconstruction of life. So, despite failing bodies, rampant disease and squalor, they were still able to maintain a harmonious humanity that is always at the core of Korean society. What else could they do? The tent city mantra seemed to be, "We have enough enemies; we do not need to be our own. And Lord if we are, then love thine enemies."

"*Oma?*"

"Yes, Sun-hi."

Sun-hi was quiet for a moment. It was another bright spring day in Busan without the usual humidity. On the contrary, there was a delicate crispness in the air. The sky above the harbour was a deep blue and the mountains their usual startling emerald green. The slopes were silent, lending the valley some peace that it could borrow but not keep. It was another simple day in the makeshift tent city with no laughter to animate it. The sea could be heard in the distance, but even the waves lapped the shores haphazardly. The mood was generally solemn as it was every day since the fire and as it would be for months and years to come.

Mother and daughter were sitting on crates at the side of their makeshift tent-home, in front of other makeshift homes. The small open space on which they had placed their crates was their only yard and bathroom combined. Nara refused to do her cooking here and moved her pot to the central kitchen that they shared with some thirty or forty other families. Somehow, despite water shortages, they combined rations and made every effort to stay clean by washing their hands and, if possible, other parts of their bodies, at least until they could build proper facilities with the help of the G.I.s, which in truth, they did not really expect to happen.

Everything here was makeshift, and everything was temporary, for if anyone tried to imply or insinuate the "tent situation" was permanent, they would be excommunicated by the group for blasphemy.

"I heard," Sun-hi hesitated but saw Nara was listening carefully. "I heard Joon's *omoni* was going to try to start a school."

Nara looked down at her daughter with interest.

"A school? What do you mean?"

"Well," Sun-hi corrected herself. "Not a school exactly, but Joon's mother was a teacher once, you remember? Well, she wants to teach the children," she said more precisely. "With the way things are, there does not seem to be any hope we can, any of us, ever go to school again," she continued, looking a little dejected. "Joon's mom says it is a waste of our young minds. So, she wants to teach as many as can come."

Nara's face brightened, pleased that the pursuit of education was on her daughter's mind, and still very much alive in the collective unconscious of those living in tent city.

"And?" Nara teased.

"I would like to go," Sun-hi said quietly. "And, Young-min too."

Nara paused and asked, "Where will Joon's mother teach? Her tent is no bigger than ours, with barely enough room to fit her family."

"Yes, *Oma*. She will teach out in the open, at the edge of the city. We'll gather crates or we'll each bring our own, and she will try to find something to write on. She says she will start next week."

Nara did not say anything right away. She paused to give

it just a moment of thought and then replied, "Hmmm," accompanied by a slight almost imperceptible nod. Nara did not look at Sun-hi, but that was enough for Sun-hi. With that small and arbitrary nod, Nara had given her daughter the Korean version of a wholehearted approval. This was fireworks as far as Sun-hi was concerned.

As Nara watched Sun-hi run off to find Young-min to give her the good news, it brought back memories of her own school days. Nara's eyes welled up with tears, the kind that appear when there is nostalgia tainted with the gnawing ache of regret.

School was over on this dry day in 1930. Streams of freshly released students poured through the wrought-iron gates where the group broke either to the left or to the right and rushed off into the distance as far away from the building as possible. The older students slung their books, wrapped with a belt, over their shoulder and loitered along slowly toward home, while the smaller students scooted their way through the older students like a school of krill, trotting happily, playing tag, squealing, and splashing in the puddles, all of them that was, except Nara. Nara was still inside.

Min-joo lingered outside the main door, hesitating over whether or not she should stay and wait or go. Her legs, dolefully indecisive, left her unbalanced, constantly teetering from one side to the next. Her uncertainty, like her wobbly legs, was from waffling between loyalty to her friend and from fear. The fear was palpable. She was afraid of awakening the beast inside the building, redirecting its attention on her, lest it find her guilty by association and be ready to mete out further punishment. Min-joo and Nara had become close friends since they started in what the Germans called *kindergarten*, a word similarly used by the Japanese. Both came from noble or well-to-do families forced to send their children to the state-run school in order to start their education at the proper age. If Nara and Min-joo had not attended the state-run school, they would have had to wait until they were eight years old before receiving a formal education in a missionary-run school or a poorly funded, nearly destitute Korean school. By attending the state-run school, they were able to start at the age of six, and so they did.

As Min-joo waited outside the school door, she heard loud, quick successive snaps followed by crying and whimpering. There were shouts and threatening words of discipline and something about loyalty to the Empire. More snaps. *Snap, snap.* The strikes seemed to let out a familiar hollow flat sound and with that Min-joo knew that Nara was being whipped. The strike landed with a blunt sound that meant Nara was being hit on the back of her legs. Then, a few strokes later, the sound shifted. The whip seemed to land with a louder, lingering *smack* that meant the stick had popped back. Nara was being whipped on her back now. She was ordered not to let out a sound on threat of a harsher beating. It must have been excruciating, but Nara restrained herself, allowing only a whimper that crushed Min-joo. She covered her ears and crouched down until her arms clutched her legs and she was egg-shaped on the ground. Balancing on her heels then the balls of her feet, she rocked herself back and forth. It seemed a long time before Nara finally emerged out the school door, staggering.

Min-joo leapt up and held her friend, careful not to wrap her arms around her back but over her shoulder. She supported her limp body and scurried her down the stairs away from the school, and though Nara's legs dragged, she knew how critical it was to get past the wrought-iron gates as quickly as possible. The teacher would be too lazy to chase after them once they were past the gates and the thought to extend her punishment would pass as soon as Nara was out of sight. So, with all her strength Min-joo pushed Nara past the iron bars.

"You should not have said that," Min-joo said sadly. "If you continue like this, we won't survive."

"He was telling us lies," replied Nara, tears streaming down her face as she limped home.

"We know that, but we must learn the truth at home. Trying to convince them of their tyranny is like teaching a dog how not to eat its own dung," Min-joo said with the nationalistic tone she hears at home, in particular the reference to "tyranny" — a word that most young children her age would know all too intimately by then. "It is bad enough everywhere. We mustn't suffer at the hand of the teacher too."

"Oh Min-joo. We already do. He calls us 'rats' to our face and insults our culture and our history," said Nara. "He laughs at us for being bold and then tells us we're ignorant and stupid."

"He says that 'the Mikado brought enlightenment to us,'" Min-joo said in perfect mimicry of the teacher, complete with official tone.

"Min-joo?" Nara looked at her friend in surprise.

"No, no," clarified Min-joo. "No, I mean that ... ummm, what's the word he used with you today?"

"'Sarcastic,'" Nara recalled.

"Yes, I mean that *sarcastically*." They hobbled along a little more, slowly now that they had made some distance between themselves and the iron gates. Nara could barely walk from the throbbing. Blood oozed down her left leg, but she did not notice it for the pain in her back.

As they walked along, propping each other up, Min-joo added something that must have been on her mind all day long. "My father cannot seem to renew the permit to operate his business. He talks about it every day now. The permit is no good soon and he says every document requires another document and some documents don't even exist. I don't understand any of it, but..."

"But he can't get a license anymore," helped Nara.

"That's right, he can't, and if he can't get a license, he can't operate his business. Soon, he will have to sell or close it,"

Min-joo said softly. "This is what father says over and over when he thinks I'm not listening."

"He will have to sell it to a Japanese immigrant. No one else will be able to buy it," Nara said sadly.

"Of course," Min-joo said, nodding.

"My father tells me that they closed another newspaper," Nara added

"How does he know?"

"In their last issue, the newspaper wrote about how they were forced to close down by decree of the proclamation of something or other," replied Nara.

"Closing another of our newspapers?" Min-joo said. "Oooh, enlightening," she added, *sarcastically*.

At home, after Nara went to bed, her father raged. "I don't send my daughter to school to bow to displays and charts to impress upon her such lies that that island is the oldest and most powerful nation in the world!"

"I understand," Nara's mother replied. "But…"

"They don't really teach that the Mikado is really the divine commissioned ruler of all mankind, do they? What form of barbarism is it to lie to children like that?" he yelled.

"Shhhh," his wife begged. "Shhh!"

"What form of brainwashing is that?" he continued.

"Shhh! Please! They will hear you!"

"I don't care! I'm the head of this household. I am in my own home and in my own country, damn it. I should be able to say whatever I want about my own country!" he bellowed. "I should be able to rage when they beat our children like that! Nara is only a child. A child!"

"Shhh! Husband! I know, I know," cried Nara's mother, looking forlorn and trying to keep her voice down. "Do you think my heart does not ache for what happened? Do you not think I am angry inside? Look, Korean children must bow before the photograph of the Mikado to show loyalty."

"My daughter will bow to no foreign emperor," Nara's father fumed.

"Shhh! Listen!" Nara's mother pleaded. "Listen, while I suffer for what Nara has suffered, we must be cautious for her own good."

"Her own good is not to be whipped by a thug," Nara's father grumbled.

"Husband, stop, please! Listen, I have heard one young boy who refused to worship the image of the so-called 'heavenly ruler,' and he was sent away to prison. He was no more than ten or eleven years old, and in that village, no one has seen him since."

"That's ridiculous," said Nara's father.

"They heard screams from the prison. Coming from a young voice. It went on for hours. Then, for a while, they could only hear muffled whimpers, then, again blood curdling, terrifying screams."

"A boy of ten or eleven?" he questioned. "That is inhumane."

Nara's mother's face went dark, and she fell silent. Then, looking straight into her husband's eyes, she whispered, "Is it really so hard to believe?"

Nara's father also fell silent. Both knew the bitter truth. If this anecdote was true and such a boy existed, and such a boy refused to bow, then indeed there would be no doubt of the punishment. Nara's parents shed tears for the abused boy, now surely dead. They felt sorrow for themselves, and for their nation, and resolved to take Nara out of the state school.

"I will go to the missionary school tomorrow and inquire."

Within a few days of Nara's thrashing, she transferred to a missionary-run school even though her father had to deal with the authorities to withdraw Nara from the state-run school — the authorities wanted all noble Korean children to attend their schools in order to 'enlighten' them — and, more to the point, he had to attend to his shamanistic beliefs. Still, it was obvious to Nara's father that the missionaries were good-hearted men who were inwardly critical of the ruling regime though outwardly neutral. At least, he knew they represented a sympathetic group that would educate Nara in an environment of a "loving God" as it was made evident to him. Though this was not ideal, as it would implant foreign values to Nara, it was more satisfactory to him than the other option. For him, it was important that his daughter receive an education, that she read and write, do arithmetic, and learn about the modern world and its brave new technologies, for he fully believed they would not be occupied forever. When the day came for revolution and release, he wanted Nara to be ready for the outside world.

Within a few days of Nara's transfer, Min-joo followed.

When Nara first laid eyes on a missionary, she was not at all intimidated as she had anticipated she would be. Rather, there was a somewhat comforting familiarity, as if they had met before. But it was not just that. Rather than the alien clothing typical of men from the West, with their European jackets and pants, this man wore a long black robe that gave him the appearance of a monk. Nara had also never met a monk, but at least she had seen them in pictures. In Nara's young mind, the robe the missionary wore lent him a sense of credibility at an age when she could not easily distinguish between an angel and a demon. Her conclusions about him were confirmed as she approached him; he was standing on the stairs that led to the school's entrance like a tall statue, the statue of a god. In hindsight, he was probably not so tall, nor was he a god, but when she looked upon his face there was a chaste perfection of spirit with a unique serenity about this man. It was tenderness that conditioned his disposition, and his soul was quiet. When they were finally within close range, he extended his hand to her in a slow and attentive manner so as not to startle her. She did not know why his hand started to stretch towards hers, so she stepped back a moment. Anticipating this, the missionary, with a reassuring nod, pulled her gaze back to his face, then looked down at his hand. He bent a little and reached for her hand, which lay still by her side. Once he grasped it, he shook her whole arm up and down to exaggerate the motion, all the while smiling a big friendly grin. This foreign gesture filled her at once with a sense of dignity and discipline. It was also funny to have her arm flipped around like that and though her lips were twitching, she managed to suppress a giggle.

To go to the missionary school, she had to wear what they called a "uniform." She did not mind, for although they described the clothes as austere, they were, in fact, not that different from the *hanboks* in her wardrobe, except she felt her *hanbok* or traditional dress, despite its bright colours, was more demure. Her uniform was a half-length white frock, plain and almost intentionally unbecoming in cut, as if she was going to be cloistered away like a nun. The only adornment was a turned-out bib in the back that was also white, making the additional detail and cloth almost negligible for not being able to see it flap in the air. She wore her hair in a traditional manner, split down the middle with each side pulled down smoothly, then tied in a tight bun in the back, which suited the school as well.

At first, the two girls were worried that the school would indoctrinate them into a new belief system that they would have to guard against, but by some strange coincidental ebb and flow that sometimes hangs thick in the universe, the values the missionaries talked so often about seemed not merely vaguely familiar, but resembled those values in their homes and in their tradition. Nara and Min-joo were not sure what to make of that. *Love, respect, family, hierarchy, forgiveness, and above all, sacrifice must be universal,* thought the young girls. *Although, it does not always feel so universal right now.*

What surprised them the most, however, was how the missionaries had learned to speak Korean. Some of the missionaries had almost mastered the language with its ghastly moods, deference to cultural norms, subservience of speaker, and syllabic domination. The girls thought they had wandered into a surreal world. It was not easy to grasp the high, middle, and low forms of their speech and the nuances in tonal adjustments dependent on to whom one is speaking — someone older, younger, or of a higher or lower class. It was a strange thing to hear, and it was an even stranger thing to watch: Korean words coming out of a white man. But it gave them a deep respect for these people who tried so very hard to communicate with them.

As the two girls adjusted to an entirely new school with new and sensible rules, they shimmied their way hesitantly into new friendships. They recognized similarities that were easy to identify: a burdened, overwrought sense of familial loyalty, a hardened displeasure at the Occupation, and a common aestheticism that ran deep. But they were searching more for differences as the germination of young personalities was now beginning for many. Petty differences and jealousy sometimes developed into hostile bickering or worse still, bitter scraps, typical of any schoolyard anywhere. Nara welcomed the normalcy of it. It was an all girls' school yet, with the brutish and sometimes competitive play in the schoolyard, one might think otherwise. Still, despite occasional hostility brought on by stresses unbeknownst, there was a captivating camaraderie that imbued the atmosphere.

Though cut from the same cloth, there was a wide variation of the one culture and one language here. Even more distinct were the varying behaviours and dialects of the girls. There were a few waifs from Incheon; several broad-boned girls from the mountainous province of Gangwon; and rather simple, brash girls from Jangheung region in Jeollanam whose slang peppered their speech. They did, however, fairly represent the rural area from which they hailed, where their families lived, hard-working farmers making an honest living. There were energetic girls, plain girls, pretty girls and refined girls from Seoul proper with Mary-Jane shoes and the hyper-slurred dialect typical of city dwellers. It was easy to identify those from

Seoul by the way they pronounced their "s's." The "s" sounded closer to a "th," as if they were speaking with a lisp. It was an intentional display of overcompensation as city dwellers, wanting to sound smarter than country folk, and believing swift speech would create that impression, ended up sounding thick-tongued. An outsider might hear the way they speak and think the Seoul girls were actually speech-impaired when in fact, by local standards, their enunciation was viewed as eloquent, even mellifluent. In contrast, when the girls from the mid-region spoke, their speech sounded like frenetic whining with unnecessarily long extensions at the end of sentences that culminated in a high pitched tone typical of a *Gyeongsang* dialect. Whatever a mid-region girl said sounded more like a question full of complaint. Nara was from *Daegu*, in the mid-region. It was seen as an unfortunate predisposition, but given her pedigree, she had been taught to cut the high-pitched tone at the end of her sentences, and when she dropped and muted her sentences at the end like that, she sounded authoritative, earning the respect of her classmates quickly. And, thankfully, she did not speak like the Busan girls who sounded like they were singing a love song with every sentence.

Alongside the average girls, amongst whom the most earnest and serious in their study could be easily spotted, were also some obstinate teenage girls who concealed dreams of a life liberated. There was protest in their eyes. The narrow ideas of the current regime only made them crave freedom and the open spirit of philosophy. And when pressed into the service of the great fatherland, their gaze betrayed them, prepared as they were to make the supreme sacrifice in the cause for their freedom. Though they were young, they looked up to the men and women who a decade earlier demonstrated a remarkable degree of courage and devotion in the national movement, who gave up their lives for their country to release it from persecution. Nara's heart filled with respect for those girls who laughed and played like the others and carried on with gossip and frivolous fashion talk and the latest events, but in their hearts, were patriots as wilful as any solider. They were no different than her. Nara knew she was in the right school now.

"Hello Nara," said Reverend Armstrong. "How are you?"

"Ah, *Mok-sa-nim*, pastor, I'm good today."

"I see you and Min-joo seem close."

"Yes, *Mok-sa-nim*, we're the best of friends."

"Indeed," he said gently. "It seems she cares very much for you as you do for her."

"Yes, *Mok-sa-nim*. I would die for Min-joo." The Reverend seemed surprised to hear such solemn words come from such a young girl, but it only took a moment to remember where he was.

"And you both are looking forward to making new friends, I guess?"

"Yes, *Mok-sa-nim*. Some of these girls are inspiring to us."

The Reverend paused and seemed to debate what to say next. "Like you, they love their friends and family," he concluded.

"And their country," added Nara. Then with childlike fluidity, Nara changed the topic. "*Mo-sa-nim*, my father would like to invite you to dinner."

The Reverend smiled and replied, "I would love that. Now speaking of love, can you remember this? 'Greater love has no one than this, that a man lay down his life for his friends.'"

"This and all of the complexity that resided in Korea at the time stemmed from a new world order of capitalism and technology that inundated old Asia in the nineteenth century so the region was forced to transform itself."

"Yes, I see. In fact, we were probably part of that perpetration," said Reverend Armstrong. Nara's father smiled.

"Your English is remarkable, by the way."

"Your Korean more so."

A western-style dinner was served, which was essentially

boiled chicken and potatoes next to some green vegetables. While Nara and her family found the flavours dull, it seemed to suit the two reverends just fine.

"Many Asian nations went through periods of upheaval and left the ruling classes, including emperors and kings, in a state of disarray and their people in a state of tragedy."

"I'm sure we contributed to the disarray."

"I would not agree that religious beliefs contributed to any chaos. I think as observers you may have helped dissuade any further violence. But there is no doubt that during this time of uncertainty and political unrest, Japan found weaknesses amongst its neighbours."

"Including Korea."

"Indeed. And with a view to dominate the region, during the Sino-Japanese War, Japan seized the opportunity to defeat the Qing Dynasty in China, a long-standing ally of Korea."

"Hmmm, and if I know my history, some decade later, in the Russo-Japanese War, Japan defeated Russia."

"Correct, leading to the control of Manchuria, which borders Korea at its northernmost point."

"I suppose ambition bred opportunity, and so Korea was annexed to the Japanese empire."

"That's right," replied Nara's father.

"I suppose we should have known," the Reverend said remorsefully.

"As Americans, how could you truly know what was going on? I doubt you would have tolerated it if you knew the truth."

"I'm Canadian, actually, and so is Reverend McCrae. As any right minded person, how could we tolerate it?"

"Canadian?"

"Yes, as obscure to you as Korea once was to us."

Nara's father smiled again.

"Canada is located north to the United States. We're neighbours."

"Not like Korea and Japan, I hope."

"No, not at all," he said. "Canada and the U.S. have lived in peace for a long time."

"So Canada must be a big country then."

"One of the biggest in the world."

Nara's father looked wide-eyed. "One of the biggest and yet unknown to me. How could that be? Is it beautiful?"

"Very."

"And where in Canada are you from?"

"I'm from a small town in British Columbia, which is a province in the western part of the country, and Reverend McCrae is from Ontario, which is in the eastern part of the country."

"Sounds like you are from far apart."

"Yes and sometimes far apart in too many ways." Both reverends nodded.

"You must miss home."

"I miss fishing. I lived near a beautiful lake. But we are glad to be here because we feel we are truly doing God's work. It is a time of turmoil, and we want our work and prayers to have an impact."

"Indeed, it is a time of turmoil and oppression, I'm afraid. We need all the prayers we can get," Nara's father said kindly.

"As you know, though, I am not a political man. Missionaries pray for all."

"Understood, *Mok-sa-nim*. Understood. A man of religion should not take sides on political matters. It would be — shall we say — inappropriate."

The Reverend wanted to respond to that to clarify his meaning, but he hesitated and decided to remain quiet.

"And Father, why did we never invade them, then?" asked innocent Nara. She had not understood most of what her father had said to his guests.

Her father looked at her stunned by her rather profound question and could proffer no good answer. There was only one Korean mantra he could give in response. He replied, "*Sadae kyorin.*" The words were familiar to young Nara, but her vocabulary was not elevated enough to understand fully what her father was trying to tell her.

"In effect, *sadae* means 'an attendance on the great' and *kyorin,* 'good will to neighbours,'" her father continued, also for the benefit of his guests. He was implying that the Korean mindset with respect to invading other countries did not exist. The cultural aestheticism was harmony and to live mostly in peace or more accurately, "To put it simply, it never occurred to us to go to war," he added.

However, as a landowner and nobleman, Nara's father knew the "best defence, after all, is a good offense." And now, more than ever, no doubt Nara's father harboured an opinion deep within his heart that there should be a national conscience of a more assailing attitude where none existed before. Why his countrymen did not was about as grand a mystery as could be.

There was a loud banging on the door of the school that prompted one of the women missionaries to open the door cautiously. As she did so, a group of rough-looking uniformed soldiers pushed themselves inside.

"We're looking for Reverend Armstrong or Reverend Mc-Crae."

"I'm Andrew Armstrong," the Reverend replied. "Can I help you?"

"We understand that you are harbouring enemies of the state."

"I'm sorry?" the Reverend said.

The other uniformed thugs went from class to class rounding up some of the older girls. The guard shouted at one of the girls, "Where are you from?"

The girl answered, "Seoul," another answered, "Buthan."

"There, liar! You're from Seoul. Go stand over there," and he struck her on the side of the head.

"Please stop! What are you doing?" the Reverend demanded.

"Quiet!" barked back one of the guards.

"Do you have any papers? On what authority are you here?" the Reverend asked firmly.

"We don't need papers," growled another guard.

"You do not have the authority to be here without orders," the Reverend asserted. "I want to see your orders."

"Quiet!"

It did not take long for the Reverend to understand what was happening. As the Reverend made note of the students the soldiers were singling out, his face turned a ghostly grey. They were rounding up teenagers from Seoul and from Jangheung region. He must have heard some of the patriotic whisperings that came from these girls, and Nara recognized every one of them.

A day later, the Reverend went to see the students at the police station.

"They seem well," the Reverend said after he had returned to the school. Nara had seen the Reverend arrive through the main doors and had run to him for news.

She looked up at him and pointedly remarked, "You mean they haven't been beaten yet."

The Revered averted his eyes and nodded his head.

"What did you do?" asked Nara in an almost aggressive tone.

The Reverend said, "I've told them at the station that I had contacted the embassy and notified our ambassador of their arrests. We still don't know if they have any proof of their charges that the girls are so-called traitors."

"They don't need proof, Reverend," Nara said.

"Yes, but by contacting the embassy, it makes things more official. Do you know what that means, Nara?"

"Yes," Nara replied, somewhat reassured. She knew that meant that the police could not mete out any punishment as they wished, especially without any proof of wrongdoing. They needed to follow protocol, whatever the official protocol might be, because they were now being watched by an outsider.

The Reverend offered up a small anecdote to help ease the

tension. "Listen, when I went down to the station to check on the girls, I saw a little boy who was detained for protesting the arrest of his father. I couldn't believe my eyes to see someone so young put behind bars. He seemed about your age, maybe only a little younger, around nine or ten, I guess."

Nara was surprised too. "He was protesting?"

"Yes, right in front of the police station, he was protesting," said the Reverend, smiling.

Nara chuckled.

The Reverend continued. "Then, when he was asked, 'Who put you up to this?' the little boy looked up at the Police Chief, who I'm told is a former captain in the imperial army, and pointed straight at him, shouting, 'There is the man who made me do it!'"

Nara laughed. She would very much like to know that little boy and shake his hand.

"I suppose they were not amused." She paused and shuddered. "What happened to him?"

"I asked the police to let him go."

The Reverend suddenly realized this brief anecdote, meant to put a smile on little Nara's face, could not end happily. He understood that the police had noted a disruptive man inside that little boy, one who would grow up and cause a lot of trouble one day. He could see the urge to quell that now, early, before the child grew up to be an idealist or a radical. The little boy had been flippant and naughty and brave. While it was marvellous, it was dangerous.

There were persistent rumours that at night, imperial guardsmen knocked down doors and hauled suspects out of beds at the point of their bayonets and took these people somewhere in the dark of night from which they would never return or be heard from again. Named by tortured demonstrators, co-conspirators and innocent bystanders alike, they were easy to track down since each Korean had been required to register their names through their local municipal government, and subsequently been assigned a number associated to their identity and whereabouts. This was probably what had happened to the boy's father, and one day, what might happen to the boy. The Occupation had denied them their name, and the disappearance of a people solely identified by a number was thus facilitated.

"And did they let him go?" Nara said suspiciously. She did not trust the police. It was well known that the police were given almost limitless power, accountable to no one, and able to exercise the most medieval techniques of torture and punishment. The force was made up of men of the basest nature, who sought not just easy money, but victims for their sadism. What other explanation might there be for these men to leave the comfort of their homeland to come to a foreign country, under the guise of serving their Emperor, where they were charged to maintain order and keep the peace by whatever means was necessary? It seemed to Nara that the empire, in its infinite wisdom, had sent scum to uphold the law in her country.

"Yes, they let him go." With that, the Reverend got up quickly and turned to his office.

A month after the Seoul girls were released, there was another banging on the front door of the school. The day was bright and hot and the rising sun was beating down on the grounds of the school while the inside scorched from the trapped heat. The day was like any other.

"By Imperial Ordinance Number 229, we are here to close down the school. We have been given reliable information that the school is not following the state curriculum and is corrupting young minds. This will not be tolerated. We also charge that this school is a front and is harbouring conspirators and traitors to the state. They will now be arrested."

"Now wait a minute," the Reverend said in English.

"No English!" the soldier barked, and pushed the Reverend back with the point of his gun, then turned to his right and nodded to the soldiers. The soldiers started to rifle through the classroom turning over desks and throwing books around. Sheets of paper flew everywhere like beat-up wings as they drifted down to the floor haphazardly.

The Reverend started to push back at one of the soldiers, but the uniformed thug thrust an opened scroll into his face. Reverend Armstrong took it in his hand and started to read, and with each line, his shoulders slumped. He looked as if someone had punched him in the stomach, winding him. He was nearly completely hunched over by the time he finished reading the document.

The other missionaries came rushing out of their classrooms as the Japanese guardsmen went from classroom to classroom, ransacking the entire school. The students and teachers huddled in the middle of the main hall, waiting to see what would happen next.

"What's going on?" Min-joo whispered to Nara.

Nara did not respond, then suddenly collapsed with a quiet thud into a heap on the floor.

"Nara? Nara! What's wrong with you?"

Nara's eyes had rolled back in her head, and she was feverish and mumbling.

Min-joo looked over to where the missionaries were guarding the hallway and tried to catch someone's attention.

"Reverend," she said desperately, "I think there is something wrong with Nara."

It was the tale of the magpie and the mountain peaks.

Once there was a girl named Nara who decided to explore her home's surroundings. And so, she started to walk. Without much regard for where she was going, she continued to walk for hours and hours, past hill and dale until the scenery started to take on a rather unfamiliar look with snow-covered rocks cropping up from hidden undergrowth, the landscape now completely cloaked under heaps of snowy blankets. She had managed to climb a precipitous pine-clad mountain hidden in a grey-white mist. There was no rustle, not even the sound of a bird, which heightened her inner apprehension until those feelings passed into actual fear. It was this fear that made her conscious that she was lost and had no inkling in which direction home lay. As she wandered about on the mountainside, nervous and alone, she heard a low grumbling of some creature in pain or in despair. She went closer to where the sound was coming from and saw, to her surprise, a great white bear, crouching down in an awkward position. She had never seen such a creature before. The bear looked as if he was in distress but Nara could not see why.

"Bear, are you alright?"

"Who are you?"

"I'm Nara."

"What are you doing here?"

"I'm trying to find my way home. I got lost."

"This is not your home."

"No, it is not my home. But, are you alright?"

"No."

"What's wrong?"

"I'm caught in this trap."

Nara could not see any trap. She looked as closely as she could without agitating the bear further, but she could not see anything that could be ensnaring the great beast so.

"I'm sorry Bear. How are you trapped?"

"This thread of silk, can't you see? It is wrapped around me, and I can't break free."

How could a thread of silk tie up such a large and powerful creature as this? she wondered.

"Here, if I may approach you, perhaps I could help," Nara offered cautiously.

"Come," conceded the bear.

As Nara got closer, she caught a glint of the silk thread and was able to see that the bear was indeed entangled in its web. Nara let out a deep breath and the thread fluttered, bending to her breath. She looked into the eyes of the bear, which appeared gentle, but they were also hopeless and sad. She was so close to the bear now that she could feel his breath on her, but the thread did not yield to his breath the way it did to hers. She slowly lifted her fingers and intended to pull with all her might at the thread, but as she raised her hand, the thread wafted. So, instead, she wrapped her index finger around the thread and plucked at it. At this, the thread instantly unravelled, freeing the bear.

Immediately, the bear sprang to his feet, fully restored. He puffed out his chest and extended out his body on his four paws, stretching hard. Nara jumped back and looked at the bear with a pondering expression.

The bear immediately thanked Nara for her kindness. "As my thanks for setting me free, let me give you something in return." With this, the white bear handed her a vial of a few drops of water, which, when she looked inside, looked like a wide ocean.

"You wish to go home?" asked the bear.

"Yes," replied Nara. "Very much so."

"The vial of water will help. Take it with you to the next peak," the bear pointed to the second peak in the mountain range. It looked bleak and desert-like.

She traversed to the next mountain peak with the vial in her hand. Though she was tired, she carried on with only the hope of returning home alighting her path.

The wintry scene of the previous peak gave way to a primeval heap of rock wall and air soaking of heat and dust. The heat was hostile and a deathly silence cut the air except for the occasional screech of what was probably an eagle or hawk. Above the skeletal treeline was only the scorching red sun. Nara climbed her way to the top of the peak, and here, she encountered a dragon, though not as enormous as one would think. It lay passive, panting heavily, nearly dead.

"Dragon, are you alright?"

"Who are you?"

"I'm Nara."

"What are you doing here?"

"I'm trying to find my way home. I got lost."

"This is not your home."

"No, but the white bear sent me to this peak. Are you alright?"

"No."

"What's wrong?"

"I'm dying of thirst." Indeed, the dragon looked parched and dry, having assumed a rather brown, dusty hue.

The talking jaws of the beast revealed sharp fangs that could easily take her with one bite, but upon hearing this, Nara immediately pulled out the vial of water the white bear had given her and tilted the few drops into the dragon's mouth.

Immediately, the dragon sprang to his feet, fully hydrated and restored to his former sunset-coloured, throbbing self. He puffed out his chest and smoke streamed out his nostrils at the same time, while little sparks flew out from the corners of his mouth. Nara jumped back and looked at the dragon with a curious expression.

The dragon immediately thanked Nara for her kindness. "As my thanks for quenching my thirst, which will last me ten thousand years, let me give you something in return." With this, the dragon breathed a great fire, which was so large it lit up the peak as if the whole mountaintop was ablaze.

When the flames finally extinguished, there remained, in its place, a golden nest. It was about the width of Nara's arm span and cool to the touch; she was able — though barely — to carry it.

"You wish to go home?" asked the dragon.

"Yes," replied Nara. "Very much so."

"The nest will help. Take it with you to the next peak," the dragon pointed to the third and final peak in the mountain range. It was the highest peak of them all. It gleamed as the sun cast just the perfect glint on the highest point, making it shimmer like an emerald. Nara took a deep breath, thanked the dragon and went on her way.

She traversed to the next mountain peak with the golden nest in her arms. Though her arms were weary and her body heavy, she carried on with only the hope of returning home alighting her path. When she finally reached the top of the third peak, the grass was lush and the air, cool and refreshing. The pine trees smelled of forest purity and the scent fell away into the rising mist. She saw small herb flowers in bright periwinkle and yellow growing on vaulted, swelling caverns and a small waterfall, dropping into a pool not far below. She halted and sat across from the water to quench her fatigue. Then as she sat, she spotted next to the waterfall what seemed like a cave with a door. She lay down the nest, jumped up, and then ran to the rocky steps that led to the door. She climbed eagerly to the door and turned the knob, but she it would not open. It had a large golden keyhole, but she could not see through it. No matter how hard she tried, she could not open the door: she turned the knob this way and that; she pushed the door; she leaned on the door; she punched the door; she even kicked the door with the toe of her boot, but nothing helped.

Suddenly, out of the corner of her eye, she caught sight of a magpie perched on a rock formation next to the wild herbs. He looked rather enormous and out of proportion (as all magpies tend to look) compared to the dwarfish surroundings. He looked at Nara as if curious, and twitched his head this way and that way, but she seemed only to be a momentary distraction. He went back to what he had been doing before. He hopped from one rock to another, then hopped back and forth, and then flew in all directions. It was as if he was looking for something. Nara found his behaviour odd enough that she had to ask, "Magpie, what are you doing?"

"Who are you?"

"I'm Nara."

"What are you doing here?"

"I'm trying to find my home. I got lost."

"This is not your home."

"No, but the dragon sent me to this peak. Are you alright?"

"No."

"What's wrong?"

"Wait, aren't you afraid of me?"

"Afraid of you?"

"Yes, most people are afraid of magpies."

"I just encountered a great white bear and a dragon."

"Yes, but I'm a magpie."

"Indeed."

The magpie grew silent and more curious.

Nara asked again, "What's wrong?"

The magpie willingly responded, "I cannot build my nest. I cannot find the right materials so I'm looking for them." The magpie certainly did look lost and homeless.

Upon hearing this, Nara immediately showed the magpie the golden nest and gave it to him. The magpie was surprised and pleased.

"Ah! What a fitting nest!" The magpie immediately thanked Nara for her kindness. "As my thanks to you, let me give you something in return." With this, the magpie hopped into the golden nest and as he settled, there were, suddenly, great tremors. The entire mountain shook as if the earth quaked. Trees swayed and rocks tumbled. Great slabs of the mountain crumbled down, and Nara fell to the ground from the shaking. The magpie lit up and great flames appeared from the nest, a fire so large it lit up the peak as if the whole mountaintop was ablaze. When the flames quieted — but not extinguished — there was a great Phoenix in place of the magpie.

The Phoenix was magnificent to behold. He emitted a godlike glow and had the brilliance of a thousand jewels. He spread his wings for the first time and it was as if the light on the mountain changed. He transformed himself and his surroundings with such magnificence that Nara fell back in awe. He flapped his wings gently, just to test them, and that cooled the air while the motion sounded like the trumpet of angels and the chimes of children all at once. He remained in the nest for a few moments, and then with his beak, he passed a key to a stunned Nara.

In a resonating, booming voice, the Phoenix asked, "You wish to go home, Nara?"

"Yes," replied Nara. "Very much so."

"Here, take this key. It will open the door to the cave and the path to your home."

Overjoyed, Nara took the key from the beak of the Phoenix. Nara thanked the fearful magpie and went back to the cave as the Phoenix took flight.

At the door of the cave, she took a deep breath, inserted the key that the Phoenix gave her and then she woke up from her dream.

The missionaries, intent on watching the guards carefully as they swept through the school, and keeping a wary eye on the younger students that they had herded into a group, seemed oblivious to the older girls that had clustered around Nara. The one named Eun-hae approached and leaned in close. Nara seemed to be moving her lips, so Eun-hae put her ear to Nara's mouth. Eun-hae gasped and with a strange look pulled away, slowly remarking that Nara was saying strange things.

"What kind of strange things?" asked Min-joo.

Eun-hae leaned in again, straining to understand. A scowl stretched across her face and she weaved her brow, uncertain of what she heard.

"Well," she came up slowly. "Well."

"What?"

"Well, Nara seems to be saying things that I don't quite understand. She's..."

"How can she be talking? She looks like she has passed out."

"No," said Eun-hae. "Noooo. I think, ummm, she's saying things that..."

"What? What?"

"That a *mudang* would say."

Eun-hae said this last part very cautiously as if she could not believe it herself. The older girls within earshot looked at Eun-hae in disbelief.

"What are you talking about?" one of them asked. "Nara is not a shaman."

"It seems to me she is mumbling words in some ancient language," Eun-hae said and shook her head. She waved at Ok-cha who was standing across from her.

"Ok-cha-*ya*, come here."

Ok-cha scurried over. "What?"

"You studied the old language? And Shamanism?"

"Hmm-huh, yes," she whispered back, confused. "Is this the time to be asking me this?"

Eun-hae hurried to the point, "Listen to Nara."

Ok-cha bent her ear close to Nara's lips. After a moment or two, Ok-cha looked up, white as a ghost. Indeed, Nara was in a trance and indeed, both Eun-hae and Ok-cha agreed Nara seemed to be uttering the words of a healer.

"What? How?" beseeched Min-joo.

Eun-hae let out a short exasperated breath. "What I mean is Nara seems to be saying things a *mudang* would say. I think she's wishing spirits a safe journey to higher realms."

"What? That's crazy," Min-joo said.

"Shhhhh!"

Nara's eyes were rolled back and she was still mumbling when suddenly a melody broke from her lips. The older girls looked at Nara with wide eyes, trying to suppress their shock and avoid the attention of the Japanese guardsmen as they trolled the hallways.

"What's Nara doing? Why don't you wake her?" Min-joo pleaded.

"She's singing," said Ok-cha.

"What?"

"She's singing a *dano-gut*."

Min-joo did not know what a *dano-gut* was.

"She's praying to a mountain deity. I know. I've heard my grandmother say these prayers before."

"What?" Min-joo was in disbelief. "That's absurd. Nara wouldn't know of such things."

"Doesn't her father practise Shamanism?" asked Eun-hae.

"Yes, but..."

"She must've heard some of these chants at home."

"Yes, maybe," agreed Min-joo. "Yes."

"She's probably just in a state of shock," justified Ok-cha. The girls all nodded. That seemed to help explain this odd behaviour.

"We need to rouse her. The soldiers will be back soon."

Ok-cha grabbed Eun-hae's hand. "That will not be safe for Nara."

"We have to rouse her or it won't be safe for any of us."

Min-joo shook Nara gently by the shoulders, whispering her name and pleading for her to wake up. Within a few seconds and without so much as a twitch, Nara sat up and asked, "Who are those men?"

Min-joo stared at her dear friend for a moment and said, "They are the same men as before."

Nara nodded. She recognized most of them.

"Do you know what just happened, Nara?" asked Min-joo in a slow and methodical tone.

"What do you mean?"

"I mean, do you know what just happened to you?"

Nara, confused, looked back at Min-joo. "What do you mean?"

"You, you — you looked like you were just in a trance," Min-joo stuttered.

"What?"

All of a sudden, there was a scream down the hallway. "They are taking away Sook-min and Hye-kyo again!"

"And Hae-soo."

A loud murmur of protest shuddered through both the students and the missionaries. "Where are you taking them?" demanded one of the Reverends.

Min-joo reached for Nara's arm and clutched Nara's hand with her own shaky one. Nara trembled. There was nothing they could do.

As the guardsmen marched by, they rounded up some of the older girls and led them to the back of the building where they were forced on to waiting trucks while everyone else, including the younger girls and the missionary teachers, were pushed outside to the front of the school.

"By the order of the imperial military and sanctioned by the authority of the government, promulgated on such and such a date," shouted one of the uniformed guards, "we are ordered to close down this edifice and ask for the occupants to depart immediately for their safety." And with that, a few days later, the missionary school was burned down and the missionaries, including Reverend Armstrong, were sent back to Canada.

At some point between reading the missionaries' biblical tales, as well as the traditional Korean fairy tales about unmannerly tigers, imps, and monsters soothed by persimmons, Nara had succumbed to what she feared most upon attending missionary school. To this power known as God, Nara surrendered with all the passion of her youth. A faith in Him rewarded her with all He had to give: forgiveness, revelation, salvation, or at least the knowledge of all these intangible things. But in return, there were things He expected from her, wanted inexorably from her: obedience, unwavering belief, and immovable faith, and if necessary, to lay down her life for Him. What she had to give God in return seemed more difficult as the expectation was without exception; it was obstinate and firm: forgiveness for obedience, unwavering belief for revelation, and immovable faith for salvation. To Nara, these were harsh conditions even for the most faithful but were less so than those meted out by warlords and colonialists. These were conditions that she willingly accepted for the hope of His promise, for at least His conditions gave her an identity, strengthened her, and called her "Nara" by name.

83
HOME OCCUPIED, HOME LOST

IT WAS SPRING, BUT THE DAYS bore the sticky strangling heat of summer. Men with large, black-brimmed, horse-hair hats cooled themselves with traditional hand-held fans, waving them purposefully at their face as small beads of sweat rolled down their foreheads. Children ran through the streets oblivious to the heat but stopping to pant on occasion, while the older folk took shelter in whatever shade they could find.

The streets were full of vehicles, mostly army trucks, but there were also cars as large as boats clumsily bouncing up and down the barely paved streets. Most of the cars were the same unruly squared shape, typical of the mid-1930s. They were all black and hearse-like with white-walled tires. It was as if there was only one car manufacturer and one tire company, and no one to think about paving the streets to accommodate these vehicles before bringing them over. Trams bumped along in different parts of the city, but the lines did not reach here. Still, the pedestrians did not notice, continuing to bustle along in the port city, shuffling in all directions in rapid succession, madly going from market to home to shop and from there to the harbour to inquire with the fishermen after the day's catch.

Almost a quarter century had passed since Korea had been shackled by the menace that hung over it like a musty stench locked in by the oppressive heat. Nara had set out alone on this spring afternoon that was like any other afternoon. She knew what she was doing would be frowned upon by stranger and kin alike since girls, particularly teenaged daughters of noblemen, were strictly forbidden to leave their homes alone, but she sought the open air, overwrought as she was by boredom and chores. She knew if she were caught, the punishment would be severe, and she regretted the risk of bringing even the slightest shame on the family. Still, she undertook a walk in the hope of finding some trinkets, or a book, to help her pass the time when she was at home alone. *If I had something to read, I wouldn't have to be here,* she justified to herself.

She strolled through the groups of street vendors, stopping a while to watch the crowds. The peddlers became merchants by virtue of throwing down blankets and placing miscellaneous wares on them. Often, the merchandise was scavenged from burned-out villages, then repaired (or not) and sold. There would be old, scorched photographs of strangers, small knick-knacks in metal boxes that had probably been jewellery boxes at one time, bits of unrecognizable objects, tattered shoes, broken dolls, chipped dishes, and kitchen supplies. Occasionally, hidden under the blankets, would be contraband: old books rescued from bonfires or incinerators that were now commonplace across the country. Most precious of all were the history and storybooks. These were extremely rare and the few merchants selling these either treasured them and sold them for a high price, or were fearful of them and sold them for nearly nothing. Today, on Nara's walk, there were no such books to be found.

Instead, she encountered a peddler selling kitchen supplies, and Nara took a casual interest but was quickly pleased to find cooking pots that miraculously did not melt in the extreme heat of a grenade impact or a village fire. Nara stopped to look and found a small grey pot with a deep bowl and a black handle. The hard plastic handle had melted just a little, but the pot was in perfect shape. Nara could almost picture the kitchen and the grandmother who must have used it to cook meals for her family at one time. At this, Nara's gaze fell to the ground for a moment, a moment to pay homage or a moment to reset and forget, but she returned back almost as quickly.

What Nara liked most about this cooking pot was the size. It was just big enough to make soup for a small family for one day, but no more and no less. When she was younger, her mother and grandmother cooked without reserve and had plenty of leftovers. Each meal was a feast, and there were ways to keep the food fresh for days, mostly by putting it in deep, properly dug and properly kept tunnel-like holes. But, now, as the Occupation, or "oppression" as they called it, pressed down harder on all classes, and prosperity diminished for the indigenous noblemen, keeping food was a waste because there was no refrigeration like this possible. Every meal had to be finished or thrown out. Nara bought the cooking pot and carried on.

The street peddlers, upon noting that Nara was a buying customer, started to heckle her, calling her to their stall or blanket, beseeching and waving her over. Nara carried on, uninterested in what they had to pawn.

Sometimes, Nara found a small blanket or stall that was worth stopping in front of. It was not the stall of a merchant selling factory-made products, or a poor wretch hawking scavenged wares, but a "someone." A "someone" who worked hard and applied his or her God-given gifts to make goods that came from their heart or hands or simply from a sheer will to survive. It could be a woman selling clothes she had made from leftovers she found behind a textile mill, a carpenter selling carved bowls, a weaver selling blankets, or a man selling clay pipes that he kilned himself.

On this day, as Nara hurried along, she passed a woman selling handmade earthen pots — large ones fit for fermenting *kimchi*. Some pots stood almost as tall as Nara, while others were of a more modest size. Nara stopped to admire them. She had seen countless earthen pots made by countless potters, and many more stunning, intricate earthen pots punched out by factories, but these remarkable pots showed a true mark of skill. They were thin at the top — not too thin, but elegantly thin — and thick in the middle and perfectly flat at the base, which was important for the vegetables and marinating juices. They were neither glazed nor did they have detailed carvings, but they were perfectly shaped and would certainly yield excellent condiments. And that a woman potter had made them was particularly fascinating to Nara.

The woman told her that her artisanal skills, now her trade, had been passed down to her by her father who was killed near Seoul about a decade and half earlier, supposedly along with authors, professors, and other Korean artists for defying the despotic Japanese directives on art and culture. "He would not give up our craft," the woman explained. "They wanted him to show them and when he refused, they wanted him to do it their way."

Fifteen years ago, Nara thought. *Around the time I was born. That would have been around the time of the independence movement.* For a fleeting moment, the woman became a little teary-eyed, and Nara knew all too well what the woman had meant. Nara also knew that merchants often used their tragic stories — and there were many tragic stories — as a selling ploy, leveraging pity and the human heart to move merchandise. But this woman seemed distant and sad and ashamed to be overcome by her memories so easily. Nara looked deeply into the woman's onyx eyes and the tears, now discreetly wiped away, left a glint that made the pupils shine like crystals.

Nara willed herself to this woman in that moment, feeling that they shared an intricate and complicated sadness that came from a labyrinth of acrimonious experiences, the kind of sadness that strangles the soul. It was the kind of sadness that can only come from seeing man at his basest, and witnessing inexplicable injustice. But it was the woman's shame in being weak that made her strong and noble in Nara eyes.

Nara did not have any money left to buy an earthen pot, but she offered to trade the cooking pot she had just purchased. The woman looked at the young girl and then at the cooking pot and smiled. "The one you have in your hands will serve you better than any of these," she said, pointing at one of her creations. "Go. Shoo, before I chase you away."

Nara bowed deeply, a gesture usually reserved for only the most honourable greeting, then glanced up at the woman and slowly and reluctantly trotted away. As she got a few yards away, she turned back and saw the woman looking at her with those sad eyes again. The woman paused and it seemed as if she was about to lift her hand. But then she dropped it and looked away as another customer approached. Nara kept walking and turned back again, but lost sight of the potter woman as the crowd blurred between them.

Nara made her way home through the centre of Daegu, over short arched bridgeways that crossed over small canals. She was tired now and a storm was brewing above the high peaks visible from Beomeo-dong neighbourhood, but she was close to home. She found the streets here deserted, not a wagon or car in sight.

Nara arrived at the gate at the front of her house, and though it was not unusual to see cars on her street, one was parked immediately in front of her home. She thought that was odd and then froze, realizing that her father must already be back from his daily errands and could be receiving guests. She slipped to the back of the house where there was a narrow alleyway and climbed up one of the large mature trees that lined the perimeter of her home.

Homes of noblemen were generally large, the equivalent of several thousand square feet, typically spread out over a single ground floor and spanning wide across with rarely a staircase in sight. Homes in the south were typically built in an "I" shape to allow for circulation while houses in the north were built in the shape of a quadrant or a series of adjoining quadrants. Nara's house, therefore, was unusual in this part of the country as it was built as two quads. Quad homes had exposed, banal, exterior stone walls that were often surrounded by trees and that belied the intricate interior, full of life and activity. At the centre of the house, naturally, was the courtyard, the middle of the main quadrant. In the centre of the courtyard there was usually a square area of dirt or a large flat stone, which was the hub of activity. It was the only area of the house that was not under the cover of a roof, and family members crossed the courtyard to get from one room to the next. They gathered there, gossiped there, played games there, including jumping up and down on traditional see-saw contraptions. The courtyard thus balanced outside living with inside living seamlessly. Flanking each side of the courtyard were nondescript rooms that were used as bedrooms or studies and reading areas while the kitchen and bathroom were usually off to the side of the home closest to the source of water, like a well or a pump. More often than not, the home sat on stilts or the rooms at least were propped up. This was to accommodate the *ondol* heating system that spread air through ducts beneath the floors of the rooms from a central oven at the other end of the house. Each room had a sliding door made of rice paper and a wood frame, but more often than not, the doors were left open to allow voices and conversations to carry across the courtyard. If the home had multiple adjoining quadrants, it allowed room for servants' quarters. Nara's home had a dining area, living area, multiple sleeping areas and washing areas, and most important, it had trees both inside and outside the walls of the home.

One particularly faithful tree was both a familiar arrival and departure point. It offered itself as the sacrificial limb, providing Nara with a perfect escape route in and out of her house, and in and out of the outside world. From the centre of the tree, on a specific branch she knew well, she was able to launch herself without too much force to land quietly on the roof, which hung low in this part of the quadrant. On this day, she managed to get on to the roof with an ever so soft landing. She proceeded to climb down one of the posts, fearing her father might have already realized she was gone. After having gently eased herself down, she tiptoed to the inner courtyard and was startled to see a strange man standing there with his two hands clasped behind his back and a piece of paper clutched in one of his gloved paws. He was wearing western clothes: a black jacket, straight pants, and a funny looking cloth around his neck. When he turned around, she stepped back and could immediately see he was a Japanese official. Surprised and forgetting her own break-in only moments earlier, she confronted him, demanding to know why he was in her house.

The man was of short stature, nearly as small as her, so she could almost look him straight in the eyes. He was stubby, though not fat, and had a funny, prickly-looking moustache and a strikingly large, flat nose; he had pale white skin and longer hair than most officials, wearing it past his ears. He wore a black derby hat to match, which was almost out of style now in the West, and in Europe, but still often seen worn on the heads of Japanese businessmen. In his left hand, he held a black cane slantwise to the ground, but he did not lean on it. His chin was up, so Nara could see a layer of fat around his thick chin, which, when held up like that made him look snub-nosed. His lips were barely visible, so if one were to draw him with a pencil, a line at the bottom of the face would do with just the slightest dastardly curl at one end, the cause of which was either a deformity or a naturally cruel heart. He furrowed his brow, which accentuated how deep the lines went in his forehead, and clearly he longed to appear domineering.

Nara repeated herself. "What are you doing in my home?"

The man looked sternly at her and replied in Japanese, "Speak Japanese, you insolent little brat. If you speak that rat language, I cannot understand you."

Nara glared at him and replied in Korean, "You are in my home."

The man did not respond and looked coldly back at Nara.

Nara continued, "I will speak the language of this home, the language of my father."

The man clearly looked immensely displeased at Nara's brashness. If she were not so young, this kind of behaviour would merit blows from his cane and possibly even arrest for treason for going against the so-called protectorate with such belligerence. But this official seemed to know that this was not the battle to fight. He was here for bigger fish.

At first, Nara beamed mildly at having put this little man in his place, knowing her words would have gotten her a few thrashes if she had said the exact same thing out in the middle of town. She thought he held his tongue for shame, but then she realized that she had not won any victory at all. There was something larger looming. *Where was father?* she wondered.

"By decree of the Oriental Development Company, the imperial military is seizing without further notice the residence of Han Tae-yun."

Years earlier, a law had been passed that all property of Korean noblemen must be transferred to the colonialist empire if it became necessary for strategic reasons or for the good of the state to do so. In return, the Korean household occupying the property at that time would willingly give up ownership and all rights to the property in exchange for housing provided by the state — of course, only if such housing was available. Such ordinances rendered citizenry impotent and being a Korean unfavourable. It was inelegant and savage.

That night, Nara and her family packed up as many personal belongings as possible. With tears in her eyes, Nara looked wistfully at her beautiful room. It was small quarters but warm and inviting. All of her mementos and precious treasures, everything from smooth stones to little carvings, were placed in perfect order and with purpose on her vanity, while the thin walls were covered in skilful calligraphy drawn on delicate, handmade rice paper. Her pillow was a well-worn roll, but the flower patterns in fuchsia silk embroidery were still vibrant and looked as if no dream had ever laid its head upon them. Her quilts and blankets were thick and luxurious and also had beautiful, vibrant, silk flower patterns. Her writing desk had been made from a light wood, likely bamboo, but it had been lacquered over in a stunning black tone and was adorned with shells. Typical of traditional Korean tables and desks, it was low on the ground, barely a foot or two off the ground in fact. When Nara sat at it, she kneeled or crouched, getting so close to it that she knew every dent, every scratch, every mark like a close friend. Nara had written countless personal letters, poems, and even songs on that writing table. She had read many books, cried many tears, and dreamt of her future leaning on this desk. It was a gift to her from her father who had had it shipped from Seoul after one of his journeys when he decided she would be schooled at home after the missionary school was burned down. This desk she could not carry, and she would miss it.

She opened her cabinet, which was a stand-alone ornate piece of furniture, also of fine workmanship, designed to hold clothes like a closet, but was more like an intricate work of art. She started to pull out her *hanboks*, rubber shoes, undergarments, and socks. Korean socks were bulky and therefore strangely uncomfortable, particularly since they had to be stuffed into small, narrow rubber shoes. The socks and shoes were both white, which did not seem to make much sense for walking in dusty streets, but at least they looked nice. Fortunately, Koreans had mastered the art of laundry and failing a proper cleaning, there was always beating the clothes with a rolling pin.

As she packed, Nara's room gradually became bare and without character. It no longer looked like Nara's room. She removed as many things that were precious to her as possible so as not to leave anything for the daughter of some General or the son of an official who would have no idea what the trinkets meant. The walls were now merely blond wooden frames made of bamboo posts that rang a hollow if you tapped on them with a knuckle.

She had always meant to burrow a secret tunnel from one of the corners of her room to the outside, but always knew that would be impossible because of the rather sophisticated heating system below the floorboards. She had longed to travel after hearing so many stories of foreign countries and strange customs, but she often felt an inward barrier, like a kind of vault, was closing in on her. When that desire to explore distant shores overtook her like some hallucination, she lulled herself by reading about tropical marshlands or lush wildernesses. But, when confined to close quarters and reading about these places was no longer enough to satiate her fanciful stirrings, she believed that the tunnel would birth her way to the outside. There was, of course, no need for a tunnel ever since she struck up a friendship with the tree in the courtyard and the forbidden branch that yielded the fruit of freedom and knowledge.

Yet, for all of those musing over distant shores, now all she longed for was to stay in her home, to never to leave the quiet sanctity and security of the four walls that was her family, the sanity of the quadrant that was the only home she had ever known.

As she packed the last of her things, including a photo of herself that was taken by a foreigner not long ago, she thought if she had burrowed that tunnel, she would stuff it with her things in the hopes of someday returning to her father's home and reclaiming it as the rightful owner. The trinkets that she would put there would be the stake in the ground and the deed to the house.

But today was not a day of victory, but rather the day to

surrender the house and everything in it, including her family's history, her family's memories, and her family's pride.

Armed with all they could carry, Nara's father, mother, and four servants, stepped out the front doors of their home, cast out of Eden, and made their solitary way to a house operated by the state. There was nothing else they could do. Later, Nara would find out that the Japanese steward of her father's finances had reported to the ruling government that Mr. Han had tried to transfer a large sum of money to Beijing. Mr. Han had claimed that he was trying to support family who migrated through Manchuria, but the Japanese government believed this to be a treasonous plot against the Empire and a threat to the emperor, so Mr. Han's home was seized and his finances frozen.

Nara's mother, with large tears in her eyes, looked back at her home and nearly turned to a pillar of salt were it not for the car pulling up with the new occupants inside, filling her heart with hatred. Her eyes turned glassy and her demeanour cold. It seemed to Nara the storm that was brewing earlier that day was one of fire and brimstone that was about to fall from the sky and she was right, as war approached.

As the colonial administrative policy shifted more strongly towards assimilation (*dōka seisaku*), within only a few days, Nara was ordered back to the state-run school. Nara trembled at the notion. She was no longer allowed to be home-schooled, for her own good, of course. If she did not attend school, she would miss out on the important lessons that would enrich any loyal subject of the Emperor. All girls of her social background were required to have a proper education, to learn how advanced and kind the Emperor was, or so it was explained to her. She could even continue to learn Korean and Korean literature, as an elective: there was nothing to stop her, as long as she had the time between the other required courses that were part of the state-run curriculum, naturally.

The thoughts of leisurely rambles through town immediately dissipated. The craving for adventure and the impulse for muse-like flight were too fantastic and upsetting now, replaced by a cold, rigid brooding that hung over the family and Nara's dampened passion.

Nara had no choice but to return to the state-run school. But returning to that school only served to bridle and temper her sensibilities. She felt the oppressive tyranny like the overbearing heat, and it bore down on her hard with every line read aloud and every verse recited. The monotonous five-syllable Japanese songs in language classes sapped her strength while, worse still, the history classes were full of error and misrepresentation. A missionary education combined with home-schooling had given her leave to read copies of old history books written by indigenous scholars. The new ones, it seemed to her, were meant to spread a contagion of lies, half-truths, and monstrous tales, and she retired from each day at school or more correctly, from the dripping attacks, with a shiver of repugnance.

Then, one day, in a life of many bad days, she experienced what would be one of the worst days of her life.

It was hazy but bright. The autumn equinox had passed and as the hours moved forward, the light shortened its stay. The hibiscus in bright shades of orange and pink were long gone and only some periwinkle fronds dotted the countryside. As Nara crossed the town on her way home, the blue hue changed to dust and dry dirt. She walked with her usual purpose and decided to stop in to see Min-joo. Min-joo had been assigned to a different school as the state system introduced districts and divisional lines to manage the population of young students and ostensibly provide a higher quality of education.

She detoured and veered behind the main street of town to a narrow alleyway where Min-joo's family now lived since they lost their business. She shook off her dreary demeanour as she approached the threshold of the door and gently knocked, hoping her friend had returned from school. She knocked again; no answer. She waited to see if anyone lit any of the rooms inside or the dark base of the doorway, but no one came. Dejected, she carried on.

The town was eerily deserted, a stark contrast to the usual bustle. Nara continued on her customary path with the obvious air that she was no longer content with her meanderings through morose and gloomy streets, brought on mostly by the sorry feeling that she had missed her friend. Then, as she sauntered into the middle of town, she caught sight of a man who looked very much like her father. The man was surrounded by five imperial army soldiers wearing baggy navy-blue uniforms with shiny gold buttons going down the front in pairs. Except for the occasional passerby scrunching down and running bent over to a hiding spot, there didn't seem to be anyone else in sight. Nara stopped cold.

She gasped. It was him. Under her breath, she uttered the word, "Father," then put both hands to her mouth, clamping it shut. She slowly inched her way closer, as quietly as she could, then managed to get within earshot, hiding herself behind a wide wooden post.

The soldiers looked drunk with power and hungry for blood.

"Move out of the way when imperial soldiers of the Emperor walk down the street!" screamed one of the colonial soldiers. "Do you understand?"

"Answer him, you scum!" yelled another solider.

Nara's father remained silent. He stood tall and unmoving, his head held high.

One of the soldiers knocked off Tae-yun's black hat, which caught a small draft and drifted slowly to the dusty road below. Tae-yun still did not move, and the soliders started to laugh at the skull-cap that covered his topknot.

"Ah, old-timer! You still have a topknot!" taunted one of the other soldiers, while another chimed in, "You know, an edict was passed a long time ago banning those!"

In the meantime, the first solider, who was looking for trouble, was clearly in a state of adrenalin-induced rage.

"Shut-up!" He yelled at the others. "This Korean rat did not move out of our way. He walked down the middle of the street as if we were not here, as if we were invisible, as if this was *his* street!" the solider rambled at his comrades. He then turned his attention back to Nara's father and said, "Do you own this street, rat?"

Nara's father continued to remain silent, still with his head held high.

A soldier who appeared to be of lower rank yelled, "Answer him! Answer him!"

Nara's father replied, "If we are rats, then you are the parasites that live off of us, drinking our blood, wallowing in our labour-induced sweat, and spreading disease everywhere. If we are rats, we should eat you colonialist cockroaches and put an end to your filth spreading."

At this, one solider forcibly thrust the butt of his rifle into Tae-yun's gut. Tae-yun appeared winded and he crunched over slightly. Nara bit her lips to keep from crying out. She did not want to endanger her father further by revealing herself thus weakening his position. She would not be his Achilles heel. She would not allow them to exploit that.

Tae-yun's reply only added fodder to the flame, and the soldiers grew more agitated at the insult.

The first soldier, with a face like a madman, bellowed, "You call us parasites and cockroaches?" He yelled it so loud he nearly lost his voice, and as he shook from the scream, dust kicked up from his uniform.

Tae-yun turned his head and looked the solider in the eye and said, "Yes, you are a parasite." The first solider turned a crazed red, and the others pointed their bayonets directly at Nara's father now. The solider spoke slowly. "If you're going to call us parasites, then at least do it in Japanese. Speak Japanese!" he growled low and harsh.

Tae-yun looked again directly at the solider and said, "I don't speak the language of parasites." Then, turning away, he added, "But, if you end the Occupation, then for the sake of diplomacy, I would surely speak to you in your language."

The solider, despite his flashy uniform, was a rather lowly village idiot. Not understanding the point, he simply yelled, "Treason! Speak Japanese or I will cut you down on the very spot where you stand!"

"No."

"Speak Japanese!"

"No." And then Tae-yun chuckled.

"What is so funny!" the first solider screamed.

"You."

"What do you mean?"

"Why should I speak Japanese when all along you are speaking Korean to me?" Tae-yun chuckled again.

The first solider was now engulfed in an anger-fuelled madness. He screeched like a vulture and began stabbing Tae-yun through with his bayonet. There was no warning. There was just rage. In a mob-like frenzy, the other soldiers joined in and they too stuck Nara's father through with their bayonets, over and over again. They punched him and kicked him, and Tae-yun sunk to the ground. As he sank, he closed his eyes and looked as if he was trying to sit down to meditate, although in fact, his body was heavy and his legs no longer able to bear his weight. One of the soldiers grabbed at his topknot, and with his body limp, Tae-yun's head flipped back. In a stroke of blind insanity, the solider holding the hair pulled out a knife and sliced Tae-yun's neck straight across, as if he wanted to cut off the head completely. Tae-yun's body dropped into a sitting position, cross-legged. Then, one or two of the soldiers shot off their rifles into Tae-yun's body, the force of which flung him down where he lay lifeless now on the dusty, blood-soaked ground. The sound of the bullets popped through the flesh of the corpse and clapped in Nara's ears.

Still hiding behind the wooden post, Nara's face was covered with tears while her hands stayed firmly secured over her mouth for fear of letting out a devastating cry. She sank to the ground, trembling uncontrollably. She brought both her knees to her chin, rolling herself into a ball, her hands still firmly pressed over her mouth. She tried to pray, but the words would not come. She did not feel God. He was not close, not at all. She sat there in utter and unspeakable shock for hours. She wanted to crawl through the dirt and dust to her father, to hold him, heal him. But she could not as the Japanese soldiers hovered around, mocking his dead body. She trembled until her muscles atrophied, and she could tremble no more. Her face was soaked with all the tears she had in her reserves. Her body stiff, she nearly died a slow agonizing death as she felt her heart shatter, her father lying only a few metres away.

Nara bore the weight of this horrific tragedy on her slender shoulders and did not speak for nearly a month after having witnessed the grotesque scene.

They wrapped Tae-yun in long sheets of cloth and covered him to spare Nara the sight of the struggle, the bruises and blows to the head, the long gaping holes left by the bayonets that speared him through, the bullet holes and the final death knell, the cut to the throat. But the neighbours did all this not realizing she had borne witness to the murder, only a few metres away from where it happened.

When she saw her father's body for the last time, swaddled in white sheets and lying in his coffin, she longed to lay her hands on him, to heal the wounds, and take away his suffering. Of course, she could not. So, she closed her eyes and envisioned opening a tunnel to the land of the dead and sending him off to a higher realm of peace.

During her period of silence, as if performing a *jinogwigut*, a ritual done by a female shaman for the dead, Nara willed herself into the land of a fairy tale and in her account of this tale, saw her father go through apotheosis. Like a phoenix, he crouched down and lit up like a bonfire metamorphosing into a god-like figure before her eyes. He looked like a glowing Buddha or Christ, emblazoned like the burning bush.

She whispered, "May an angel guide you to Paradise, Father."

When a loved one is lost, one loses a part of one's mind and a good chunk of one's soul. When it is through tragedy and injustice, the grief is not a sore that eventually heals over leaving a small scar over time. No, this kind of grief, brought on by tragedy, is like a gangrenous infection, eating away at our will and weakening our resolve. So, it was no mystery when, only a few weeks after burying her husband in the family's ancestral burial mound, Nara's mother fell ill. She coughed blood relentlessly and withered away slowly with tears still in her eyes, mourning her husband all the while. To Nara, there was nothing ennobling about illness as it only accentuated human weakness and brought man down to a mere physical level. Nara's mother had wanted to think only of her love for her husband, trying to measure her loss philosophically, understand what it meant in the face of the universe, and in the context of injustice. But she could not. She was instead forced by her body to focus only on her physical self. Illness makes us all too aware that disease is detrimental to human dignity, to being human.

With a grieving heart for her husband and desperation for her only daughter, Nara's mother fought a brave and hard fight. Unwilling to die and leave Nara alone, her mother lived long past most anyone with this type of affliction, yet, despite her battle, the illness ravaging her body eventually won. After several weeks of coughing up every last drop of blood in her body while fever burned through every pore, God took Nara's mother by force, and her soul could do nothing more than to surrender.

Thus, for the second time, in a brief period of time, death paid a visit to the front doors of Nara's household. This second time, perhaps because Nara had known her mother's death was imminent, or perhaps because of the experience of her father's death — whatever the reason — Nara felt detached, and somehow, she seemed no longer to have tears to shed, not even from the contagion of others' grief. But, she did feel grief — immense grief. She was struck by her mother's passing, but, to Nara it seemed her mother's death was more beautiful, for the death felt quiet and spiritual and bore a precise justification so though solemn, it was not mournful, nor as deeply shocking as had been her father's. Her mother was ill, she had traversed through the worst of it, and then had an opportunity to make peace with God. At the end of this struggled journey, she would surely meet with him once again.

As the neighbours and villagers who knew the family came to pay their respects and mourn the loss of the matriarch of Nara's family, all the side-glances and hushed chirping, interlaced with the frequent mentioning of her name, did not escape Nara's attention.

"What will happen to Nara?"

"Any word from her cousins? Perhaps an uncle or an aunt?"

"We have heard nothing. We sent news to the only family left and there has been no reply. We fear they might have been captured or they fled."

"Fled? No, it couldn't be."

"Yes, perhaps to Manchuria."

"I would assume right away that they must have been captured or perhaps even murdered like her father."

"Shhhh, she mustn't hear."

"Oh dear. Oh dear. What's to become of her?"

"Usually, there is a grandmother around, at least one of them."

"No, all the grandparents are deceased."

"It can't be."

"I believe it is."

"It can't be. All of them?"

"She must be old enough, no?"

"No, she's only fifteen. Not old enough to be alone. Another year, maybe two."

There was a stop in the buzz for a moment, and then one of the women simply stated the obvious. "There is no one. She will have to go to an orphanage."

There was a mild gasp that rose quietly in the air. Someone else mumbled, "Those places are no good. They are no good at all right now."

Many of the villagers there at the wake nodded. "It is not safe in those places."

Others shook their heads in disbelief. "That is no place for the daughter of a nobleman. No place for anyone, particularly our young women."

As each villager bowed deeply to the urn, bowed shallowly to Nara, paid their respects, and said a small prayer, they filed out the door one by one, giving a small sympathetic glance to Nara as they left. Nara bowed back, for there was nothing else to do.

It was on this day that Nara's connection to her home was cut. Her childhood home had been stolen away from her family against their will. She swore to herself that she would never let this happen again for when her home was taken, so was everything else — her name, her family, her future. Her father had been murdered, her mother had died of grief and illness, and she was left without a home or a family.

Four days after the death of her mother, Nara was transferred to an orphanage by the state, and all the possessions of her house and all the wealth in her family's name was turned over to the government of the Emperor for safe-keeping.

The woman owner of the orphanage had a boundless appetite for gossip. Born of the weakest ilk, she adored idol talk of the cheapest kind and was easily flattered. So, it was not difficult to sway her into becoming a co-conspirator for the imperial military. Within a week of Nara's arrival, the matron had struck a deal to sell Nara and another girl to the military. Rather than nurture the orphans in her care, this wretch helped the military find sex slaves out of her own orphanage, making victims of the already deprived and the already stricken. Under the dark of night, the girls would be taken.

It was still early evening, perhaps nine or ten o'clock, but winter's short hours deprived the day of light and it was already black outside. Nara lay in bed trying to fall asleep like the other girl who shared her room, already asleep from the fatigue of a hard day's labour. When Nara first arrived, she was surprised she was in a room with only one other girl while the other orphans shared a larger hall. But she and her roommate were older while the others were still children. It was indeed rare for an orphanage to have children older than twelve years old. Most children, by that age, had been adopted, put out to work, or ran away.

A rustling outside the window caught Nara's attention. Then she heard someone whisper her name. "Nara, are you there?"

Nara leaped up and stalked quietly to the window.

"Min-joo! What are you doing here?" Nara said, happy to see her friend.

"Just a visit!" Min-joo said, equally happy.

"You'll be in trouble. Your father will be angry with you if you are caught for being out like this! And so late! You shouldn't be here," Nara warned.

"Help me in. I'll visit a little while and go home. No one will ever know," she insisted.

Nara nodded then slipped out of her room and scurried to the front door of the orphanage. Strangely, there was no sign of the matron.

Min-joo crept in and gave Nara a hug. There was no need for words. Nara and Min-joo tiptoed quietly back to Nara's room and sat on her bed whispering and giggling and sharing happy stories and memories. The girl in the other bed snored away, oblivious to their chatter. Nara was thankful to Min-joo for taking such a risk to visit her, unable to come during the day because of the restrictions the orphanage imposed on visitors.

Some time passed and the dark of night fell harder. The girls could hardly see each other, but their soft voices carried with familiarity to their ears. Nara then bounced up and announced to Min-joo that she had to go the bathroom. "It's just across the hall and around the corner. I'll be right back."

Min-joo sat on Nara's bed and hummed a soft melody while she listened to the girl in the next bed sleeping peacefully, though not quietly. A minute or two had passed. Min-joo had not noticed, but the matron, moments earlier, had opened the front door after an almost imperceptible knock. There were some muffled voices and an exchange of indiscernible banter followed by quiet footsteps approaching Nara's bedroom. Startled, Min-joo jumped under the covers to hide.

Without warning, the covers on both beds were ripped off the bed in one fell swoop. Min-joo's mouth was covered first with a sweaty palm and then bound with a rag, and in the same stroke, her head was covered with a hood. She was lifted up out of the bed and slung over someone's shoulder. She tried to scream, but only a loud muffled sound came out. It was the same for the other girl. Min-joo heard the sound of an immense struggle and then a heavy thud and another thud. The struggle seemed to stop. Min-joo kicked her legs to try to break free, but they were immediately grasped and tied together, and she could not wriggle any further.

Nara came out of the bathroom unaware of the commotion, but upon seeing the strange shadows emerging from her room, she halted immediately and hid behind the wall in front of the bathroom. Even though it was dark, she could see two bodies slung over the two men's shoulders and then she watched them head quickly to the front entrance with the matron of the orphanage traipsing behind them. Nara could not see who the men were and could not tell who they had slung over their shoulders. She held her breath and stayed hidden as she waited for the shadows to leave. The scene was so frightening and bizarre. *What was going on? Is it? No, it cannot be. Is it?*

Nara watched motionless as the woman mumbled some rubbish to the men while they handed her a small envelope. She closed the doors of the orphanage while the men with the bodies disappeared into the night. Nara could make out the sound of a motor car as it pulled away, and then watched the woman turn on her heels and return up the stairs to her quarters. Nara hurried back to her room anxious to reunite with her friend.

"Min-joo," Nara called out quietly but desperately.

Nara looked around the room and even though it was dark, she could see there was no one there — not Min-joo and not her roommate. She strained to see in the dark.

"Min-joo, where are you?" Nara said, panicked. "Min-joo, come out from hiding. I'm back now. Are you under the bed?" Nara looked under the bed. She was frantic. She looked everywhere in the small room and lifted the bed sheets again and again, flapping them in case Min-joo was between them like feathers in a set of wings. She looked for her roommate, patting her bed again and again to reassure her there was no life in it. Her roommate was gone too. The kidnapping took all but five minutes but it would result in a lifetime of nightmares. Nara collapsed on her knees to the floor. She rocked herself back and forth in shock.

"Min-joo, where are you?" Nara started to sob. "Min-joo."

❦4❦

FACTORY

THE REALITY OF ASSIMILATION WAS NOW inescapable. Everything that was Korea had all but been completely rooted out. Poets, playwrights, politicians, professors, scientists, had all been gathered up and vigorously "dealt with." Trials of the enemies of the Emperor were carefully played out with a well-developed script, a plot full of intrigue and espionage, and ritually performed night after long night. Subsequent reviews of the state's performances were published in the newspapers, twenty of which were colonialist. There was only one newspaper left that was indigenous, which was censored and government-run anyway. Articles were eloquently composed depicting the trials as humane examples of the Emperor's mercy, yet also clearly conveying the fact that any form of treason would not be tolerated. Koreans had had to concede that the poets and artists carried dangerous weapons indeed in their arsenal, and that such articulate and pointed weaponry aimed at eradicating oppression were treasonous ploys that surely could not be tolerated.

Jae-sun had arrived in Busan from Seoul. Seeking community and not sure where else to go, he had turned to the only place he knew where he would be accepted. He was thus promptly hired as an accountant for one of the largest textile mills in the country and though not a nobleman, his employers recognized he was from an educated family of some stature. He did not relish that his father was once a communist sympathizer, particularly uncomfortable in this political climate. Nevertheless, Mr. Lee had helped his son through his life with favours not easily bought or sold, but bargained at a high price. The position in the textile mill was one of them.

Nara had noticed him at Sunday service, a handsome gentleman with mannerisms that spoke eloquently to his good breeding and good connections. She sat through the service quietly contemplating how to cross paths with this gentleman. It would be highly inappropriate for Nara to approach him directly, a perfect stranger. She would need someone, a middleman (or woman) to make the proper introductions. But there was no one in whom she could confide, so she decided it would have to be left to fate, if destined at all.

The next afternoon, on leaving his work, the newcomer stood on the top of the stairs of the factory building leading down from the balustrade. From that vantage point, he spotted Nara, a pretty young woman, who had, it seemed to him, a strong gait and bright disposition. She was just passing the factory's gate and appeared to be alone. Jae-sun had also seen her the day before and had wished to approach her. He hoped she would welcome his greeting with an inquiring look that would open the door to a possible friendship. Nara was moving at a brisk pace as if tasked with an occupation, and Jae-sun knew that if he wanted to catch up to her, he would have to increase his pace. He approached her quickly and all but put out a hand to her shoulder, though he would not dare touch her out of respect. But, as he got within earshot, Jae-sun, about to utter a friendly word or nod his head, if only to acknowledge to himself his filled heart, inwardly gasped as he lost his nerve and tongue in tow. He hesitated as he sought to regain self-control but he was suddenly panic-stricken for fear Nara would notice him hanging there behind her, all tongue-tied. Jae-sun gave up and abandoned his plan of introducing himself. He passed her with bent head and a hurried step.

Nara had heard footfalls rapidly following after her and though she should have been anxiously guarded, she had caught in her periphery a glimpse of Mr. Lee, and thought that if he was chasing her so vigorously he must surely have reason or business of some kind. Otherwise, he would not have made his presence known so obviously. Yet, as she was about to turn to acknowledge him with only a nod and no more, he hurried past with nary a glance. She was confused but could deduce only that he was rushing to an errand and had not noticed her ambling in front. This childlike play, reverberating with innocence as they each tried to catch the other's eye in the course of their normal work, stretched on for a long time. The church service they both attended faithfully each week, of course to worship God, also gave them the opportunity to chance upon each other, and when their eyes did meet, then what a stroke of luck for them both. Months passed like this but neither spoke a word to each other, and no common friend took notice to bother to introduce the two callow and doe-eyed parties until, of course, a keen Mrs. Pyon finally caught sight of a glimpse and a blush.

They were meek at first and fiercely tempered their heightened emotions. They each carried the necessary air of cold cordiality, but it was clear both felt a distinct and similar connection that brought them to intimate places in their hearts and history. Mrs. Pyon had a done a fine job. Her most proper introduction hit just the right social note and left the couple shed in the most positive light in the prying eyes of friends and neighbours. Community acceptance of any pairing would be a far gone conclusion, thanks to Mrs. Pyon.

After months more of careful and light discussions of things common and mundane, the two were able to cross the next threshold to familiarity and family. Mr. Lee, of course, could not help but wonder how a young woman was alone in such a large city, but her articulate speech and knowledge of current events belied her situation. It was not hard to see that she'd had a good education and came from a good family, and eventually, the question had to be asked. Indeed, when the time came time for the invested parties to reveal themselves fully, Nara told Jae-sun her short but potent story.

"That very night, I didn't have a choice. The matron thought I had been the one taken. After that, I had to run away from the orphanage, or I would surely be sent off or even killed. I had small trinkets, rings, and even a necklace that I had managed to keep. She would have stolen them from me if I had not hidden them in the floorboards right away. They sustained me until now. I made my way down to Busan, catching rides on carts, walking long stretches, and managing at one point to stow away on a railcar for some distance."

"Why didn't you stay in Daegu?"

"It was not safe. I had to leave. My family was well known, and at some point, someone somewhere would eventually have recognized me. It is a large city, but not large enough."

She did not mention that in her desperation to flee, she did even think to stop at Min-joo's home to report what she saw. Though by then, only hours had passed, to Nara, it was like a dream. No, a nightmare that she did not—could not—revisit. She was traumatized and an uncontrollable self-preservation drove her away as fast as possible. She only had one thought, which was to survive, and she pushed away any other thought that would pose as an obstacle. Something she would come to regret deeply and painfully.

"Hmmm, and for a young girl to be alone, wandering about with no place to go..." Jae-sun agreed.

"It was bad," Nara added.

Jae-sun nodded, understanding completely.

"When I arrived here, I managed to find a Mission and within a few days, thanks to the missionaries, I started to attend their nursing school and..." Nara said.

"And this church," Jae-sun finished her sentence.

"Yes, and I started working at the hospital, mostly bandaging and cleaning up, but helping the doctors when I could. I guess I learned quickly and that helped."

Thus, filled with days and months of provocative conversation, Jae-sun entered Nara's world of pain and sorrow and fell in love with no return.

The wedding was a simple affair, much simpler than Nara had dreamt it would be. She had always expected the pomp and circumstance that an occasion like this entailed. She would be wearing a traditional gown, beautifully adorned with the reds and blues of a streaking cosmos and looking like a grand peacock with the head ornamentation, and her groom in handsome pantaloons and the traditional short green jacket and black hat. They would have a table spread with a feast of dates, chestnuts, red bean, rice cakes, and sweets piled as high as their chests, along with *banchan* of green vegetables, savoury bites of meat, sour pickles, spicy bean sprouts, and a cornucopia of countless other dishes, as well as tea steeped from leaves brought from the mountains to the west that faced the Manchurian side. They would exchange deep bows that would see them prostrate themselves, foreheads to the floor both to each other and then to their parents. Finally, they would retire to their room surrounded by their family and friends just on the other side of the thin walls.

But, it would not be this kind of wedding.

Jae-sun's father did not approve at first, until he inquired extensively after Nara's family. When he found out what he needed to know, he eagerly blessed the union for even though Nara no longer had any wealth, she had a name. Bearing her father's reputation, which was worth more than gold, Nara was assured safe passage into the home of the Lee family.

In fact, if Nara's father were still alive and under different circumstances, it would have been Mr. Han who would not have approved.

Nara had resigned herself to wearing the only dress she had, but Jae-sun had arranged for a gown to be custom-made as a surprise wedding gift. It was traditional, but did not have the long luscious bands of silky fabric that hung from the arms, seen only when bride's arms were clasped together and the elbows were raised. The fabric would drop like drapes for the customary bow. The extra fabric was available at a high premium — a little too rich for a former communist father — but Nara gladly wore the gown. It was a kind and generous gesture and she knew it was expensive for a now humble family.

The reverend presided over a small ceremony attended by Jae-sun's father and many members of the congregation. Times were changing with the influx of missionaries and ideas, so the ceremony was closer to a western-style wedding. A new world order was blowing across the East, and in only a few short years, traditions were being replaced by the new paradigm. Still, Nara and Jae-sun bowed deeply to each other, to honour each other and some part of the past. With the exchange of vows and rings that the congregation gave as gifts to the couple, Jae-sun and Nara started their lives together.

"*Yo-bo.*"

"Hmmm," replied Jae-sun.

"What about you?"

"What do you mean?"

"I mean, your family."

Jae-sun looked up from his work and stared at Nara.

"You know all about me, where I was born, where I went to school."

"Yes, I know. I know, when as a child, you fell asleep and the birds ate the grain in the fields and you got the beating of your life because it was your job to chase the birds away. I know when you were eleven you accidently mistook *soju* for water and gulped it down so fast, you ended up drunk enough that you passed out within an inch of your life."

"Exactly," Jae-sun replied.

"But I mean, your family. You don't speak of them often."

"Well, you know I didn't know my mother. She died in childbirth."

"Yes, I know. I'm sorry." Nara paused. "I don't know. I guess." She paused again. "I guess I mean your father."

Jae-sun's father was born into the old world, and flung into a new one too quickly. He had an almost superstitious belief in revolution, but he grew tired of protests for he saw himself as a pawn and not a knight or a bishop. Although protests were mechanisms long used for revolution and change, and had factored significantly in historical movements like the French and Bolshevik Revolutions, which permeated the psyche of the region, in these fast changing times, it seemed futile to chant slogans and take to the streets in Korea. Most of the time, the chants and slogans fell on complacent and indifferent ears and reaped more jeers than cheers. With that being the case, the change Jae-sun's father hoped for simply did not happen. So, from foot soldier to policy maker, he became a communist sympathizer, and in providing pivotal advice in backroom dealings, he quietly rose in the ranks to effect the change he had long envisioned for his country. But it was misplaced and short-lived. As Jae-sun grew in years and maturity, he diverged further away from his father and his views, disagreeing at every turn of how best Korea should move forward one day.

But they converged on one point: that the dream of a free Korea could only be wrought through confrontation and not collaboration. Then, one day, Jae-sun's father abruptly, and without explanation, left the communist party. Jae-sun had asked about it on only one occasion, but was shut down with such a look of anger that he knew he could never raise the subject again, deferring out of respect and fear to his elder, his father. Jae-sun, like Nara's father, longed for his countrymen to demand the return of their rights through aggressive action, certain that the only way to loosen the grip of the Occupation was to do so by sheer will and brute strength. After he left the communist party, Jae-sun's father no longer agreed with his son on this point and they diverged again. Jae-sun's father, like many of the Korean elite, felt there was no other choice but to succumb to the agonizing conflict of loyalties and collaborate with the ruling Japanese. It was a psychological burden that Jae-sun's father quickly learned to bear.

"A story for another day," was all Jae-sun said in reply to Nara's question.

About six months after they married, Jae-sun received news from the general manager of the factory that it was being shut down. No further production would be taking place in Korea and all work would be moved to Japan. It was the largest and last functioning textile mill in that region of the country, and the number of skilled workers would be needed in the factory in Japan. There seemed to be a mass migration of workers going to Japan at the time, some voluntarily, some conscripted as slave labourers. Who fell into which pot and how it happened was bewildering, but one thing was clear: some were in Japan willingly, and others were not.

"No need to worry, Jae-sun. We guarantee that we will protect your position as an accountant. You will not be the senior accountant, unfortunately, but as a junior manager, you will still be provided a very comfortable situation," said the *sokai* government official who was in charge of the deployment office.

Nara found herself leaving her home once more, but this time, she was not leaving merely the edifice, but her country.

During the voyage, they had often had to rub off the layers of sticky sea air and salt that continued to accumulate as they approached the dock in Port of Osaka. The water near the city's harbour was swollen and dark, the waves ominous and threatening as they rushed relentlessly forward. A multitude of ancient sampans and wooden schooners clustered beside freighters and steamships, and there was a long pier against which the ship docked. The muddy tide went as far up to the edge of the swampy undergrowth where no one bothered to manicure or clean. The rest of the harbour, further up, seemed well groomed however. Nara thought how strange that the surface of the water seemed pristine but in the lower part of the pier, there was stench and repulsive rot. She held her nose.

"Discarded fish parts and guts," Jae-sun said when he saw the look on her face.

The Osaka docks were a frenzy of languages, people, smells and sounds. The noise was almost deafening, the harbour filled with the shouts and grunts of masses arriving or getting ready to leave. Jae-sun could only see where the waves were higher than elsewhere, and when looking at the beach, noticed the crest breaks backwards, not forwards.

Jae-sun, Nara, and the other passengers did not know what all the different languages being spoken were, but they could distinguish the different tones and words. Here, Japanese competed with German, English, French, and Russian, a cacophony of the new world: ancient Japan meshed awkwardly with modern commercialism. In the near distance, they could see warehouses flying the flags of a dozen countries, vibrant and smartly patronizing as they flapped in the wind. The flags were intended to welcome the various sailors, generals, and politicians who approached their shores. The glaring omission, of course, was the Korean flag, but in those days, Japan was determined to absorb the colony, as Korea was one of their biggest suppliers and trading partners.

Still, despite all this frenzy of activity near the harbour, there was only a shadowy hint of life and a foggy ghostliness that descended down onto the docks and surrounded them. They became aware of their breath, which was weightless, and imperceptible like the near breathless sleep of the dying. Upon disembarking from the ship, Jae-sun and Nara craned their necks to see if they could spot the representative from the factory who was supposed to show them their quarters and give them their orientation. A small flood of factory workers, many of whom Jae-sun recognized, started to pile in behind him. Just a few metres from where they stood, there was a lurching roar of military trucks. Truck wheels turned and squealed to a stop as the military trucks came to a stop just in front of the growing group on the dock. Japanese soldiers unloaded from larger trucks with canopied backs and dispersed, surrounding the passengers. Other vehicles fitted with loudspeakers cruised the docks blaring, "This ship is being evacuated to the factory. Everyone must go to the factory now. You are labourers of the Japanese empire by official order. Please report to the depository."

As the soldiers started to gather around the workers, Jae-sun tried to reason with one to explain to him that he was a manager and could oversee the entry of all the passengers. He had papers signed back in Korea showing his position and level of authority. Additionally, he knew the names and positions of many of the workers here on the dock. But the soldier pushed the useless papers away and flung them back into Jae-sun's face. The soldiers would not hear anything about it and herded the groups of frightened workers, pushing them to a central depository at the end of the dock to be processed.

It was a situation, as in any slave labour, devoid of humanity. Standing on the reeking dock, with the darkness falling and wind whispering heartlessly at their ears, Jae-sun and Nara looked over their shoulders back at the ship. Without passage back home, they were to work as labourers in the factory; there was no choice. The sting of this betrayal coursed through Jae-sun's veins like venom, and he read the callousness and depravity exactly for what it was: despotism and brutality run rampant.

Each day, they experienced an uncontrollable, overwhelming fatigue from overwork and impossible sleeping arrangements. Men and women were assigned different labour, and so they were conveniently separated: mothers from sons, husbands from wives, and so on. The women worked inside the factories on the machinery, making textiles. The men worked outside, performing grunt labour: shovelling, digging, moving dirt, filling holes, constructing, building, or burying.

Jae-sun, more than Nara, was ravaged by hunger, but always siphoning off a part of his ration to smuggle to her. He managed to sweep off a few extra grains of rice from the tables during the daily meal and hide them in the lining of his dusty overalls. He desperately wished to devour them on the spot but summoned the will to save them until morning to share with Nara in the one moment they caught a glimpse of each other as they passed in the daily line up beside the barracks, before they started again at their work. Despite his determination to save these precious grains of rice, to Jae-sun, exercising the willpower to do so sometimes seemed a ridiculous exercise, serving merely to give him a sense of dignity, which, ultimately, was useless in a factory where he was doomed to spend the rest of his short life.

Yet all around him were former teachers and students, politicians and playwrights, construction workers and trolley conductors, who were knowledgeable and alive to the world. Ignoring the stench of the barracks and the backbreaking labour, they would converse, share ideas and even allow themselves to hope for something better, sometime soon. But Jae-sun wanted no part of that kind of talk, for it was cruel to hope.

He remained indignant, and embittered. There had never been a management position waiting for him. It had been a lie. There were no Korean managers anywhere in Japan. Not one. He felt foolish and gullible for having believed that it might have been possible. It was clear, upon their arrival in Osaka, that the state-sanctioned policies against them were severe, demolishing all hope of prosperity and advancement. Jae-sun, and all the others that had been shipped there with him, had been thrown into a world of hard labour and a banal yet surreal form of ethnic discrimination without life preservers.

After their one meal of the day, Jae-sun got up to return to his station at the building site, but as he wobbled past the makeshift kitchen where they prepared the slop, he spotted a small, damp, and rotting clump of radishes on the filthy cold ground just beneath him, just barely out of arm's reach. Salivating, he knew the radishes would provide a little energy for both Nara and himself. Eyeing the scrap of rubbish warily, he strategized how he might reach for it without tipping off the guards, and more importantly, not tipping off the other workers. Heaven knew if they grabbed the radishes before him, they would devour them on the spot in front of him. He coughed and then coughed harder. He coughed so hard, he keeled over and clutched his knees. Then, he sneezed and held his stomach. He inched his upper body ever further down to the ground so as to be able to give his arm the furthest reach and therefore the best chance possible to grab the radishes. He coughed more, covering his mouth with one hand, while the other groped for the fruit of the forbidden tree. His fingers spread and stammered their way around until he felt a cold, squishy, wet something and realized that indeed he had managed to grab the coveted radishes. He got it. He nervously stuffed the small clump into his pocket, wiping his mouth of the spittle that had spewed from his coughing with his other hand. As he walked out of the mess hall, he looked down to avoid any eye contact with the guards as his beaming face would betray him.

The foreman of the factory in which Nara worked was unjustifiably indignant. This vain man had great overblown ideas about the power of his surly glance. He was beside himself with rage when Nara repeatedly faced what were meant to be threatening glances with a humble, deprecating smile that eventually got on his nerves. He kept a close eye on Nara, looking for the slightest error to pounce on her and be able to mete out some severe, often fantasized punishment. But despite his small mind, the oppressor understood the power of a mob and out of an inadmissible fear of sparking off a riot on which he would have to file a report and tarnish his perfect record, he held his tongue and his lash, at least for now.

The dawn brought a pleasant crispness to the morning. It was serene. This was the only part of the day Nara would look forward to: the walk between the barracks to the factory floor, the one hundred and fifty-eight steps in the early morning calm when Nara felt free, even though she walked in a strict line formation. It was the only time they would be outside, able to breathe the cool fresh morning air and feel the weather, whatever it may be, on their aching skin. Once inside the factory, it would be polluted, dusty, and mostly sweltering, whatever the weather, except in the middle of the coldest time of winter, when, of course, it would be freezing. But it was the stagnating heat that bore down hard on even the most dauntless.

The factory had two windows, one at each end. The window at the far end was small and closed over with what seemed like rice paper, like the kind used on wooden door frames. It still let in light, but it was a muted light. The window closest to Nara's station was high up above the scaffolding of beams of wood and plaster where they stored old bolts of fabric, non-descript boxes, and scraps of miscellaneous metal parts. The window was enormous and dirty but by coincidence was punishingly positioned to let in the sun as it made its way across the sky. The window was positioned that way so the light it allowed into the factory could confirm the integrity of the colour of the fabrics. Natural light was the only way to ensure quality control and though it would seem workers stuck inside all day long would welcome the light, instead, it was received with dread. During the summer months, around midday every day without fail, the sun would fill the factory floor and start to bring it to a low, rolling boil. The burning red sun was vicious and the heat that came with it made the work exponentially laborious.

Today was no different. As this summer day progressed, sweat like running water rolled down Nara's face and those of the other women. Their clothes were soaked through and despite the whir of the machinery, moans of despair could be heard echoing across the floor. Some women started to tremble from dehydration and others coughed from tightening throats as they gulped back the thick heavy air. With the sun beating mercilessly through the window, it was so hot that day that even the doors and hinges twisted from the heat. It was a surprise the machinery did not also twist, affecting the calibration.

With the mercury climbing to blistering levels, Nara trembled and her vision grew more and more blurry as the day wore on. As the machinery continued to weave threads into textile, Nara's fingers, wet with sweat and no longer agile, could not always keep the threads apart, so the threads would snag, causing the machine to hiccup. It did not seem to result in uneven snags or other visible imperfections in the fabrics, so Nara would breathe a sigh of relief on the two or three occasions this happened. But, suddenly, Nara saw that two threads had crossed over. She immediately caught the thread and slowed the machine by lifting the heavy lever as she did hundreds of times a day. Delicately, she separated the threads before restarting, but her fingers slipped, and the threads moved back, knotting ever so slightly just as the tooth-like crenels chomped down. The machine lurched and halted, at the same time as Nara's heart stopped. Then everything else came to full stop on Nara's side of the factory, and all went silent. There was no whirring, no whizzing, no clamping sounds, no banging and no snapping. Nara could not understand. Everything appeared all right. But she calmed herself, knowing from experience the machine just needed to be restarted and production could continue. Due to the stoppage, the foreman jumped up from his nap in his cool office where a fan blew all day, while from upstairs two managers descended in rapid succession down the metal frame spiral stairs. They scurried to Nara's station.

"What happened?" screamed one of the managers.

"The threads. I separated them, but they went back," Nara said directly but quietly.

"What?" yelled the other manager, almost spitting into Nara's face.

"Let me see your hands!" cried the foreman.

Nara lifted her hands, sweat still dripping from every pour.

"Your fingers are wet like a sweating pig's," he spewed.

"Do you know what you've done, pig?" accused the first manager.

Nara did not actually know. It seemed if they only took a look at the machine, they might discover it was perfectly functional. She thought to herself, *Please just restart it.*

"Answer him," barked the foreman, pleased at the opportunity to exact revenge for all the looks and innuendos.

"I don't know," Nara replied meekly. The three men scoffed, mumbling something about dumb animals. She continued to respond, "If you look, the machine is still..."

"Shut up!" yelled the second manager, who looked darkly at Nara, full of hate and disgust. "Try and explain yourself, if you can," he taunted, growing ever more hostile. He nudged the first manager and gave him a little shrug as if hinting to him to play along. The first manager fully understood this was a moment not to be lost. It appeared they agreed they ought to make the most of it.

Nara remained quiet but weaved her brow briefly so it was imperceptible.

"These machines don't fail. They are built to run perfectly. The only reason they would not is because some stupid animal can't work on them. Now, explain yourself," he insisted.

The foreman squeezed her arm to encourage her to speak.

"I separated the threads, they moved back and the machine reacted."

"The machine! The machine reacted? Ha!" cried the second manager striking her across the face. Nara glared back and his anger became uncontrollable. He yelled as loud as he could so all the other factory women could hear. "Foreman, she is to be locked in the box until I tell you to let her out!"

"Yes sir!" the foreman replied obediently and grabbed at her by the elbow to take her away.

Nara resisted, confused. She did not know what was happening. She pulled her arm back from the foreman's grip, and he pulled her back towards him harder. They were already jostling as Nara resisted even more, and then the two managers got into the fray.

"But..." and before Nara could finish speaking they began to beat her on the dust-covered floor of the factory in front of the other workers. There was no hiding their brutality. By meting out a thrashing like this, they intended to show the others that their power would be undisputed. One of them punched her across the jaw while another kneed her in the stomach and yet another struck her on the side of her head. When she fell to the floor, the three kicked and stomped on her, swinging their legs as far back as they would go, striking her with the full impact the pendulum movement yielded. Not one of the perpetrators beat her with any hesitation; two of them seemed to enjoy this with a perverse sexual pleasure, while, the other descended into an animalistic frenzy. She could not fight off the blows and certainly could not avoid them, and only a few minutes after that, she almost stopped feeling the blows. Almost. Her eyes shut and she saw sparks, then great bursts of light play out before her in her head. Even a patriotic song seemed to trumpet in her ears. This was followed by burning sensations in her stomach and her back, and blood oozed from the gashes in her head and dribbled down her face. In a daze, she thought the blood was water. She would have started to laugh between her tears if it were not for the agony. She could see the metaphor of this act in a microcosm that played out larger across her nation: she was a little morning calm beaten down by a ruthless rising sun.

On her hands and knees, Nara shimmied her way out of her cramped dormitory quarters. The room was so dark it was hard to tell if it was centipedes crawling on her roommates or something else, but one thing was for certain — the thin bedspreads that acted as mattresses were infested with ticks. Everyone who shared the room was covered with little red bites that itched severely. And, the *clicking,* scratching sound was unmistakable: cockroaches infested the walls and the room and sluggishly lay in ugly clumps all over. At night, many of the disease-ridden roaches were caught in thin, weak, spindly hands, followed by disgusted whimpers, "No matter how many I catch, I never get used to it."

The smell in the room was bad too. Once locked down, no one could leave the quarters to access the latrine. So, there was a constant putrid odour of urine, vomit, blood, oozing pus from injuries, and even feces, that no one noticed anymore. As Nara crawled her way out, climbing over top of some of the other women who shared her room, she spilled out into the corridor and vomited on the tiles outside, which, while not unusual, happened more and more frequently. Some of the other women were ill, and the Zainichi labour guard came around to check on the one who was coughing up blood and running a fever.

"I need to get a message to my husband. It has been almost two months since I was last allowed to see him and talk to him. We were allowed see each other that night, but since then, I have not received any word."

"Two months is normal."

"But I used to catch sight of him in the mornings during the roll call almost every day. Now we have not crossed paths for all this time. There has been no news from his side of the camp. Is he well? Is he alive?"

"Shhhh, not so loud."

"Please, can you get a message to him?"

"I'll see what I can do," the Zainichi labour guard replied. There were many Korean guards who oversaw the function of various groups, sharing the same language but little else. They were Koreans who lived in Japan, choosing to live and work there for low wages and poor treatment. This particular labour guard was responsible for monitoring the labourers for illness and to report anomalies and of course, deaths. Other Zainichi guards sometimes served more sinister functions, but survival of the more comfortable kind after all did require a total loss of morals.

"Thank you, thank you. Yes, please."

"I'm not making any promises. I will see what I can do," she replied cautiously. "What's the message?"

"I'm pregnant."

There were rumours. Nara had heard news that a great war had begun. It was raging all over Europe — a horrific war, unlike anyone had ever seen and as it raged on, Nara gave birth to Sun-hi.

Merely a few days after giving birth, Nara was back on the factory floor while Sun-hi spent the first five years of her life in a childcare facility set up for the labourers' children — a sterile, dank, and lifeless room void of angels, fairies, and tales of adventure.

It was not long before Japan saw what was happening in Europe and took the opportunity to expand their aggression and their territory, executing a campaign in Indonesia and in Hawaii bringing the war to the Pacific side. There was no discussion of it on the factory floor where the ears of supervisors and factory thugs could hear. It was either forbidden or masked over and like so many things here, not discussed. But in the evenings and at meals, rumours and news got around. Some of the workers overheard kitchen staff, some heard delivery drivers, some overheard managers talking, and many saw the subdued chaos outside the factory walls. Nothing was as it should be. People walked around with their heads looking up at the sky. It was rumoured that Japan had struck Hawaii, which meant a direct attack on the United States. It seemed so outlandish that Nara almost did not believe it. It seemed impossible that Japan had bombed an American military harbour. Why would the Japanese attack the United States? Were they mad?

She sighed to herself. *No need to answer that, I suppose.*

❧ 5 ❧

MIDWIFE

A THIN LAYER OF ICE ENCRUSTED the inside of the window of her crowded room. The heat from all the bodies was not enough to stop the cold from creeping into Nara's bones. But this was better than summer nights when the blazing heat rose up from the floors and pushed down from the ceiling, strangling everyone inside. Blurry-eyed, she woke thinking she had heard the muffled voices of men stealing into the hallway. It was a recurring nightmare that crept into her sleep often, so terribly often. She pushed it aside, believing she was dreaming. Nara breathed out a long, slow breath, and a fog formed in front of her. She grimaced from the bitter cold and rubbed her hands frantically. Then she thought she saw two figures push aside the Zainichi guarding the floor. The Zainichi seemed to cower, but then she lifted her arm and pointed in Nara's direction. Grabbing that same arm, the two figures dragged the Zainichi toward Nara's room and in a harsh tone, demanded to know "which one?" The Zainichi strained to see in the dark. No, Nara was not dreaming. Who was the Zainichi looking for? The woman slithered her way to Nara and pointed at her. Nara trembled. The men stomped their way towards Nara, stepping on the other women who lay on the ground in their tracks as if they were piles of dirt.

Both men were dressed in traditional kimonos but with heavy western-style overcoats. They were out of place in the factory. While they did not look like noblemen, they did not look like scoundrels either. All that belied their status were their hands, which were not smooth, but rough, even chafed, and the kimonos hidden under the coats were not of silk, but of cloth.

They growled at the Zainichi and then grabbed at Nara, pulling her up to her feet. Nara looked at the men. All they said was, "Come with us." Nara pulled her arm back, refusing to move. She froze from the terror brought on by the night and its darkness. Her head spun with confusion, never having witnessed something so mysterious happen in the factory in all of the years she had suffered there. She knew she could not ask what this was about. She remained silent, but her shaking body gave away her fear. Her legs were weak, and suddenly she was no longer able to stand. She started to fall, landing with a thud on the ground. Then, one man grabbed her left arm while the other grabbed her right, roughly jerking her to her feet. The other women in the cramped room gasped but said nothing. A few sobs could be heard and someone whispered, "Nara," inadvertently. Nara tried to free herself, but the men had already started to drag her out of the room.

She knew she was being pulled through the cold, but she could not feel anything. The air bit her, and her breasts, which hung out from her sack-like dress, tightened in the icy wind. She was not wearing shoes, and her toes ploughed through the frozen snow leaving a thin trail next to two sets of heavy shoe prints. The metal gates creaked open. It was the first time in years — Nara wasn't sure how many — that she had been outside the gates of the factory. It was not entirely impossible to go outside the factory walls. In fact, from time to time, some men and women were sent on errands under guard, and some left the compound daily. But Nara never went.

Just outside the gate, at the front of the factory, a black car was waiting. The smoke from the exhaust lifted in the air like a ghost. One of the men opened the car door, the other flung her into the back seat. Nara shivered from the cold, from the terror. She would have fainted if not for suddenly feeling the warmth in the car. She had not ridden in a car in a long time. She could not remember when, but it did not matter. She remembered the last time men came in the dark of night to steal another young woman away. There was not anything good about that.

She struggled to get out of the car. She could not leave the factory. Jae-sun and Sun-hi were still there. She screamed. She kicked. She wept. One of the men who had entered the car from the right, put his hand firmly over her mouth while the other man, who had entered the car from the left, slapped her with the back of his hand and pushed her, forcing her to sit in the middle, between them.

The two men sat silently on either side of her while a driver with a black hat and leather gloves drove away. The driver glanced at Nara in the rear-view mirror but quickly averted his eyes back to the road, disinterested now that he knew what the package looked like.

One of the men took out a handkerchief from the inside overcoat pocket and tied it around her mouth, which was wet with tears, while they each took an arm and pushed against her legs with their own so she could not move easily. One of them, the shorter, stout one, started to speak to the other. Nara was, of course, nearly fluent in Japanese because of attending state-run schools and working in the factory, but the way they spoke was foreign to her. They had a colloquial slang and words melted together. She could see they were not well-educated, if at all. But how did that explain the car and the overcoats and the handkerchief? Her head swam with possibilities.

"Take out the knife."

Nara's eyes grew wide.

"It will keep her quiet."

Nara squirmed as hard as she could and tears flowed down from her eyes. She could not stop thinking about Jae-sun and Sun-hi. However, as the car drove on and Nara squirmed violently, it became slowly obvious that the men were actually trying *not* to hurt her.

Nara could not tell how far they had gone, but they seemed to be driving for a long time, over muddy, bumpy roads, far into the quieter areas of the city. Finally, the car stopped and Nara saw a house with glowing lights coming from between every wall. It was a traditional, well-maintained Japanese home, larger than all the other houses around it, with curved roofs, dark wooden beams and bonsai in the windows. A small garden featured an ice-covered water fountain and small bushes covered in snow.

When the car pulled up, a woman who was crouched down on both knees, slid the door open and bowed until her forehead touched the tatami floor. There were candles and lanterns burning, so while the outside was pitch black, the inside of the Japanese house glowed. Glowed like hell.

The two men pulled Nara out of the car. Nara continued to sob and tremble. What was this place? Why was she here? The three dragged themselves up the stairs to the hard wooden porch, and then finally, through the door.

The two men who had grabbed her and taken her away from the factory and her family, now threw her to the tatami floor and then bowed deeply to a man dressed in a rich shimmering kimono made of the finest silk. Nara knew the silk well. He was standing in the middle of the room with his arms crossed, his back turned to the servant men. He growled at the two lowly servants as he turned to face them. He could feel the cold wind they brought in on their overcoats. The servants bowed deeper, shuddering a little and cowering a lot.

The man in the silk kimono, the master of the house, waved his hand to send them away.

They did not need to be told twice. The servants scurried away like insects. Nara stood up immediately.

She looked around to see sparsely furnished but nevertheless well-heeled surroundings. The hard wood beams were polished and gleamed, and the floors did not creak. There were silk wall hangings and intricately carved armoires. It was a home well-groomed. Nara would have been reminded of her own childhood home for the sheer opulence of it, but nothing of it was familiar.

There was another servant standing in the corner, better dressed than the others.

In the backroom, Nara could hear the muffled voice of a woman. She strained to hear her — it seemed that the woman was in agony, repressing screams. There was a gagging sound; then, suddenly a low, long growl followed by a shrill screech. The master of the house slung his arms behind his back and grimaced with disapproval. The women servants scurried around nervously, and it became clear to Nara that the woman in the back room was in labour.

The wealthy homeowner seemed startled at first to see Nara on her feet, refusing to bow or cower, but then he seemed to resign himself to it as if it was strangely befitting. Instead of commanding her to bow down — which a man of his stature would not do anyway, merely expecting it with no need to say it — he observed her like he was trying to figure something out. He looked at her sideways, glancing at her as though she had disappeared and then reappeared right before his eyes. He lifted his hand and waved it in front of him, as if waving away an imaginary fog, and announced abruptly, "You're a midwife."

Nara was stunned. Then, she felt immediately relieved. Now she knew why she was brought to this Japanese man's home.

"You're what you people call a *mudang*?"

She collected herself but she still stuttered, "No, not a *mudang*. I'm a nurse."

"You were taught by the Christian man."

"The missionaries?"

"Yes, and their mystical powers," the man asserted.

Nara was insulted. No Christian had mystical powers.

"Medicine," was all she replied.

The Japanese man ignored her. It was obvious he did not relish that a Korean woman was about to help his wife and that his baby, his firstborn, would be at the mercy of Nara's "kind."

The man nodded at his servant standing in the corner, and the servant continued to explain, "The factory owner said you are a nurse trained by 'the Christian man.' The stories of your healing powers reached his ear and passed on to us."

Nara did not have any idea what the servant was talking about.

"The master's wife has been labouring for too long. Days. We believe she is dying. The birthing mat is soaked with blood and her sweat and her tears. It is wet with her pain. Her screams are raising the *yokai*."

"*Yokai*?" Nara was unfamiliar with the word.

"Ghosts. Shape shifters."

"Shape shifters."

"*Yokai*. The woman will bring a curse upon the master's household if she does not stop with her pain and screaming. She is calling for trouble. Do you understand? She is waking the dead."

Nara frowned in disgust but did not say a word, shutting her lips together tightly. That man's wife was in labour. That was all. Who was waking the dead? If anything, she was bringing in life.

"You must help him."

"Him."

"Yes, were you not listening? With all of her screaming, she will bring a curse on the master and his house." Nara looked at the servant and blinked, reminded that servant or master, it did not matter. All men were the same.

She looked back at the wealthy homeowner, who had already turned to leave without so much as a word. The man's back scooted through the screen and Nara lost sight of him as the screen door slammed behind him.

Nara knew that if she did not help the Japanese woman, she would no doubt be cast out on to the street with no way back to the factory, where Jae-sun and Sun-hi still slept. And she knew that if she called for help, no one would come to her aid. And even if she could walk back to the factory, she did not know the route and it seemed a great distance. She needed to return to Sun-hi. She could not abandon her daughter. So, Nara could not refuse.

She moved into the back room where the woman in labour was lying on a mat, her screams desperately muffled, in an effort to acquiesce to the demand for silence dictated by her culture.

Without looking at the servant, Nara paused and then slowly asked, "And what if the baby or woman dies in childbirth?"

The servant looked up and said plainly, "Of course, you will die."

"And if the baby is stillborn?"

"You will die."

Nara shuddered. The injustice was raw and inescapable but not new. She did what she always did, she prayed, uttering Psalm 143, "Cause me to know the way wherein I should walk; for I lift up my soul unto thee. Deliver me, O Lord, from mine enemies." God had His way of answering.

"Do you think the woman would do the same thing for me?" Nara was not sure why she asked that out loud. She simply blurted out what she was thinking. The servant looked at Nara bewildered at such a question and gave her a look of derision. Though he did not utter the words, Nara could almost read the servant thoughts: *Of course not. The master's wife would not do the same thing for you. What a stupid question.*

Nara could see the woman in labour was mad with pain and delirious. She ordered the servant to bring hot water and towels. The woman lifted her arm towards Nara when she saw her, almost begging, as if she saw Nara as an angel come to help her. The woman's head and entire body were dripping with sweat and mucous and fluid was everywhere. She bore down and then seemed to fight the urge to push, letting out a great moan and then a reluctant, stifled scream.

Nara hovered over the woman and put a cloth on the woman's head as she slumped back down onto the mat. Nara prayed again. Then, she laid her hands on the woman's womb and chanted, "*Neh sohn, yack sohn ya. My hand is a healing hand.*"

When these words, "*Neh sohn, yack sohn ya,*" were said aloud, they had a soothing rhythm, like a gentle lullaby a mother might sing to her baby. The emphasis had to be on just the right syllable and said in such a way that it was truly like a chant — one so melodic that one could not help but focus only on the beauty of it. Repeated over and over again, with hands on the injured body, it had the makings of a shamanistic mantra.

And then, Nara remembered.

A factory supervisor's young child had fallen and hurt her arm. She had screamed so hard and was in such pain, the young girl would not let anyone touch her. Since Nara was a nurse, she could see by the way the child was favouring her arm and holding it in an L-shape against her chest that the little girl had a dislocated shoulder. She had approached the child slowly and given her the gentlest look. "You look like a doe," the child had said pointing up at her face. Out of her pocket, Nara had pulled out a cross she had made from an old piece of wood; she gave it to the little girl to hold. As the girl held the wooden cross in her good hand, Nara had set the shoulder right, snapping it quickly back into place while the child was distracted by what was in her hand. The child had given her a startled look, almost fearful, like a child looks when whirled around on a father's shoulder, the thrill too enticing to ignore. The little girl had frowned for a moment and it seemed she was about to cry, but then her face softened and she smiled.

Nara rubbed the girl's shoulder, "*Neh sohn, yack sohn ya.*"

The factory supervisor, a hard and evil man, had looked at Nara suspiciously but also with relief.

His young daughter leapt into her father's arms, with no awareness of the kind of man he was, and cheerfully chatted to him now that her arm felt better. He gave his daughter a kiss on her forehead, let her down, and patted her away.

The supervisor had looked through thin eyes and thin lips at Nara and asked what she just said. Nara had translated, "My hand is a healing hand." She had not meant that literally, of course. But, he was an ignorant man.

Then, not long after, a factory co-worker had fallen ill. She had clutched her stomach and groaned in agony while writhing around on the floor. Nara had asked the woman what kind of pain it was and the woman described a thorough cramping at the side of her stomach. The woman's groans had been so volatile, that some people, including the factory manager, thought she would die. To Nara, it seemed the co-worker had food poisoning. At first, Nara thought this a strange diagnosis since they all ate the same horrible grub, but then she had simply shrugged, rubbed the woman's stomach, and chanted, "*Neh sohn, yack sohn ya,*" followed by a brief prayer. Those around her could see her lips moving, but no words were coming out of her mouth. The warmth of the rubbing had caused the woman to defecate what was bothering her, and she was well once again.

Shortly afterward, another factory worker had fallen to the ground, convulsing as if possessed by a demon. Her eyes had rolled back in her head and her body had shaken uncontrollably. This had also not been the first time she had done this, and every time, the factory managers would kick her and beat her, and every time, it was as if the worker was not there, as though her soul had emptied from the body. Nothing worked, and after the first couple of incidents of this demonic behaviour, all the managers had developed a fear of the girl. Nara had seen this at the hospital when she was a young nurse. The missionaries had explained that this was something called "epilepsy." There was no cure, but episodes could be avoided if the patient was not stimulated by swirling colours and quickly moving images. When the latest episode stopped, Nara had held the girl, soothed her and stroked her head, and chanting, "*Neh sohn yack sohn ya.*" Again, she had followed this with little prayer. Her lips moved, but no words came out. She had then risen from the ground with the girl still in her arms and said to the factory manager that the girl needed to be stationed outside. She should shovel dirt or clean the kitchen, but should not be separating threads on the dizzying looms. The factory manager had looked at Nara in disbelief, but heeded what she said, seeing her as some kind of wizard. After the exorcism, the girl had started working in the kitchen and the epileptic seizures stopped, and Nara grew in legend.

Then a woman had gone into labour. She had become pregnant after being raped by one of the factory managers but was accused of sleeping with one of the men in the quarry on the other side of the factory during visitations. She was sent to the infirmary, but the labour was going badly. A Zainichi had rushed to get Nara and delivered her to the infirmary. Nara had drawn upon her only experience with childbirth, which was when she had given birth to Sun-hi. She had no magic solution, no mystical powers. Upon seeing Nara, the two nurses tending the pregnant woman had started to move away from the bed, but Nara grabbed their arms and pulled the nurses closer to the woman, indicating they should not go anywhere.

She had lain her hands on the woman's swollen belly and said, "*Neh sohn yack sohn ya,*" and again, bowed her head and prayed. As she was rubbing, she felt a little movement, a kick from around the midpoint at the right side of the tightened belly. Nara had known immediately that the baby had not completely turned. There was probably nothing that could be done. She told the woman to stop pushing and explained that she herself would push down for her with her hands. So, Nara had pushed the area where the leg had kicked and felt around for the bulbous head. Feeling something similar to a head — and hopefully it was not the baby's bottom — she pushed it down. She had not known what she was doing; she had only guessed.

It likely had nothing to do with what Nara was doing with her hands, and maybe more to do with the prayer she had said earlier Nara thought, but after nearly an hour, the baby had turned. It had been a miracle. The baby had squeezed headlong into the world, bringing with it a pool of blood and placenta and every hope it was ever going to have. Nara had delivered her alive and the woman, though near death, had survived. This had sealed Nara's reputation as a mystic healer, a midwife, and an apprentice of "the Christian man."

The Japanese woman continued to wail and pant as sweat poured down her face. Nara felt her belly, and there did not seem to be anything wrong. The baby was turned. To Nara, it seemed that it should only be a matter of time. She was puzzled. As another contraction approached, the woman suppressed her scream and summoned all her might in order not to push *too hard* for the immodesty of it, and Nara frowned.

"This is your first baby?"

The woman nodded her head feverishly.

This time, Nara got close to the woman's face and looked straight into the crying woman's eyes and said sternly, "Do not pay any attention to your fool of a husband."

The woman quieted and looked at Nara.

"Do not listen to the whispers and anxious footsteps behind the walls."

The woman could hear Nara.

"Scream all you want and push hard."

The woman could see Nara. She seemed to see Nara morphing from woman to angel, angel to woman.

"Scream. There are no *yokai*. Now push hard!"

Through the night, the woman pushed as Mother Nature

intended, shaking off any false sense of decorum and womanly modesty. This was not the time.

Afterwards, Nara held the baby, head in her right hand, his bottom in her left. She looked down at him, at first with a soft gaze. He looked like any other baby she had helped come into the world. He wriggled innocently in her hands, unable to steady his unproportionally large head and puffy face. His small thin legs flailed and kicked the air. He gurgled a bit and sleepily opened his eyes for a moment before shutting them tight again. Nara's gentle gaze quickly dissipated like fog, and her face darkened. He was still covered in birthing fluids and mucous, and he was bloody and slippery. She stared at this creature with curiosity and suspicion all at once. She suddenly held him like a rabbit about to be skewered as he writhed in her hands. She knew that before long he would grow up and his views of the world would narrow into a deluded sense of superiority, echoing in his cry the yearning of a nation hungry for power and domination. He would learn to hate her. In her arms lay yet another generation in which nothing would change.

ම6ම
"RAGE, RAGE AGAINST THE
DYING OF THE LIGHT"

BY NIGHT, THE FACTORY AND ALL the government buildings were completely dark. From time to time, flares dropped from the bombers would light up the sky and then the windows of the buildings could be easily distinguished, and the buildings' towers would throw quavering shadows across the courtyards. Like thunder following lightning, a barrage of fire would then emblazon the sky as shells burst and were made brighter by the reflection in the now visible clouds. Allied planes circled high above, beyond the range of Japanese anti-aircraft fire, but at the same time, prevented by the bombers from descending to an altitude where they could return accurate fire. From all indications, the government buildings and factories were indeed the main targets. Until recently, the Allies had been blindly dropping their loads over the region, sometimes hitting industrial zones and even civilian areas. But, lately, the Allies had gotten good at understanding the landscape and their aim had become highly accurate. At least, that was how it looked from the small windows of Nara's dormitory. The Axis powers became befuddled at how Allied aircraft passed their radar undetected, and were completely unaware that the Americans had developed a prenatal version of what would someday be stealth technology. Thus, the air superiority of the Allies seemed all but absolute.

By this time, west of the Caucasus Mountains, the Axis powers were in a state of utter collapse. Their forces, scattered from

Italy to the south and Russia to the north, were retreating from the soft lines in the sand they had meekly drawn weeks earlier. The Germans were in disarray, unable to handle the Allies flowing down the continent like spreading wildfire, clearing the land like it was plagued with disease, as entire divisions and infantries surrendered one after the other like dominos. Axis tanks and artillery were unable to withstand the barrage of fire from the Allies above, while small villages all across Sino-Russia burned by the hundreds.

Despite the daily rain shower of bullets that popped on the soil when they landed, it was clear that in the land of the imperial Emperor, its citizens conspired to believe there was nothing happening in the rest of the world, and certainly not in nearby Korea. It had become obvious to Nara that millions of people were in willing denial of what their own government was doing. There was a tacit agreement that either there was absolutely nothing happening at all or whatever might be happening was perfectly all right. Like the Germans whom the factory managers often whispered about, their own government and ruling class had given the ordinary Japanese citizen plausible deniability and kept them blind like fools. And why not? The role of the ruling government at the time was to maintain the peace and stroke the insecurities of an unaware population that prostrated themselves willingly to be subjugated to blissful ignorance.

Then, as quickly as it started, it was over. Sometimes answers to universal tremors come slow, stretching over decades or centuries or millennia, but sometimes it does not take long at all. After the war, Nara finally heard about the radical transformation in military technology the Americans had developed in the aftermath of Pearl Harbor. Some people described the transformation as an "improvement" or "development," but "improvement" made Nara think it was agreeable to make military advancements. But she could not deny it was certainly effective in killing, which, she supposed, made the weapon better at what it is supposed to do. If only humans could transform as easily. *Of course, with weapons like that, it doesn't give us much chance*, she thought.

The Allied forces liberated Korea from Japanese imperial rule but left it divided. Nara would rather take a country divided than a country in bondage. In the eternal reverberations of the universe, like Newton's first law of motion, an object keeps moving until another force exerts on it and changes its direction. In this case, the force that was exerted led Korea back to independence and Nara and her family on their journey back home.

The rumours were true. The Americans had indeed built a bomb like no other that turned humans into ghosts and breath into shadows. It was so fierce, neither demon nor angel alike could do their job in catching souls, whether damning them or rescuing them. And so, with this, came the unceremonious surrender of the Japanese empire.

In Korea, the Japanese government disbanded and disintegrated, and in Japan, forced to hang their head at this capitulation with vengeance in their hearts, a mass wave of insanity overcame the population and it fell into temporary chaos. While there were countless suicides by Japanese officials and industrial leaders — acts meant to regain their honour — there were "unofficial" murders of refugees to silence them, which only added dishonour and blood on already soaked hands. The Allies sent armed units to Japan to mediate the transition of workers when factories were shutdown, and the slave labourers were freed, and Nara and Jae-sun and Sun-hi were reunited. There, in the autumn of 1945, they packed their few belongings and prepared to head out of the factory into freedom.

There were hundreds of labourers streaming out like a tidal wave ahead of them. On their way out, Nara and Jae-sun both turned slightly to acknowledge the factory foreman sitting on an overturned trash can, watching the exodus with boorish loathing. It seemed he could not believe his country's decisive defeat and its utter failure to satiate his personal appetite for power. He looked partly bereaved, but unable to change come hell or heaven, he remained firmly hostile. Nara almost skidded past him, but he stood up when he saw her. She was face-to-face with the foreman whom she considered the lowest example of a totalitarian oppressor, vacant of purpose, and empty of any worth.

The foreman looked at her with wide eyes that goaded. A sharp diatribe with this soulless creature would be a wasted effort. But she intentionally brushed shoulders with him as she passed and said, "*Mansei.*" It was only one word, but it spoke volumes, and in reflex, Nara closed her eyes in tribute to her homeland.

When she opened her eyes again, there were several stares directed at her. Factory managers were going about their business within the fence walls, and many Japanese locals were passing by outside walls. It was a usual day in unusual circumstances. Some of those staring at her looked away as soon as she made eye contact with them, but a few eyes remained fixed on her long enough to remind her of where she was. Imperialist design was near rot, and the poison dripped from the lingering stares of disapproval. Many walked away shaking their heads, while others looked like they would spit on Nara if she stood closer. Jae-sun could read the dare in the taut muscles of Nara's neck and was now cautious, not for himself, but for those around them. He knew the look in Nara's eyes meant she would not go quietly.

"Only a few months ago, like so many before me, you would have flogged me or sent me to prison where I would be tortured and ultimately put to death for so-called treason, for this act of patriotism, for uttering this one word," Nara said quietly, her tone icy. "But the world is watching, old man. The world is watching."

The foreman's smirk dropped and he stepped aside.

"*Mansei,*" she repeated. *Long live Korea.*

Jae-sun turned toward the foreman and grinned as he pulled

his wife close to him, gently nudging her to his other side, away from the foreman. Then, taking their bags, he grabbed Sun-hi's hand and led them away, pushing past the rude spectators and pallid faces of the factory managers still milling about.

Nara and Jae-sun headed to the port, their intended destination, with purpose and pride. Along the way, they saw all the labourers and workers who had suddenly been set free. The streets were flooded with a people who had no citizenship, no home, and no work, left to fend for themselves, to scavenge for food and shelter. Fortunately enough, Nara and Jae-sun had scraped together enough money and hidden it well — most of it earned by keeping the *yokai* away from the wealthy homeowner, who had paid Nara an offering so as not to raise the eye of bad spirits. Some money had also come from others grateful for her healing hands, and the rest had come from selling whatever was on their back or from trinkets found in dust heaps.

They bribed a sailor to stow the family away on a boat destined for home. They did not have enough to be ticket-holding passengers like others, including some of the labourers who had voluntarily come to Japan to work. So, hiding behind cargo trunks filled with machine parts and crates filled with other goods, they would be able to manage passage across the East Sea to the Port of Busan. During the voyage, they might be able to mingle amongst the rest of the passengers as long as no one asked for their papers. To be safe, Nara, Jae-sun and Sun-hi came out from hiding only in the evening and at night to search for scraps of food and to stretch their legs. They wisely elected to use extreme caution if they ran into anyone.

Night crept in. The moon's silver gleam swam upon the open sea. After Sun-hi fell asleep, Nara and Jae-sun carefully emerged and then stood at the prow wrapped in a blanket they had found while trolling the bridge deck earlier. They felt a mounting, salty wind, and they looked down to the waves thrashing as the ship pushed on with a clap and a gush of foam. They did not have view of what they had left behind, but looked only to the open sea and listened carefully to the stories the ocean had to tell to them. The wind blew harder and made them feel both refreshed and a little deaf. But, it washed over them, this feeling of the free wind, and, for the moment, all their anguish sank like a rock to the depths of the sea and turned to joy.

On a freighter, this trip would take no longer than a day — maybe two days at most — but on this rickety tub, the trip took much longer. It was apparent with its small girth and slow bearing, coupled with the stops along the way, that this would be a multi-day voyage. They had been at sea for already a second day, and at nightfall, as Nara was about to emerge from behind her crate, she caught sight of another woman crouched behind a crate that was diagonal to the one Nara and her family were hidden behind. Nara had not noticed the woman before and was startled. It was obvious the woman had also not noticed Nara's family, or if she had, she may have mistaken them for legitimate passengers. The woman hobbled out, for what looked like the same reason as Nara's, to look for food. That night, Nara resigned herself to the safety of her hidden spot on the ship and did not venture out, for fear of running into the woman and betraying her location. She put her finger to her mouth as a signal to Jae-sun and Sun-hi that they would be staying in this evening.

Nara had a clear view of the woman and over the next couple of days, she quietly observed this shadow woman. The woman was fevered and frail, and she seemed much older than Nara in her face. It seemed as if all human dignity had been stripped from her, like fur pulled off a live animal. In her eyes, misery and suffering languished on the pupils' surface, like scum or algae on standing water. She was limp and broken — utterly broken. Though she appeared ghostly, Nara could tell she had her full faculties by the way she cared for her wounds, as though she had cared for them many times before, and there appeared to be many. It seemed some had healed over countless times, but some were still healing. She had bruises on her face and neck like she had been strangled. Welts and cuts covered her arms in circular patterns that looked like cigarette burns. There were scars on her neck, upper back, and shoulders that ran deep, as though someone had tried to skin her alive. Her legs were wobbly twigs that looked like they had been seized and bent with an inconceivable force. Having seen her walk, Nara could see the woman's legs barely supported her. She teetered back and forth, each step an agony. She obviously had dislocated her hip or knee or both at some point and that neither was ever put right. She wore a tattered dress, one too large for her, and it was clear that it was never meant to be a piece of clothing, merely something to cover her body, cover her shame. Once in a while, because it was too big, the dress would slip down and off her shoulder a little, and when that happened, the woman's eyes would fill with tears and she would grit her teeth in almost uncontrollable frustration, as if all the world's burden perched on that slightly revealed shoulder. Seemingly unable to bear revealing any skin, she would grab at the cloth and pull it up high around her neck, cursing it for failing her. If Nara could see beneath that tattered dressed, she gathered that what she witnessed on the woman's arms and legs would be worse on the woman's torso and back. She did not wish to see and refused to imagine, but she felt certain her body would be covered in welts, bruises, burns, and gaping scars, and in the holy regions, inconceivable horrors. Curious still, the woman clutched her stomach all day and night, never removing her arms from her midsection. She clutched herself as if she were her own baby, as if she needed to rock herself, protect herself, and reassure herself that she was really there. The area she clutched was lower down, near the blessed region. Nara supposed the woman was going through her monthly cycle and must have had cramps, severe ones. It was the only logical explanation, but not the only explanation.

Because the woman was making extreme efforts to conceal herself, Nara did not want to betray that she had seen her and had been watching her with genuine concern for some time. For though Nara also suffered greatly, this woman looked like she had traversed the most evil regions of a dark abyss, and had been rejected by heaven with no angel to watch over her. Looking at her, Nara's heart filled, not with pity, but with deep sorrow.

One evening, as they neared the Busan harbour, Nara noticed the woman did not steal out at the usual time. The sun had set already for some time, and Nara thought the woman must have fallen asleep for there was no sign of her. She decided it would be safe to come out. It was her turn to look for food while Jae-sun kept watch. As Nara emerged from her hiding spot, she heard a gasp, and then very clearly, her name.

"Nara."

The sound, a dull monotone. There was no joy in the voice that spoke her name, only the articulation of a fact.

Nara whirled around astonished. She was startled to see the woman standing just a foot or two behind her.

"How do you know my name?" Nara stammered.

"Nara. It's me."

Nara looked hard at the woman trying to place her, questions running through her head. *Have I met this woman before? Where have I met her?*

"How do you know my name?" Nara whispered, still a little shaken from the surprise.

"Nara, it's me."

"I'm sorry, I do not recognize you. Have you been watching me? Did my husband tell you my name?"

The woman looked back at Nara with a profound sadness in her eyes, for this made her realize that she was no longer there, so beyond the point of recognition that the woman she once was had indeed gone, and her name and identity with it.

"Who are you?" Nara asked again quietly.

"Nara, it's me. Min-joo."

"Min-joo?" Nara's eyes lit up and just as quickly went dark. Before she could utter her surprise, her joy, her sadness, her fear, she fainted, collapsing cold onto the ship's deck. To see Min-joo again and realize this was her dear friend, this woman who seemed to have suffered the most unspeakable ordeal, caused Nara's soul to lift out of her for a moment, as if it was ready to depart and allow Nara to die.

They moved to the upper deck, ostensibly to search for food, but it was Min-joo's story that kept them there, long after they had given up the pretence of looking for sustenance.

Min-joo told her about the sound of footfalls in the corridor outside her room, or the continuous opening and closing of doors, when the soldiers were drunk or angry or half-crazed by the war, that was the habitual backdrop of nocturnal terror for countless nights.

"I would say, 'Please God, don't let them come in. Block the door with one of your angels or send the Angel of Death to rescue me.' And if the soldier passed by my room, I would be relieved," she sobbed. "Relieved that he moved on to the girl in the next room or the room after that." Years of guilt were etched deeply into her face.

"During the day, the manager kept the barracks open from eight in the morning to five in the afternoon. It was like it was some retail shop that kept regular office hours. We were merchandise, and it went on all day, every day. The daytime was bad, but the rapes under the dark of night were unspeakable. The soldiers were not supposed to access the barracks at night, but a small bribe helped an eye turn blind. The dark veil gave shelter to evil and the soldiers morphed into demons, with no light in sight. The worst nights drunk and angry soldiers would hone in on one victim and a tide of men would rape, mutilate, and beat the woman in the most gruesome and barbaric way. Then at dawn, someone's daughter, someone's wife, someone's sister, a woman with a name, was left there alone, broken, bloody, near dead. If she was too broken, she was left to die. If she was reparable like some object, they would send her to the infirmary and eventually send her back to be forced to do it all over again."

As Min-joo spoke, Nara trembled. "The sound of muffled sobbing was constant, and it was mostly suppressed of course, but on occasion sobbing turned to hysteria. The hysteria made me quake, for I knew that whatever was happening was not merely a crime, not merely a sin, but the kind of thing that makes shame itself hide."

Often that sobbing was hers. Often the hysteria was hers and more often it was from the hundreds of thousands of other girls and women trapped in countless camps and colonies in this unspeakable slavery.

"Most days, my nerves gave out. I would say, 'If only they would slice me up or stab me through. Could they not have just this much mercy to kill me?' But there was no mercy in sight. There was no God and no mercy. And, indeed, many women did kill themselves. By the time I got there — how many years now? — we were left only with bed sheets and the wood frame of the bed, but a desperate woman can do desperate things with just a few items on hand," Min-joo fell silent and tears dropped to the ship's deck. "One woman, a few doors down from me, tried to hang herself with bed sheets, but the noose kept slipping through. She made several attempts, but each time, just before she lost all air, the noose would slip through again. On the last attempt, she fell to the ground and passed out unconscious. When she revived the next morning," Min-joo paused, "she was brain-dead." She paused again and trembled uncontrollably. "It didn't work. She was still alive but brain-dead."

Nara lamely tried to console her by adding, "Lucky, then?" She did not mean to seem cold, only realistic.

"If she was brain-dead, I guess," Min-joo said, then added,

"but, you don't want to know what they do to girls like that." She shivered.

"I had heard that in the early days, the soldiers would go into the rooms with their full uniform, weapon included. This was poor judgement. The women would grab at the weapon and kill the solider and then kill themselves with it. Since those initial mistakes, weapons were not allowed in the rooms. A small solace to those mutilated by knives, but no solace for those who wanted escape. Then, I had heard there were magical potions that some soldiers whispered about. The potions made them feel numb about the war and helped them feel empty. I longed for some of this mystical concoction to numb my broken body, numb my broken mind. Nothing and no one came to help. I was alert and aware, and I longed to be dead."

Min-joo trembled as she remembered the vile acts forced upon her small body, and she sweat with fear at the memories.

"Do you know why I'm here on this ship, Nara?" whimpered Min-joo.

Nara shook her head slowly, unsure. She knew the ship had arrived in the port in Japan directly from Burma and South China. Min-joo must have made her way from the front lines in one of those places, perhaps Rangoon, and stowed away on this ship, staying hidden the whole time. Min-joo must have hoped she had boarded the right boat, but Nara then assumed Min-joo probably had not cared which boat as long as it took her far, far away from the barracks and those men. Nara tried to stop the large tear drops from forming a small puddle at her feet, but she never took her eyes off Min-joo.

"I was allowed to escape because I survived for so long, that's why. They thought I was some circus freak because I lived through the abuse for so many years, and as a sort of amusement, they let me go before the foreigners came. Almost all the girls in my barracks died within a few years, and wave after wave of new girls arrived until the sources started to dry up, I guess, and then they tried to keep us alive a little longer. We were able to bathe — well, we were forced to. And we had access to medicine. But still, within a few years, most were dead from disease or illness, or worse, from the mutilations or forced abortions. The abortions were bad. They were barbaric and forced. Some would die from the complications after. "Oh," she moaned. "Oh, sometimes the bleeding didn't stop. And she would scream, scream so loud. Or after the procedure, sometimes she had a gaping wound and a soldier would say she was 'useless.' But most of the time, no procedure was needed. After all, why stop even if a girl happens to be pregnant? So, she miscarried. And there were many miscarriages. And if the baby stayed in there, sometimes they didn't bother to try to abort it. They'd just killed the girl as if it wasn't worth the effort to save her, as if she was to blame for getting pregnant." Tears streamed down Min-joo's face unabated. "Can you believe it?"

"Some girls contracted severe disease in their areas. When a soldier saw disease, they called it her filth, so occasionally, if they could get away with it, instead of sending them to the infirmary, they would bayonet her through the...," she gasped. It was too vile to say out loud. "But do you know? The manager of the facility would be angry at the woman for soiling the sheets with her blood, as if she were menstruating or something. Once dead, he tossed the body out with the rotting garbage behind the barracks. What remained of her would be burned in the incinerator with all the other dead girls. She turned to ash, as if she never existed," Min-joo paused again with disgust and horror in her eyes. "Can you imagine? As if she never existed."

Min-joo trailed off in thought, trying to make sense of things as though she had been trying to make sense of it for a very long time. She started to mumble, unable to bear the weight of her memories. It was as if her mind was short-circuiting.

"The night they took me away was a mistake. I wasn't supposed to be there."

Nara looked at Min-joo and could not utter a word.

"Do you remember, Nara? I was only visiting. I was visiting you. I wanted to comfort you and keep you safe. I was only visiting."

Nara held her head in shame knowing this was the truth. She could not speak. She could only weep. All that happened to Min-joo should not have happened and it had happened because of her. The guilt bore down like a bitter winter wind that blew through her. Her body trembled to her very core. She convulsed and started to retch, as if to purge herself from the guilt.

"I did not regret it at first. I pitied you for your loss. You should not have lost your father that way, and then the injustice to lose everything: your family, your name, your home. And to be sent to some roach-infested orphanage. I still had my loving family. I felt guilty. I thought I deserved some pain too. But, but so much pain?" She paused. "I, I just..." She couldn't finish. Min-joo fell silent for a long time.

"That was the last night I saw my family. Everyday, every-day, I think about them. I so often wanted to tell them that I was still alive. I would imagine my mother and how she must have wept for me. My heart breaks, Mama, Mama," Min-joo cradled her stomach again and rocked herself. "I dream about my family and know, know, no," she stuttered. "How much they must have been looking for me, never to find me. Never to be found..." Min-joo rambled. "My father must have searched every street and looked down every alley wondering if I was there," Min-joo said, continuing to sound confused.

Nara gritted her teeth and clenched her hands. Min-joo's pretty face was now reshuffled. It was no wonder that she had not recognized her. Her mouth and her nose were distorted, presumably from many beatings. Her nose had been broken on more than one occasion, and now it was permanently swollen and misshapen. She was gaunt, obviously malnour-ished, and much thinner than when Nara had known her many years ago. Of course, they had both aged, but while both were still young, Min-joo looked old, so old. It had been almost a decade since the rift in the universe and their destinies split onto different paths. But, it was not simply the physical changes that had made Min-joo unrecognizable. Nara no longer recognized Min-joo for whoever Min-joo had been — her wisdom, her kindness and her gentle ways, and all of her characteristics no longer dwelled on her spirit. All those things that made Min-joo were taken from her the day she was kidnapped. From then, her mind was gone and all hope was gone. And, without hope there is nothing. All that was left was a body. And now, that broken and limp body too was almost completely gone. The woman who stood before Nara was not Min-joo. She was a shadow, with barely anything left of the young Min-joo she had known long ago. Nara took a deep breath and waited for something, anything to redeem all their souls. She waited to be smote down from the heavens, for great lightning bolts to rain on her, for death to strike. But nothing happened, and all she could do was weep once again.

Min-joo continued talking, but now she did not care if anyone listened. She had been alone for years, when no one heard her cries, when no one stopped to listen or cared to hear. After years like that, she was used to talking to herself, to comforting herself. Now before Nara, she had regressed to brighter days for a moment, before her fateful kidnapping, which left her sad now, mourning for her lost family, her lost innocence.

"She would cry every night for me. I know, Mama. You cried every night with me. You cried like I did. You cried when they grabbed me. You cried when they did those things, Mama. They did awful things, Mama, and you cried." Min-joo wept uncontrollably. "I cried out for you to help me. I cried to you, I cried to Daddy, I cried to God, but no one came. No one. I know you couldn't come. I know. Why couldn't you come?

God, where were you? God, where are you now?"
For a while, Min-joo stayed locked in her dream, far, far away.
Nara chose not to wake her, and fell into a hell all her own.

The strong wind continued the next day and rocked the ship
mercilessly. The sea sloshed and thrashed as clouds scattered
quickly across the night sky. Both Nara and Jae-sun came
down with varying degrees of motion sickness and they teetered on the decks even though the ship had a heavy passage
and remained steady.

Although it was pitiful to see them with their shallow stomachs
and sunken eyes, the refugee children on the ship survived the
journey much better than their parents, including Sun-hi. To
Sun-hi, Korea was a land of fairy tales and paradise where the
birds were more beautiful, the trees were taller, the land more
abundant, and the sky without effort was a bright, dazzling blue,
able to reveal its true self when not shackled behind a mask of
factory smoke. From the women-folk around her, her mother
most especially, Sun-hi had heard endless accounts of joyous
festivals full of dancing, games, and songs. She had dreamt of
eating the tantalizing food so spicy and bold that was often
described to her in great detail as they ate whatever scraps of
food and mush they could find. She had heard wondrous tales
of tigers and persimmon, crows and lovers, frogs and fortune,
and simple girls marrying gentle princes, and Korea, she believed, was a land of freedom. She who was Korean was not
born there, but she was finally going to the loving embrace of
her country and into the ancient communion of her ancestors'
spirits who called out to her from across the sea. To Sun-hi, it
would always be the land of fairy tales, no matter how squal-
id and decrepit it had become by apathy and despotism. The
wisdom of her ancestors whispered into Sun-hi's ear and she
knew well in her heart that it had not always been like that,
and that one day, the fatherland would rise out of the ashes
and become resplendent once again.

"Kazuko," Nara called out to her daughter.

"Yes, *Oma*," replied Sun-hi.

"You are no longer Kazuko. Do you understand?"

"*Oma*?"

"Your name is 'Sun-hi,' your real name."

"*Oma*." Sun-hi obeyed, bowed, and wept tears as if she had found God.

There was no other explanation needed. The Occupation was over, and the 1939 *sōshi-kaimei* Name Order no longer existed. Sun-hi had been given the name "Kazuko" at birth, but she was resurrected as "Lee Sun-hi."

"Sun-hi," echoed Nara into the wind, raising her daughter's name to the heavens to be blessed.

As the ship broke the water nearing Busan harbour, the immortal slopes of the mountainous backdrop emerged out of the distance and appeared like a mirage. It was almost impossible to fathom they were still there, still the same, never moving, always standing. Nara found the familiarity and constancy of nature confounding. The mountains looked strong, lush, and green. They were dazzling. Against a clear blue sky, the mountains stood majestic as if to show those embarking on the shores that this land had a backbone made of rugged peaks able to withstand whatever came upon them in stealth or in will, and to welcome back prodigal sons and lost sheep. The sight of the mountains brought an indescribable flood of emotion to all the passengers; it swept over the entire boatload of souls as they only just realized that it was not Charon at the helm taking them to Hades, but Christ at the oars taking them into heaven. At the sight of Paradise, they wept.

Arriving, it was intoxicating and invigorating. And just as immediately as their bliss surged, they dropped onto their tattered homeland in despair. Nara, Jae-sun, Min-joo, and Sun-hi had nowhere to go and had nothing but the clothes on their backs and barely enough money and trinkets for few meagre meals. The four wandered in the countryside through swampy marshes for a couple of days with their dreams in tow. Finally, they returned to sandy banks of the beach to camp in the glassy night air.

It was already midday, and Nara and Min-joo were trying to remember the good days. But with all that Min-joo had suffered, there was only misery gaping in the space between the two women. The searing past welded forcefully with the present only served to strain an already tenuous friendship.

"No, what revolution was there?" Min-joo cried out. "After the March First Movement, there was a wave of nationalism and demands for independence, but what then? The nation quieted after only a few short years. Was that all the energy we could muster for our freedom and independence? After the imperial military quashed all dissension, our brave countrymen fell either into cowardice or worse still, into appalling apathy."

Min-joo stopped speaking here and looked at Nara expectantly. The nobleman's daughter looked back at Min-joo like a humble match girl. Nara could not say a word. She felt shame. Of course she knew their countrymen must have fallen into pathetic apathy, otherwise, how could they stand by and allow themselves to be treated like ignorant sheep? How could they listen to a full generation of Korean-blooded children speak more of the language of the imperial military than their own? How could they stand by and tolerate the kidnapping of tens of thousands of their women and girls who were forced into sexual slavery, never wondering what had happened to them? How could they endure their government being run by foreign ministers, or that their newspapers had been closed and replaced with propaganda? How could they have allowed their lands to be stolen?

The marvellous propaganda campaign had worked witchcraft with the rest of the world as the Emperor's media machine kicked itself into high gear on the world stage before the western and eastern powers so they would not know the difference between the truth or a lie. How could they have known? But surely the Koreans themselves had not believed the propaganda?

Nara had been away for years but even before, she had seen the evidence: there had been a gradual but clear shift from protectorate to full absorption of the culture with assimilation as the mechanism to get there. Every decree, every behaviour, every law, every proclamation had repeatedly disadvantaged the Korean citizen. Abominations like these should have caused such outrage as to warrant a national strike, a teardown of state-run schools, the burning of government buildings, the destruction of land, the picketing at media outlets, a series of walk-outs and protests, and downright utter chaos. But, there had been silence across the nation for nearly a decade or more. Yes, there would have been deaths and a merciless reaction from a savage dictatorship, but blood was the mortar and bones were the bricks for building homes on the tenets freedom — at least, was that not how it was supposed to be?

Yet, the fire of revolution had extinguished under the deceiving blanket of peace and defeat. The calm waters could not bear any more waves. The militant reaction and subsequent brutality and massacres had quelled the Koreans. Shamefully, liberation had to come from the outside not unlike someone opening a jail cell. Her countrymen had become prisoners in their own land. And then there was Min-joo and all the other hundreds of thousands of Min-joos left behind.

"They were defeated," Nara said sombrely. "We were defeated."

"Gave up. Resigned. Surrendered."

"Yes."

A strained silence followed.

Nara thought of the woman potter she had talked to in the market in Daegu, years ago, when she was younger. She remembered the woman had something doleful in her eyes from grievous experiences, the kind of sadness that clenched the soul. But here, looking at Min-joo, the sorrow was not merely a despondent bleakness: in Min-joo, the despair had strangled her and left her barely alive. Her sadness was raw and so utterly and bitterly painful, nothing, not anything, would ever be the same again. There would only ever be agony.

"Min-joo, look! A steeple," was all Nara could say as she pointed to the sky.

On the third day, when all hope seemed lost, Nara gazed upwards like she had seen the Canadian missionaries do when she was a little girl. At first, she closed her eyes briefly as if in prayer but more because the sun glared brightly. Then, when she opened her eyes, she instantly saw a steeple with the familiar symbol that surrounded her at school. She knew that the path to take was towards that symbol.

The doors of the church flung open and gently shut behind them, birthing them into a new life. It was like a warm blanket when they were invited in to take refuge in the basement, and finally, after years of turmoil and years of homelessness, they had a peaceful place to rest their weary heads and forsaken bodies. Tonight, they had the warmth of home to lull them to sleep.

"*Uhs-suh,*" said the minister softly. "Welcome."

Out of honour, self-respect, and to earn their keep, Nara and Jae-sun immediately undertook to be the caretakers of the church. They had a desperate need to do something for the church that sheltered them, something functional and mean-ingful to contribute where they could until they could figure out what to do next.

"*Mok-sa-nim*, please. Allow us."

So, they became the keepers of the church, maintaining the building, managing the office, doing the accounting, and keeping relations with the foreign missionaries, all the while finding God, losing faith, and choosing it all back again.

"*Oma! Oma!*" cried Sun-hi as she rushed to her mother's side.

"Yes, Sun-hi, what's wrong? Why are you running?"

"Min-joo," Sun-hi panted. She had tears in her eyes. "Min-joo is ill."

Nara dropped the pail of water and mop she was holding and ran as fast as she possibly could to Min-joo's room. She looked very fragile and very ill. Min-joo seemed to suffer from an unknown infirmity. Her body was covered in sores, and her mouth was dry, making it impossible for her to eat. It seemed to Nara that Min-joo was sick from the decay of organs inside her body, and not from a virus or infection. It could be the kidneys or the liver, perhaps even her brain. She suffered from sudden bursts of fevers, frequent loss of consciousness, then uncontrollable coughing and pain in her chest. Not being able to eat was pitiable, but she could not even draw water, which was horrible, since Min-joo was shrivelled and gaunt.

Min-joo had wished to marry. She dreamed she had healed from her past, from the present, and married someone sound and sturdy who had no notion of all the dreadful things that had happened to her. And even if it had come to light, she would not be destroyed. She would enter into a healthy old age having been redeemed by her imaginary, darling saviour. She knew she would never feel the joy of hearing the laughter of her own children; that dream was too outlandish because of all the damage that had been done to her body. But there were orphans she could adopt. Ah, the orphanage. That damn orphanage. She cried even in her delirium. Tears rolled down the sides of her temples and carried with them the bitter salt of regret.

What could they say to each other at such a time and in such a place when all the barriers between long-lost friends were only just coming down now and all the sadness and guilt still there?

"Will you remember me, Nara?"

Nara stared at Min-joo. "Min-joo, you'll be fine. Shhh."

Nara tried desperately to help Min-joo. "*Neh sohn, yak sohn ya.*" She searched the deepest recesses of her memory to remember any cures, any medicine, anything at all, but for all her training, for all her miraculous hands, she could do nothing. She was useless. She was no *mudang*, after all. She stayed with Min-joo, never leaving her side, moistening towels for her forehead, listening to her moans, begging God for answers, already knowing He would not respond.

"Will you remember me?"

"Min-joo. My dear Min-joo. I will never forget you. I could never forget you. You live with me."

The church called in a doctor but he took one look at Min-joo's frail body and the damage done to her and cinched his mouth shut. He took the stethoscope slowly off his ears and shook his head with sorrow. He must have guessed what might have happened, and he was filled with pity. He never said a word, not to anyone, and left Min-joo at peace.

After long nights of dismal pain along with long days of fevered passions and waking nightmares, Min-joo finally prayed her last, and in the quiet of the night, as quiet as on the night she was stolen, with a still mind and empty heart, she stopped her fight and gave up her soul.

There were flurries of snow outside that dampened the sound of the world. It was as if the world was giving Min-joo a moment of silence. The cold winter wind kicked up again almost as quickly as it stopped, and the draft blew through the cracks of the church basement letting in the Angel of Death and a bitter freezing bite. A part of the sun extinguished for Nara that day, and it would shine that much less brightly to her for the rest of her life.

Unable to the bear the crushing weight of her own remorse, Nara cried like she had never cried before. In her arms, she cradled her dear friend — Min-joo who had waited for her on teetering legs outside of their school; Min-joo who had giggled with her at night and shared girls' secrets and a woman's dreams; Min-joo who had become her only family after the death of her parents, bringing peace to her in her time of need and loss; Min-joo who had been mistaken for some girl with no name in an orphanage, stolen from this world and hurled headlong into a life indescribable; Min-joo who had suffered so much but deserved better, far, far better.

Min-joo was dead, and Nara wept bitterly. She held Min-joo against her chest, rocking her back and forth. "Min-joo. Please, Min-joo. Stay with me, my sweet Min-joo." Tears landed on Min-joo's face, and Nara gently wiped them from her cheeks. Then she held Min-joo's face between her two hands and looked closely upon her; she could see her again. Death had lifted the veil, and Min-joo was beneath.

"There you are, Min-joo," Nara cried. "There you are." She held Min-joo tighter. "There you are, Min-joo. There you are. You were there all along." Almost inaudibly, she sang a short lullaby in Min-joo's ear and then bid her farewell.

"*Ye, ahnyong-hee ga-se-yo*, dear friend. Goodbye, Min-joo. Goodbye, dear friend."

In the spring of 1948, Nara's second daughter Young-min was born and life began anew.

৳7৩

AN EXECUTION LIKE ANY OTHER

SIRENS ROSE UP AND HOWLED AT the dawn that breeched on the horizon. Gunfire could be heard in spurts, but the shooting sounded random, as though there was no known target. Then, a low rolling hum plugged the air, and to Nara, it felt like her ears were muffled with water from the baritone crooning that became louder and louder as a formation of bombers dragged closer. Her region was not the target and thankfully the posse moved on northward. Somewhere in the distance, a heavy bomb dropped and split the serene night. It was 1950 and the Korean War had begun completely unexpectedly, and when it started, no one told the peasants, workers, or farmers; in fact, no one told the general population. It was unexpected but not entirely as surprising as the death and destruction in the weeks that followed, which was further marred by months and years of shock and disbelief.

But within a few days and weeks of the start of the conflict, a mass migration of people, an Exodus out of the north, started to flood southward out of the war zone, tens of thousands of people forcefully displaced from their flattened villages and fields.

The landscape was littered with orphaned children — naked, burned, and alone — along with widows or widowers coping with fissures in the only structure they had ever known up until then: their family. Dotted all along the northern edge of the country, from Russia to Seoul and its surroundings, were either the dead or the lost souls. The massive scourge left behind from the incessant bombing of the northern part of the country left the landscape unrecognizable, yet there were still people ever resilient, who packed whatever was left and pushed onward to safer grounds.

There were makeshift tooth-like battlements and embrasures across the countryside where the front lines were once scratched into the ground to hide the non-political loyalists of the republic and their military — the South Korean soldiers — from the enemy. The crenels, shaped like rectangles, allowed enough gaps to see the enemy approach, but the muddy mounds were an eventual giveaway for soldiers in wait. While the soldiers gradually abandoned the structures, most of the embrasures were left standing as remnants that served as reminders of the ongoing conflict to the civilians who simply went about daily life as best as they could.

Bombs drifted down into villages, decimating them, and the mass migration of people continued for nearly two years as the front line vacillated back and forth between points South and points North. At one time, the only bastion left was the perimeter around Busan, which was held by the UN forces and finally pushed back north thanks to the strength of the West's military. All of this Nara could see from the church belfry at the top of the small hill where she now lived.

"Nara-*ya*."

Nara heard someone calling. She turned and saw Mr. Lim. Mr. Lim.

Nara froze.

What was Mr. Lim doing here? This was a miracle. This was a nightmare.

Oh my God. Nara stared.

Mr. Lim had spent all his resources looking for Nara and heard that she was taking refuge in a church. "Nara, do you remember me?"

"Mr. Lim." Nara tried to suppress her profound shock though she turned pale as a ghost. She bowed deeply to Min-joo's father, as deeply as she could bow. She pushed back the tears, swallowed a gulp of air, and straightened herself.

"Mr. Lim, it is an honour to see you again." It would have been culturally discordant to respond in any other way than stoic and steady.

Mr. Lim looked at Nara gently, yet aching for answers. "Yes, it has been a long time."

"You have been able to find me."

"Yes, the missionaries keep good records. I was actually looking for Min-joo, but stumbled upon your name. Then, I thought if I could only find you, I would find Min-joo. Do you know what happened to her?"

"I'm glad you found me, Mr. Lim."

Mr. Lim looked extremely sad at seeing Nara. It seemed to bring back more pain and more memories than he had expected. Tears started to well up in his eyes, but he pushed them back. "You look well, Nara."

"I'm well," Nara responded quietly.

"I'm glad for it," Mr. Lim choked. He cleared his throat. "I had hoped to see Min-joo with you. You both disappeared around the same time." He shuddered lightly, his face despondent.

Nara did not reply. She did not know what to say. It was as if the world had stopped to play a cruel joke on them both, then stood by to watch their galaxies collide.

Mr. Lim saw the flash in her eyes and pressed her. "We all thought you both ran away together." His voice suddenly faded. "At least, that is what we had hoped. At least, that you two were together for each other." His voice lifted a little.

He paused then added tremulously, "To keep each other safe. To keep each other company." Again, his eyes lit and dimmed with each word and each thought. These words and thoughts had been played over and over in his mind for years. Hopes lay buried in his words and his wishes permeated his mind and dreams. Years of searching, doubt, anger, and despair all culminated here, and yet, the words were few — typical of the culture — appropriate for the hierarchal relationship between the people involved in this discussion. In these few words, though, was a universe of pain.

"We had hoped you would be together," he repeated, the pain in his voice palpable. "But, it does not seem it is the case. Min-joo did not go with you, I understand."

Nara still did not know what to say. She never dreamed she would see Min-joo's father ever again. Nara was a grown woman now, married with her own children, yet here before Mr. Lim, she was still a child and cowered to his higher, elderly authority, not willing to make eye contact and fearful her face would betray her. Her mouth went dry. Her hands grew sweaty, and she breathed heavily but quietly. She quaked at what seemed to her now the hardest juncture in her life. It was a crossing of paths that happens for an unknown but purely deliberate purpose in the face of the expanse. It was destiny. And Nara was unable to meet it.

"I'm sorry for your suffering in the factory. I heard you were conscripted," Mr. Lim said quietly.

"Yes, but I am here," Nara replied with the full weight of gratitude bearing down on her.

Mr. Lim winced a little at that. "And Min-joo? You were together. She came with you on the same boat."

Nara did not have the heart to answer him. What could she tell him? After all that he had lost. After all that so many people had lost. She could not bear to tell kind Mr. Lim the truth. She could not tell him that she had fled the orphanage and did not even think to stop to let him know what happened to Min-joo. She had been so full of fear, so traumatized by what had happened that she had no thought but self-preservation and had run away as fast as she could. She had been but a child herself, terrified and needing only to get as far away from the orphanage as possible. And now, how could she tell him that his daughter was raped day after day in militarized slavery? How could he survive such news? He would sink into madness and may never come out of his rage and regret. And the blame — the heavy and immense blame —would be rightfully and squarely placed on Nara. Nara did not want to tell the truth. She could not bear the truth. She did not tell him the truth.

This was an appropriate time for a grand lie, and so she proceeded with the deceit. She told Min-joo's father the same story she had told everyone else when they arrived in the Port — that Min-joo had also ended up in a factory in Japan similar to her, and at the end of the war, she too had come back to Busan. They had met on the boat as fate would have it. At hearing this, people would reply, "God works in mysterious ways," and praised Him.

Nara had devised an explanation for this remarkable coincidence. She explained certain types of labourers from different factories were meant to be put on the same boat by the government; for example, coal miners from different mines were all put on the same boat; this was the same for seamstresses or textile factory workers. This was not true, but it was all made to conjure a believable coincidence particularly given the confused organizational skills of the imperial government of the day, which was a well-known fact. All was in chaos at the time and yet, also in some kind of dystopian, twisted order.

She knew Mr. Lim would fume at the thought his daughter toiled and would spit in disgust at the maltreatment and the injustice of it all, but in months or years, no matter how long it took, he would eventually pass through that like passing through the River Styx. And at the end of that journey, he would ultimately be able to forgive even if no one asked for forgiveness. It would take a long time, but at least, he would be at peace.

So Nara proceeded to uphold her grand tale and kept Min-joo virtuous, or so she initially thought. But like any sin, the gratification was short-lived and unsatisfying while the pain, consequences, and punishment bore on long in Nara's heart.

Nara told Mr. Lim some of her own stories sprinkled amidst the narrative as if they were stories told to her by Min-joo. This too added such colour that it could only be perceived as the truth. Mr. Lim had tears in his eyes, and his jaw clenched at hearing about the beatings and the conditions under which Min-joo laboured, but he listened politely and intently.

"Of course, there was much sickness and disease both in the factories and on the ships returning home," continued Nara, leading him to the end of Min-joo's story.

Min-joo's father nodded his head to indicate he understood how she must have died.

"It was not so long after," Nara could barely hold back the tears now. "She coughed up blood for many days before," she paused. "And then…"

Min-joo's father held up his hand. He heard what he needed to hear.

With his head hanging low, "*Gomupsumnida,* thank you." was all he said. Tears dropped from his face to the ground as he got up to leave, but before doing so, he gave Nara a deep and respectful bow. With this final gesture, Mr. Lim's long search was over. All his resources spent, all he had left in the world was gone — his name extinguished and worthless, his wife dying from grief, and now he had nothing but the memory of his beautiful Min-joo. But when he left the basement of that church, he had the answer he needed, and he was able to walk away without looking back.

Nara got up and hovered in the doorway watching Mr. Lim disappear into the distant light, and as he faded out of sight, "I'm sorry," was all Nara could whisper in return. Quietly, she cried bitter tears. She stood motionless at the threshold, aching to run after Mr. Lim to thank him, to bow to him, to grasp him, to hug him as hard as she could. She wanted to throw herself on the ground begging for him to take her life in exchange for his loss. She wanted so very much to pay the price for the irreplaceable Min-joo. She needed to die and put things right. She needed Mr. Lim to forgive her.

That would be the last time she would see Mr. Lim or anyone in Min-joo's family. There was no family left. Nara kept her gaze on his figure as long as she could, until he was a shadow in the dust, and then, a distant memory.

That night, Nara hugged herself as she lay curled in her bed whispering, "I'm sorry, I'm sorry," over and over again.

She was sorry for all of Min-joo's sufferings. She was sorry Min-joo received no justice for the crimes against her. She was sorry for Min-joo's father and his loss — a cross no one should have to bear. She was sorry she lied to him and in doing so, dishonoured Min-joo's memory. Nara knew that only in talking about what had happened to Min-joo, only in speaking the truth, in acknowledging the shame, in stating clearly that it was not Min-joo's fault but that of the men and the governments and ruling people that failed her, would there be any healing. Nara knew all that. Lying about it only made it worse: worse for the women who had suffered, worse for history, worse for the governments that had turned a blind eye, and worse for the very government that actively sanctioned such atrocities. But most of all, lying about it was worse for the truth. For this, and so much more, Nara was sorry. She rocked herself until the dawn brought the calm of the morning and for the sole comfort to which she could cling for the rest of her life: the belief that that she had brought closure to kind Mr. Lim, and a measure of peace, who deserved more than her grand lie but justice for the truth.

Suddenly, flights of ground-attack planes with unrecognizable markings on their wings flew over in a northerly direction, so low the roar made a droning sound like a bumblebee caught in an ear canal. A violent flash suddenly illuminated a grove in the distance, and revealed a thick brush where the enemy could easily hide if not rooted out by light like this. Footsteps of soldiers were timed to the thunderous clamour of the air raid.

Scattered companies of infantry were running true to form, as if getting their bearings from instinct and not orders. Men from a platoon jumped ahead of armoured vehicles that held back from deploying out of its belly all manner of weaponry. Mortars started spitting fire in the direction of the deep woods. Gunfire splat in all directions, and the church at the top of the hill observed on. One of the explosions was so powerful that it managed to blow out the pane of a window in the sanctuary. All the lights in the church were already out, but Nara hastened to blow out the candles.

"Quick, everyone, down to the basement."

The next explosion, the closest so far, shook the church to its foundation.

"Get down! Get down!" Jae-sun called.

"But the altar and the cross!"

"Leave them! We must not be in the crossfire! Go down to the basement! Hurry!"

Jae-sun glanced at the shattered window and then at the altar, the candles, the cross, and the bibles. There was nothing to be done. The area was now being subjected to a chaotic artillery barrage. Tanks, with their turrets pointed in the direction of the forest, left a trail of smoke and a number of small fires blazing behind them. One of the tanks plowed into a tree and came to a halt. Men started to spill out of it, all the while blasting a hail of bullets at an invisible enemy.

Eventually, the American-led UN forces pushed out the communists from Busan and pushed the line back North, while some remained caught behind the enemy lines.

The North was concentrating their forces for an assault. There were nearly twenty thousand men, tanks, and heavy artillery moving towards the 38th parallel, but the Allies, including the South Koreans, were demoralized and scattered. At about half their regular strength, there were small spurts of insurgent attacks but nothing sustained to allow them a foothold or to leverage the ground they had gained. The battle now was essentially at a stalemate in the trenches. The divisions were caught in small pockets and neither side seemed to know what to do with the growing number of prisoners. Eventually, on both sides, they killed them all in waves of massacres and buried them in mass graves strewn along the North-South supply route. The air superiority of the Allies was clear but without boundaries or front lines, they would bomb random areas of both friends and enemies. Criminal logic was the only strategy at play, and the most challenging of all situations had to do with the spies who infiltrated every camp and every battalion. As it was with all brothers, the language spoken was not a giveaway to the lay listener and physical appearance was also of no help. There was nothing that helped separate a friend from foe, for a North Korean seemed the same as a South Korean, and mistakes were made.

"I'm going to the market," said Jae-sun.

"Is it safe?"

"I should go. We need supplies. Anyway, it's quiet now."

"If you insist, then here is a few *won* we saved. Get a small gift for Sun-hi."

"Sun-hi? No, we must be prudent."

"Her birthday is approaching."

"She should be giving us gifts," Jae-sun chuckled.

"Jae-sun, *eh-ga chak hae*," stated Nara.

"Okay, Okay. You're right. She is a good girl..."

"And endured so much," Nara added.

"Hmmm," he grunted.

He passed through the edge of a small group of ramshackle houses, many of them lopsided and in disarray with darkened thresholds and only bits of light aching through the cracks. He got to the main road on the way to the daily farmers' market where there would be some vegetables, when he encountered some farmers, with their wares on their backs and in buckets.

They were the very same farmers who would sell him their goods at the market, so he decided to walk with them on the short journey to the centre of town.

He quickened his step with a bit of a hop, as if dancing a jig, which was a bit conspicuous amongst the group of down-trodden farmers. The air was heavy, rank with vapours on the plain and the almost imperceptible sound of bursting shells far off in the distance that echoed because of the mountain range that repeated the groans of the world like gossip. The echo of the exploding shells reverberated again towards the group, carrying with it only bad news.

As his group of farmers plodded down the dusty main road, Jae-sun caught sight of what looked like a small military vehicle and a few soldiers marching alongside of it. Initially, it seemed the small military band would cruise past them, but instead, the soldiers slowed by this group of meagre pedestrians and a gloomy disaffection washed over them all. When the soldiers approached the farmers, the air between them bore a delicate ghostliness, for the farmers had seen soldiers like this before, and the soldiers brought the front lines of the war directly to the tips of their dust-covered toes — tiresome and foreboding truths that bore heavy on them all.

The vehicle stopped and let out a few additional soldiers like rats flooding out of a bin. They stopped the farmers and the usual check of bags and bushels followed, along with the routine demand for any papers or documents and the scrutiny behind the insipid and conventional string of monotonous questions.

When the soldiers had finished with the spot check, the lead military officer who had been hanging back from the group during this initial screening process came forward. He had long since jumped out of the vehicle and was already far along with observing each one of the farmers, wives, children and Jae-sun from a distance. The Colonel appeared to be a highly decorated soldier with multiple colours on his uniform. He had a face without emotion and a tall, broad body. The smoke from his cigar puffed up above him, creating a grey cloudy circle around his head. It looked like he was a mirage flickering in and out of clear vision. His stare was glassy and hard, and he seemed to be sharp-witted and cruel.

The low-ranking soldiers had already interrogated the farmers and had asked for Jae-sun's papers and had long moved past him after he had answered the usual questions satisfactorily, but the Colonel was not satisfied.

Like a recurring nightmare, a familiar scene played out for a second time in Nara's life. But this time, she would only hear about it through anxious, sad-eyed gossip.

"You there."

"Me?"

"Yeah, you. Come here."

Not knowing at all the rank of this officer, Jae-sun slowly approached the South Korean man wearing an officer's uniform. It looked different than the ones he usually saw as it had more coloured tags on it.

As Jae-sun slowly made his way through the crowd, each step bringing him closer to the Colonel, Jae-sun suddenly recognized a higher responsibility to himself and his countrymen than the dreamy almost unrealistic outlook of his youth. He suddenly found himself in a serene relationship with his surroundings. He passed into some kind of daze, dreamlike and phantasmagorical. He walked past the farmer carrying the load of barley on his back, the woman toting the basket of vegetables on her head with her baby strapped to her lumbar, the many women with their many baskets, and the farmers with their various loads, going about their daily lives, knowing there was a war just at the edge of their fields and near their homes, but doing what needed to be done from one minute to the next in order to survive and carry on. Jae-sun gazed upon their faces in awe. Their faces were worn from worry, fatigue, and frustration at what they could neither label nor name, but what would be considered malfeasance. Their faces showed the markings of defeat and sorrow, but there was still the hint of a soulful music within, the rhythm of their daily routines that animated them. Jae-sun found himself enamoured with them. The enthusiastic impulses of his youth in pursuing a profession that would give him reason to boast and feel superior among these hard working people, or the wish to turn his back on such base and backwards uneducated kind, suddenly dissipated into the afternoon sun. As he reached the Colonel, he discovered the great story of life right there in the midst of these farmers, these simple people who were not faced with a thousand decisions to cloud their judgement but with one: how to feed themselves and survive. Everything changed in an instant. Jae-sun's sense of intellectual morality shifted from particle theory to religion in a matter of mere steps. God was here and not over there. He did not dance around in the cosmos, but toiled in the fields. God did not choose random paths and random wishes. He was specific and direct. With Him, there was no chaos. All those years of suffering in the labour camp and starving for food had not made Jae-sun realize this at all, for he had not been looking for God, he had been looking for food. It was being amongst the people in ordinary life that revealed to him that without the beauty of survival, the beauty of nature, of poetry, of children at play, there was nothing. His soul opened.

The Colonel asked him who he was.

"Lee Jae-sun."

"And Mr. Lee, where do you live?"

"In the church."

"In the church? Which church?"

"It is located at the top of the hill, just about a mile or two back."

The Colonel strained to see if he could catch a glimpse in the distance. He could not.

"Is it Catholic?"

"No, but we believe the Catholics may have built the edifice. It's Protestant."

"And you live in that church?"

"Yes, in the basement. I'm the accountant and caretaker."

The Colonel gave Jae-sun a curious look.

"So, Accountant, what are you doing here with the farmers so far away from home, looking like that?"

Jae-sun looked at his clothes. He was wearing his usual scruffy clothes, but at one time, the clothes would have looked like a suit. Without the western jacket, it might even look like a tattered uniform, perhaps even a manipulated uniform, one that projected to disguise him almost too well.

"It is my old suit."

The Colonel again gave him a curious look.

"An old suit or an old uniform?"

"Sir?"

"I'm just curious what a gentleman like you in a suit is doing here with the farmers. You don't look like you belong to this rag tag group."

Jae-sun did not follow. He did not understand the Colonel's line of questioning.

"Sir, if I may. What exactly do you mean? I'm here minding my own business. I was on my way to the central market when I came upon the group of farmers. I simply thought I could buy my vegetables directly from them but find myself walking with them to the market."

The Colonel gave his head a little jerk to signal a couple of the soldiers standing by. The Colonel then shifted the conversation in such a way that Jae-sun's instincts knew the situation was not right.

"Tell me, what do you think about the communists?"

"The communists, sir?" Jae-sun was taken aback. He found this question outlandish, but he must have had a glimmer of recognition in his eyes.

"Yes."

"I'm not sure I follow."

"The communists. Do you think they have the backing of

Stalin?" The Colonel eyes goaded Jae-sun to respond, despite his disinterested tone.

"If I may, sir, I'm not sure what you mean. You're asking a simple man about Stalin?"

The Colonel nodded his head in acknowledgement that he was, indeed, asking a strange question. "I am asking an odd question then, am I?"

"If you don't mind my saying so."

"You, there. Farmer," the Colonel called over to one of the farmers carrying bags of barley and rice — one on either side of the wooden pole slung over his shoulders.

The farmer looked nervous, but sheepishly replied, "Yes, sir?" And then cleared his throat.

"Farmer, do you think the communists have the backing of Stalin?"

The farmer's eyes glazed over. He looked flustered, as if he was being asked a question in a foreign language and had no comprehension of the question whatsoever. After letting the farmer sweat it out a minute or two, the Colonel held up his hand, indicating the farmer did not have to answer.

"Lee Jae-sun," the Colonel called lightly as if calling a friend.

"Yes, sir?"

"What do you think?"

"I'm sorry sir, but..."

"Humour me, will you? You seem like a smart man. You're dressed in a suit and speak so eloquently, I just want to know what you think?"

"Well, I just..."

"Please, I'm sure you have some theories. You look like a scholar. Hmmmm?"

Jae-sun hesitated, but the Colonel looked bright-eyed and curious. So, he thought about his answer, assuming the Colonel was looking for an academic answer, which Jae-sun was perfectly equipped to give. But Jae-sun had read the question incorrectly.

"From what I know, the Soviets have not suffered severe battlefield losses in the war thus far."

The Colonel perked up and listened. "Yes?"

"I would imagine, however, that it is not the loss of life on their end that concerns them," said Jae-sun.

"Oh?" The Colonel rubbed his chin while Jae-sun continued, "I imagine it is the Korean military brigade fashioned out of ex-guerrilla remnants that concerns them."

"Ex-guerillas," the Colonel repeated, intrigued.

"Yes, as well as Kim's inability to shift strategies when things don't go as planned."

"Hmmm, indeed," agreed the Colonel. "Like?"

"Like the fall of Seoul."

"The fall of Seoul, last year?"

"Yes, when Kim was not able to secure Seoul, the South did not capitulate and the conflict continued. The North, specifically Kim, simply didn't know what to do. At least, that's how it seems to me."

"You think so," the Colonel said as if pretending to be surprised, but most certainly suspicious. He concluded that this so-called civilian spoke too easily and too knowledgeably of communist thought, so much so it seemed, in fact, to ooze from his pores. His mannerisms and bearing gave a strange leftist slant to his posture, observed the Colonel.

"Yes, that's how it seems. But the communists still managed to limit the southern advance and eventually all that was left was a small perimeter around Busan and Daegu."

"The South, you mean," clarified the Colonel.

"Yes. Until, the Battle of Incheon."

"Yes, of course," the Colonel nodded his head as if in agreement. "Incheon."

Then, with remarkable dexterity, the Colonel, without any warning, changed his tone from a light to a stern key, the fluidity of which was not lost upon Jae-sun. The Colonel now opted for the role for which he had practised as military officer all these years and ordered his contingent of soldiers over to him. The dozen or so soldiers surrounded Jae-sun immediately, pushing aside the farmers and others looking on in surprise. Most did not look at the soldiers but rather at Jae-sun with their gaping mouths and startled expressions. Noting the expressions on the faces of the farmers, Jae-sun realized, in an instant, how this must have looked and he acknowledged to himself that he was about to pay for the sins passed down from one generation to the next, from his father to him. Jae-sun then understood that he must have looked out of place. The soldiers might have thought he was hiding amongst these men, and was not *one* of his countrymen. He had probably sounded like he knew too much about strategy, too much about the front lines, too much about Kim Il-sung. His father's connections to the Communist Party years earlier had not helped and his intellectual fortitude and his atypical behaviour, along with his upright and confident gait, might have made him seem far from home, though home was only a mile or two away.

Jae-sun initially bent his head as if mildly defeated, but then he lifted it almost as quickly and held up his hand. However, before he could say another word in his defence, to explain his background and how he was able to surmise so much, the Colonel cleared his throat, looked Jae-sun straight in his eyes and stated loudly so it was clearly an official proclamation, "Lee Jae-sun, you are a North Korean spy."

Justice no longer relied on the superfluousness of truth nor on the intervention of God's law, but rather on the ill-gotten, so-called "confession" of the accused, and sometimes, whether in war or in peace, just on the whim of a man. In Jae-sun's mind, the Colonel's logic smacked of sophisticated assumptions and deliberate self-deceptions, a mind clouded by the events of the day and by punishments meted out in a childhood long past. Jae-sun lifted his eyes and laid his gaze on the beautiful mountainous horizon. He craned his neck, hoping to see the ocean, but his view descended only upon the dusty road behind the soldiers and at his feet. In the moment when hope can no longer be sustained, one had to take lodgings within the recesses of the mind where the only light that is left can be found. It was the place where one could let go the coveting of one's own life. It might be that one protested this because of pride, or of anguish for the body and the pain inflicted upon it, or out of fear. But in the moment, one is as free as one can ever be, released from the shackles of this world, free from the slavish body, and brought to the cause of humanity, even if that cause was to maintain one's own humanity. It was selfish and yet entirely self-deprecating all at once.

Jae-sun looked upon the Colonel as if he was a logician who was calculating to the last, his imagination bound to rationalism and unable to recognize beauty, love, freedom. He listened only to the words he chose to hear, and concluded Jae-sun was an enemy of the state, determined through his own brand reason mixed with obscurantism, a dangerous potion even under the best of circumstances. Jae-sun knew the intellect must be bound up with imagination, but not the other way around. Imagination stood on its own. It did not have to be bound by intellect.

The Colonel gave the order to fire and at once five guns answered almost in unison with a sixth popping off just a bit late. But it all seemed a farce. The farmers could see and hear the rattling off of gunshots, but it was as if firecrackers were spitting. It was not. At first, there was a wild and panicked reaction, with initial cries to "Get down!" together and high-pitched screaming. Many fell instantly to the ground while two or three simply ran away. But almost as quickly, the pandemonium stopped. It was as if they had seen this sort of thing before and knew there would be no other shots. So after the initial cries of surprise, there was silence, not a whisper, whimper, or sigh amongst the loosely packed crowd of peasant farmers. Children came out from behind mothers' skirts, baskets were picked-up from the ground, vegetables recovered from where they rolled, and clothes spanked to get the dust off. Immediately, chaos returned to order and petrified faces resumed their passive state.

Without so much as a trial, evidence, proof, or shadow of doubt, Jae-sun was summarily executed, on the dusty road leading up to the central market amongst his countrymen and in what Nara would later describe as, "Judicial murder. My husband died because no one could figure out which side of the border he stood on. Up until the year or two before, he was just Korean. A year later he was killed, mistaken for a North Korean spy. What does that mean? *North* Korean?"

The end of the war finally brought hope to a country that had been ravaged and abused for so long. Nara swelled with pride at thinking about how much they had survived. She knew, thanks to the country's birth and upbringing, they would rise out of these tribulations stronger for the hardship much like someone who had a good childhood but had fallen on bad luck for a spell.

To celebrate the end of the war, a special congregational meeting was held at Mrs. Noh's home as the leaves started to turn and the late summer crocuses started to dot the landscape.

"I must say, if we didn't have a solid foundation, recent history would have brought us forth as lost, indignant and mad, chaotic and ignorant," said Mrs. Pyon.

"True, true. I believe our dynastic traditions, stretching back into the past, as you say Mrs. Pyon, will be our foundation to find a way to exert our influence on the world," chimed in Mr. Poom. "We must gain control of our manufacturing and thereby, our economy."

"Technology is the way to go."

"How do you propose we do any of that?" cried Mr. Suh. "With the UN on one side and the commies on the other?"

"Well, let me say, we are not like coveted man. God and the devil may want our soul, but we have the free will and choice to make our own destiny," said Nara. Nara felt within the fabric of the nation what long existed in its inhabitants was a beautiful form and poetic vision that produced resilient thinkers and technicians. Upon seeing her countrymen — specifically the people in this room — unafraid, unwilling to bury their pain, but choosing rather, to own it and thrive in it, was somehow strangely inspiring to Nara. Other countries might have wallowed in madness.

"Even though this war is done, we're still recovering from the last one," said Mr. Suh.

Nara drifted for a moment. It was true. The shock of the Korean War that just ended was raw; not enough time had passed for the experience to ferment and manifest in dreams and nightmares. It was not that they ignored it, but that it was so close, so unbearable, and the gaping wound had not scarred over yet. Speaking about this war so soon after it ended seemed almost taboo and disrespectful to those who could not be here: most in the room did not want to speak of it in front of Nara.

However, thoughts went easily to the war that took place during the midst of the Occupation. It could not be helped. They lived the times, suffered under it, and it lingered long and hard on them. Scars from the Occupation were left on the people, while one large scar was left on the land from the Korean War — the new border.

"We knew nothing," said Mr Poom. "The newspapers were state-owned. The media was state-owned. The teachers were state-owned. We just had no idea what was happening."

"That's not true," spoke up Mrs. Noh. "That's not true. We all struggled to receive news from the outside. Many of them seeking news paid a high price to get the truth back to us," her gaze fell to the ground. "But we did not know enough."

"Yes and when it was all over, what did we find out? We found out that the Axis powers were combined forces of the Third Reich, Imperial Japan, and Mussolini," stated Mr. Suh.

"Japan allied with the Nazis?" said Mr. Poom.

"Why are you so surprised?" Mr. Suh demanded.

"I know. But, it's unthinkable."

"As far as I'm concerned, the Nazis and Mikado are good bedmates," slurred Mr. Suh.

"Well, I suppose at the time they shared a similar ideology. I have no pity for them. People were suffering under their occupation all over Europe," said Mr. Poom.

"All over," corrected Mrs. Pyon.

"Even their own populations," offered up Mrs. Noh.

"Do you suppose," Mrs. Pyon's voice dropped. "Do you suppose the Japanese knew what their German counterparts were doing?"

"What do you mean?"

"I mean the Nazis. What they were doing."

"You mean to the *Yudaien*."

"An atrocity..." Mrs. Pyon covered her mouth.

"What do you think?" asked Mr. Suh.

"I don't know. How could an empire who claims to be so magnanimous know and not do something?"

"Bedmates, that's how."

"You don't know if they knew."

No one was sure, and they averted their eyes.

"The end of the Axis is the thankful demise of this criminal union. I assure you, no one weeps," concluded Mr. Suh.

The room fell quiet and the vengeful fire in the eyes of some of the good Christian men showed they were not so far from hell after all.

Nara thought it would be a good time to change the subject. The air was growing thick with memories and politics. "Ho! Everyone!"

The friends looked up.

"Now that my house is built, I wish to invite you all there for an upcoming congregational meeting."

The mood in the room shifted like the wind, and everyone perked up quickly.

"Ah!" cried the Pastor. "How wonderful Nara. Indeed, yes,

yes. For when should we schedule it?" Nara had already given it some thought and calculated that she would need probably some weeks to prepare. She immediately replied, "Shall we say in a month or two? In November, perhaps?"

They were eager to share in Nara's happiness, and the room buzzed with genuine camaraderie. The upcoming gathering would be a nice occasion to inaugurate Nara's new home and for the group to celebrate the end of the war in a small but meaningful way.

৫8৩

SUN-HI

SUN-HI COULD SEE HER MOTHER WAS horrified as she watched her friends run screaming in the direction of the fire. But young Sun-hi did not understand why her mother was not more concerned about her own family and her own home.

Sun-hi tugged on Nara's skirt, "*Oma, Oma!*"

Nara just looked down at her in a daze. "Stay put, Sun-hi. Don't go near the fire. Stay home and take care of your sister. I will be back soon."

"*Oma, Oma!* Where are you going? Please don't leave us."

"Stop! Sun-hi, you must be strong. You're the eldest daughter. Show some courage. Stay here and watch your sister. You will be safe."

"Don't leave us, *Oma!*" Sun-hi cried.

"Look," Nara scolded again and lifted her arm towards the direction of the fire. "The fire is far. It will not come here. Now stay with your sister while I go help our friends. They need my help. Now, stay here!"

"But — I'm afraid."

It was too late. Nara hadn't heard her. Sun-hi watched her mother rush off in the direction of the homes of her friends and disappear in a cloud of kicked-up dirt and dust.

Sun-hi never forgave her mother for abandoning them during that fierce night of fear and ferocious fire. She had been left to fend for herself and her sister, who was still too young to understand what their mother had done. When Nara had left, the fire was so far away that it had never occurred to her that the pernicious thing would eventually descend on her threshold and plunge itself into it. But, for Sun-hi, when it came to life and death, Nara had chosen her friends above her family, and for a young girl, nearly a teenager, still struggling to find her way in the world, Nara's actions had shown her how much value she had in her mother's eyes. Nara had left her daughters to fend for themselves. The scars of this choice would last and Sun-hi would never forget.

Despite the fire, Busan was rapidly growing and even faster now that the war was over. There were still hundreds, if not thousands of soldiers who were posted in Korea, most of whom were stationed near the North Korean border, but many were still in the south, protecting the harbour.

Though the government was not quick, they were not entirely slow to respond to the devastation of the fire and went to work to rebuild that part of Busan. Tents were being replaced by homes and buildings at a brisk enough pace, but because such a large part of the city was destroyed, rebuilding would take years. To support the family, Nara went to work at one of the nearby hospitals and as the renowned midwife and healer of "tent city," occasionally she made handsome sums of money or brought home fine food or gifts after she delivered babies or helped heal the sick. She would turn around and sell the gifts, and even some of the food, in the booming parts of the city. Some of the gifts she received were rare items, salvaged from the fire and kept by the household for precisely such a need. By doing this, Nara was able to make a surprisingly healthy even relatively prosperous living for herself and her two girls.

Sun-hi had grown to be a young woman of peculiar beauty — her dark hair parted down the side, which was unusual, since hair was usually parted down the middle. Her nose was thin and her brooding eyes stern. Despite her baggy clothes, it was becoming apparent she was no longer the scrawny, shapeless girl she was when they first came to tent city. She would have retained her cheerful disposition since she was quick to humour and smiled with ease, had it not been for the fire, the factory, and all the devastation, all of which had not been nurturing grounds for that sort of character. When a young child, her eyes had often lit up for no apparent reason and she would burst out in song, but as she grew her voice had assumed a curt and hard timbre with an imperious alto that gave her a domineering air, making others feel servile to her whims.

She had grown quickly in the tent city's squalor and dust heap that was measured in terms of hope and future. She was already an idealist, bitten by lofty notions long before the swift value shift that happens to so many who attend university and become immersed in it — like some odd baptism — Darwinism, Pascal, and a Newtonian universe, where the Bible and mainstream society are cast as the backward enemies and foreign thought the path to enlightenment. The only influence that was not taught was Marxist theory — socialism would not be given the soil here in which to take root as South Korea germinated. No, it would map its paths on roads known as "Democracy" and "Capitalism."

Sun-hi sat next to her mother and kissed her on the cheek. "*Oma*, we can't live this way all the time, lingering in the past. It is done. We want to live!"

Nara looked sadly at her daughter, knowing that Sun-hi truly believed in this idealist sentiment of forgive and forget, and to live each moment to its fullest. Hardship had changed Sun-hi's outlook but not toward dismay and discouragement, rather, she raised her fist, and opened her mind and heart. The combination was radical and ironically antagonistic to those around her who loved her, whom she viewed as being almost undeniably ignorant, her mother a relic.

"We are going through a necessary historical change, Sun-hi. It's unavoidable. It is the conditions of a growing capitalism for one and socialism for the other. It is what separates our country inextricably. Nothing, not a petition, not an appeal, not a treaty, not a miracle will change that. It only sharpens the struggle of our country, what we came out of, what we are going through, and what will come."

"*Oma*, times have changed now."

"Times have changed, and yet nothing has changed. It is important to remember where we come from to know where we are going and not to repeat our mistakes. All these things you're saying, well, they used to arrest people like you. They used to torture and kill people like you, people like me."

"*Oma*, they don't do those things anymore, random arrests and false trials. Those days are over."

"Those days are not far behind us."

Looking at Sun-hi, Nara felt distance from her own flesh and blood. Sun-hi was so confident, fearless, and full of hope and happiness, even defiance. Sun-hi wrote petitions and appeals on scrap pieces of newspaper or food wrappings to the local and provincial authorities asking the United Nations to broker a deal as if the country's unification was as simple as gathering a few men into a room and negotiating a peace treaty and a unification pact. Such an idealist.

"In the North, where Marxism has now taken hold, those things continue. The theory sounded utopic, even melodic to the down-trodden and powerless. The theory was about equality, sharing, a world without religion — all of which must have sounded marvellous, but in my mind, it killed your father, Sun-hi. Who knows, maybe it killed him long before the bullets when it caused a rift between your grandfather and him, and a part of your father withered away. I am surprised you have so easily forgotten what this war has done to us, to our country. Why come down and invade us? An ideology that feigns freedom and equality but fails to deliver these at the most basic level is doomed. It may thrive now in some remote pockets of the world...."

"The Soviet Union is not a remote pocket," corrected Sun-hi.

"It may thrive in some areas of the world, but it will fade away like yesterday's storms, taking with it countless lives from the gulags to ghettos. Extremism on any side of the spectrum is chaos. I say the same thing about fascism. We do not need to look so far in history to see what it engendered." Nara paused. "The world war was a perfect example of how both far left and far right can live under the same roof if they are selfish and power hungry enough."

"Oh, *Oma*, I'm not some communist!"

"No?"

"No, and I'm not some fascist either."

"No?"

"No! I'm an artist!"

Despite Sun-hi's optimism, Nara was acutely aware that the tents were a poor home for a sixteen-year-old girl. The thin veils of the tents exposed more than covered, and were open to wandering and curious eyes. It had become unsafe for Sun-hi as she started to blossom into a young woman, and Nara sought a way out for her.

At Sun-hi's exclamation, Nara saw an opportunity and simply grumbled, "You cannot attend art school, it is simply not practical, but how about nursing school?"

"Nursing school? No. No." Sun-hi looked appalled.

Nara took a deep breath, frustrated at her daughter's lack of interest in practical things. "It's a skill-set, an occupation. You can get a respectable job after that. Nursing is a very respectable occupation." Nara paused and calmed herself.

"You became a nurse only because you had no choice."

Nara pursed her lips and glared at her daughter. Sun-hi hung her head and sealed her mouth, smart enough to know the difference between defiance and foolishness.

Nara sighed again, then continued. "The missionaries gave me a gift. I learned about the body and science and learned that things are not about chants and incantations, but real ailments and afflictions and because of it, I can work today."

"You were destined for that, Mother."

"We make our own destinies."

"You're a healer. You think I didn't hear the rumours in the factory? The whispers. All those women gabbing about how you helped the sick? I'm not like that."

Nara had dreamed for more for her daughters, for a brighter future. She knew Young-min and Sun-hi were bright. Young-min, despite her loss of hearing, still thrived in this frenetic world, finding her own way to communicate with those around her, which proved as effective, if not more effective as speech. She could not read letters yet — the tent city was not conducive to sustained study — but she could read lips and people's emotions. And this was a gift.

During the years in the tent city, Young-min had grown from a bouncy five-year-old to a keen and highly observant eight-year-old. She was not able to access formal education — finding an institution to support her special needs was not only improbable, but indeed impossible. But, living in tent city, Young-min had learned a lot about human nature, about relationships, about turmoil, and responsibility. Nara would often catch her washing dishes, mending clothes, or feeding stray dogs with such intensity, as if Young-min was trying to squeeze as much meaning out of every moment as possible. Still Nara was no fool. She knew that Young-min would never be able to go to school. There were no schools that could accommodate her youngest daughter's needs. If God was willing and with any luck, Young-min would marry someone with a particular heart and sensibility — someone who would be mindful of her disability, but not mind it at all. Or, she would remain a spinster and live with Nara for the rest of her life for she would not be able to work, not for lack of skill, but for lack of compassion for those considered disabled. Young-min was deaf and nearly mute. Who would give her a chance?

And Sun-hi? She was highly intelligent and together with her artistic sensitivity and compassion, she could be a good doctor, or even a lawyer, fighting for the rights of victims and those without a voice. But Nara looked at the squalor around them, and sadly, was acutely aware of the limitations of the tent city. There was not enough of a foundation in the tent city to serve Sun-hi. No foundation had been laid *within* Sun-hi, and no foundation upon which to build, so, even though colleges and universities were sprouting like buttercups, it was already too late to set Sun-hi on the path of something so lofty as law or medical school.

Nara could not deny that Sun-hi was missing fundamental skills — skills that should have been nurtured in a secure and sustained environment over a period of years. At no time did Sun-hi ever have this in her short life. As a toddler, she bounced against the walls in the barren facilities of the factory for lack of any stimulation. As a young child, she had received sporadic spurts of education and whatever else she could soak up in the church basement. Yet, somehow, she had managed to learn to read and write and calculate. She showed promise, but it did not matter anyway, Nara sighed. She did not have the money to send Sun-hi to medical school — certainly not that much money.

"The country is not in need of more nurses. I want to go to university and become a fine arts major. I want to learn about art history and maybe someday teach it," Sun-hi insisted.

"Art history? Do you think the country needs more artists?" This time, Nara was blatantly sarcastic.

Silence followed, and Nara wove her brows together in frustration. Then, she added, "All right. How about going to nursing school and then studying art history on the side?"

Sun-hi frowned.

"I will pay." *This she could manage*, Nara thought.

During these years in tent city, by providing medical services, Nara had managed to save a considerable sum and before long

— though she was not sure how much longer — she would be able to rise from the squalor and move on.

Sun-hi brightened up, and they had a deal.

Seoul had become a city of unequal balance as it rested on the precipice of a sharp ledge suspended between tension and peace. War had ravaged it and pounded on its doors relentlessly and yet, it had risen itself out of doom. It had a finely tuned dystopian quality, teetering between the futuristic yet the strangely old-fashioned, between old world Confucianism and a brave new world. It was an odd mixture of west and east with a hint of uncertainty and whiff of self-doubt. Hollywood movies permeated, and Doris Day and Rock Hudson were household names. British music had invaded and a new generation existed that did not have any memory attached to the earlier atrocities of the assimilation campaign. As Sun-hi put it, "Marching into modernity she goes." Whether that meant her or Korea, either way, Sun-hi reaffirmed that life had finally changed.

Sun-hi did attend nursing school and most of those years were filled with long periods of study, occasional solitude, and finding her way. There was still the natural ebb and flow of meeting new friends and letting them go when they changed or she changed. It was the usual rhythm of students finding their voice through the teachings and readings of others. Some ideas latched on while other ideas never stuck at all. Sun-hi often remarked to herself how friendships at university only seemed to exist between those who agreed with your way of thinking. It was hard to be friends with someone who did not agree with you or the way in which you perceived the world. This approach to human relationships seemed closed minded to Sun-hi. She was an artist, after all, caring little for any particular political or philosophical stripe. *In tent city,* she thought, *you could be friends with anyone,* for ideas were not the foundation of friendships. In tent city, suffering, hunger, and life experiences trumped academic theories.

While Sun-hi went to nursing school, Young-min, only nine years old then, stayed close to her mother side, relieved but sad that Sun-hi was away. She missed her sister greatly but there was a quiet lull that swept over their small household upon Sun-hi's departure. Young-min was deaf, albeit partially, but she was not blind. She could see the rift growing between her mother and sister from a relatively early age. Sun-hi and Young-min were eight years apart, born in different times and different worlds. The one born under Occupation and forced-labour, the other born in a free country to free parents with free will. Sun-hi barely knew the warmth of her mother's bosom whereas Young-min grew up strapped to Nara's back, as was traditional, lulled and strengthened daily by Nara's movements and warmth. Nara had the time and freedom to hold Young-min tight and close to her heart. Sun-hi had been separated from her mother during her early years in the factory in Japan and though they were eventually able to live in closer proximity than ever, they could not be further apart. Sun-hi's early hardships made her anxious and impulsive, but she was also courageous and fiercely independent. Young-min grew up secure, but it also made her passive. This was not because of her hearing disability, but more because of her natural demeanour. She was quiet and reserved, a shadow in Sun-hi's bright light. Young-min greeted everyone with an enthusiastic wave and a wide grin, but it was Sun-hi who lit up a room. Nevertheless, Sun-hi was protective of her younger sister, and watched over her like a guardian angel. And Young-min? She was the only one who understood Sun-hi, knowing that Sun-hi was calling out for help every time she flew into an argument or harped on about changing times. The monsters inside Sun-hi would not let her go. Young-min was the only one who could see glimpses of what Sun-hi could have been but had never been given a chance to be.

The sisters understood each other, not because of words, but because of history.

By 1962, Sun-hi was just beginning the final year of her studies. After reading novels about worlds fantastic and unfamiliar, Sun-hi had added to her art history interests and pursued studies in literature. So, with a youthful thirst, these particular courses kept her interest in school as she finished her nursing program.

It was in a European literature class that Sun-hi found herself sitting next to a good-looking man with well-chiselled features and a dark brow. He was brooding, even mysterious. They were both leafing through a newly published Solzhenitsyn and grimaced at various excerpts in *One Day in the Life of Ivan Denisovich* as if they were Denisovich themselves. The starvation, the camps, the gulag — the pain was as close to their hearts as if they were reading their own biography.

She knew then that she wanted to get to know Jin-Chun, and without further thought she immediately introduced herself, something that could never have been done in times gone by.

A young ambitious writer, Jin-Chun had distinct thoughts and opinions of his own not commonly shared. He lived more intensely than others, while at the same time was fearful of his own freedom. His view of the world seemed to suffocate him and freely entrapped him. He suffered from strange troubles and ailments, though it was hard to tell if they were of his own doing or happened upon him. And yet his troubles were like breeding microbes adding to his discontent. He appeared to shun people, a behaviour easily confused for loathing, but inwardly, he longed for the company of like-minded people, only to him, there were so few. He understood the beauty of art, old world philosophies, Gnosticism, and the new psychology of Freud and Jung. He was a poet, and expressed his emotions in verse and his thoughts in narrative tales of worlds created by the imagination. He was restless and brooding, and appeared to luxuriate in melancholy, but in truth, he wanted nothing to do with it. Though pessimism ruled over his days, allowing a morose gloom to envelope him in loneliness, he would have so much preferred the light of the sun and the ardour of society to bathe him instead.

Sun-hi thought, *It must have something to do with his childhood.* But as they were all children of those war-torn days, who did *not* have "something?" And she left it at that.

Yet, Jin-Chun was an energetic and inspiring student. The rumours were true that he had a fine grasp of the Dravidian grammatical foundation of *hangul,* the Korean alphabet, without any formal training, and was always able to deftly articulate the finer points in any debate of almost any topic. There was a sentimental part of him he kept hidden away from all the others except Sun-hi. As it was, Jin-Chun was not at all in sharp contrast to Sun-hi for Sun-hi too was sharp-minded and pointed.

Later, someone realized — (it was unclear who) friend, foe, or a family member — that the dark Jin-Chun whom everyone knew, and the bright-minded Sun-hi who they also knew, converged in one manic figure. He was a living conundrum of swirling uncertainty and imbalance. The heights of exhilaration and the depths of despair rolled together the black and the bright, mixing to create a constant state of grey.

"Mr. Hwang, what are you reading?" The professor peered over his glasses at Jin-Chun sitting to his right in one of the middle rows.

Jin-Chun cleared his throat. "Reading, sir?"

"Yes, reading. I thought it must be more interesting than what I'm saying about iambic pentameter."

"I'm reading Goethe, sir." In fact, Jin-Chun was not actually reading as much he was writing. He drew inspiration from all manner of sources, and at the moment, that was Goethe. He read whatever inspired him with gluttony.

"Goethe, Mr. Hwang?"

"Yes," Jin-Chun replied.

"*Faust*, Mr. Hwang?"

"Yes, sir."

"In fact, I see you have a few books on your desk, Mr. Hwang."

"Yes, sir."

"And?"

"I have Goethe and Wordsworth, sir, and Blake."

"William Blake? *Tiger, tiger burning bright. In the forests of the night,*" the professor recited in English.

"Yes, sir."

"Hmmm, Mr. Hwang, what is your position on this notion of Romanticism?"

Jin-Chun looked up from his writing and stared at the professor for a few moments. "I think my position is unequivocal."

"Unequivocal, Mr. Hwang?"

"Yes, I am a humanist."

"A humanist."

Jin-Chun did not need more encouragement to speak and off he went. "While I claim some deep assent to one principle, that is the intellect, sir, you can convict me of ascetic allegiances to the soul. I affirm and honour nature, love, beauty, freedom."

The professor listened curiously. "Go on."

"But, that is not to say that I accept happiness, in fact, I reject the enjoyment of life."

"You reject the enjoyment of life?"

"Life is not meant to be enjoyed; one must suffer it. To accept that as truth is true asceticism, for suffering is what comes easiest to one's life as such there is a reason for it. We must bear it, overcome it, and conquer it, but few of us do. We enter life suffering, and we exit life suffering."

No one in the classroom seemed prepared, even as devil's advocate or as a debating exercise, to refute that for they had all suffered and this was the truth of the matter. There was credence in what he said, they all agreed.

"We come through the canal in what seems to be excruciating pain, crying to the heavens and our mother. Such is the agony that we have no recollection of it. And at death, we are hurled into the abyss suffocating from mortality with the Grim Reaper's hands around our neck, with no perception of the pain as we enter the threshold and beyond. Surely, if suffering bookends our lives like this, why should it be any different than the story in-between. I prefer a withdrawal from the sentimental, from Romanticism, and from the pleasures of the body. It is moonshine; it is delusional." Jin-Chun spoke quickly with an elevated heartbeat and flushed cheeks, excited for this forum to banter at will.

"For in our culture, as in so many," he conceded, "there is no nobility at the end of sensuality's stony road. The body's needs soil the mind, cause souls to decay, calls upon death early. The only goal worth pursuing is the noble search for the Bodhi, the divine, by an abdication from desire but with a spirituality that is bound to nature, free from the slavish body. If I'm an antagonist for saying so, then so be it. And, in Romanticism, there are reason-denying powers. Abandon those. Like the great principles in physics of force and movement, link the intellect with the soul and there you have humanity proper."

"Interesting doctrine, Mr. Hwang," the professor paused. "Humanity proper would indeed benefit from a link of the soul and the intellect. To blazes with the body, I suppose, Mr. Hwang?"

"To blazes, sir."

"Interesting Mr. Hwang. Now please put down your books — and your pen — and join the rest of humanity proper, will you?" As he said so, the professor spread his arms out like wings as if to embrace his class. He was denoting to Jin-Chun that the class was his community for the hour in which Jin-Chun must be his captive audience.

Sun-hi loved Jin-Chun's ambition and his insecurities, and of course, it did not escape Sun-hi that he was a rather handsome example of a man. Though not rich by any means, he had the air of a gentleman, who kept himself carefully groomed. He almost always wore a clean, ironed shirt with slacks and a belt. He occasionally wore a jacket and always shined his shoes. There was a fierce brilliance in his dark, proud eyes. High cheek bones and flared nostrils made him look aristocratic and haughty, but he imbued this look with a watchful stillness and deep reflection. Jin-Chun's views were so unique and compelling, Sun-hi could listen to him ramble on for hours about whatever struck his chord: Nietzsche, Buddhism, Beethoven, *Ben-Hur*. The little money Sun-hi received monthly from Nara and that Jin-Chun received from his poetry, they would spend on books and read them voraciously, as hungry for knowledge and inspiration as they once were for food and nourishment. On the rare occasion, they would splurge on a movie to watch Cary Grant, Marilyn Monroe, or a run of *Casablanca* in one of the city's movie theatres, clasping one another's hands as young lovers do. They shared their love of garlicky noodles, sticky rice — not the fluffy stuff — and the inland version of *kimchi*, that is, without the squid. They went to poetry readings and long walks through the city, which was an ever changing urban landscape, getting lost as street directions changed from one week to the next. Then, one day, they decided to marry and it occurred to Sun-hi to write her mother about him.

Oma, I have met a wonderful man whom I love dearly. He is an aspiring poet and editor, brilliant and kind. We have decided to marry in the spring. I am asking for your blessing. Would you come?

By the time Sun-hi was in her second or third year of her nursing program — she wasn't sure exactly when — Nara and Young-min had moved to Seoul as well. As tent city started to shrink and more and more people moved away — finding their way — so did Nara and Young-min. After nearly six years in tent city, Nara had accumulated enough savings to start fresh somewhere else. They moved to Seoul to take advantage of more opportunities to grow, to do better, have steadier job prospects, and truthfully, to leave behind bad memories and bad air.

When Nara received the letter from her daughter, telling her that she was going to marry, she collapsed on the floor of her apartment and wept — her ascetic, both hierarchal and bound to strict obedience, expected nothing less of her daughter. After several days, she called her daughter on the phone. "You will not marry someone poor, Sun-hi."

"He just got a very prestigious job, *Oma*."

"Oh? Where?"

"He's the new editor of a highly esteemed *moonhak*, literary magazine, *Oma*."

"An editor?"

"Yes, and the youngest ever for the publication. It's amazing what he has already accomplished."

"An editor can't make that much money."

"No, but..."

"I had hoped you would marry a doctor or a businessman. You're attending nursing school. I just thought..."

"He's not rich, but he's smart and..."

"And poor."

"*Oma*. I love him and I will marry him."

"No, Sun-hi, marriage is not about love. It is about everything else but love. It's about home, family, power, money, society, community. It is about cooperation. Have I taught you nothing? You must improve your own situation, and then, together, hopefully improve both your situations. Combined, it is about survival."

"Survival? What does that have to do with marriage, *Oma*?"

"Survival, Sun-hi. Yours, your family, your future children. Marriage is about success and sustaining the family for the next generation, and if possible, taking the family to the next level in the ruling hierarchy. That is why the noble class only marries within the same class so as not to dilute the power."

"You're talking like an ancient. You don't know what you're saying. You're just speaking like an old-timer, caught up in the past."

"Yes, and how quickly you have forgotten all we have suffered."

"We're not of the noble class anymore, *Oma*. I have never felt like a *yangban*. I grew up poor. We're simple people now. Commoners. Whatever was stolen from us will never be returned. You must accept that! It's gone!"

"And so, you must marry someone who can take care of you. A businessman or a lawyer, a somebody."

"He is a somebody. He is going to be a great man, one day, *Oma*."

"Someday he'll be great? That's a promise? And I guess he'll still be poor. Love won't sustain you. Familial responsibility and honour — these are things that keep things running smoothly in a well-oiled society. When that simple construct breaks down, everything else falls apart. You must not dwell on a dream, not on 'someday.' You must marry someone who is rich today."

"For you?"

"For *you*." Nara was crushed. Her voice suddenly shook, then dropped to a hush. "For *you*, Sun-hi."

There was silence. Nara felt like something had pierced her through. Sun-hi too.

"I'm marrying Jin-Chun. I hope you will come."

Spring had arrived and upon its entry, April stood in the threshold between the cool of March and the warmth of coming summer. Sun-hi had a simple wedding ceremony, partly paid for by Jin-Chun's family, partly from whatever Sun-hi had saved before Nara cut her off. She wore a white chiffon gown with an empire waist and a beehive hairdo. There were no traditional elements to speak of: no colourful silk sleeves, no tea, no bowing, no hats, no pantaloons, just the trappings of a typical western-style ceremony, which was the way things were done by then. The wedding was attended by friends, writers, editors, students, and Jin-Chun's father. Nara and Young-min were not there.

In a way that only made sense to the heavens, sealed in the fateful crevices of the constructed walls of mortal space and time, history had a way of repeating itself. Jin-Chun sat in his office smoking a cigarette that was loosely clutched to the side of his mouth while he typed fanatically away on his typewriter. The blue-grey smoke drifted in a loop above his head, and lingered low and heavy, filling the room with a strong film. *Click, click, click* slapped the letters madly against the paper as the sun streamed in through the floor to ceiling windows typical of an office building built in the late forties.

The building was old by the day's standards as new edifices were popping up almost overnight throughout the city, but the furnishings, including the vinyl-covered chairs, the laminated white desks, the heavy steel green cabinets, and paisley wallpaper gave the space a distinct newer look of the sixties. The walls were covered in framed articles and posters about protests and demonstrations as well as clippings from foreign newspapers. The office had the usual pleasant hum from buzzing busy people, ringing phones, and the *clickety-click* of several typewriters.

Suddenly, a loud clamour came through the fifth floor offices of the *moonhak* magazine. At first, there were several bangs at the front door down the corridor, away from the main work space, but as someone scurried to open it, a group of military police charged through. The other journalists and assistants working in the office jumped up from their seats, startled by the intrusion, blindsided by the commotion. They were wrangled together and lined up against one wall. One tall, ominous-looking police officer charged into Jin-Chun's office and grabbed his arm, slinging him out of his chair and rammed him against his desk. He bellowed only one state-ment: "You are being placed under house arrest for treason."

"You can't be critical of the dictatorship and expect there not to be any repercussions, Jin-Chun."

"I thought we lived in a free country now," replied Jin-Chun to his colleague and friend through the bars of the holding cell.

"Free. What does that mean?" Dae-sun replied, looking back at Jin-Chun through the bars.

"I'm the editor of a literary magazine. I publish literature. It's poetry, fiction, articles."

"Poetry, fiction, and articles that are critical of the President."

"Dictator."

"He is also an economic genius! Korea is booming, we're industrializing, and people are becoming more prosperous. One day, history will not remember Park the Dictator, but Park the Innovator. It will be thanks to Park that we will advance. Anyway, you cannot print stuff like that. Some of the poetry you print definitely does not sound like innocent rambling verse about love and nature."

"Many are pastorals."

"About heirs to cultic thrones, melting Icarus' wings, suffo-cating sheep, lips full of venomous nectar?"

Jin-Chun shrugged.

"And what about this one," Dae-sun said, pulling out another piece of paper reading from it: "'It is a painful sight — the anguish of the flesh — for the wounds of the body only served to reveal the most metaphorical of decay, the envenomed cor-ruption of the mind. This is how it is with government in which the steely hand of power-hungry forces burrows through the healthy core of society and manages only to achieve a poor reflection of what was once a grand Korea. Good intentions are corrupted and fall unfamiliar when the mechanical hand of corrupt leadership touches the organic soul of a country and it drains it of its first nature, which is to follow its will. Is that will the will of God, the will of a benign creator, the will of a collective archetype, the will of society? Does it matter? In the end, because the venom of power can be lethal even in the heart of leaders with the best intentions, like eating of the fruit of self-will, puffery, and decay, the initial dreamlike society withers and dies.'" Dae-sun rustled the papers and fisted them as he held them at his side. "Basically, what he's saying is 'No more utopia, no more Korea of days of old, thanks to the regime.'"

"That writer of the article is allowed to express his opinion in a free society."

"Who's the writer?"

"It doesn't matter. What he ends up saying is entirely different from what he meant to say which is to speak of hope, I think. He should have spoken about a society aspiring to become more than what it is seemingly allotted to become. A divine being did not cast Korea in a specific role, victim or victor, power or pauper: we can become whatever we want to become, but the writer didn't give us that. He didn't say we become more by clutching fate by its thick neck and pushing it aside to determine our own destiny, to rise up from wherever the hell we were pushed into and to lift ourselves out of the filth, despite the naysayers, to the sky's very limit. We live in an emancipated society where no one occupies us any longer. We have been free for a long time now. No more foot soldiers from the north or the east or the west trample our soul."

"Soul?"

"*Soil*. I meant *soil*. No more wars, no more destruction, no more cultural assassination, no more outsiders telling us what to do. No more foreigners drawing a line in the sand for us anymore. And now, how dare we let this happen? Now, we have an insider, one of our own, trampling on our souls."

"Soil."

"No, souls."

"I see. That's what the writer didn't say."

"Yes, that's what I didn't say and I should've."

Jin-Chun's colleague, Dae-sun, it so happened, was also the assistant dean of the arts department of a local college. He was also a keen reader of the magazine and he followed Jin-Chun's writing career closely. He knew some people in the European Commission, so through one of the embassies, either the French or the British, he leveraged some pull and had the military police release Jin-Chun from his arrest. And thus it seemed to Jin-Chun that foreigners still garnered more influence in their country than their own, and so, not much had changed, after all.

The harassment and threats of arrest continued as Jin-Chun continued to publish pieces that were viewed as disruptive and treasonous to the government. Jin-Chun continued to *click* away on his typewriter until the cigarette smoke that swirled in his office dissipated when the state police finally ransacked the magazine and it became unsafe for Jin-Chun.

"Jin-Chun, you continue to publish articles that are critical of the government."

"Are they untrue?"

"President Park certainly did not purge the leaders of the other parties."

"Oh?"

"Of course not."

"Then just the members of other parties then."

"You claim that he's some kind of dictator. He's not Kim Il-sung, man."

"I don't know. Those two seemed to be pretty close before the war. Perhaps they were just playing *janggi* chess."

Without further discussion, the police guard thrust a hard punch into Jin-Chun's stomach. "You insolent fool." Coughing hard, Jin-Chun straightened up and wheezed as he tried to take in some air. This time, the guard grabbed Jin-Chun's head and threw him to the ground. After several kicks to the lumbar, stomach, and face, Jin-Chun coughed up blood, which oozed from the side of his mouth. His teeth were red and several had become loose in the back from the blows. He spent the night convulsing on the jail-cell cot, his muscles stiff and aching from a couple of broken ribs, a dislocated jaw, and a bruised spirit.

Unable to control the publication through bribes, threats, and coercion, the regime eventually closed down the magazine. It was time for Jin-Chun to leave.

"Si-oux san mary," said Sun-hi's friend, Su-wen.

"What?"

"Si-oux san mary,"

"What are you saying?"

"The recruiting program. They are recruiting nurses from Korea. The government man said that there are not enough domestic nurses there, so they're recruiting from schools like ours."

"From all the way over here? From Korea?" Sun-hi asked skeptically.

"Yes, from here, from the Philippines, from European countries, from everywhere."

"It's strange, no?"

"I don't know. They need nurses, so, I'm going to Si-oux san mary."

"You mean Sault Ste. Marie?" helped Sun-hi. "Yes, yes. I remember now. I heard of the recruiting program. It's in..."

"Canada. Yes, that's it. I'm going there. Where is that?"

"You're going, and you don't know where it is?" Sun-hi said surprised.

"Yes," Su-wen said proudly. "I'll be able to make more money and there will be more opportunities for me once I get there." She did not sound nervous or apprehensive. She seemed to view it as some kind of adventure.

"But what about your family?"

"They want me to go. I can help them by sending back some money."

"So, you're going to leave Korea?" Sun-hi still sounded surprised.

"Yes, and go to Canada," insisted Su-wen. "Where did you say it was again?"

"It's near the United States, just above it on a map. It's a big country." Sun-hi thought of the missionaries her mother so often spoke about. They were from Canada. *It must be a wondrous place,* thought Sun-hi.

"Hey, how do you know Canada?"

"I just know."

With thoughts of kind missionaries clouding her view and bright ideas dancing in her head, Sun-hi applied. Indeed, she had become the nurse that Nara had expected, highly skilled and in demand. And just as the threat of further arrest, beatings, and possible trial for treason loomed high, Jin-Chun and Sun-hi experienced divine intervention. She secured a nursing job in Canada, just in time. She would go to Canada as one of the hundreds of nurses of the late sixties who were part of the health worker migration. This was Sun-hi and Jin-Chun's ticket to a new life, free from persecution.

☙9❧

HARSH LESSONS

IT WAS DIFFICULT TO TALK TO anyone. The only thing for certain was that everyone looked upon him and others like him with suspicion. When he first arrived in Canada, Jin-Chun found a tale that was written for him already: one of conspiracy, humiliation, and tragedy, fabricated by cowardice and misunderstanding. Once the editor of a prestigious and rebellious literary magazine, Jin-Chun was now working as a hospital custodian, unclogging toilets and mopping mucous covered floors, or cleaning up the vomit of patients and the shit of visitors. The filth was stagnating and the stench saturated his nose, but this was the only job he could get. The sight of the sick and dying, and their smell, overwhelmed him, but it also provided great fodder for his writing *and* his drinking.

On one of the first days on the job, he found a pub where he could dine for cheap. But there was only the unfamiliar and unpronounceable. The server brought over bread and butter to the table along with the cheese and vegetable sticks Jin-Chun had inadvertently ordered.

Not knowing what to do, Jin-Chun looked around the restaurant. Other diners seemed to be eating the bread with something inside so he took a piece of cheese and put a piece of bread on top of it. It toppled and was unsteady in his hand. Eating with his hands seemed strange to him. He managed to take a bite.

Awf! Jin-Chun threw down the bread and cheese onto the

plate. He started to retch and cough. The cheese tasted like sharp ammonia, a bit putrid, and the bread had a texture similar to an unthreaded silk worm. He gagged and gulped down some water to rinse away the taste. With water dripping down the side of his mouth, he coughed a little and then shut his mouth tight. Although this was not the first time he had eaten bread, this bread was strange. It was not hard and crusty, but soft and thread-like. As for the cheese, it was the first time he tried it. It was horrible. The cheese had a putrid smell. He could not understand why people thought *kimchi* smelled so bad when cheese had an unbearable stench. He looked at the butter on the table. It was unlike anything he had seen. He lifted the plate to his nose and retched again, nearly throwing the plate down from surprise and disgust. Everything around him smelled like vomit. The smell of the creamy butter hit him at the back of the throat. It smelled milky and putrid like a baby's regurgitation. *How can they eat this?* he wondered.

He slouched in his seat, disappointed. He gnawed at the vegetables that were familiar enough.

After a few minutes, a basket arrived with more bread, in between which was a perfectly round piece of meat, and some deep fried sticks on the side. Jin-Chun looked suspiciously at the meal in front of him. It was a hamburger and French fries but he had never seen either up close before. He had seen commercials for such a meal on TV. In the advertisements, the hamburger always looked so good, dripping with juices, bold and smoky. But he did not know what a hamburger actually smelled like or tasted like. He took a whiff, and it smelled like a muted version of the back alley of the restaurant: an old, murky, greasy smell. And while it was unpleasant, in truth, he was relieved it did not smell like the cheese or the butter.

It did not look as good as the hamburger on TV, but the meat was as perfectly round as ever. He knew about ground beef, but in Korea, they did not have that. They just cooked everything as it appeared in nature, nose to tail. A gizzard was cooked as a gizzard. A tongue was cooked as a tongue. If they mashed it up, it was not intended to mask the meat in any way. He imagined there was stuff in the ground beef he would not eat if he knew what it was. But, coming from what was once a poor country, he appreciated eating and using everything. He just was not sure about the round shape of the meat.

He took a bite and found it greasy and bland. He felt like he was eating a cup of melted lard with the texture of undercooked barley. He dumped the hamburger back into the basket in which it arrived over the deep-fried sticks, and shook his fingers so the juices would drip off.

He leaned back, so his head rested against the back of the booth. Frustrated, he looked up at the ceiling of the restaurant, expecting to find something above that might provide answers to some very basic questions, but only saw stucco and wooden beams.

He perked up a little when the server brought over his beer.

Jin-Chun recalled that in the Book of Moses, people sinned against God because of food. They disparaged the food in the wilderness, constantly longing to go back to Egypt, where, despite the slavery, there was honey and meat.

Thank God, however, that manna eventually fell from the sky.

As the weeks and months passed, Sun-hi noticed her husband would only find comfort in nursing a bitter, martyrish sacrifice in his isolation. In fact, he was so wholly alone, one could cut the loneliness that lay thick on his desk. In small-town Vancouver of the sixties, who would ever understand Shamanism or Gnosticism? There was no one. But he relented. At first, he needed to. That was his character; that was how his mind worked. He needed to talk as he had always done: boisterous, opinionated, brilliant. Like anyone striking upon good ideas, he wanted to share them. So, he talked to anyone who would listen and sure, there were a few bright-minded, or more correctly, open-minded, kind and patronizing individuals, but they could not sustain the onslaught of mantras about bodhisattva, karma, and nirvana, never mind being able to pronounce these things. With his thick, drawling, foreign accent, it made it even more difficult to understand him, and as people withdrew, unable to face their own shortcomings about such esoteric things, or to sustain kindness for his foreign tongue, Jin-Chun withdrew himself from society.

How could he not? The first dozen places they visited, they could not rent even with good honest wages. Something about "it's already been rented," even though it had been available only a half hour earlier and other potential renters traipsed in behind them. Or they "could not rent to them because their accents were too thick and they preferred to rent to people they understood." Or, on more than one occasion, the smell of their food was objectionable, but pets were allowed.

The search to find a place to live, a roof over their head, never mind a home, had become quite a revelation and put a fresh perspective in Sun-hi and Jin-Chun's minds with a new found resolve. They had lived in homes built on long and forgotten histories, on lands obliterated in wars and now they resolved that they would live in a home built on their flesh, blood, tears, and dreams. Like typical immigrants, they saved their money, penny by penny, tear by tear, and by then, Sun-hi realized why immigrants were so good at saving. It was not just the tendency of immigrants of all stripes who had survived through unspeakable difficulties in their homeland to be frugal; it was this cold mirage called "money" that gave back the leverage that their accent and appearance took away from them. By the time Sun-hi discovered she was pregnant, they had saved up enough to buy their first home. They found a place on a small street near Kingsway, an area that was a sort of multicultural ghetto in Vancouver, where Italians, Chinese, East Indians, and other ethnic minorities owned homes, rented out rooms to their own, and lived. They lived amongst each other, away from the white people, for at the time, they gave off an odour that did not come from their food.

Jin-Chun continued to write, but the underlying quiet hostility towards him and his kind known as "immigrant" started to wear down on him. Increasingly, Jin-Chun — who was already disconnecting from the world — was in an almost constant state of inebriation when he was not writing or at work in the hospital where Sun-hi was a nurse.

At a time when johns trolled Richards Street for prostitutes and West End beach apartments were considered low-income housing, there was a motel on Kingsway with a tacky red neon sign that had a bar that sold cheap drinks and even cheaper company. The exterior stucco walls had once been white-washed but were now a faded ivory and belied the seedy interior that smelled of booze and sex. Frequented by the lowest dregs of society, this was no place for a bright talent, a genius even, but the nearly homeless misfits were the best company that Jin-Chun could afford at the time. He mingled with a swamp of ignorant, sometimes drug-addicted shadows who in their inebriated stupor feigned to understand his deep philosophical drunken ramblings, but still managed to come off as patronizing. During Jin-Chun's many broken diatribes, evening after evening, various low-minded drinking companions would listen intently as if studying his words like chimps learning sign language. Occasionally, someone would hold up one arm in the air in the fashion of an ancient Greek scholar and hold an imaginary toga in the other arm while mouthing-off unrecognizable words that came out like dribbling idiocy. Evenings hit their peak when intoxication and words, already a deadly mixture, removed the thin film of opacity and revealed the mockery beneath: most nights ended badly with racist slurs hidden in friendly cajoling: "Hey man, I don't mean to offend ya', but ya' all look the same to me," and, "You're what? Korean? What's that?" and "Ah fuck, I can't tell you guys apart." But drunk, Jin-Chun could laugh these comments off and the next day wake only to the usual headache. Though, despite the numbing effect of booze, of the experience he was sure. Alcohol numbed the pain inflicted by bigotry, but it did not take it away. Jin-Chun commiserated with the wretches in the bar as if they were like-minded people, brothers-in-arms, wallowing together in the pile of the judged and rejected, dealing with the shitty hand life had dealt them. But in the end, they too stabbed him in the back; he was betrayed even by the lowest bottom-feeders in society. Jin-Chun cringed at that. He cringed at what he remembered, pounded his fist on the table, unable to explain anything about anyone anymore.

"Why did we come here?" Jin-Chun raged in the living room in the middle of the night, after one of his drinking binges.

Sun-hi did not know what to say. "Keep it down, you will wake the baby."

"Why did we come?" he yelled louder.

She lashed out. "If we didn't come, you would have gone to prison or worse. They could have put you to death."

"I would rather have died for my beliefs, honourably criticizing the regime, than wither away here!"

"Then go back!" Sun-hi bellowed, forcing the tears back, her heart aching and full of regret too.

"How can I go back? We don't even have enough money for groceries. We pay for our house and what's left? What's left?"

"Your drinking money! Your smoking money!" Sun-hi fought back.

"They hate us here! They look at us, and they hate us. We don't belong."

"That's not true," cried Sun-hi. "Those drunken bastards who can't see past their own face, those assholes you call drinking buddies, they don't know us. But the rest, the ones who see us for who we are, the government..."

"Ha! The government only sees us for our tax dollars and our cheap labour. That's what they want. To keep us working in service jobs, cleaning up after them, cleaning their shit and paying us next to nothing to do it. Your mother was a factory slave. How does it feel to be a slave yourself?"

"It doesn't have to be this way. They don't all feel this way," stumbled Sun-hi, stunned by Jin-Chun's drunken comment about Nara. "I have friends. I've made friends!"

"Do you feel that walking down the street or going to the grocery store? Do you feel that when we need help or when we offer to help? No one is going to help us, and they certainly don't want our help."

Sun-hi grasped for answers. Choking back the tears, she recited all the patriotic brainwashing she had received since arriving.

"All of us," she repeated emphatically. "We all add to the tapestry here."

"*Tapestry?*"

Sun-hi did not mean to say 'tapestry.' Even she knew that sounded laughable.

"What in the hell are you saying? Is that what your so-called friends tell you?"

"What's wrong with that?"

"Are you mad? Like all our goddamn colours woven together! Isn't that just some fabric made in a slave factory?"

Sun-hi didn't respond, taken aback yet again by Jin-Chun's cruelty in bringing up the factory. And anyway, she had meant "diversity." But the word "diversity" had not yet taken root in the general conscience or embedded itself in the Canadian conversation yet, so it was easy to confuse. No one used that word back then.

"You're ridiculous talking like that. We don't belong!"

"Yes, we do, Jin-Chun. Yes we do," broke down a sobbing Sun-hi. "If you think that way, you're only agreeing with those ignorant bastards. But they will wither away and die one day, and a new generation will..."

"...Will hate us just the same."

"No," Sun-hi paused. All of a sudden she heard her mother

in his words. As memories gushed in her head together with the rush of tears, she remembered one small anecdote Nara told her about a Japanese baby who lay gurgling in her arms after she helped bring it into the world. He lay so innocent in her arms, but Nara knew that one day, that child would grow up and would not hesitate to spit on her or even kill her if they met in a prisoner of war camp or in a factory or crossed each other on some street. From this generation or the last, not a lot changed.

Sun-hi continued to argue. "Like an oppression or occupation that fails, prejudiced, narrow-minded ways of thinking will wither away and die because people will not stand for it. We work hard and we belong here and..." Sun-hi heaved a great breath and cried bitterly. She was not even sure of what she was saying, but even though she did not really believe what she was saying, she had to believe for what else was there? They had been in Canada almost three years. This was her home now, and without hope, there was nothing.

Some weeks after this, Jin-Chun fell ill. The bartender at the local bar threw him into a taxi after midnight one evening and when he got home, he looked as if he was simply in yet another drunken stupor. When he stumbled inside, Sun-hi got up to go to bed, now that he was home. The usual look of fatigue and helplessness commingled with a heavy dose of tears filled the room as it did almost every night. She looked worn from taking care of the baby, taking care of the home, and taking care of their beaten down souls. Frustration and loss was woven across her face, and she knit her brow and pursed her lips at the scent of booze that wafted from an alcohol-soaked Jin-Chun. But when she finally lifted reluctant eyes to look at Jin-Chun, she could see he was stiff and running a high fever as his eyes rolled to the back of his head. For the next forty-eight hours, Jin-Chun looked like he was on the threshold of death. He was so feverish and sweating, the bed sheets soaked through.

Sun-hi guarded over him as if she were fending off the Angel of Death with her will alone, for she knew what the Angel looked like, and knew it well, for having seen it too often in her life. After fizzing up his intestines with Alka-Seltzer, she wrapped him in heated blankets and force-fed him a porridge of wet, soupy rice for the next two days until his tormented body recovered to a normal temperature.

At the end of the weekend, Sun-hi had to go back to work. She could not stay home; the job was too important and to take a day off was work-suicide. She took her daughter to the babysitter and left Jin-Chun to fend off death by himself. He sat up in a daze and waited in bed until her return. He sat there for eleven hours until Sun-hi and Lauren finally passed through their creaking doorway. He thought they had been out only a few minutes, an hour at most. At the end of what had been a long day for Sun-hi, she saw that her husband had not moved a single muscle or a single inch from where she had left him that morning. The convalescence had knocked him down like a blow to the head, and he was collecting his sanity back from the space in which it had scattered, waiting for it to descend back to him like tossed up leaves floating down from the sky. After another small bowl of porridge, this time sprinkled with a bit of soy sauce for salt and flavour, he shimmied back down under the covers, and Sun-hi tucked him in like she would a baby.

For all her survival instincts, her practical nursing training, and her savvy, for Sun-hi, Jin-Chun's illness was the first time she realized she did not know what to do. It was not that she did not know how to treat the illness; it was that she did not know what to do if it got worse. She did not know the system. The experience was eye-opening, and it frightened her. She heard her husband's words ring in her ears: "Do you feel that we belong when we need help? No one is going to help us." She worked in the system and yet where could she go? To her hospital where she worked? Of course, that was where she should go. She certainly could not run into the street and cry for help. She was not in war-torn Busan or in a tent city any longer where a cry for help would bring streams of neighbours out with sticks and batons. Here, if she ran into the street crying for help, neighbours would look at her as if she were mad. They would not come to help. To the contrary, they would close their curtains and lock themselves behind the doors of their stucco homes. They would call the police, not to help her, but to get the raving lunatic off their streets.

Instead, there were steps, processes. There was a system. But would that system be conducive and sympathetic to her kind? Yes, maybe if she went to the hospital where she worked. But elsewhere, would they do everything they could to save his life? She trembled at not being entirely confident of the answer. For the first time, they were totally alone. They were left to fend for themselves in a place where one look at their hair and eyes decided it all, where one look decided whether or not they would receive treatment of the best and generous kind or care administered void of compassion. For humanity could be measured by degrees, could it not? She witnessed it every day. She witnessed it at work, on the bus, in the city, in the parks, everywhere. All that talk in university about humanity, love, aestheticism, and Romanticism seemed ridiculous now, highfalutin nonsense. Superfluous, abstract notions about the intellect and the soul faded here in this moment. Sun-hi recognized in the dark of night and the light of suffering, the world in which she lived, such notions were all talk of roses and smelled of sour vapour.

She knew the limits of her helplessness and shrank from testing it. She shrank from crying, and instead, she did not weep or speak but rose with spasmodic effort, with rigid limbs and a rigid soul. Her heart hardened and with an immovable face, she clung to one certainty — absolute resistance to the indignity of having to ask for anything in the world and ask anything from it.

On that night, Sun-hi resolved that she needed to right a wrong and mistook that for affluence and wealth. Never realizing the words of her mother had taken seed in her, she finally manifested in her life what her mother had told her all along. Nara had said, "You must improve your own situation, and then, together, hopefully improve both your situations." Then Sun-hi remembered what Nara had said about marriage. "It's not about love. It is about everything else but love. It's about home, family, power, money, society, community. Life is about success and sustaining the family for the next generation, and if possible, taking the family to the next level." And finally, Sun-hi might have understood what her mother was trying to tell her. As a survivor of a great fire that destroyed her childhood home and a survivor of two wars, "risk" was doing nothing. Sun-hi was good with numbers, sharp, and she was tent-city fearless.

So, by the time her baby daughter became a toddler, Sun-hi had an apprenticeship to life in which the freedom to grow led to prosperity.

❧10❧

1972 VANCOUVER

THE RAINS HAD CEASED ABRUPTLY AND an extraordinary brightness and clarity overtook the scene, particularly above the trees and hilltops. The mountains stood out sharply as three-dimensional engravings against the blue sky. Grouse Mountain looked fresh and green, and wisps of light fog lingered just above the waters between the mainland and the North Shore. Lions Gate Bridge looked impressive, stretching across like two long arms of a slumbering giant, spanning across the inlet with ease. But this freshness remained only in high elevations perched in the heavens and not down on the ground. Down below, everything was withered, dried out, and drooping. The deciduous bushes in Stanley Park were spindly and skeletal while the boxwood was a dull grey-green shade. It was the first time Nara visited the park since coming to Vancouver, but even in the colourless thrust of the late fall, she thought it was beautiful. Burrard Inlet was clean and clear and reminded her of Busan, except for the wet chill that came endlessly from the North with the jet stream rounding the Juan de Fuca Strait. It was the kind of cold that got inside one's bones and left behind a solid case of the shivers.

Nara walked along the seawall pushing the small, light stroller with her granddaughter sleeping inside. Not so long ago, she had received a letter from her estranged daughter Sun-hi informing her she was a grandmother. Since the birth of the baby two years ago, things had been difficult, the letter said.

In fact, since they immigrated five years ago, everything had been hard, and so, without further words of reconciliation, requests for forgiveness or closure, Nara was bluntly asked if she would consider moving to Vancouver to live with Sun-hi and help raise the baby. *By the way, your granddaughter's name is Lauren*, was all the letter had to say about the baby, leaving off anything descriptive or remarkable about her.

Nara had not even known Sun-hi was pregnant. To say the letter was a shock would be an understatement. There was surprise, joy, disappointment, and deep repugnance. The gall of Sun-hi's request left a bitter taste in Nara's mouth. How could Sun-hi not have bothered to let her know that she was grandmother? How could she have waited for two years before telling her? And now, she wrote only because she needed help.

Nara had cried a little with the letter in her hand. Not a lot; there were worse things. But the few drops that had fallen caused the ink to run in streaks. Some words had blended into each other making those sentences incomprehensible, and in some parts the words had become meaningless.

Nara had pondered over the name of her granddaughter. She remembered how they had struggled to recover their Korean names after the Occupation, or fought with their lives to keep them, and now there was "Lauren." It was an entirely western name without even the hint of Korean intonation or meaning. "Lau-ren," Nara had said over and over. "Lau-REN, LAU-ren, LAU-Ren." *At least it had two syllables*, she had thought, as she tried to put emphasis on the separate syllables in different ways in an effort to imagine how to pronounce it correctly. It had sounded foreign to her, but as with everything else, she knew she would learn to adjust. To her surprise, adjusting to life in Vancouver was about the same as adjusting to the factory work Japan or to the Korean War. It was a little harsh, a little cruel, and a lot different.

Right around the time Sun-hi moved to Canada, Young-min had married a young man of a certain sensibility and jovial personality whom she met at their church in Seoul. His mannerisms were marked by large hand gestures and strong facial expressions that came naturally to him and Young-min was drawn in. They married at City Hall in a brief ceremony with no one attending except the officiator and Nara as the witness. With this unlikely and almost miraculous turn of events in Young-min's life — one that no one around her ever truly expected — Young-min's journey continued with a husband at her side. And because of this, despite their mother's objections, Young-min secretly wished Sun-hi a safe and wonderful journey as Sun-hi embarked on her own adventure, going headlong into a new country with nothing except Jin-Chun, a good dose of hope, and huge amount of courage. So, as both her daughters entered new phases in their lives, Nara was left alone in her small apartment with no family around her, again. When Nara received news from Sun-hi in Canada, knowing that Young-min was settled with her husband, she was fine with once again moving to a new home.

Nara continued to walk in the direction of Lions Gate, then under it and around the bend until West Vancouver was at her back and she was facing English Bay. She was greeted by the waters of the Pacific as they gently lapped up against the stony shore covered with green-black seaweed and various forms of algae. The beach was not like the soft sandy beaches lined up near turquoise water she had seen in photographs of foreign places like Hawaii. No, these beaches were rocky, ungroomed. Nara paused for a moment in awe at the smattering of logs that had washed up onto the shore. She had never seen such a thing. She looked in wonderment, not knowing where the logs could have come from.

The sound of the waves hitting the rocks carried a steady rhythm. As she strolled, Nara caught herself occasionally closing her eyes not from fatigue but from the lull of the slow lapping sound of the waves as they rolled into shore, the sound of freedom. She breathed in the air deeply, as if she were breathing for the first time. The air was clear and fresh, so different from the low hanging fumes that seemed to smother the tent city, or that fell heavy and dense after the air raids in Busan, or the dust that hovered over Seoul. She gazed out at the beautiful Pacific Ocean and was struck by the knowledge that this ocean touched her country too, that these very waters also washed along the shores of her beloved Korea. The connection was comforting, and startling. It amazed her to see how the world was connected like this in both a physical and metaphorical sense, not separated by oceans but connected by them. She wanted to stretch out her arms, to put her hands in the water and reach across to home. Then, she caught herself. "I suppose this is my home now," she said out loud. And, she could not deny it, Vancouver was a small piece of paradise.

She had come to the city excited at the idea of starting a new life. Yet, at the same time, her heart was filled with the fear of starting over. In the weeks leading up to the first airplane she would take in her life, she had been overcome with anxiety and it had taken every bit of strength she had to pack her bags, leave the rest of her possessions and life behind, and board the plane.

She would miss Young-min, though they hardly saw each other at all by then. But, with reserved and even taut emotion, she was cautiously ready to embrace Sun-hi again and welcome her back into her life, though it was in fact Sun-hi who was welcoming her. Nara thought her granddaughter would be the bridge to unite them and she was enthralled at the idea of having a granddaughter at all. To Nara, Lauren was a symbol of her own survival, that she had made it, that a new generation was even possible when once generations could have been lost.

A week before her flight, Nara had decided to revisit Daegu. She had gone back to Daegu a few times since the war for other reasons, but had never ventured close to her old neighbourhood for fear of dredging up buried sorrow. On this trip, believing it would be the last, she had made a conscious decision to walk past her childhood home knowing she would never see it again, having heard it was back in Korean hands, owned by a rich businessman, a supplier to the exploding shipping industry. She had felt glad about that but deeply saddened too by the memories of how that home had been stolen from her family.

She had been curious about how well the house might have been kept. She could never afford to buy back her father's stolen home though it had not been for lack of trying or lack of dreams. After the war and the fire, though she had fearlessly gotten back on her feet and did well enough, the amount she would have needed to do so was unattainable.

The injustice of having lost her ancestral home in the first place and *how* it was taken from her family was so great, there was not enough emotion left in her and no words sufficient enough to say anymore about it. There was nothing else to do but to blame God, or forgive Him.

She had stood in front of the gate and remarked that little had changed. It still had the massive front door with its large, carved wooden medallion placed in the middle that hardly showed any wear at all. The rounded black tiles on the roof were still intact and the pillars standing tall at each side of the front wall were still strong and indifferent. The only change had been the vegetation surrounding the house: the bushes had grown fuller, the trees taller, and the plants larger, all showing a more mature leafiness. She had stroked the trees in the front wistfully, saddened that she could not see the trees in the back. She had wished she could just climb that "tree of life" — the one that was just outside what used to be her bedroom — just one more time. She had wished she could whisper to its trunk and strong limbs, "I'm okay." She had looked one last time at her childhood home with longing. It was so heart-wrenching, she was almost relieved to leave.

When she had arrived in Vancouver and finally settled in, she found herself more content than she had expected. She was happy to live with Sun-hi again, and though they had not reconciled, she felt a rare warmth that only comes from being with family.

As she rounded the bend of the seawall, and walked closer to English Bay, the seawall seemed to embrace the water, encompassing it round like a womb. It was as if the seawall was a pair of arms that hugged her, and Nara was an embryo against the wall of Mother Nature whose heartbeat she could hear with each swish of a Pacific wave washing up against the shore. She felt as though the glint of the sun and the swaying trees honoured her, approving of how far she had travelled on such a short walk. Right around English Bay, Nara stopped and blew her prayers to God. Again, there was no answer save for the rustle of the wind through Stanley Park's trees.

Later that day, in the grocery store, Nara smelled the melons and strawberries, which were in season, and saw the spinach leaves were large and dark so they were probably rich in nutrients though a bit grainy to the tooth and slightly bitterer than the lighter variety. She could not find any rice but picked up the few things she needed to prepare dinner. She asked a stock boy if they had any soy sauce but he only looked her up and down and then walked away. As she stood in line, the cashier looked over her, or rather, looked past her. "Next," was all she said and Nara was bypassed by the customer standing behind her. He stepped in front as if she was not standing there, like she did not exist. *Doesn't he see me?* Nara wondered. The cashier might have noticed that the man jumped the queue, but if she had, she chose not to do anything about it, and if she had not noticed, well, all the worse, for that made Nara invisible to the checkout cashier too. The cashier processed the man's basket of groceries and he paid and left.

"Next," was all the cashier said again, and now the woman standing behind Nara passed in front of her, nudging Nara in the shoulder as she did so. Nara was not sure if the nudge was intentional or not, until the woman gave her an icy glare daring her to say something. The woman mumbled something, but Nara could not make out the words. It was unmistakable; the woman was speaking to her.

With a strong Korean accent, Nara said, "I'm sorry," to apologize for not hearing the woman.

The woman responded sharply, "You people. Get out of here. Go back to where you came from."

Nara's head jerked back in surprise. The words spun at her like knives, piercing her. Nara understood these words well. She had learned English from the missionaries so her comprehension of the language was good, and it had gotten better over the last few months. But she did not understand the reason for this woman's words. The lady with yellow hair had fire in her fair blue eyes and a palpable disgust for Nara oozed out of her. Why was she so hostile, so full of hate? She did not even know Nara.

Nara suddenly became immensely conscious of her behaviour. She was afraid of doing something ridiculous and being laughed at. In her short span of life, she had survived two wars, the Occupation, the attempted assimilation of her country, the loss of a lifelong friend to rapists in organized, militarized sexual slavery, the loss of her father and husband at the hands of murderers, her mother to a sickness and a broken heart, and a massive fire that levelled her city and took everything she owned. Then, at a ripe old age when most people were getting ready to settle down, she had moved, with great courage, she thought, and every iota of her strength, to a new country and there she was, in a supermarket on Granville Street, scorned like she had never been before. She had been humiliated by a man half her age with twice the gall, and then by a cashier, a young woman who had barely started in life. And, now she was being mistreated by a yellow-haired woman who looked like she must have had a good childhood in a good home in a good neighbourhood — so, with a life like that, why was she so full of anger? Nara did not know if the woman or the man or the girl had had hard lives or if they each had experienced an event that caused them to be less than they could be, but even if they did, this did not explain why she was being judged for how she looked and despised for no other reason except for being her.

The yellow-haired woman's words rang in her ears. She trembled from fear and anger, shook from embarrassment, and had no words in *any* language for this kind of treatment. She was in disbelief that this could be the same place from where her beloved missionaries had come. The missionaries who looked upon her with kind eyes, compassionate hearts, and gentle souls, who elevated her sense of humanity and love, who introduced her to her God and brought her steps closer to salvation. Unknowingly, the missionaries had instilled in Nara a narrative of a beautiful, kind-hearted, open Canada – one that she could love and one that would love her back. How could this be the same place they came from? And yet, this encounter would be the first of many such encounters in a world of men and women who had likely never travelled far beyond the four walls of the Lions Gate Bridge to the West, the North Shore Mountains to the North, Richmond to the south, and Surrey to the East.

It was here in this random grocery store on a random street in a random city, that Nara's oppression had come upon her full circle. It was in this moment that she realized that she would never truly find home. Go home? This was supposed to be home now. The journey would end here, and it was no place for her.

Now there was nowhere upon which to lay the foundation for a bright and happy future, nowhere to upright the walls of a place safe and secure, nowhere to put a roof over a family that was intact and at peace, and let in the warmth of love into the rooms of her hollow soul. *Ah, this place will be built over these sorts of ashes, will it? This form of decay.* And this realization crumbled inwardly upon Nara's heart.

She went back to her daughter's house, went into her room, and looked out the window, squinting at the brightness reflected off the high clouds. She grasped onto the curtains, pulling them down with her as she collapsed to the floor in bitter misery and disappointment. She was too old for revelation of this kind; she was too old for tears, and she did not deserve to cry like this any longer. She had already paid the hefty price of all that had fallen upon her like curses from God. Now, tears, like brimstone, fell through the night. She did not weep loudly, she did not whimper, but she pounded her chest with her fist. She hit herself hard, as if punishing herself. Did she need to feel the physical pain? *Please, I can manage the physical pain.* Her mind became numb, her heart too. She pounded her chest harder. *How dare I allow myself to dream, how stupid. How dare I believe things could finally be different? How foolish.* All night, she beat herself.

It was impossible to think about her experience that day and not think back to her past. The Occupation had forcefully suppressed her identity, and now, it was happening all over again. Who was Nara to those in the grocery store, in this city, in this new country? She had no identity for them and they showed her no other side of themselves. It would be a sad and limiting lesson for them both.

Not long after arriving in Canada, Nara found a job. The fish factory was not a bad place to work. Nara processed the fish after the heads and innards were removed. She did not object to cutting the heads off or gutting the fish at the front of the assembly line, but on most days, she ended up on the side of the line where she needed to filet the fish in pieces according to the cuts the customer wanted. Sometimes, she worked further down the factory floor where she packaged them up, but no matter where, the assembly line was highly efficient and familiar — like her, nearly all the workers had done something like this before. Her shift started at the time when the day is darkest, before sunrise, when the fish first arrived from the ships just having docked in port close to the factory. The smell upon first entering the factory was expectedly overwhelming. The entire building was soaked with a briny smell and a swampy version of the big blue ocean filled her nostrils, but as offensive as it was to smell fish guts at four-thirty in the morning, it played on her youthful years, reminding her of the Busan Harbour, and she was all right with that.

Coming home on the bus though, there would be the looks and the words, of course, until Sun-hi finally bought a car and they were able to drive to work. Both Jin-Chun and Nara came home together after spending the day with fish. By the time Nara was back home from her shift, Sun-hi would leave for her shift at the hospital. Nara's turn to take care of the baby would start, while Jin-Chun's drinking shift began not long after.

Jin-Chun's drinking seemed to have gotten worse, but at least he was no longer working as a custodian in the hospital. In the end, he could not clean up after other people. He could barely clean up his own mess. He joined the fish factory at the same time as Nara. Part of his job was to lift and toss the one hundred pound fish from crate to conveyor belt, which was hard and strenuous, even back-breaking work, but it was lighter than lifting the broom. Jin-Chun often thought of himself as the fisherman, maybe even a saviour.

Nara barely spoke to Jin-Chun but not because she disapproved of him any longer. There was just too much distance and too much history that had not been resolved. They both brooded in silence in the others' presence, neither willing to bring up the past, to forgive, or ask forgiveness. The talk was always banal and the tension was palpable but not intolerable, and so it went on like this for years.

In the early months, he had berated Sun-hi for bringing Nara over.

"You agreed!"

"She rejected us!"

"We need her."

"You need her."

"Lauren needs her."

Nara had lain awake in her room downstairs in the small house, trying to remember the good times but none could be found. Lauren was usually able to sleep through it all, but when the fighting began in earnest, Nara would bring Lauren to her room and cradle her. Fast asleep, Lauren's mouth would curl up and pout while small bubbles came to her tiny lips. Though her eyes were closed, the child had smirked a little at the ticklish sensation of the popping bubbles, and Nara had smiled. Holding Lauren in her arms were the only good moments she would have in that house that should have felt like home.

Lauren was awakened by her teary-eyed mother. As Sun-hi picked up Lauren, she slumped over her mother's shoulder, wanting to sleep, but soon realized she was being taken away. Her father was in another drunken stupor. His eyes were blood-shot and murky, barely able to focus. They were dead and fiery all at once. It was like looking at a defeated demon still raging but slothful and impotent of any power. He was thirsty, and there was never enough of anything to quench his thirst. It was pitiful but frightening. He did his best to stand up tall while continuing to yell about things Lauren did not understand. Her mother stormed out of the house not saying another word, buckled Lauren in the car, and drove off. Lauren looked out the backseat window at her father who was now darkening the threshold of their front door, holding the sides of the doorframe with both hands to steady himself. He looked angry. He looked sad. Sun-hi drove. She did not drive long. She went to the nearby grocery store and parked across the street. There, they stayed for a long time. There was no sound, and Lauren dozed off. It was unclear how long she slept but when she woke, her mother was still in the driver's seat, not having moved an inch. But she had been crying and crying a lot. The night was still and cold. The engine had been turned off for so long, the window was now covered in mist while a fog dispersed with each breath.

"When can we go home, Mommy?"

Sun-hi did not respond for a moment, trying to clear her throat, but making no effort to conceal her pain.

"I don't want to go home."

"Why not?"

"It's not like a home."

"It's warmer than the car."

Sun-hi turned the engine and put on the heat for a few minutes. Lauren dozed off again. When she woke, it was still pitch dark outside so she knew it was still the middle of the night. Sun-hi was still in the driver's seat, still crying even though Lauren could not see her face.

"I'm tired, Mommy. I want to go home."

"I'm tired too."

At some point, much later that night, Sun-hi turned the ignition and took the longest drive of her life, back down the street to the house. She did not have anywhere else to go, nowhere to turn, no one to help. She had played out every possible scenario in her head and realized there was no escape. Her money was tied to her marriage. She was in a strange country, with strange customs and strange attitudes. It was hard enough to survive the radical change together; it would be impossible alone. She had a young child who depended on her, and while her husband did not lift a finger in rearing her, still she knew she could not raise her as a single mother. No matter the misery at home, Sun-hi concluded that the cost of liberty was too great and the misery of being alone would be worse. No matter the hell at home — the psychological beatings, the emotional torture — she measured and weighed all the options that night sitting in the driver's seat of the family car and made the heartbreaking choice to give up freedom for compromise. She must have also recognized the guilt she bore like a cross. He was here because of her. Maybe it would have been better for him to go to prison for fighting against corruption, or even to die in Korea for his beliefs than wither here all alone. But of this, she was not entirely sure. Sun-hi understood the brain of the beast as well as the heart of the man she married. He was troubled. So was she. As Sun-hi pulled up in front of the house, there was relief but it was not hers. This was not the outcome Sun-hi had wanted out of this evening, and while carrying Lauren in her arms, she crossed back through the threshold of her home, her pride shattered and her hopes dashed.

Nara emerged from her dimly lit room in the basement and came upstairs, stopping just at the top stair. She was wide awake and with a woven brow, she looked at Sun-hi briefly. She had spent the night anxious and afraid for herself, afraid for Sun-hi. She had paced her bedroom back and forth and wrung her hands and read the Bible and prayed again and again. Sweat had beaded itself along her brow, and her heart had pounded all night. When she heard the door open, she had gasped and steadied herself. Slowly, she had ascended the stairs. Now here, at the top, there was nothing to see but tragedy. She could see in Sun-hi's face an agony that revealed surrender. She saw Sun-hi accepted the choice she made, but hardly the sacrifice it had entailed. There were no words, so she turned and went back downstairs. Jin-Chun was lying on the couch. Upon hearing the door open, he jumped up and tried to stand. As Sun-hi passed through the living room, she all but glanced at him and walked with such haste, she struck him in the shoulder, nearly toppling him. Jin-Chun staggered and found his balance, though poorly. He mumbled something and retreated to the couch. It would not be the first time that they would teach Lauren a lesson about choice and sacrifice.

Nara looked at her granddaughter teetering on her legs and hopping gingerly over the cracks in the sidewalk while throwing her arms out like she wanted to fly. Nara smiled as they promenaded down their neighbourhood street like it was a grand boulevard in Paris or Rome. The girl's hair bounced and caught the sun's glint, and her thin legs were marked up with scars from falls, scratches, and childhood. Lauren ran ahead and then hop-scotched back to Nara and jumped ahead again. At one point, Lauren turned, looked at Nara, and then waited for her grandmother to catch up. Nara stared at Lauren and tried to place the feeling of déjà vu that suddenly washed over her. The familiarity of her granddaughter and her movements seemed to stretch back into the past. Lauren had stopped on an oddly shaped section of the concrete sidewalk and was balancing somewhat precariously on one leg. With outstretched arms, Lauren closed her eyes and tilted her head up to the sun. Lauren smiled a sweet smile that curled up on one side of her mouth and she basked in the light of the mid-afternoon sun, innocent and carefree of the big bad world around her. Nara startled. She tilted her head and screwed her eyes, for her vision was not what it used to be. She looked at Lauren who was like a mirage now, with the glow of the light over her head that made her seem a bit of a blur. Nara shook her head then took her index finger and rubbed the inside corner of her right eye. She then closed her eyes and pinched the bridge of her nose. She opened her eyes, lifted her gaze, and having reset herself, she took another look. Lauren looked exactly like Min-joo. Nara could not believe it. There was such a strange and uncanny resemblance that Nara's skin tingled at the similarity. She saw Lauren clearly now, but she also saw Min-joo.

"Gamma? Are you okay?"

Nara was far away.

"Gamma?"

"Yes, yes," Nara returned. "Let's go back in. I think Mommy and Daddy are waiting for someone to visit."

As they went back into the house, Nara had a sinful thought. It was like Min-joo had reincarnated in the form of Lauren. It was ridiculous of course. There was no such thing as reincarnation. Nara was not a Buddhist and never gave any thought to such mystical things. But the notion of second chances was not foreign to her by any stretch; in fact, such an idea was entirely consistent with her own beliefs. How stunning the similarities still.

But, that was how it was with Koreans and Korean grandmothers. There was a juxtaposition of their Christian beliefs with ancestor worship and belief in walking spirits as well as their ability to tap into a universe that everyone could see, yet no one could see except them. It was a universe of tall, beige tombstone markers covered in ancient scrawls, of temples and shrines, of large bells and courtyards, of old homes and villages. It was an Elysium where the ancestor spirits dwelled. And whenever Nara rubbed Lauren's aching tummy, and chanted, *"Neh sohn yack sohn ya,"* with her eyes shut and head down in prayer, it seemed to Lauren that Nara was calling upon the spiritual world to let her hand be a healing hand. But by the same breath and manic faith, Nara was praying to God, asking Him to heal Lauren.

There, in that small act of rubbing a belly with head bent in deference, was a living example of how children were stroked treasures and altars upon which to worship and pray. While all parents imbued a love that knew no end, by submitting to the inexplicable drive to provide for them, Korean parents drew with determination the future of their children from their own needs, sacrificing all for the needs of their sons — and their daughters — with half-madness and half-godliness. Whether sensible or not, Koreans puts their children first, even at the sacrifice of health and happiness so to the third and fourth generations and generations to come, hard-earned blessings there would be.

Likewise, it was — and still is — a society based on gossip and hearsay that forces one and all to be a good story worth telling, not a story worth repeating. It was that strong gossip-based society that encouraged Koreans to save face, to do well, to desire to have successful children and a respectable, honourable family. It was this that helped Korea survive all those occupations. It was this that would help Korea to thrive.

By contrast, in countries where they sold off their children like commodities for sheer survival or even profit, they ended up destitute and suffered greatly. In countries where fathers sold off their young daughters to marry old men without remorse or sold off their young sons to toil in field and factory without conscience, ended up selling their future and their souls for scraps in this commodity exchange — a few meagre coins for a priceless child. What a price to pay. Indeed, it was irrefutable that it was a vicious cycle where poverty and pain bred poverty and pain, but the failure of the family unit was the equivalent to the failure of that society. If the value of a child was reduced to something so vile and dirty as money and commodity, and the family unit was no longer sacred, the nation had a disease rotting at its core, and it would never be able to lift itself out of the sickness of despair and destitution. The only commodities that made a nation wealthy had little to do with blood and flesh.

As for Sun-hi, she was never traded or bartered for. Nara fought for her, and she had been, and still was, fiercely loved.

"Go on to your room now, Lauren," said Sun-hi kissing her on her forehead mindlessly. Nara strolled back downstairs listlessly, heavy in thought, while Lauren scampered away knowing she should not be told anything twice. Lauren saw her mother as a ghost. Not an evil spirit but one living amongst her fairies and girlish haberdasheries. Her mother was a spirit far away.

In the middle of the small living room papered in a disintegrating damask pattern, there was a sturdy rectangular table, hard as a rock with rounded legs. It was a coffee table but reminiscent of dining tables back in Korea. On the coffee table was a thick ledger full of columns and numbers hand-written in fountain blue ink, nicely sharpened pencils, a pewter coloured business-card holder, and two cups of cold tea. Water boiled on one of the elements of the stove, ready to be transformed into a hot beverage at a moment's notice. When the doorbell rang, it gave a quick start and then a weak tinkle. Jin-Chun and Sun-hi breathed out a sigh of relief. Jin-Chun approached the door, tugged on his shirt, cleared his throat, and nodded to Sun-hi. "Ready?"

A few light clouds drifted across a pale blue sky and turned silvery white by a sun that had lost much of its glow as it waned by the weight of the day. A stout man, wearing a relatively inexpensive suit — one would not say "cheap" for the office the man would hold — stood in a sideways pose as if already half-way through the door or perhaps half-way out. A dull green tie clung to his clean shirt. Even with the door wide open, his eyes scanned the neighbourhood first and finally haphazardly landed on Jin-Chun's grin.

"Welcome, Mr. Roberts," Jin-Chun said, grabbing the man's hand and shaking it up and down with great zeal.

"Please excuse me for having made you wait," the man said politely.

"No, no, it's not an easy street to find. Very obscure."

"Hmmm," the man grunted.

"Please come in. Please."

As they moved into the living room, the smoke from the cigarette that Jin-Chun had been nervously smoking only moments before was just starting to thin, and the man took a deep breath as if to drink in the last of the grey strands.

"Ah, here, allow me," Jin-Chun stuck out his packet of cigarettes.

"No," the man said reluctantly. It looked like he would have gladly taken one. "That's fine, thank you."

Sun-hi bowed slightly then welcomed Mr. Roberts into the living room while Jin-Chun tactfully extended his arm out to the armchair, the only armchair", and then tactfully extended his arm out to the armchair, the only armchair, in the room. The man called Mr. Roberts plunked himself down into the chair without further thought, while Sun-hi and Jin-Chun slowly lowered themselves into the folding chairs they used at the kitchen table.

"Thank you for coming, Mr. Roberts. We could have met you at your office. It would have been no trouble. We certainly do appreciate that you..."

"Ach, my office is small, barely big enough for my file cabinets, my desk and me," he chuckled. "I like making house calls from time to time," he said giving a wink and a nudge to the air.

Jin-Chun did not know what that meant, but Sun-hi nodded.

"Anyway, it's just as easy enough for me to come here," Mr. Roberts said in a rather jolly tone.

"Can I offer you something to drink, Mr. Roberts," asked Sun-hi. "A cup of tea perhaps?"

"No, that won't be necessary, Mrs. Hwang. This should not take long."

At last, everything was in order and ready for business. Mr. Roberts had already keenly remarked on the ledger lying on the table. "Permit me to take a closer look at your numbers, will you?"

Both Sun-hi and Jin-Chun eagerly offered up the book like it was being presented at the altar. The ledger had a grainy, fake leather cover and perfectly lined pages in which carefully fixed numbers, ready to be examined, had been neatly written down. The fake leather indicated that it was best they could find at the price they could afford and that it had some importance to them.

The man took out a calculator from his inside jacket pocket and punched at a few buttons with his stubby finger all the while hemming and hawing. Sun-hi wrung her hands discreetly while Jin-Chun rubbed his foot on the scruffy floor where the old carpet had completely worn out.

Long minutes passed in silence. The three people sat huddled around the coffee table as though warming themselves around a flickering fire. They looked at each other for any perceptible movement or familiar, readable expression.

"And the contract?" the man asked suddenly.

Sun-hi immediately lifted up a carefully clipped set of papers from the table that was on top of the tallest pile of even piles of paper, neatly organized long before. The care by which these papers were organized indicated nothing short of obsession. She handed the contract to him and looked him straight in the eye while doing so.

He thumbed through the pages, occasionally licking a finger or two to gather up the corner to turn to the next page. He put both the contract and the ledger down on the table together to get a different perspective of the numbers dancing off the pages. He followed the numbers with his finger and leaned with the other hand on the table for some support.

"Are you feeling better, Mr. Roberts?" inquired Sun-hi.

Without looking up, the man said, "Oh yes, yes. That was a scare indeed, wasn't it Mrs. Hwang?"

Sun-hi nodded, but the man did not see her agreeing. He continued to speak in an almost inaudible tone, "Couldn't thank you enough for alerting the doctors the way you did, Mrs. Hwang. Could have been bad."

Sun-hi did not respond. She was humbled and thankful.

A few more long minutes passed, and Jin-Chun had gotten up to pace a little. The room was damp and humid. With thin windows and poor isolation, there was always a moist draft. The weather was overcast on this day, with bursts of sunshine that would scream through the window from time to time quickly followed by low clouds that would shut out the brilliance. The atmospheric pressure seemed to drop heavily every time it was about to rain and today, it was so oppressive, it pushed on the heart and brain and made breathing difficult.

Jin-Chun looked outside and saw a swallow flutter so close to the large living-room window that he was afraid it would crash into it. Its wing tip brushed the glass just in time and the swallow shot straight up with a quick thrust, averting danger.

Finally, the accountant looked up with a face that reflected his satisfaction at the state of affairs the closer look afforded.

"Mr. and Mrs. Hwang, all the numbers look in order. The contract is a standard contract, nothing to worry about. You have enough savings, and if needed, it looks like you would qualify to borrow the rest. The store's numbers look sound to me. It should be no problem to operate that business should you decide to buy it."

The dream of owning their own business was upon them. With a little English and a little capital, the grocery business seemed the most attainable. While the store was in an area that seemed somewhat unsavoury, Sun-hi and Jin-Chun saw the opportunity in it. Hard work and extremely long hours might deter many others from operating a grocery business, but what most could not see was that an area like that desperately needed a decent place to shop. Everyone deserved fresh fruit and vegetables, after all. And if that did not make them a living, then well, the cigarettes and packaged goods would. High inventory turnover meant high cash flow and profit.

Sun-hi and Jin-Chun nearly jumped up from the news. Their faces glowed with such exhilaration that the accountant almost got carried away himself, but he quickly tamed his own emotions. He realized that such a simple thing as looking at numbers and reading a contract meant people could change their lives. The legal terms of the contract, and understanding whether or not the numbers made sense, must have daunting for this couple. Mr. Roberts felt a small sliver of humanity creep into his heart, and he felt happy to have been able to help.

Once again, Nara was awakened from a light sleep. There was

a persistent noise coming from upstairs in Sun-hi's bedroom. At first, there was just the one bang on the wall and then several rapid successions of bangs. There was a boisterous rout of shouts and cries and muffled words of protest. There was no doubt what it could be, and Nara felt the blood leave her hands and her face, and her heart palpitated nervously. Initially, she lay on her pillow paralyzed, hoping the argument would stop as it usually did after several minutes. She paused and closed her eyes to pray, but the fierce banging continued to pump anxious scandal through the house. She had refused to get up as it had become a disturbingly repetitive nightly ritual, but the persistent banging forced her out of bed. The rattling had become so strong, that while normally she would not, she picked up the Bible in her hands this night and hurried to the top of the stairs.

Sun-hi had also awoken from her slumber and had leaped from her bed, horrified to see what Jin-Chun was doing. In hot desperation, Sun-hi was flaying her arms and swearing at Jin-Chun, beseeching him to stop and accusing him of madness.

Jin-Chun had taken a large hammer and was striking the flimsy wall again and again, exposing the weak drywall behind the thin coat of white waxy paint.

This was another episode of what had become regular tirades of drunken violence and explosive badgering. This time it had gone further and was wilder and more chaotic. Like Cronus eating his children, Jin-Chun ate away at his family in a furor.

Sun-hi was repelled by the smell of sour alcohol that seeped through Jin-Chun's pores. Mixed with the stink of cigarette smoke clinging to his clothes and skin, he smelled like he was embalmed in formaldehyde or some chemical concoction that made him repugnant.

If he had not been so inebriated, he would have seen a picture of himself that would have made him regurgitate. He was hammering the wall with such violence and drama that it was absolute madness.

"What are you doing?" screamed Sun-hi.

"I'm breaking down the walls in this house, woman!"

"Why? Why? What are you doing?" Sun-hi continued to sob.

"Walls! Walls!" Jin-Chun repeated in a frenzy. "Walls!"

"Stop it! Stop it! We can't fix it! We can't fix the walls!"

"I don't want to fix them, you stupid woman! I want to break them down!"

Sun-hi continued to plead with Jin-Chun, knowing that after the alcohol-induced rage was over, the walls would be torn down, and they would need to rebuild again. Again and again. *Why so much rebuilding? Why so many homes destroyed?* She started to spasm and convulse.

Nara peered into the room and saw Jin-Chun push Sun-hi onto the bed. With increasing horror, Nara slowly opened the door, knowing that entering Jin-Chun's bedroom would be considered an appalling affront to the head of the house. Sun-hi grabbed onto Jin-Chun's pajama pant to pull him away from the wall to keep him from striking it yet again, and suddenly, he pounced on Sun-hi with the hammer still in hand. They began to wrestle, an inextricably uneven match. With grim caution, Nara proceeded closer to their bed when suddenly Sun-hi bit Jin-Chun in the arm as hard as she could. Then, as quick as a lightning strike, the brawl turned into a murderous scene. Jin-Chun screamed from being bitten and raised the hammer over his head. With wild, blood-shot eyes and demonic ferocity, he glared down at Sun-hi and opened his mouth as if to consume her. Gripping the hammer even harder, his anger fell squarely on his wife on whom he blamed everything. All he had wanted to do was smash the walls until there were none left standing. Nara caught the look in Jin-Chun's eyes and saw the hammer twitch downward. A strange look flashed across his face, and for a moment Nara thought he was going to smash the hammer on Sun-hi's head. In a split second, Nara screamed as loud as she had ever screamed in her life, louder than during the fire, louder than in the factory, louder than ever: "No!"

Startled and still asphyxiated by the demon within, Jin-Chun looked up to see where this great succubus had come from. Upon seeing Nara, he suddenly morphed, his body swollen and fierce, and took on the form of a Herukas, a Tibetan deity and blood drinker who leads beings away from ignorance to enlightenment. However, Jin-Chun the Herukas was not the gentle guide to enlightenment. The blood drinker stared with large crazed eyes in Nara's direction. He looked like he wore a great colourful mask, adorned with bullish nostrils and a large red mouth, inside of which were long, sharp yellow teeth. He had smoke piping out from those nostrils and from every pore like a dragon. Without hesitation, he flung the hammer with incredible force in Nara's direction.

No one could remember exactly what happened next, but Nara lay on the ground with a deep and horrific gash at the side of her head, which bled profusely. Her eyes were shut and she was barely breathing. The Bible lay next to her right hand on the floor.

It was a profound peace of mind that Jin-Chun sought, each time he gulped down half a bottle of vodka, trying to reach a state of *moksha*, a state of liberation. But, while the alcohol-addled state left him empty and unhindered, he was far from free. It was not an ancestral form of shamanic thought that brought him to seek some form of freedom. To the contrary, it was a base, natural, hammer-like banging that throbbed in his mind. It was well known by Tibetan Buddhists that the moment before achieving enlightenment, a mountain does not look like a mountain anymore and a river does not look like a river. But once one passed the threshold and entered a state of enlightenment, a mountain was again a mountain, a river again a river. But it was not the same mountain and it was not the same river. And so similarly was Jin-Chun's transformation.

The post-drunken stupor was anaemic and even macabre. At the corner where death and light merged, Jin-Chun held his head in shame for when he came to, he was puzzled by the blisters and scrapes all over his hands and arms and did not remember what he had done. He did not remember he had thrown a hammer and struck Nara squarely in the head, and nearly stole her life from God. Nara lay unconscious in a hospital bed, the same place where he had cleaned corpses and shit in the bathrooms.

The moment he struck Nara was the moment a mountain became a mountain again, and a river became a river again, but not the same river and not the same mountain. Like waking out of an induced comma, which was an intentional disruption in the participation in life, he stumbled headlong into an unintended path of spiritual awakening and rebirth. For so long, he had heard a desperate scratching against his soul, which was guilt or madness or abuse or something else, but it was putting him in a state of bondage with himself, and no amount of alcohol or fist fights or self-hatred was going to release him. This horrendous moment of disdainful contempt for Nara's life — any life — had given him the clarity he needed. A bright spark had flashed across his mind as though the hammer had hit him in the head and not Nara and woke him nearly to death. He had an involuntary urge to achieve a stillness of mind that could not be cheaply bought, but only hard-earned through a long struggle to fight one's physical needs and dependencies. Indeed, he had an absolute need to quiet that desperate scratching against the soul. In epic form, at such a grand scale that it brings to mind the Ramayana, improvising all the way, Jin-Chun made up means of salvation through trial and error. After years of raising swords against one hidden monster to another, from one anguish to another, and failing to extinguish his target, he finally bound himself to soteriology, to agape, to a love that never fails.

It was not a fluid process, but he clod with abrupt, uneven steps from the old romantic aesthetic of the pastoral of love, peace, and contentment to an acceptance of suffering. He finally remembered that life was not meant to be enjoyed; one must suffer for it. But Jin-Chun had lost sight of that for so long. He had surely suffered life, but he had not accepted the truth about suffering. Rather than bear it, overcome it, conquer it, he succumbed to it and tried to escape it. Not wishing to suffer, most people looked for cheap thrills, laughed at silly jokes, made funny faces, and settled for momentary pleasure. Jin-Chun drowned himself in pools of alcohol and lost himself in inebriated clouds. But eventually, he would acknowledge that he entered life suffering and he would exit life suffering all the while never giving up the noble search for the Bodhi, the divine, with an abdication from desire but with a spirituality bound to nature, free from the slavish body.

He pulled himself out of the quagmire that the old enslavement put him in and started to lead a disciplined life of purification. He cleared his mind and sought the truth or at least something worthy in the present life and did so with nothing but virtue in the heart. There was no voice inside him, not even God. There was only a full kind of empty, just as it needed to be.

The man that Sun-hi had married was not the same man, but he was the same man with whom Sun-hi would finally cleave and eventually find peace.

Looking into a kaleidoscope, one can see the fragments of colours and lines assembled to compose geometric patterns, and yet as fluidly as the figures came together, one immediately discovered there was no formula to be followed. Then the shape falls to pieces at the slightest tap of a finger on the side of the tube to be replaced by another complex and equally sound geometric pattern of the same elements entirely dissimilar to the first. Equally valuable, equally fragile, equal. This was no different than Jin-Chun's change from a raging alcoholic to a brooding writer to old man monk. All the same and all different in one single tube. That was not evolution, not even enlightenment. That was God's relationship with man. That was a kaleidoscope.

❦11❧

THE TREE OF KNOWLEDGE

NARA LOOKED AT THE SEASONS DIFFERENTLY here. There were not four distinct ones like in Korea. Seemingly, in Vancouver, there was only one — the rainy season. If it was spring, the rain felt cooler, if it was summer, the rain felt heavier and the air muggier. In fall, again the droplets cooled the air to a distinct and nippy chill, and in winter, the rain was cold. But it was rain all the same. In spring, whenever the sun did finally come out, Nara admired the different species of birds and even came to distinguish them pretty well. Along with the birds, she could not miss the burst of blossoms on the fruit trees, especially the cherry blossoms that lined First Avenue or Nanaimo Street. Where she lived now, she noticed the different buds and the surge of life in the coniferous trees. She breathed in the smell of the pine needles that perfumed the air and acknowledged that it was far more pleasing than air filled with smoke.

In autumn, she was in awe of the burst of colours in the trees like fireworks of red, orange, and yellow booming and sparking in slow motion. The sight was intoxicating and she walked amongst the trees full of wonder. It was only now that she was able to see things for what they were — the details of the trees and the different species of the birds, the various kinds of leaves, the movement of light, the sound of rain. Before, she could not be bothered with any of that. She had been too busy with the living and the dying and the dead. Nothing then had held her attention for long due to the frenetic pace of her life that forced fate to work on her side to ensure survival.

With Lauren at school, Nara was alone in the house now, well-settled into retirement, and left to her dreams and histories. In the quiet of the day, she walked around the house feeling like she was more like a shadow or a ghost than a live human. The rain pattered down on the rooftop, the usual melody, the same as it was yesterday, and as it would be tomorrow, eternally sweet and melancholy.

It had been years, a decade even, but her head still throbbed. It had taken a long time for the gash in her head to heal but heal it did, and she ended up with a large mushroom-shaped scar that ran from the left temple to the top of her ear. It formed a bit of a crater in her head that she covered with her hair. She would massage it from time to time as a healer would and when she did, it looked like she was in deep, meditative thought. She continually massaged it, figuring if she could not heal herself, it would be a cruel and absurd joke.

As she lingered in her room, her hands absentmindedly rubbing her scar, she suddenly thought of Jae-sun for the first time in a long time. Her body felt weary, betraying the deep inner sadness that she thought she concealed well, when in fact, it was as apparent as the afternoon sun.

She did not know why she thought of him out of nowhere, but memories have a way of lurking then rushing back at the least likely time. For all they had gone through, there was more bitterness than sweetness that remained for Nara. He was her first and only love and not being able to share the twilight years of her life with him made her sorrowful. She thought of how long it had taken them to reveal their love to each other, how they danced around the social restrictions and played the enterprise of love just right to ensure they had the blessing of the community around them. She thought of the sacrifices he had made for her in the factory, scavenging food and bringing her trinkets he had found in the dust heap so they would have something when it all ended. He had held her tight when she went into labour, never leaving her side despite the objections of the factory foreman and the manager, whom he had fought off with such violence, no one dared touch him until Sun-hi was safely arrived in the world. He had stood up to the iniquities of reproach and taken severe beatings for Nara for he could not tolerate such ill treatment of his wife and his family. He had been her rock and her strength, and he would have been her cornerstone until the end. He had been Nara's healer.

If he had been alive, would they have built their home in a different part of Busan? If not, would she have left the house when the fire raged on or stayed with their girls? Would they have moved to Vancouver together? Would Sun-hi and Young-min have been raised differently with their father around?

Nara sat in her green rocking chair and the questions continued for hours, while her thoughts meandered through the murky streets of Busan and the dusty streets of old Daegu. She talked to Jae-sun and reminisced with him about hard times, happy times, and times best forgotten, as though he was a walking spirit. But there was no reply. Today, like all her days, was filled with stark memories that only stoked heart-wrenching regret.

In the quiet of the night, the sound of her beating heart were words enough, for it prevented her from sleeping as it had for years. Each beat of her heart reminded her she was alive and all those others who were not: a murdered father, a murdered husband, a murdered friend, a sickly mother. The pounding in Nara's ear, the sound of the pulsating blood coursing through her body, was like a drumbeat of suffocating memories.

When she did fall asleep, she was plunged into terrible nightmares or strange and awkward dreams. The nightmares transformed into monstrous fairy tales with deathly giants, hot-eyed dragons, and dizzying heights from which she would fall and fall and never crash. But, for all the garish dreams, she would never return to that fairy tale of long ago and which she knew was the only one that could help her find her way home. The bear, the dragon, and the magpie stayed hidden in their peaks and she could not find them again. And, from time to time, she would see a figure in the distance, in the land of blessings and peace. The figure would be walking through the brush slowly or dancing on tip toes in the cool breeze through wheat fields but always getting further away from Nara. Nara would call out to the figure, "Hey, there! Who are you?" But the figure never looked back.

This night, like all others, she found herself surrounded by loneliness, the pitter-patter of rain on the windowsill thumping in tune with the pounding of her heart. In the room next door, her grandchild slept peacefully, never to know the places Nara would visit night after night. Tonight, as she thought of Jae-sun, she lay her head on a tear-soaked pillow and hummed lullabies until her heavy eyes finally let her rest, this time until morning.

Sun-hi and Jin-Chun had successfully built their business. And, by the time they had moved to North Vancouver, Nara's role in the family was sealed: she was cook, cleaner, and caregiver. She did not know herself any longer. Just as she would have given anything to exchange toiling in a factory in the blistering heat, she found it equally humiliating to be reduced to house-servant in her daughter's home. It was just as unbearable. It was not the obligation that tormented her, but the undying desire to live her own life.

But there was never any outward complaint. She hardly uttered a word now. There were no words left to be said.

Sun-hi was always working, and indeed, the affluence she sought soon followed. Nara had observed that at one point along the way, Sun-hi must have felt a heightening discontent with the wearing futility and strain of a small and mechanical life. Perhaps she resented supporting an expensive drinking habit; perhaps she did not want to be robbed of choice, which would mean sacrifice; perhaps she simply resolved to do better, or perhaps, she finally met God and feared Him for the first time. Nara did not know where Sun-hi's drive stemmed from, but she saw a vigour and fire in her daughter that she had not seen before. Sun-hi and Jin-Chun set out a plan, analyzed the numbers, mortgaged their house, and took on methodical and measured risk by buying their first grocery store, and then another and then one more. It was a typical immigrant story that fulfilled the stereotype. Koreans owned grocery stores and dry-cleaning businesses and that stereotype started with people like Sun-hi and Jin-Chun who were probably amongst the first. They did it well, and as success came, others followed.

As it turned out, in the months that had followed the last outrageous drunken episode that saw the end of Jin-Chun's journey through purgatory, and back with the living, Sun-hi had recoiled from the shock that her mother had nearly been killed by her husband. At one time a reasoned and balanced person, she had acted out of impulse and behaved like a torrent, questioning, ever questioning for weeks. She had gone deep into herself, haunted by the realization that there was so much death around her. For a short while after the incident, Sun-hi's mind had whirled like a dervish. She had never meant to form a new determination but the indignation had sunk deep, and the turbulent experience had dulled her passion into remembrance. If anything could have induced her to change, it was that the prospect of death always lurked at her door. More than ever, she had craved power over her sensibilities, power over the weaknesses that poverty thrust upon her family, and the unassailable quest to quench what she did not have, which was ever-lasting life.

She had burst out with anger and hatred toward Jin-Chun. It had taken a phoenix-like transformation, but finally, after a long journey through her own kind of hell, Sun-hi had finally forgiven Jin-Chun. It had not been a cathartic forgiveness of the religious kind, but it was about as close to the experience as godless Sun-hi was going to experience. The love she had for Jin-Chun floated closer to the surface, and though the depth was gone, its breadth spanned far along the history they shared. They had both accepted there had to be darkness in order for there to be light.

As for Jin-Chun, thanks to rising before dawn to go to work at the fish processing factory, he was now able to wake early every day, around four in the morning, to write, helping him find a new serenity. A couple of hours later, around six in the morning, Sun-hi and Jin-Chun, hand in hand, went their solitary way to labour at their store: to stock the shelves, clean the vegetables, put out the litres of milk, and cut and package the meats. It was hard work, but it was theirs to bear. Both having tasted knowledge, their nakedness now finally obvious to them — the work was theirs, the business was theirs, and all the worries, responsibilities, and successes were theirs. As the business grew, and the scar on Nara's head healed over, Jin-Chun finally came out of the darkness and into the heavy burden of light. Nara's family had at last deciphered life in Canada and thrived.

One could see why all the trees were bent in one direction and had lopsided tops. The winds blew in a constant northerly direction and the rains softened the flora and the sun dried and set them like a bad haircut. It was important to understand certain things pointed in certain directions. It helped in adapting to the climate much more easily. The headwaters at the Capilano Suspension Bridge had changed in the years since they moved nearby. Once swollen and dark grey, it used to roll threateningly, rushing in a furious anger, foaming and bubbling over white froth. The water was quieter now; the riverbed adapted to the currents, so the noise of the torrent of water almost had a pattern to it. It was a matter of deciphering the pattern. Though the waves still pounded, they were less deep and the rapids more predictable. One needed to see the direction of certain things and point that way. Of course, if one went close to the lashing waves and went about it the wrong way, one might still get the thrashing of one's life; one might even get carried away by the current. But finding the rhythm of the river, there was no need to fear the waters. The waters, then, could not harm you.

One day, at dinner, the family bantered about the usual: "How was your day at school?" and "Business is good," or "Business is bad," or "The government wants to introduce some additional tax." Topics bounced around from books to news to pop-culture: "Is Darth Vadar supposed to be communism?" "Is ET the prophet Elijah, carried up to the heavens on a bike?" As they pondered these questions, Jin-Chun looked outside and sighed.

"The tree looks dangerous."

"What?"

"That one. That tree looks dangerous." He pointed at it accusingly as if identifying a criminal when, in fact, it was perfectly innocent.

"Why?"

"Look at it. The branches are growing into the electrical wires."

Sun-hi got up to take a closer look. There were three trees in the front yard. Typical of Vancouver, these trees loomed large. In fact, almost all trees in the city were hundreds of years old and towered above most of the houses and buildings. These trees, in front of their house, were no exception.

Sun-hi could see that the tree in the middle was strangely shaped, like a crucifix with two longer branches extending out on both sides. It was growing in-between the electrical wires dripping with raindrops. Against the dark grey hue of the evening, with the black concrete beckoning below, the tree's precarious position made the situation look ominous.

"Hmmm, looks dangerous."

"Could be a fire hazard."

Sun-hi did not answer but went back to her dinner.

"We should do something about it," Jin-Chun continued.

"Before our house burns down?" Sun-hi stated dryly, barely looking up. She did not intend to be sarcastic but that was how it came out. Jin-Chun knew better than to reply to that. Nara lurched forward as if rear-ended in a car, but immediately got a hold of herself and remained still.

Sun-hi shrugged it off. "Well, we don't have time right now. We'll have to deal with it later."

"If lightning strikes or there's a wind storm, that's going to be big trouble. It will fall on everything. It will destroy our roof, our *house*."

"Well, right now there are other misfortunes with which we need to deal with. We need to fix the refrigeration system in two stores. The milk has gone bad in both, and we need to dump it all. There's the lightning that we need to fear for the moment." There was nothing else to say.

Though Nara had become quiet over the years, and though she rarely spoke more than a few words at a time, she heard everything.

It was only recently that Nara had been able to get a glimpse of what Sun-hi saw in Jin-Chun. Now that he had come out of the whirlwind that was the fury of Erinyes. Like the creatures found in Greek mythology, Jin-Chun had regenerated.

Nara had disapproved of him for so long and that might as well have meant death for Jin-Chun in her society, in the world she knew and understood. But now that she finally approved, she never said so. When Jin-Chun had struck her with the hammer, Nara perversely accepted that as an equalizing blow, and now they were even. It did not seem to make sense, but to Nara — and even to Jin-Chun — it did.

Week after week at church, she spoke about the trouble with the tree. She spoke of the woes it was causing and the fear it instilled like it was a nouveau prophet threatening life as they knew it, daring to rewrite the laws, and great stories about the wind howling through the branches late at night, like a voice crying in the wilderness. It was a menace that continued to grow and spread. It needed to be stopped. Eventually, certain gentlemen in the congregation felt they could do something about this. They would need some equipment and some time one Saturday, but the job could be done.

The congregation of this church was very much like her congregation back in Busan — a mix of intelligent and simple people, all of whom suffered in some way back home, who had come to Canada and suffered in other ways in their new home. There were many in the church who reminded her of her old friends. One woman in particular, Mrs. Kim, reminded Nara of Mrs. Pyon. Ah, effervescent Mrs. Pyon; how Nara missed her. In fact, Nara thought of all her friends, Mrs. Pyon, Mrs. Noh, Mr. Poom, even Mr. Suh — all of whom must have surely passed by now, except maybe Mrs. Pyon. They had all lost their homes that fiery night and Nara thought of them often.

A few weeks later, while Jin-Chun and Sun-hi were at work, she had the churchmen come to cut down the tree that seemed to be a thorn in the family's side. Nara was pleased with herself and even had a small hint of pride at being able to solve a family problem all on her own, to contribute in her own way. She brimmed with excitement. "I have a surprise for your father."

"What is it?"

"Some men from the church are coming to cut down the tree in the front."

"The one growing through the electrical wires?" asked Lauren.

"Yes," she beamed.

"Oh, that *is* a surprise," agreed Lauren. Lauren too had heard her father complaining on several occasions about the tree. He had, actually, complained for weeks. He was going to be so happy to see this problem resolved.

Nara began her day the same as usual, putting away the dishes, sweeping the floor, dusting the furniture, and making breakfast. She fluttered around the house anxiously and finally, later that morning, the churchmen arrived. They came with heavy equipment and heaved up a tall ladder. One of them started to saw through the thick branches while others hoisted ropes and tied off sections of the tree so that when it was ready to fall, they could control the direction without having to worry about which side of the trunk to cut. Whistles and shouts filled the neighbourhood along with the steady hum of chainsaws throughout the day. The whirring and whizzing seemed to conjure notions of concocting some potions and magic spells, while the loud raucous yelling to "Be careful with this" and "Ho! Watch for that," were the various incantations uttered over the bubbling mix.

The men worked throughout the day. They were not actually lumberjacks by trade and had never cut down a tree before and this one was large indeed. Douglas firs certainly grew to great heights, their branches waving in the winds high to the heavens. And yet, despite their majestic and noble bearing, they were humble and quiet trees.

Nara fixed the group of men some lunch, but the sky started to grow dark and clouded over so they ploughed forward with the execution. Before long, the tree was whittled down to a thin trunk, scarcely a shadow of itself with almost all of its branches cut clean away, and the top lopped right off like the head of John the Baptist. Then, one section at a time was cut down so that the tree now stood maybe ten metres high, about half its original height. Lauren looked at the tree and remarked at how odd the front yard looked. Removing the branches seemed to leave everything looking bare and exposed.

Suddenly, the hum of the chainsaw ceased immediately followed by loud whistles and shouts. It was around three in the afternoon, and they were ready to cut the trunk and topple the tree as safely as they could surmise. The churchmen pulled hard on the ropes as the tree started to wobble, and in matter of a few seconds, there was a loud crack and then a strange whining sound. A few seconds later, there was an enormous crash — like the sound of crackling fireworks combined with thunder under the overcast skies as the tree let go of its will and succumbed to its death as it hit the ground. Everything fell silent for a moment.

Lauren could not bear to watch. Oddly enough, she suddenly felt sorry for the fallen tree. As soon as it crashed to the ground, she wished it had not been cut down at all. The front yard now looked utterly empty and lifeless, where once the tree stood, awesome.

When the churchmen saw there was no damage anywhere and the tree now lay across the street, whoops of satisfaction and cheers rolled up from the street, a mob satisfied by the verdict. Nara seemed pleased. She could not wait for Jin-Chun and Sun-hi to see what she had done for them.

The churchmen proceeded to cut the log. Breaking it into pieces would make it easier to shred into wood chips or transform into firewood. The log made cracking sounds as if still wailing at its small limbs being splintered into pieces by the chainsaws. There was something oddly savage about treating the body this way. The tree, only hours earlier, lively and bowing wistfully in the wind, was now completely void of beauty. Its demise seemed to make even God culpable in this murderous act as it lay bare across an altar.

The churchmen had done a good job at cutting off the branches, and taking away any semblance of the tree's identity. It certainly no longer resembled a crucifix; it no longer looked like anything, really. They broke the main trunk into smaller pieces, leaving no hope of resurrection. All the sum of the parts made the tree, but it would never be whole again, never grow again. All the pieces of wood were the same wood from the same tree, but it was no longer the same wood or the same tree — like a kaleidoscope. It was indeed as if the tree had sacrificed itself for the peace of the family, the forgiveness of all their sins.

The hornbeam tree at the back wall of her childhood home had been her accomplice in liberty. That tree had provided an escape route from her bedroom when she lived in Daegu in her family's ancestral home. Nara recalled this tree now and how as a teenager she had climbed on its sure and steady branches — as garbled and intertwined as they were — to go and explore the outside world and all the things and people in it. If it had not been for that tree, she would probably have a different, narrower, simpler view on life. She went to bed that evening wondering if someone had cut down her tree by now or if it had grown old and weak like her, or if it was bigger and stronger. She wept for her hornbeam tree, not knowing what had happened to it. She wept thinking about her childhood home. And, most especially, she wept, for her family was ungrateful.

Nara was in the kitchen again. There was something lyrical about her movements as her hips swayed back and forth while she kneaded the dough that would soon be turned into dumplings for that evening's meal. She grimaced when she hit a particularly hard lump as if the dough suddenly had an evil spirit in it. She worked her hand though it gingerly, grinding the knot out between her fingers, adding her signature to the fairly simple and mundane mixture so it would come through in tonight's soup. She would call out from the kitchen to plead for anyone to come and help, and every time, there would be no response. She had a strong, resonating, beautiful voice that could have been heard above the flames that could have cut through the smoke of a burning city.

As monotonous as life seemed to have become, it seemed more tiresome in the stark absence of gratitude when there was every need to be grateful. There was not a word of encouragement or recognition. She was what was expected of her and no more.

Jin-Chun's reaction to the fallen tree was unjustified. First, he had been shocked; then, a quiet simmering kind of anger emerged in his face, followed by disappointment. His was an expression of acerbity that was truly painful to behold. Jin-

Chun recognized his error and said it was his fault for talking so openly about wanting to cut it down. He had not really wanted to cut down the tree. Having acquired a sincere Buddhist sensibility, he felt a soul resided in that living thing. Like Peter in denial, all the while betraying the Lord, Jin-Chun awoke in the morning to mourn and regret his words and actions. When he vented about the tree, he was merely expressing a worry for the electrical lines that had given him cause to fear. But even though he said it was his fault for speaking about it, it was obvious that the words he spoke did not reflect the expression on his face and the burden of guilt fell squarely on Nara, and he bore a sin more for throwing that burden on Nara than for speaking about the tree. Nara knew it, Sun-hi knew it, everyone knew it.

Nara's sadness in this home was solidified after this day. The cloud that descended on her like a dark apparition covered all of her light. Whatever light was left in her eyes died out.

His soul still yet divided between monk and demon, Jin-Chun asked the cut-down tree for forgiveness for wishing for its death, but when it came to Nara, forgiveness was left on the table. The contrast was genuinely ridiculous, but made perfect sense in this familial dichotomy.

Nara went over to the cupboard to take out a cooking pot to start boiling the dumplings. She reached for one of the larger pots but needed to move some smaller ones out of the way. One of them fell and hit the floor with a quiet thud. Nara looked at it curiously but also desperately. It was similar to the one she had bought as a teenager at the market on one of her secret adventures outside in Daegu. It was the very one rescued by Sun-hi from the fire. Nara had kept it all these years, bringing it with her to every home in which she lived, including all the way to Canada. She would never have left it behind. Nara always made sure to place that particular pot in a safe corner of the cupboard, never really wanting to use it, as if to preserve it so that it would last forever. Anyway, it was not big enough to cook her soups or her stews for the family, so best to keep it as is.

The cooking pot lay innocently on the floor, looking neglected and dejected. It seemed to emanate a sense of calm surrender, as if it knew it was fortunate to have survived this long, knowing it had been randomly chosen and saved with no thought given, except that it was there. There was no free will in it — it had no soul. It had no choice but to be saved. So, there was nothing more it could do except to serve and do its function well. To do any less, would be a sin. But how it was chosen was as random as anything, and there would be no answer to the question of "Why this pot?"

And, this was the same question that Nara carried with her all along, since Min-joo was stolen away that night in the orphanage and Nara was saved. "Why her?" It was as random as any event in life could be. One is saved, another is not. Nara bent down to pick up the pot and holding it by its handle, she thrust it back and forth like a sword as if to check its mete and then clutched it like a stuffed animal.

At thats moment, Sun-hi entered the kitchen but hung back to observe her mother with the cooking pot. She blinked once at the pot, almost jealously, though she knew it was silly to be envious of a cooking pot, and she turned her head in embarassment. Yet, she did not know the answer to "Why this pot?" either. She did not understand or see that the randomly saved cooking pot was somehow a metaphor that carried a deeper meaning for her mother. *What was it about that damn pot?*

In her heart, Sun-hi was aware of at least one part of the answer. It was not just that that pot was the only thing to survive the fire. It was the only thing Sun-hi had saved of all things she could have saved but didn't. Things more beautiful, things more valuable, things that deserved to be saved, but were not. She had rescued that pot from the flames of the fire for no reason except that it was there. It did not do anything to deserve to be saved.

Sun-hi slowly approached Nara who was deep in thought as she cradled the silly pot. She looked up at her daughter. "This cooking pot is the only thing left," said Nara.

"The cooking pot is all that is left, *Oma*?"

"Yes," said Nara and then mumbled something incomprehensible.

"I don't follow, *Oma*."

"It's all that's left Sun-hi. That's all you bothered to save."

Sun-hi flushed with anger and insult.

"No, I'm left. *Oma*. Me and Young-min. *We* are left."

Nara didn't respond. She wanted someone to save Min-joo.

"The Busan fire burned down our house while you left us to fend for ourselves, and fend for myself I did. What's left is me. Now look at our home. This house. Here, Mother. Look around you."

Nara glared at Sun-hi and then turned her head away, unable to look at this beautiful child who had become a brute of a woman, her own flesh and blood who found things too hard to remember and did not understand. Or was that Nara?

At the same time, Sun-hi could not believe she was saying so much for no reason. Where did this outburst come from? She immediately fell silent. Of course, she had every desire to tell her mother what was seething in her heart and eating away at her like gangrene, but she could not reveal her soul. Thus, a lifetime of resentment easily slipped through a thin layer of asperity.

Nara let go of the cold metal pot that clunked down onto the kitchen floor like a dense brick carelessly thrown and landed on her heart. She shivered and got goose bumps.

"Auntie Young-min!"

Young-min waved hello and bore a big grin for her niece.

Lauren was happy to see her aunt again. They did not see

each other often, but whenever Young-min came by to visit, it was as if a spark lit up across the threshold.

Young-min had distinct lines that gave a landscape and story to her face. The lines were not wrinkles, but milestones carved outwardly on her face. She wore a long, black jacket and baggy navy trousers, with her hair tied back in a ponytail, any loose pieces pinned squarely back to the side of her head. There were already some small patches of grey, but they only served to give her a rather noble look. She had a pinched, thin face, with big oval eyes that looked frightened or more correctly, frightening. And she wore heavy, dark clogs that were in stark contrast to the rest of her bearing. She said they were more comfortable than regular shoes.

Until Young-min was married, Nara had taken close care of her, feeling a special obligation for the shortcoming that had fallen upon her young daughter from the heavens. Even as she grew into a young woman, that protective instinct had never subsided. She regretted Young-min's hearing loss, but most especially, she regretted leaving Young-min and Sun-hi when she saw that their house had in fact burned down, and she had fallen in terror at having nearly lost them both. This was a guilt that Nara pushed far back into her heart and almost never let out. When a young man who seemed like a fine gentleman came to woo Young-min, Nara was startled at the miracle. The prospects of finding an appropriate suitor for Young-min surely could only have happened by divine intervention. How could Nara, or Young-min, refuse?

Young-min had married her husband because she could feel his heavy footsteps approaching. She knew he did that intentionally so as not to scare her when he neared and this sensibility appealed to her. He was humorous and cheerful, with bright black eyes and a gleaming smile. She fell in love, more for his love of her than her love for him. He found Young-min charming and lovely, caring little that she was mostly deaf. When first courting her, he liked to talk closely into her ear, with words both innocent and naughty, full of flirtation and indulgence. But, unfortunately for every good quality he had, there was another that was easy to loathe. He was the master of the game. Pleasant but boisterous, he shook hands on every occasion with everyone he met, displayed his colourful feathers and a puffed-up chest, and proved to be as admired by the young men as he was by the ladies. And in time, this had become intolerable for Young-min.

She had wanted to take revenge on him for the hurt he had caused her. She had also wanted desperately to shame him but she knew she could not, for his charm belied a soul. And she had finally grudgingly realized that if he had any soul, it would be shallow and any blow to his character would simply fall flat.

She had taken solace in the fact that there were no children, neither together nor from his dalliances. Offspring of any kind would have made things unpleasant. Of course, he was always deeply apologetic. But eventually she could only look at him as though he were a stranger who rambled something about a moment of weakness and the enormous despair he felt over the pain he had caused. Young-min had only stared at him with empty eyes. With a deaf heart, she failed to acknowledge his excuses and after nearly a decade of marriage and long years of doubting his fidelity, Young-min left her husband and came to Canada to share in her sister's household cares. Now, Young-min was ready to move on again.

"Lauren, I've come to tell your mother that I would like to move to the Okanagan." She pronounced Okanagan as "Ok-can- again," since this is how she heard it.

"Okanagan? Don't you like it in your apartment?"

"I do, and I like working with your mom and dad. But, it is time," she signed. It had already been maybe five or six years since Young-min had arrived in Vancouver to help her sister in her business, as well as in other ways, and to spend more time with her mother. In return, Sun-hi had done as much as she could to help Young-min settle into her new home, giving her work well-suited to her skills by managing the books of one of the businesses, which did not require the sense of hearing, just good sense. She found her a small apartment which gave her younger sister as much freedom as possible. Young-min did not live as close to Sun-hi, and therefore Nara, as she would have liked, but this distance was just enough to give her the autonomy that she needed for an adult now, she did not want to have the sympathetic and saddened eyes of her mother cast upon her every move.

When hearts' desires were given voice, the universe inevitably answered. For even while living with her back-stabbing husband, in her heart she had hoped to live with her mother again one day. But now, in Canada, in a world that did not judge her the same way for her disability as Korea, she thrived well-enough without Nara and also without whatever else pity garnered.

"It's time to move?" Lauren clumsily signed back. She didn't have enough practice at the language, but had learned enough to get to know her aunt. Like her conversations with Nara, the words were simple and oscillated between one language and another.

"Yes, there is a place in the Okanagan . Quiet, near the lake where the fishing is supposed to be good. With my hearing the way it is, I think it would be better for me to live in the countryside."

Go someplace quiet? Isn't that a strange thing for Auntie Young-min to desire? thought Lauren. *Away from people, I guess, she means.* But Lauren did not know.

"Anyway, speaking of that, I heard *Oma* wants to move too."

"Gamma wants to move?"

"Yes, so I thought," Young-min signed.

"To the Okanagan?"

"No. Well," Young-min paused, "At least not as far as I can tell."

"Then where?"

* * *

"She is leaving us?"

"She felt her job here is done."

"Her job?"

"Yes, she feels like a servant."

"A servant?"

"Yes."

"So where is she going?"

"She's moving to Powell Street."

"Powell Street? Isn't that Japantown?"

"Yes," Sun-hi could see what registered in Jin-Chun's eyes. "I'm well aware of the irony. But, it's what she says she can afford on her old-age pension. I told her that we would…"

"She would rather live in a small apartment in Japantown than live here with us?"

"Yes."

"In Japantown, rather than in our house?"

"Yes."

There was nothing more to say.

Nara took each step up to the apartment laboriously, her legs heavy from guilt. The stairs were old and uncertain. She had moved to a small apartment in a low-income co-op building on a small strip of Powell Street know as Little Tokyo. The building was barely kept up, barely lit, and as rickety as the boat that had brought her home from Osaka. Her apartment was really only a room big enough for a bed and a small dresser for clothes and toiletries. It was all she could afford and refused any help from Sun-hi, feeling it was an insult, as if she could not take care of herself. She shared a bathroom with other tenants and a kitchen with the rest of the building, which was located down on the main floor. On a small, melamine counter at the side of the room, she stacked a few dishes, her one set of utensils, two pots and a pan, as well as the resilient cooking pot.

The roomed smelled of mould and sweat. Old, musty blankets were rolled up on the bed, odd knick knacks left behind by the previous tenant were covered in dust, and books lay untouched on the shelves. There was even an old china doll with a broken arm and broken skirt revealing a hollow inside. The face was pretty and intact. She had a tiny nose and ruby red lips that glistened and light blue eyes that were almost imperceptible, having faded over time. Her hair was perfectly kilned and yellow like a lemon, and, as it is with all china dolls, smooth and without texture. Her skin was milky white, like the face of a geisha.

Nara picked-up the porcelain doll and looked carefully at it, observing every possible, flawless detail. She thought it was so pretty, so smooth, so dainty, so white, and so cold. She hugged it for a moment and then threw it against the wall with an almost violent force, as much as she could muster. It shattered with a shrill clink. The head tore from the body and landed with a light thud onto the floor. It was upturned and appeared to look straight back at Nara.

Nara looked at it in surprise. Why had she just thrown something she found so pleasing against the wall like that? It was like she did this outside of herself. A moment of uncontrollable anger or hatred boiled in her quiet soul, which she thought had been subdued by old age, yet cried out from time to time. She hurried over to the corner and picked up the broken pieces and piled them in her small hand. She intended to glue the pieces back together again. But maybe later.

It was six months before anyone saw each other again. If it was not for Lauren's constant haranguing and whining, it would never have occurred to Sun-hi to take her to visit her grandmother, certainly not after such staunch rejection of them. Lauren wanted to see her Gamma and Sun-hi almost felt pity for Lauren, if she was not so bewildered by her.

Lauren had a sensibility about her that Sun-hi did not

understand. She was very similar to Nara or at least similar to someone from an age long forgotten; indeed, she looked extremely familiar like someone Sun-hi had known long ago. Sun-hi never did manage to place who, the way Nara had. And Lauren was becoming curious and spiritual even though Sun-hi had chosen not to teach Lauren about such things.

Nara would argue, "She's a child; she needs guidance."

"She will find her own way."

"No, you need to guide her, at least."

"She will make her own choices."

"And when she chooses?"

"Whatever she chooses, I will support it," replied Sun-hi and then mumbled under her breath, "*I* didn't have any choice."

But Sun-hi did have a choice. Even though she had grown up in a church and survived by the good graces of God-fearing people, she deliberately pushed herself away from that belief system, which she perceived as either false, hard to believe, or close-minded. It was unclear if it was the rules, the way of thinking, or the faith that she could not accept, but with eyes wide open, Sun-hi had made her choice and Nara had accepted it.

Sun-hi dropped off Lauren at the front of the decrepit building where Nara was waiting and drove off with barely a glance. Nara rushed to hug Lauren and welcomed her to her small and humble home.

Upon seeing Nara's small dimly lit room, Nara thought she saw a flicker in Lauren's eyes. Was it pity? Lauren was sad but at the same time, Nara could see her granddaughter seemed embarrassed to feel sorry for her. However, almost as immediately as her heart fell, Lauren's spirit lifted. Brightening the dark room were two flower arrangements, one on either side of the room. They were deliciously fragrant and fresh and the foliage almost shimmered. How lovely they were! The dainty daffodils and wide-eye gerberas danced while the snapdragons and irises stood tall, surrounded as they were by rich glossy green fronds that bent to the will of the pins holding them. The arrangements were so banded in colour they made the room glisten in a strange and beautifully subtle way. If they were outside, the sparrows might twitter and the pigeons might coo with approval at the sight of them.

"Gamma! The flower arrangements!"

"Oh yes, do you like them?"

"They are beautiful."

"Thank you Lauren."

"Was it hard to make the arrangements, Gamma?"

Nara believed the world had a way of pushing particular issues in the same and repetitive direction with a strange swirling of fate. Consequences constantly conspired to bring things back over and over again, contrary to the wishes of the victims and bystanders. In an immensely ironic twist of fate, Nara made friends with her Japanese coworkers in the fish factory, one of whom became a good friend, Mrs. Mutsumoto, who reminded Nara of Mrs. Noh. The similarities in appearance and mannerisms were uncanny, except of course, the "clearly Japanese traits," whatever that meant. It was Mrs. Mutsumoto who helped Nara get a room at the co-op and it was Mrs. Mutsumoto who introduced Nara to the Wednesday Ikebana Club on East Hastings Street, just behind Oppenheimer Park.

Nara's arrangements were beautifully displayed in black porcelain rectangular dishes, large enough to bake casseroles, though it seemed this was the wrong function for the dishes, for even dishes and pots have their true purpose.

The fragrance rendered memories of far-off dreams and the same mistiness laid itself upon Nara's senses, the same kind of mistiness as she had felt when she walked along the harbour and she saw that passersby could only see the beauty of the completed work but not the turmoil and horror from which it sprang, whether they were observers of history or nation building or flower arrangements.

"Finding what I wanted each arrangement to *become* was hard, and learning to let them *be* was harder," she quipped, "But, it was easy to stick the flowers in the needlepoint holders."

Lauren laughed.

"And flower arranging is much easier than bringing a tree back to life," Nara was able to quip.

Lauren delighted in the day she spent with her grandmother, finding her surprisingly well equipped and highly tolerant of the frightful unknown. Of course, for Nara, the trip across Burrard Inlet was one of the easiest journeys she had ever taken.

⟡12⟡

GRANDMA

A LOW SWEET HUMMING, THE COMBINATION of church bells mixed with the drizzle in the dark air, sunk and dissolved in Sun-hi's ears. Sun-hi had taken Nara to church despite the fact that their grocery stores rarely closed on Sundays. In her life, she would close the main store only twice; once, when she fell ill with pneumonia, and this time.

Sun-hi crossed the street and walked as far as the marketplace on Commercial Drive. From there, the church was about two blocks down the street on the left where Nara had already hurried ahead and gone inside. But every time Sun-hi came to the front of the church, she changed her mind about going in, and instead, circled around the maze of streets of old houses that made up the neighbourhood. It has been a long time since she had been in an area with such rundown homes. These Grandview-Woodlands houses had crumbling stairs and broken windows, held up with a bit of masking tape and cardboard; the neighbourhood creaked with neglect. The houses reminded Sun-hi of the makeshift homes that dotted the landscape in Busan before the fire. The houses gave off a stench of lifelessness and disrepair, and Sun-hi scowled. She did not like being there.

In times gone by, this area had been bustling with local Italians, their rolling words lifting up off the pavement, and the strains of opera music piping out from the various shops. On one side, there had probably been a chemist, doling out remedies from the old world — the latest rage in Venice, no doubt, a bit of nutmeg mixed in squid ink and crushed fresh basil. And on the other side, a notary's office, the cousin of Guido the barber, the best.

One could almost hear the gaggle of shopkeepers and patrons, all talking about their sons and daughters, the proud display of familial feathers boisterously boiling over to passionate aggression, unlike with Sun-hi's clan where a small amount of flattery was necessary to smooth an exchange up to a right proper discourse.

Though the houses did not tell the tale, the shops spoke volumes that the area was becoming gentrified. In several windows, there were displays of desserts and rolls, and the delectable scent of freshly baked bread and buttery pastries was comforting to Sun-hi now that years had passed and adaptation had taken hold. She could not be sure if her senses had evolved, but Jin-Chun would say her tolerance surely had.

In the middle of the row of shops on that section of the street was a large grocery store that still had an old faded sign that said, "Alimentari di Galazzo," hanging just below the new one. It was obvious it was kept there as a piece of nostalgia. People crowded in and out of the open storefronts that spilled out onto the street as outdoor stalls, carrying small bags of fruits or vegetables while some middle-aged ladies squeezed the oranges and tasted the grapes, while inside, small children ran between the aisles of olives and Sriracha. The bare, splintery floors were being swept with an old broom by a student, when at one time, a silver-haired grandmother with a black handkerchief tied over her head fifties-style and black hand-knit sweater draped over her shoulders would have been behind the counter. Sun-hi sighed and thought she should be minding her own store, aware of all the business she was losing today.

It had also been a long time since Sun-hi had stepped foot in a church. It stood here on the corner, beside the busy, heavily travelled street, an old, grey weathered building that had settled on all four sides like a dilapidated, sagging barn or warehouse. Looking at it, it was hard to tell it was a church. The belfry was situated on the roof in such a way that from the street it was impossible to see. The church did not even have a cross on the outside. If not for the sign saying "First Presbyterian," it would be hard to tell it was a place of worship. It had two stories and two points of entry, one at the top of the stairs to enter into the sanctuary and the other at basement level.

Sun-hi was tempted to enter by the basement. That would be familiar.

But she knew she had to enter properly through the main entrance, glide her way next to Nara, show loving support, and demonstrate the appropriate level of daughterly deference. Utterly consumed by her thoughts and having quite lost the thread of them, she went in and reluctantly made her way through the groups of worshippers standing in the back.

The main floor or sanctuary was crowded. People milled about between the pews and along the sides. It was an un-adorned and boring room, not beautiful like other churches with their glorious stained-glass windows and shiny grand organ pipes. No, this church was rundown, like an old-world community infused by old world beliefs. The once bright red carpets had faded to a yellow-pink and the dark wooden pews once freshly stained sported random sad grey patches while the massive doors squeaked loudly on their hinges. Of course, what Sun-hi mistook for neglect were in fact signs of good use: the carpet was well-trodden, the door was often open, the seats were sat in.

As she entered, she heard the piano that played somewhat hollow at the front of the sanctuary. Though it was in tune, it sounded like old-fashioned piano in a country and western saloon with the keys hitting strings that were shredded and worn. It was a sad melody befitting a funeral, but even without this context, Sun-hi wondered why or how anyone could feel inspired by these surroundings.

She was greeted by a number of people, all seemingly excited to see a fresh face as familiar to them as Nara. She was, after all, Nara's daughter, and by association, she was fully baptized into the community. She received bows and handshakes, smiles and compliments — the mannerisms consistent with all things too familiar and that made Sun-hi cringe inside. She rebuked the subtleties and complexities of Korean society now. Inference and implied meanings no longer played into her sensibilities and were replaced by what had become more familiar to her, like direct challenges, words, and deeds. The unconscious impact of nationality on behaviour had found its way thousands of miles across the Pacific Ocean, and Sun-hi felt like she was back in Busan again. *There is no need to feign admiration and give flattery if you do not mean it,* she thought. She much preferred direct discourse now.

Sun-hi no longer liked being around other Koreans, having gotten into the habit of thinking them as old stories too familiar to be interesting. She did not like being around them for it was like being confronted with people who had better success with following their principles, fulfilling their social commitments, and fitting into the tight attire of community order. To her, their eyes — at once gawking and curious, salivating and sinful — were no different in church than in the tent city. And how they salivated for the latest gossip, the latest titillating flaw. In truth, though, for all the other excuses and for all the superfluous justifications of not wanting to be with them, it distilled down to one undeniable truth: their existence served to remind Sun-hi of what a poor "insert any identity" she had become, whether that meant "daughter" or "mother" or "wife" or even "sister." And for this, she hated them. They did not know her. They could not judge her. Yet, even though they did not say — dared not say — she felt the heavy weight of their judgement on her, and she did not need to, for Sun-hi had become the Sun-hi she wanted to be. She was a self-made, successful woman who had released herself from the trappings of what was expected. Against all odds, against everyone and everything that had happened to her, she rose triumphant. She reflected back in the mirror what she wanted to see, not what they expected to see. She did not want the obligation of name and nation.

The children fidgeted in their seats until the wooden casket at the front was opened at the head, revealing a well-powdered woman with a stylized hairdo and little to no make-up, and they let out quiet squeals and gasps, most of them curious or shuddering at the sleeping woman inside. Mrs. Kim, the one who reminded Nara of Mrs. Pyon, had passed a few days earlier, and Sun-hi was obligated to attend the funeral or she would not hear the end of it. She was Nara's closest friend in Vancouver; there was no friend who was closer.

Sun-hi, of course, did not know any of Nara's friends, having never bothered to get to know them or to go to church, so Mrs. Kim was known by reputation alone and quite a reputation she had. Sun-hi stared intently at her face, and decided that she did not at all *look* like Mrs. Pyon. The resemblance her mother spoke of must have therefore been in something that she herself could not see, perhaps in the woman's heart, head, or spirit. In that sense, Sun-hi thought maybe she should have met Mrs. Kim if only once, for if she were truly like Mrs. Pyon as Nara said she was, well that would proffer fond memories indeed.

The bottom half of the casket was closed and was covered with a large flower arrangement. Sun-hi thought it looked beautiful, never realizing it was the handiwork of her mother. The lit candles flickered as more people milled in and started to take their seats. The piano player switched to the organ, which also rang hollow as the pastor approached the pulpit. As the organist struck the next few chords, the door to the corridor slowly opened and swung back, allowing latecomers to soundlessly make their way to a pew.

The organist played a movement of Haydn and something by Debussy that Sun-hi recognized. At that, she remembered

Debussy's most famous quote: "Music is the space between the notes." She smirked a little, thinking that could be true of a lot of things. It was always about the spaces in the "in-between," she thought, about the unspoken.

She took her place next to Nara who was in the front pew so she could be as close to the casket as possible if not for all the family members crowding near it. She sat quietly, knees together, hands clasped and shoulders slightly hunched. She wore a white *hanbok*, one of many Sun-hi had ordered for her straight from Korea. There was no shortage of beautiful silk dresses now. *No shortage of anything anymore*, Sun-hi thought with a measure of satisfaction.

The organ came to a slow stop as the pastor started to speak, his deep voice filling the sanctuary with sonorous, well-modulated tones, accustomed as it was to emphasis and projection.

But his words did not touch the ordinary human emotion within Sun-hi. Instead, his words smacked of dogma and pedanticism, a sharp contrast to the beautiful melody that Nara heard echoing in the church. As he executed a series of familiar phrases, Nara heard a frailty and rapturous longing that only rest in a holy, distant place could satiate. What was virtuosity and ascetic sermon to Nara was closed-minded and ancient banter to Sun-hi.

The crescendo of the sermon approached with the obligatory review and discussion of "Yea, though I walk through the valley of the shadow of death, I will fear no evil." The pastor bourréed to the next position in his sermon readied for the finale.

Nara's gaze shifted from the pastor to Mrs. Kim lying quietly in her final resting bed to a non-descript spot on the floor. Mrs. Kim looked peaceful and like she did not care anymore about what anyone said, or about anything at all, in fact.

The pastor spoke about the kind woman who had a rigour and dignity of character that "lit up every room she walked into." He spoke about how she survived the war, worked to support the family, and other anecdotes familiar to everyone in the congregation. How her young brother died of small pox, how her mother died giving birth to that very brother, how her older sister went to work at a military base, never to be seen again, and it was at this point that Nara drifted far away.

There were snippets of memories that persisted and odd things that impressed upon the character and lasted: a whirring sound of the fans in a hospital ward; a favourite pair of shoes that once outgrown are coveted all the more; a colourful illustration of frightening characters meandering on a yellow brick road in a children's picture book. All were fairly inconsequential. And there were stronger memories that persisted, that were roused from the darkness: the painful groan of a woman scorned for her labour; the soft ghostly voice of a friend back from the dead calling your name; the fleshy stabbing sounds of bayonets plunging through a father's broken body. All were deleterious; all were pushed back into the deep recesses of memory in order to survive the day.

How was it that even by then apologies still had yet to be uttered when so many like Min-joo were wronged.

They arrived late. Nara went to the guest room and Sun-hi went straight to her bedroom, on the main floor of their large, rather monstrous house, without stopping in the foyer to remove her coat. It was quiet there. A dim light came from beneath the door as Jin-Chun was reading in the upright chair they had placed in the far side of the room next to a large window. His reading glasses hung at the tip of his nose and he peered over them to look at Sun-hi. She had a dark violet glow that matched the shadowy forms in the room. She glided to the heavy velvet drapes and pulled at them since they were not completely closed. The drapes had a deep, lush texture that no textile factory could easily weave since velvet required a special loom. She tugged a few times to close the gap. It bothered her to see any separation between the two sides. In the morning, the light would break through.

"How was it?" he grunted, expecting no answer.

It was no surprise Sun-hi cast a glare in his direction.

Jin-Chun did not need words. He knew he should have accompanied them. But he was not inclined to do so, and Sun-hi knew it. Nara also knew it. But, he should have gone with them.

Sun-hi removed her coat and dumped it on the bed before kicking her heels off and slumping into the other chair next to Jin-Chun's. She removed her nylon stockings while Jin-Chun went back to his book, although his eyes wished to remain on his wife's legs. It would be an inappropriate time. He might have been in a passionate mood, but it was not a passionate fight he was bargaining for this evening. No, that would be undesirable. He tried to shrug it off quietly, but the earth might as well have quaked for Sun-hi could read every one of his flinching gestures. After all these years of marriage, she knew what her husband wanted without a single touch or whisper.

She was disgusted that he could shift so easily from familial responsibility and death to sexual arousal in the same breath. Yet, she also recognized that death and sexual desire were born of the same mother in another myth.

After she removed her stockings, she reached behind her neck to undo her dress but the buttons would not so easily come through the slip-stitched holes. She fumbled for what seemed like several minutes.

"The tailor didn't have the sense to sew the holes on so that we can get the buttons out," she grumbled. "Doesn't he know that when we put the dress on, we must also take it off?"

"Let me help you."

"No. Do not touch me."

Indeed, Jin-Chun had his own peculiarities, but the years had mellowed him beyond recognition. He spoke with a deep, steady, but friendly tone. When Lauren was a baby, he was always scruffy and unkempt. But later, he groomed himself into a right gentleman, his mannerisms changing with age. He had reverted back to his well-groomed youth with his iron-pressed shirts and proper jackets, so Jin-Chun was Jin-Chun again, but not the same Jin-Chun.

He could have been a social revolutionary if he had not become a warrior-like peacemaker in his heart. It seemed he had found the liberation he so desperately sought. There was a salvation or emancipation of the soul that had occurred sometime along the way.

Jin-Chun knew Sun-hi was still simmering about being left on her own to fend for herself against all those Koreans. "You know me. I'm made for the quiet of solitude and not for the bustle of community, even if a funeral. You made apologies for me, didn't you?"

Sun-hi had grown accustomed to Jin-Chun, the hermit who had retreated from society a long time ago. A sober life had grown into something of obsessive-compulsive life in his mature years. There were the occasional bursts of hand-washing he called "purification," the dread of germs like the dread of sin, and the intermittent repetition of some sentences he called "mantras," which by some Catholics' accounts could just as easily be his version of "Hail Mary." Jin-Chun had become a perfect eccentric, but, after all, something had to fill the void that alcohol had left behind.

They sat in the yellow glow of the dim lights and he had grabbed her hand. This was his way of letting Sun-hi know that she was a good wife and to thank her for sticking by him. They clutched hands for a moment and just as quickly let go. Their hands having dropped to their knees, they glanced at each other sufficiently long enough to say with their eyes that it was time to go to bed. In practice, there was no quarrel left between them. Without another look or any superfluous word, the lights went out and their backs turned.

In surrendered moments like this, late at night, Sun-hi asked herself if she really was some kind of monster. She thought about the woman she had become and in truth, she regretted almost every word and every deed, conceding she had become a maelstrom in her home. She was often a mad Chimera spreading fire and chaos all around her. But she knew she was not what her family thought. She was indeed a good wife. The best. She tolerated and survived the Herukas, known as Jin-Chun, and finally, they had found a rhythm with each other. She was also a good daughter; of that, she had to convince herself. She, who had never cast out her mother or left her alone, who had stayed by her mother's side despite all the rejections. In the mirror was not the woman she expected to see, but it did reflect back what she wanted to see. She continued to approach life like an unextinguishable fire at least partly because she could not imagine being anything else.

Long before any tree had been chopped down, Nara and Lauren's talks had defined their relationship for even though there is always a deeper and purer, more unsullied kind of love that one can have without words, the ideas and thought embodied in language were the only way to share in a family unable to see their history for their clouded reflections in the mirror. Despite Lauren not being fluent in Korean and Nara not being fluent in English, they had managed to dialogue, converse, confess. While they had talked simply, they had not talked about simple things.

They had shared an uncommon sensibility and did not delight in things the same way as others. Lauren had started to show a maturity well beyond her years and continued — increasingly — to remind Nara of Min-joo. She had even imagined that Lauren was a gift from Min-joo. It could also be that Nara had raised Lauren in Min-joo's image — similarities could happen if you dressed your doll in a particular way. Lauren had offered Nara the pleasure of repentance. Strange what the mind could conjure from under the weight of adversity.

"Gamma"

"Yes, Lauren."

"How do you know God exists?"

"Because he was there before we were here and he will be there even after we are all gone."

"Even with no one to think about Him?"

"And no one left to worship Him."

"So, even when no one believes in him anymore?"

"He will still be there."

"Because man didn't create God."

"God created man."

"He doesn't need us then."

"He needs us very much."

"But not for the reasons we think."

"He needs us very much."

Lauren went back to doing her homework as Nara was settling in for a long visit after the funeral, not being able to see herself alone during this time. She had not returned to live in Sun-hi's home, but she might as well have, since visits often turned into stays. This home was still not the place for her, but she took purpose in sharing time with her granddaughter who was more like her than Sun-hi. Nara had urged herself to preserve her self-respect, in a choice similar to one made outside a grocery store one night some years ago when — confronted with the choice to leave or to stay — Nara had inclined towards the decision to provide loving arms and a secure embrace for Lauren, for they needed each other very much.

She peered over to see what Lauren was doing. "What's that?

"It's a computer."

"What's a computer?"

"It's a machine that lets us do work quickly and talk to each other — well, sort of. At least, one day we will be able to."

"Talk to who?"

"Whoever we want."

"Where?"

"Anywhere, anytime."

"Like in Korea?" Nara asked wide-eyed

"Yes!"

"But, what if you don't understand?"

"The computer is universal. There's always a way to understand."

Nara sat quiet. The computer sounded a lot like Tower of Babel. That proliferation of message and belief and thought into a common language was as easy as fibre to cable to connection to screen. Indeed, it sounded like a new Tower of Babel in the city of Babylon. She wondered how long it would be before God came and decided to smash it down, confounding the common language and dispersing the peoples already scattered on the face of the earth.

"Can we talk anywhere right now?"

"No, not yet, but it's only a matter of time."

"I imagine before I die, I will not get to see the new world that has dawned on Korea. But I have heard great stories."

"Yes, Gamma, the accomplishments are impressive. But..."

"Are they as remarkable as they say?"

"Yes, Gamma."

"I have heard how Korea has risen from the ashes and transformed itself, no longer a pawn. Can we all raise our heads at how far we've come?" Nara's eye gleamed and she wondered.

"Hmm, yes," Lauren nodded. "So quickly too. In a single generation, Mom's generation."

Nara thought about that. *In one generation. In Sun-hi's generation? How so?*

While Nara reflected, Lauren thought of the word "pawn" and how certain countries in the world, either because of where they are located or what they have — gold, oil, metals, diamonds — were coveted or used or trampled upon or propped up. In such random locations, these random gifts were bestowed, as if gifts from God. But in that unspoken struggle, the people must be resilient enough to know who they are and what they have to withstand to instead turn it to their advantage. "Ah, yes, like in chess," Lauren said. "A pawn can eventually become a queen."

"Like a magpie can transform into a phoenix."

Lauren looked at her grandmother curiously.

Nara smiled back. She also thought about Vancouver and about Canada. How, in a generation, Canada too had undergone a transformation of its own, of a miraculous and beautiful kind, where she finally felt welcomed and even at home.

"So it's good," Lauren asked.

"Yes, it's good."

Nara thought about this for a long time. Thinking of Korea's progress, she remembered an article Jin-Chun published in the *moonhak* magazine. Indeed, she had searched for copies back then and read them discreetly. The article had expounded upon the idea of siezing one's own destiny and driving down the chosen path using an ordinary man as the example, but it had been an obvious metaphor for Korea. It spoke about how man could aspire to become more than what had been seemingly allotted to him, realizing a divine being had not cast him in a specific role, predestined yet with free will. There was always a choice. The article had been about the endless possibility of transformation. Like St. Paul, a sinner passing through the threshold of blindness into the blinding light, it was always possible to be forgiven and to forgive. It was never too late.

"Gamma?"

"Yes."

"Why doesn't God hear us when we pray?"

"What do you mean?"

"I mean when we pray for stuff."

"Well, He hears us when we ask Him for forgiveness."

"Yeah and..."

"And when we ask Him for guidance and wisdom."

"Hm-huh."

"He hears us when we ask Him to help us to forgive others when we have been wronged."

"Yeah. But I mean when we pray for stuff like doing well in school or helping Mom and Dad in their business?"

Nara responded sternly, "Are you asking me why God doesn't grant your wishes?"

"Well, no," Lauren said. "Well, I guess, yes. I mean not wishes, but like getting good grades or becoming rich."

"Ah, I'd say you *are* pretty comfortable, Lauren."

"You know what I mean."

"No, not really. And by the way, to do well in school, you need to study hard."

"I know."

Nara said sternly again, "Is God our own personal genie in a bottle, Lauren?"

Lauren looked stunned. "A genie in a bottle? No, of course not."

"Prayers are not the same thing as wishes."

"Of course not. But God can do anything. Didn't He say 'ask and it shall be given unto you'?"

Nara pondered the attitude of the new generations. "Have we reduced God from being a great, magnanimous creator to a trickster magician in our imagination?"

"That's not what I meant," whispered Lauren. She knew where this was going.

"Well, I think that's what you meant." Nara looked disappointed and she paused for a long time. She finally softened. "Lauren it is not you. It is all of us."

Lauren nodded.

"It seems we have all dared to reduce God to some fictional wish-granting genie who is kept in a bottle to be called upon whenever we want Him to grant us our whims?"

"I guess that's what I sounded like."

"And do we dare feel let down and go through a famine of faith because the wishes don't actually come true?"

"Wishes are not the same thing as prayer," conceded Lauren.

"Yes."

"Study hard."

"Yes."

"It's a fine thing to celebrate the past when one is feeling good about the present."

The rain had not stopped for twelve straight days. The wet trees hung heavy, and the grass drowned under the puddles. Day and night, the rain dashed and splashed, and finally, just as all were sufficiently weary, it broke. The clouds separated to reveal more sky behind them — a lot more sky — and just in time for Sun-hi and Jin-Chun's wedding anniversary.

"There isn't much in the past to celebrate," continued Sun-hi.

"You've lost your sense of poetry," remarked Jin-Chun.

"Poetry? I've occasionally given some thought to that sort of curiosity. But I'm not pre-occupied with those things anymore. There will always be poets like you who have an interest in probing observations and inner life, capable of expressing that inner life with beauty and thus enriching the emotional life of others. As for me, I'm a simple merchant, my dear."

"Should we do something? Maybe go somewhere."

"Somewhere?" Each year, the event passed unmarked and unattended.

"A vacation, maybe." The request was almost as impossible as it was objectionable.

Whether in a marriage, a friendship, a relationship between father and son or mother and daughter, there was the ugly and the hauntingly beautiful. The astounding and the astounded. The simple, the complex, and the stories in-between. The misunderstandings and the misgivings. The hurt, the pain, the words and the actions. Something to remark on an anniversary.

Even though a vacation was out of the question, a visit in the city would be acceptable.

"And work?"

"The stores will be there when we get back."

They went to the Planetarium and wondered if they could see anything in the telescope. They were like a young couple falling in love again for the first time. They limbered up onto the platform with the telescope and stood there listening to the gentle tick of the recording instruments, a sound associated with the passing of time. The wind lifted in the morning sky, carrying clouds that blanked out the celestial spheres to the naked eye. The clouds arranged themselves in cirrus festoons and then cumuli. A small rain shower followed, falling on the couple in gentle droplets while the pluviometre collected a couple of millimetres. The clouds broke formation for a short period but ganged up behind Jin-Chun and Sun-hi, charged in the darker, heavier variety. The sky darkened and the barometer fell. They ran as fast as they could for cover and just as they scuttled under an awning, the thunder clapped and was followed by a sudden downpour.

Jin-Chun felt he could hold the thunder in his hand and toss thunderbolts into the mist. He was not feeling godlike but more like an artist who was only in partial control of his work; the rest was up to chance and blessings. The lightning blazed across the sky and exposed the heavens in their nakedness, dark and gloomy and raw. The sound of rolling thunder rose from the mountains beyond Lions Gate like an orchestra, a crescendo that possessed the listener. The awning drummed loud underneath the rain, while the rain both crashed and leapt, like the flailing arms of someone playing the timpani. The rain jumped up from the ground, and Jin-Chun curated the scene. In his mind, a natural calm presided over the texture of the cataclysm as the bright green leaves of strong, standing trees reflected the dark pavement.

The two were dry as a bone, having made it under the awning in time. But, they looked at each other and laughed. Hand in hand, they strolled out from under the safety of the fixed umbrella and exposed themselves to the pouring rain. The onslaught continued until they reached the car by which time, they were soaked. They sat in the car, with the windows misted up, hair and clothes dripping.

Sun-hi's thin chiffon blouse stuck to her, and Jin-Chun could see through to her white brassiere beneath. Her legs were crossed, and her skirt stuck close, rising high just below her knee. It was erotic and softly beautiful that it could be this way, even at their age. They stared at each other with wet faces and wet lips. How long had they been married? If in their dreams, then, only since now.

Wisely toting a large golf umbrella, Nara and Lauren had already gone ahead for a walk. The family never went on outings together, in fact, so rarely that this anniversary ended up more as a family outing than a romantic day-trip. It was not what anyone would think typical of an anniversary, but nothing about this family was typical.

Nara had the urge to go near the water's edge, which was reminiscent of her childhood. This allowed herself to slip back into memory of familiar times. Though she tired easily now, it was good to get out after being trapped inside for so long and happy to be invited on this mini excursion. Together, Nara and Lauren meandered onto the grassy knoll, their steps squishing and sloshing as they headed to the railing to catch a better view of English Bay. English Bay — it never changed. The shape was the same as when Nara first laid eyes on it — the shape of a womb — and hopefully, likely, if God willing, it would always stay that way.

It reminded her of when she laid eyes on the Busan mountains once again as the boat from Osaka glided into the harbour bringing her back home. Nara recalled how the familiarity and constancy of nature was confounding to her at the time. The Busan mountains looked strong, lush and green. They were dazzling. The mountains had not changed. They were the same mountains, but not the same mountains. Not to Nara.

There was a tree bursting with bright green leaves just ahead and flowers that lined the path and Lauren drank in the scents and sounds, listening to the whispers of the wind as they brushed through the leaves. The floral scent lifted and hung for a moment before being carried away unwillingly, preferring to stay than be dispersed into thin air. If it could, it would stay. She looked up at Grouse Mountain and the other mountains around it and marvelled at how high they seemed to go.

Looking at the majestic mountains and thinking about this day, she asked, "Gamma?"

"Yes."

"Did God really create the universe in only seven days?"

"You find it hard to believe?"

"Yes, I mean, they say it took billions of years. Even fossils tell us it takes millions of years for creatures to evolve."

"Fossils talk?"

"And God does?"

"More than fossils, I surmise."

"I can touch fossils."

"And you don't think you can touch God?"

"I don't know. Can I touch God?"

"You tell me." Nara stared at the ocean longing to plunge in and feel the waters wrap her in an embrace as she swam to the far ends of Mother Earth to search for her lost dreams.

"I don't know. But, do you believe God created the universe in seven days and not seven billion years?"

"The Bible also says that, 'To God, one day is as a thousand years and a thousand years as one day.' So what's the actual difference between seven days and seven billion years?"

"A lot."

"Only to us."

"*Oma*, you wanted to speak to me." Before seeing Nara, Sun-hi usually prepared a speech in her mind, but each time she laid eyes on her mother, the words dissipated and were replaced by memories and emptiness.

"The flowers in the backyard need watering."

"Hmmm," Sun-hi shrugged.

"You should vacuum from time to time."

"If I had time, *Oma*."

Nara coughed. "I'm getting old now."

"Not old *Oma*. You're as strong as ever."

"No, I'm old and tired."

"You could always..." Sun-hi stopped herself. She wanted to invite Nara back to live with her, but rejection would hurt bitterly. Certainly, Nara would say no. But she longed to be with her. She loved her mother. Or at least, she felt bound to her.

"I had kept in my heart my desire to leave now. I have lost purpose. Lauren is growing up and she is an independent spirit. I don't have a reason to live close to you any longer, Sun-hi."

"You don't live so close, *Oma*. But close enough so we can..."

"Take care of me?"

Sun-hi would not say. She wanted to speak her mind, but Nara would dismiss her. It was Nara's job to be staunch and strong and uphold the image of the family, to brush aside trivialities like scraped knees and hurt feelings and old age in favour of shedding a good light on accomplishments and beaming with pride at a successful family.

"Where would you go? Back to Korea? There's no one there for you," Sun-hi said sharply.

"No, I'm too old for that. Anyway, I parted with those hopes. I know I will never see Korea again," Nara said sadly, never expecting Sun-hi to understand. "Yet the desire will always be there, and it is still painful to bear. Everything around me only seems to remind me of it somehow."

"And, so, what do you wish to do, *Oma*?"

"I want to move to the Okanagan to live with Young-min."

Sun-hi remained silent and held her tongue. Nara had left her alone in the sterile room while she worked in the factory;

Nara had left her during the fire; Nara had left her to live in Japantown; and now, Nara was leaving to live with her deaf sister who often heard Nara better than Sun-hi ever did or could. So, there it was.

Nara continued. "The silent world in which Young-min lives is similar to mine. I have no voice here. I am mute. You never seemed to understand that."

Of course she understood her mother's isolation. It was only exactly the same for Sun-hi. They all shared that same isolation. All these rejections impressed upon Sun-hi an excruciating agony that left her numb and dark. It was like being left behind again; only this time, it was in the quiet of the day and not in the path of a raging fire. Her mother could not see it and Sun-hi could not say it.

"There's nothing here that could sustain me, not the way I need. And even if disease would ravage me or illness take me, up to my last breath, I need peace."

Nara did not want Sun-hi to see her become weaker and wither away. She knew she was ill somehow — whether it was simply the ravages of old age or something else.

"I need peace for there's no hope left, only the hope of seeing..." Nara did not finish what she was saying. She was already gone.

Sun-hi thought if only her mother knew her and all she had endured. If only she knew her mother and all *she* had endured. They were both equally blind to each other's pain and yet fully awakened to it.

It was too late. Healing would not happen in their lifetime. It was apparent there would be no resolution. God was left to judge who was wrong and who was wronged, for it had nothing to do with being right.

Sun-hi did not respond, but let her mother go free. With this, Nara left Sun-hi for the last time.

"Lauren," Sun-hi called up from the bottom of the stairs.

"Please come down. We need to go Kelowna right away."
"To visit Grandma?"
"Yes. She's in the hospital."

"In the moment when hope cannot be reasonably sustained any longer, in that moment, I will turn my back on this life and take lodgings somewhere up in the peaks above here or in the valley below but my soul will no longer linger in this no man's land. That will be a sad day but after much labour in life for the least material gain gotten, I am no longer able to fend off the disease of bad memories, which surely was the beginning of my demise, for without hope, there is nothing. I have, in my small way, served the cause of people around me and will do so up to my last breath. I leave no burden behind and I sever all ties. We owe no further debts to each other and now I take my leave."

Nara was likely delirious. The heat outside was stagnating. Mid-July in the Okanagan Valley always made things brittle and dry. The air conditioning barely worked in the rural hospital, and Nara seemed to be rambling, maybe overcome by the heat. Young-min remained down the hallway, already having said what she needed to say all these weeks while Nara's frailty took her back and forth from "this place" and "that place," from the here to the place beyond. Now, these last moments would be for Sun-hi and Young-min knew that. Sun-hi looked at her mother and then lifted her gaze outside through the wide window. The heat waves bent everything out of shape. Perspective was all wrong and skewed everything in view.

Jin-Chun had come to pay his respects but hung far back, almost in the corner, and just out of everyone's peripheral vision. When he heard Nara, he thought she was referring to the terrible night when he threw a hammer at her head and nearly made her into a sacrifice. After that, he too remained silent, never asking for forgiveness or to be forgiven, assuming — no, hoping — that his silence expressed enough remorse.

But he should have said something then, confessed his regret, and rectified the reckless path that he was once on. But the moment had passed and it was time to move on. Something that weighed so heavily on both, that had been unresolved for too long, had simply transitioned from the substantial to insubstantial. The window to say "sorry," that would have closed that wound in their lives, had been slammed shut. And so, instead, Jin-Chun gave a deep and respectful bow, the only time he would ever do so, and walked ever so gently into the hallway.

As for Sun-hi, she understood fully what Nara was saying and she whispered only one word to Nara and that word was "*Oma.*" She could say nothing more.

There was, of course, a lifetime they needed to talk about — the factory, the war, her father's murder, the fire, the tent city, the husband, Vancouver. But that talk would not happen. It was never to happen. Overwhelmed by such a miserable, shared history and by such grief, there were simply not enough words. It was time to say goodbye. Ever so reluctantly and without any desire to do so, Sun-hi slowly turned around and faced the door. She paused only for a moment and then, weeping bitterly, it was Sun-hi's turn to leave.

She experienced, albeit for only a day, a mood that harkened back to childhood and it brought a sudden outburst of longing in her twilight hours to wander spellbound in a long stream of memories that emptied into the Busan harbour. Nara experienced this flashback with no less warmth and passion than when she lived it in the reality before now. Those years of violation and betrayal surged in her like the waves of the sea that had brought her boat home. She had new hopes in her dying days to tie up loose ends and close this chapter, and so she did, saying goodbye to Sun-hi and Jin-Chun while in the hospital near Young-min's house. She knew the roots beneath were strong, but with so many of her branches trimmed away and all those outright cuts through her trunk, she knew that she had been living only a semblance of a life; one that would never blossom fully or yield good fruit once again. But, in a long and storied life, she had done what she needed to do. She found God, gathered up souls, battled forgiveness with forgetting, sacrificed, and resurrected herself out of the ashes. Although her body was transplanted here, her dreams took her to the harbour far away and lifted her to a quiet place to rest her head.

In the years following the closing of her missionary school, Nara had struggled to go back to her dream to see what was behind the door of the cave, but it seemed it was lost forever. She was unable to visit her dream ever again to reveal the mystery behind the cave door that promised so much. But in her travels to her safe dreamland, she often saw Min-joo. She was there in the land of blessings and peace simply walking through the brush in the cool air on sunny days or dancing on tiptoe. Today, for the first time, Min-joo turned around and saw Nara. She reached out her arm to Nara and Nara eagerly reached back. "Oh, have you forgiven me, dear Min-joo?"

"Gamma."

There was no reply.

Lauren waited for what felt like an eternity. Tears welled-up in her eyes and Lauren felt a sharp stab in her heart. For the first time, she understood what loss meant. Finally. And it was excruciating.

She said again, "Gamma."

Still no reply.

Nara did not want to say goodbye to Lauren and so she would not. She looked at Lauren with almost a wistful longing, a recognition, with love. Lauren reached for Nara's soft, healing hands. *The softest hands in the world*, Lauren thought and held them for a moment.

"Your hands always made me feel better, Gamma."

Lauren waited again and fought back the tears. She knew this was not what Nara wanted to see. She looked at her grandmother and nodded her head. "I suppose you look forward to going home," she said, her fingers soft against her grandmother's cheek. She pulled back the tears, gulped them down out of sight, and gently stroked her grandmother's fingers as she held them lightly. Then, she bent her head close to Nara's ears and whispered, "*Neh sohn, yack sohn ya,*" and then offered a brief prayer.

Visiting hours were almost over. Nara waited for Lauren to leave.

As the sun scorched above the Okanagan valley, a forest fire advisory was posted for the area warning residents to evacuate before the fire spread to their homes. But, in Nara's room, a gentle, almost imperceptible breeze came through the window as Nara closed her eyes. She could see she was back on the mountain peak at the door of the cave where the phoenix was waiting for her. He beckoned her towards him with wings spread open as if to wrap her in a welcoming embrace. *Surely your goodness and mercy will follow me all the days of my life and I will dwell in the house of the Lord forever.* Nodding to the phoenix to let him know everything was finally all right now, she opened the door and entered.

ACKNOWLEDGEMENTS

There are not enough words to thank Inanna Publications for believing in this story and Luciana Ricciutelli, the best editor any author could hope to have, for her deft hand and deep understanding. I could not have done this without her.

Though this is entirely a work of fiction, it was inspired by my grandmother. Thanks Grenma. I miss you.

Finally, for the 200,000 women and girls who suffered in the camps under military rule. In order to forgive, one must first be asked to be forgiven. May you get the apology you deserve.

Born in Vancouver, Canada, Christina Park has been around art and letters all her life. Her writing is informed by personal experiences as a second-generation Korean Canadian, as well as by living in Vancouver and Montreal. Outside of her writing pursuits, Christina has worked for both technology start-ups and large financial corporations, including as VP of Marketing for a prominent investment management company. The biggest influences in her life are her husband and daughter. An avid traveler and would-be runner, she is thankful to have run in interesting locales where she could see things up close. Visit her website at: www.christinapark.ca.

The Myrtle & The Rose

Annie Messina
(Gamîla Ghâli)

Translated with an Introduction

by Jessie Bright

ITALICA PRESS
NEW YORK
1997

ITALIAN ORIGINAL
IL MIRTO E LA ROSA
1982 © SELLERIO EDITORE VIA SIRACUSA 50 PALERMO

TRANSLATION COPYRIGHT © 1997 BY JESSIE BRIGHT

ITALICA PRESS, INC.
595 MAIN STREET
NEW YORK, NEW YORK 10044

LIBRARY OF CONGRESS CATALOGING-IN-PUBLICATION DATA
Messina, Annie.
    [Mirto e la rosa. English]
    The myrtle & the rose / Annie Messina (Gamîla Ghâli) ;
    translated with an introduction by Jessie Bright.
        p.   cm.
    ISBN 0-934977-45-3-(alk. paper)
    I. Bright, Jessie, 1930- . II. Title.
PQ4873.E79M513 1997
853'.914--dc21   97-41902
                                        CIP

ISBN: 978-0-934977-45-6

Printed in the United States of America
5 4 3 2

Cover Illustration: "Dioscorides and a Student," miniature from an Arabic
text of 1229. Istanbul, Library of the Topkapi Sarayi Museum.

Introduction

An author who cheerfully signs books in shopping malls, answers questions at literary discussion groups or welcomes interviews on TV doesn't seem strange to North Americans, nor even egotistical. We almost expect writers to seek publicity in order to market their work and our curiosity as consumers sometimes makes them into celebrities. The same could be said of the Italian reading public. Why then would a seventy-two year old woman with little or no previous literary success who manages to sell her manuscript to a prestigious publishing house decide to hide her identity behind a pseudonym? Yet Sellerio of Palermo first brought out *Il mirto e la rosa* in 1982 under a false name: Gamîla Ghâli. The book jacket notes that the novel is most probably an original work by a contemporary woman, even though at first glance a reader might think it was written long ago and translated from Arabic. But Gamîla Ghâli was soon unmasked and the book cover of the second edition supplies the reason behind the ruse. She did not want to presume upon the success of Sellerio's re-publication of the works of her famous aunt, Maria Messina — Zia Maria to Annie. The name Maria Messina should be familiar to most students of twentieth-century Italian literature, and an introduction to Annie's book might well begin by saying something about Maria and about the Sicilian heritage of both.

Maria Messina was born in Palermo in 1887 and died in Tuscany, in Pistoia, as an indirect result of allied bombing, in 1944. Her niece summarizes her life in the Afterword to John Shepley's translation of Maria's best known work, *A House in the Shadows,*

Annie Messina

published by Marlboro Press in 1989. Annie's gentle commentary is an affecting tribute to her aunt's tenacity in overcoming the disadvantages of a provincial society "in which women were held in a state of subjection bordering on slavery." It was Maria's only brother, older than she was, who encouraged her to develop her literary talent, and she did achieve "both a public and a critical success." The brother was Annie's father and the family bond was strong. She speaks of her own "affinity with [Maria], with her aspirations and ideals." In fact, when the late Leonardo Sciascia, one of the most celebrated Sicilian writers of this century, wrote the presentation for Sellerio's re-publication of Maria Messina's works, Annie contacted him and offered some of her aunt's unpublished manuscripts. The Afterword concludes without a single mention of Annie's own literary endeavors.

I tried both here and in Italy, but was unable to find out very much about Annie Messina's life, perhaps because of my own lack of research skills. I am indebted to Italica for supplying me with a photocopy of a review from *Le Monde* [Vendredi 17 juillet 1992, 21] of the 1992 French translation of *The Myrtle and the Rose*. The reviewer, René de Ceccatty, notes that Annie Messina, the daughter of an Italian consul general in Egypt, lived much of her life in that country, studied art, worked as a translator and, like her aunt, never married. Her literary output is small. Ceccatty mentions two works published under her own name in 1938, apparently with only modest success. I was unable to find any reference to them. There is one other work in print, *La palma di Rusafa,* published by Mondadori in 1989, a sequel to *The Myrtle and the Rose*.

I do have her response to an inquiry I sent to her home in Rome, a brief letter typed on an old fashioned typewriter, and dated 10 November 1994. She addresses me as "Cara Jessie," and thanks me for my kind words about her and Zia Maria. She says she would like to tell me more but she is 84 years old and unwell. She concludes by suggesting some books on Islamic history by Italian Arabic scholars, but notes that they would probably be difficult to find here. She says that if necessary she will send me a "copiosa bibliografia" of works she used in writing this novel and *La palma di Rusafa.*

Introduction

The letter concludes by apologizing. She would like to tell me more but writing tires her. A year later when I made a brief trip to Italy I meant to go to Rome and meet her but in the end I did not. Was I too becoming tired of making certain kinds of efforts or was I afraid to intrude? I wish now I had not been so hesitant. Months later I received a letter from a friend who lives in Rome. As I opened it a tiny newspaper clipping fell out of the envelope: an announcement of Annie Messina's death on the 27th of February 1996.

Thus Annie Messina remains for me an elusive but singular figure, all the more appealing because she neither sought nor seemed to enjoy celebrity. There is no trace of a personal voice or signature in the prose of *The Myrtle and the Rose*, a welcome contrast to the self-conscsiousness of certain contemporary fiction. Perhaps this accounts for the Italian book jacket's comment that it is reminiscent of *The Thousand and One Nights*. The lucid and simple style reminds me of Maria Messina's stories. The emphasis is clearly on the narrative. There are vivid images traced with poetic clarity but description does not distract from the telling of the tale. Readers will want to know what happens next, but in a certain sense they already know or fear they know. The story reads like a fable, but it is a fable tinged with tragedy. It concerns events and characters remote in time and space, but painfully close with respect to the theme.

A surprising theme for the writer I have been describing. Not because it concerns Islamic history. Annie Messina spent much of her life in a predominantly Muslim country and Arabic history and culture are integral to her Sicilian heritage. Any tourist can see this clearly in the magnificent art and architecture of Palermo. A story set in a tiny principality dependent upon the caliph of Baghdad at the end of the tenth century, by an author well versed in art and historical research — this is not remarkable. A romantic love story written by a woman in her seventies is not exactly an anomaly. Nor is a story about an intense and exclusive love between a man and a boy unusual for the culture it represents, any more than it would be for a reader of Plato's *Dialogues*. But this is a novel by a writer who praises her aunt's simple but "impassioned protest against the oppression of women" and it includes no female characters who matter. *La palma di Rusafa* recounts the same kind of love story between a man and a boy, but here at least one woman plays an important role. As for the title of the present work, the myrtle represents manliness, the rose the innocence of childhood. The story is told with impeccable taste and the characters are complex enough to be convincing. Some are good, one at least is a fascinating villain, one a fool, one an old and wise and faithful servant, but none is so simple as to be merely an allegorical good or bad guy. Most readers will probably see traits they recognize in their contemporaries, or alas, in themselves. The fact that we can't quite identify the exact time or place only makes it more fun.

No introduction should give away the story, but a comment by the French reviewer is worth repeating. He says that the kind of love depicted in the book and the attitude toward its physical dimension is an idealistic plea for a form of love that is absolute.

I do wish to thank Dr. Wayne Husted of the Pennsylvania State University for helping me prepare this translation. His knowledge of Islamic culture and history gave me the confidence to deal with content that was largely unfamiliar to me. I would have been lost without his aid in transliterating Arabic words from Italian into English. If there are still mistakes they are mine, not his. I have yet to produce a flawless translation.

Jessie Bright
State College, Pennsylvania
August 1997

The Myrtle & The Rose

The Slave Merchant

"Oh most excellent of princes! Bulwark of Islam! Champion of the faithful! To what does your lowliest of servants owe the honor of this visit?"

Sitting tall on his roan stallion, Prince Hamid al-Ghazi smiled at the hyperbole, his lips barely moving between his soft brown mustache and curly beard. As the ruler of a small mountain principality and vassal of the Grand Caliph, his independence from the ultra powerful Abbasids was problematical, based more on personal prestige than on the strength of his army, valiant to be sure, but few in number. Besides, his kinship with Abd al-Rahman, the last of the Umayyad caliphs, and his family's late and unenthusiastic conversion to the True Faith had left him less than well regarded at the court of Baghdad. On the other hand, in times of war his loyal and frequent service to his sovereign had earned him the coveted epithet "al-Ghazi," the warrior, and this distinction together with the strategic location of his tiny realm made it an obstacle probably not worth the considerable trouble it would take to remove it.

Certainly his position would have been quite different without the massacre that had marked the end of the Umayyad dynasty. But Prince Hamid gave little thought to the past; he preferred the present. And the future, as everyone knows, is in the hands of Allah or, if you like, one or more of the ancient dethroned gods of the Kabah.

Such fulsome praise had thus made him smile. As for the question, no explanation was required. Anyhow he himself wouldn't know how to answer it even if he wanted to. It was simply a whim that had stopped him in front of the establishment where the slave merchant Butros al-Shami plied his trade in the *suq* of Bisah. That morning the prince had ridden down to this small lowland city with his personal guard, twenty horsemen under the command of the supremely faithful Hassan, as well as Ibrahim his overseer and a number of servants. His errand had been to visit the shops of the Persian goldsmiths in search of gifts for his women, particularly for Lailah, the favorite. Meanwhile the overseer would see to replenishing the palace larder with the finest of provisions.

Their program had not therefore included a visit to Butros. The prince was supplied with highly trained soldiers and efficient servants and his harem, numerous but carefully chosen, was sufficient to satisfy his robust virility, especially since the arrival of the beautiful Lailah. And yet a sudden impulse had brought him to a halt, and Hamid was not a man to waste time analyzing his impulses before acting on them.

He sprang lightly to the ground, tossing the reins to a guard who rushed up to catch them, strode past the slave merchant, now bent double in a bow, and entered the welcoming shade of the *dukkan*. Outside, where a small crowd of curious onlookers had quickly gathered, his retainers dispersed them with shouts and cracking of whips, then took up positions in front of the doorway while Hassan, the captain of the guards, and Ibrahim the overseer followed their master inside.

Hamid al-Ghazi was then forty-two years old. A strikingly handsome man, he was over six feet tall but so well proportioned that his height was noticeable only in comparison to others. Darker than the average Arab, perhaps he owed the bronze color of his skin to a drop of Berber blood, whereas Greek blood accounted for his regular features: high forehead, straight nose, large eyes in well defined orbits, a wide sensitive mouth and determined jaw whose firm line was discernible under his carefully trimmed beard. In fact at that time, around the year 1000, the vast Islamic Empire had become an immense crucible in which wars, incursions, piracy and the slave trade had commingled all the races of the known world from the confines of India to the coasts of the Atlantic, from the Taurus Mountains to the remote frontiers of China.

With long elastic strides Hamid entered the small inner room where Butros received his distinguished clients and conducted his business in an atmosphere perfumed by the spices and honey of the *hushaf* his servants offered to his guests in finely decorated cups. He seated himself in a chair inlaid with mother of pearl, which the obsequious merchant personally brought him and nodded briefly to the local no-tables who had rushed to pay their respects as soon as they learned of his presence in the city. Only then did he deign to address Butros, who was standing before him in servile solicitude, trying to figure out the best way to turn a profit from this unexpected visit.

"So, Butros, can you show me something to really grace my household?"

"My lord prince!" exclaimed Butros in consternation that such a golden opportunity should befall him precisely when he was a bit short of merchandise. (Hamid was one of his most generous clients.) "I ask for nothing better than to serve your excellence, but alas it isn't every day one comes upon a pearl of such unusual value as Lailah, whom I had the honor and pleasure to procure for you. I hear she still enjoys your favor."

"So she does. Nor would I ask you for a second Lailah. I wouldn't even want one. But come now, have you no prized slave to offer me?"

"Well, my lord, I happen to have a consignment of exceptional merchandise, right now at this moment — six boys from the Greek coasts, all under the age of ten, superb little creatures, veritable budding flowers, the stuff of connoisseurs. But I realize this sort of thing doesn't interest your lordship."

"No," said the prince brusquely. "If you've got some pretty little boys among your flowers you might propose them to the Emir Husain ibn Ali. He has a harem that could use wet nurses instead of eunuchs."

Butros laughed obsequiously, meanwhile racking his brain. "I do have a very fine Persian slave, an old woman who excels in all types of embroidery. She makes the most exquisite things with precious stones and gold and silver thread."

"Old, you say. How old?"

"Thirty, more or less, my lord. But her eyesight is perfect despite her age and she makes a very good appearance...."

"If she really is what you say she is, I could make a gift of her to Princess Shirin. She uses a lot of embroidery."

"A splendid idea, sire. She could not help but please the most excellent lady princess."

Everyone knew that Hamid had been virtually separated for some time from his wife Shirin, a princess of Persian origin whom he had married for dynastic reasons. He had given her land near the border of his realm and she lived there in a handsome palace with her own small court of soldiers and slaves. The couple's only child, Prince Harazad, lived with her. Hamid rarely visited his wife and his relationship with his now twenty-year-old son was downright stormy. Nonetheless he had always kept up appearances and the gift of a valuable slave at this point would surely advance that purpose.

"Very well, I'll speak to my overseer about it," said the prince. "Meanwhile, if you...."

He paused, frowning. From the corridor came the noise of a furious struggle punctuated by shouts and curses. It sounded as if something or someone was being laboriously dragged along by a number of people. Then there was a loud yell followed by more curses.

"Butros what's all that racket? I didn't think such things went on in your establishment. Go put a stop to it."

In fact, although rebellions and punishments were not unusual among the vulgar slave traders who displayed their wares on the corners of the marketplace, Butros had always conducted his business at a higher level. It was well known that the Syrian dealt only in prized specimens and treated his merchandise with scrupulous care. Slaves bought from him were always clean, well fed, devoid of bruises and scars, and already settled and tractable. As far as harem candidates were concerned you could be sure that when he sold them as virgins, they really were virgins, males and females alike. The first hand to fondle their firm and youthful charms would be that of the noble purchaser or of the eunuch acting on his behalf.

Hence this disturbance, certainly provoked by a riotous slave, was unusual in his shop and Butros, acutely mortified, rushed out to determine its cause. He returned at once, excusing himself profusely for allowing such vulgarity to wound the ears of the prince.

"It's a little boy we have to castrate. My servants, stupid idiots, didn't give him the calming potion called for in such cases and when the child realized what they were going to do he rebelled with all his strength. But everything is all right now. They've tied him down and there'll be no more trouble."

"A little boy, you say? And he put up that kind of a fight against your men?"

"Well, my lord, it's a long story. If I weren't afraid it would bore you, I'd tell you the whole thing. It really is quite out of the ordinary."

"Let's hear it then. I'm interested. But first go back and tell your butcher to wait. Not to touch the boy until I say to. Is that clear?"

"Yes, my lord, right away," and Butros dashed off to give the order in person, a faint ray of hope dawning in his mind. He might yet resolve this wretched case to his own advantage.

When he reappeared the prince had settled more comfortably into his chair, one elbow on the arm rest, chin on his hand. The captain of his guards squatted on the floor to his left while the overseer and servants remained standing respectfully behind him. Even the minor local notables were craning their necks to hear. In the Orient everyone appreciated a good story, and this one sounded promising.

"So, my lord," Butros began, sitting down crosslegged on the floor, "it all began two months ago when I made a trip to Ala al-Habib's well, where I had agreed to meet a friend of mine whose caravan would come through there on its way back from the Arabian coast. You know, Sire, that for us slave merchants the major source of supply — apart from wars — is actually these nomads whom, may Allah forgive me, I would not hesitate to define as outright thieves."

Multiple nods of agreement greeted this virtuous affirmation. Caravanners were mostly scoundrels who dealt in slaves, weapons and contraband, and often functioned as couriers for more or less illicit purposes. Around the wells frequented by caravans many an intrigue was woven and plenty of hot merchandise changed hands while traders swapped news and gossip.

blind if I'm not speaking the truth. With the help of my doctor, who is a very good one, I clean the boy's head wound, straighten his broken leg and set it with two splints. All this time he never moves, keeps his eyes closed. But when he finally opens them a few days later, what eyes my lord! I've never seen any more beautiful and believe me I've seen eyes of every color — blue eyes like the blond races have, black, brown, green, topaz and streaked ones. But eyes like these — never. They're huge, almond-shaped, and a clear luminous gray color like a cloudless sky just before dawn."

Butros paused to give full effect to his lyrical flight.

"So, the boy begins to get better, to eat and to talk. But he doesn't remember anything. Not who he is or his name or where he lived. He can't even recall the days in the caravanner's tent. Actually this is a good thing because I'm more and more certain he's of noble blood, the son of a powerful lord by one of his white slaves. Who knows maybe his mother was a princess taken in battle. Perhaps his father favored him and so the other concubines were jealous or his own brothers decided to get rid of him by faking a pirate raid. Anyhow it's fine with me. It looks as if I've brought off the deal of a lifetime, getting hold of an item like this for five *dirahim*. And instead I might as well have thrown away those five *dirahim* — I wish that was all he'd cost me!"

After another pause for effect Butros took up the thread once more.

"At first things don't go too badly. The boy is grateful for the care. He thanks me every time I treat him, even though he does it with a certain condescension, as if I'm the slave and I owe him this kind of attention. He'll learn, I tell myself. But meanwhile there's something that should have put me on guard. Once he's well again the boy won't let anyone touch him. Lay a hand on him and you're asking for trouble!

Lucky for me I took a good look at him while he was unconscious. Otherwise I might not even know whether he was male or female.

Anyhow he's steadily recovering and getting more beautiful every day. His head wound has healed and the broken leg has apparently knitted well and strengthened and I tell myself little by little he'll get over his squeamishness. But when he begins to understand where he is and realize from now on he's a slave waiting for a master, at that point things go bad. I try being nice to him — you know, Sire, how I observe the Prophet's commandment to be charitable with slaves. I try to reason with him. I tell him wherever his home might be, he isn't going to be able to go back again. I assure him I'll only sell him to a good master, a prince or an emir who will take good care of him. I point out it's up to him to show off his best points — who knows he might be accepted as one of the personal guards of an emir. He has the looks for it. Totally useless. He retreats into stubborn silence and I cease to hear the sound of his voice. He doesn't even cry out when I try punishment to bring him to his senses."

The prince frowned as if displeased at the idea of that punishment and Butros hastened to justify himself.

"But what could I do, my lord? And I assure you, I used a light hand on him, also because I don't like to damage my goods. But with this one nothing works, neither good treatment or bad. I tried everything. To be honest with you I like this young boy so much I even considered giving up a profit just this once and keeping him for myself as a servant."

"Keeping him as a servant — you? A boy like that?" said the prince with such disdain that Butros had to swallow two or three times before he went on.

"Well, yes. I thought about keeping him as a servant. Once I had him well trained I'd dress him up in fine embroidered livery and have him receive important guests, serve the *hushaf*, and since he's so refined, help me teach the other youngsters good manners. I thought a servant like him would give a certain prestige to my *dukkan*. But he won't even listen to me. There he stays, most of the time with his eyes closed, tied to his bed...."

"You mean you kept him tied up?"

"But what could I do, my lord? If I left that boy free he'd kill himself even if the only way to do it was to beat his head against the wall and reopen his wound. And he won't take any food either, but when I show him how we force feed stubborn cases, well then because he's intelligent he agrees to eat. But only enough to escape the humiliation I've described.

Of course he begins to lose weight and I watch my goods deteriorate right in front of my eyes. Then another disappointment. When I insist that he move around a bit I notice the broken leg hasn't mended well. It's a good half inch shorter than the other. Which means goodbye to any hope of selling him as a nobleman's bodyguard. So then I say to myself, well a lame leg doesn't matter much in bed and if he learns the art of pleasure he'll be able to satisfy the most demanding of noble lords — he's pretty enough. Why, he might even become his master's favorite.

So I think I've come up with a good idea until the first time I show him to a eunuch in charge of a large harem in Damascus. He'd come here on business and was eager to bring back something nice for his master — it turned into a real fiasco. I really did warn that eunuch to approach him cautiously because he was more skittish than an unbroken colt. Well, first he examines the child from every angle, then puts a hand between his thighs. At that point the boy goes after the eunuch's face with both hands and scratches him till he's bleeding. Don't ask me what it took to placate the eunuch. He threatens to report me to the magistrate and I have to present him with a sizeable sum as a gift. That means one more expense to write off as a loss. I don't know how I'm going to balance my accounts and then, Sire, I happen to think of your good friend, the Emir Husain ibn Ali."

"My good enemy, you mean," corrected the prince. "And after taking care of this boy like your own son, as you yourself put it, you would have given him to the Emir Husain?"

"But my most excellent prince, I am not rich. I have to work for a living. And this child whom I'd bought for five *dirahim* at the beginning had by now cost me a fortune in medicine and treatments of all kinds, without even counting the gift to the eunuch. I had to make up my losses. So I wait for the emir's overseer. He comes here often to keep his master's harem supplied...."

"That's true enough. Those unhappy children don't last long in his hands."

"My lord, it isn't everyone who can be as refined a lover as you are, strong as a lion and gentle as a dove," said the unctuous Butros, but seeing the prince's eyebrows contract into a scowl at this indiscreet assessment of his erotic techniques, he hurriedly returned to his story.

"So when the overseer gets here I have the boy brought out, securely bound this time to avoid unpleasant surprises. I turn him slowly around so the overseer can see every detail without putting his hands on him. I thought I'd taken all possible precautions. But I was mistaken."

"Why? What happened to Husain's fat pig of an overseer?"

"Alas, my prince, all hell broke loose. The overseer takes a good look at the boy, decides he really deserves all the praise I've heaped upon him, agrees with me that his rebelliousness could actually be an added attraction for his master — the emir likes to season his sweets with a bit of pepper. In short, we're about to conclude the deal when the overseer says he'd like to inspect the boy's teeth. I can hardly refuse — it's a reasonable request. He'd end up in trouble with the emir if he tried to pass off a damaged article as quality merchandise. So while a servant and I hold the boy still, bound hand and foot as I have said, the overseer pries his mouth open and sticks two fingers inside to touch his teeth — which I might note in passing, are two rows of perfect pearls such as can't be found in all the Orient, and strong besides, as we all know here from experience. And what happens? The boy jerks his head free and bites off one of the overseer's fingers."

Here the prince smiled openly, as did Hassan and Ibrahim, and so did the local notables. The idea of the emir's fat overseer with a finger firmly clamped between a child's teeth was just too comical.

"You are laughing, Sire, but it didn't look funny to me. The overseer lunges at the boy ready to kill him. My servants and I manage to get the child away from him but we have to take our share of blows and kicks. We're all shouting except for the boy. He never raises his voice. In the end I have to shell out another gift and I pacify the overseer by promising to punish the rebel, to give him a lesson that will leave its mark. Naturally I do nothing of the sort since it would be useless anyhow and the one I'd hurt would be myself. But I'm convinced things can't go on like this. There's only one thing left to do. I have to have him castrated. Of course, this means I won't get half the price I'd hope for if I sold him intact. But better a small profit than none at all. I've already had a request from the head eunuch of the sultan of Bilis. He's looking for young castrati to bring up in his own way as harem servants. The boy will still be attractive. As I told you, Sire, I'm sorry things had to come to this, but I have no choice. May Allah, who sees all, dry up my tongue if I am not speaking the truth."

As he talked Butros kept an eye on the doorway, where a servant had appeared several times, apparently wishing to say something but afraid to interrupt. It seemed the castrator was becoming impatient. But a man of the prince's status certainly could not be hurried.

It was Hamid himself who intervened. "I'd like to see the boy," he said, standing up.

"But of course, my prince, by all means. Permit me to escort your grace." Butros rose and made his way to the end of the corridor, where he opened the door and stood aside with a bow to let his noble guest pass. Hassan and Ibrahim followed, then the notables, straggling along one or two at a time. By now everyone was curious.

The room was a vast well-lighted area. There were numerous pallets along the walls, many cupboards, a large tub, quantities of pitchers and basins, small tables piled with combs, brushes, razors and little jars of different ointments. It was here that Butros provided for the various treatments and operations necessary to improve the health and appearance of his merchandise, which often suffered from the consequences of capture and transport.

Here hair and nails were carefully trimmed; males were shaved and unwanted hair was removed from young girls by applications of burnt sugar. Here males were exercised to develop strong muscles, and females were given special treatments to enhance their beauty. Here the sick and wounded were cared for and finally it was here that castrations were performed.

Over near one of the windows a boy about twelve years old, little more than a child, lay stretched out completely naked on a wide plank bolted to two sawhorses. He was bound to the board by heavy straps that completely immobilized him — shoulders, chest and abdomen — except for his legs, which were tied at the ankles to two pieces of wood, each one fastened to the plank with a pivot.

The castrator, a muscular man clad only in a pair of breeches, was sitting on a stool at the foot of the table. His right hand, holding the knife, dangled between his legs. He absently stroked the boy's leg with his left hand while he talked and joked with a group of his own assistants and Butros' servants gathered around him. Laughter and wisecracks passed from one to another, referring no doubt to the operation about to take place. However two men stood sullenly off to one side — one had a bandaged wrist, the other a conspicuous scratch on his neck. A third one was sucking two bleeding fingers.

At the prince's entrance, the laughter and talk subsided and all hastened to prostrate themselves on the floor. Hamid stopped on the threshold, regarding all that apparatus with a certain astonishment. It seemed as if they were preparing to castrate a wild animal, not a child. Then he walked over to the bound boy, looking down intently from his imposing height.

Butros had not lied. Even tied down as he was, the boy's exceptional beauty was evident, in such contrast to the coarse humanity surrounding him as to suggest he might be an essentially different creature, fallen from some unknown ethereal world into the midst of beings completely alien to himself.

Undoubtedly he was the result of a series of crosses among various races, but it would be impossible to say what mysterious alchemy of the blood had produced the color of his skin — an antique ivory, warm, luminous, somewhat lighter in the palms of his hands and on the bottoms of his feet, as occurs with darker races, but tinted delicate rose on his lips and the aureoles of his nipples as with white races. Though his limbs still retained the softness of childhood everything about him predicted the future harmony of a perfect virility.

A mass of chestnut curls with silver highlights fell back from his forehead and small well-formed ears — an indication of noble blood — and clung soaked with sweat to his neck. Under cleanly traced brows he kept his elongated eyes stubbornly closed and his thick short lashes deepened the shadows below them, accenting their delicate violet and giving him a languid air. His straight slightly acquiline nose added a proud character to a face that might otherwise have seemed too gentle and so too did the chin, which rounded out the firm line of his jaw. His mouth was rather wide and his labored breathing had slightly parted the well modeled lips to reveal the sparkle of his teeth.

Meanwhile Butros, in order to flaunt his authority and show everyone that after all he was the one in charge, was haranguing his servants: "Why didn't you give him the potion? You know I don't want any disturbance!"

"Master," one of them answered, "we tried to give it to him but he wouldn't take it. There was just no way we could get it down his throat. So if he wants to watch the show, that's his affair. Anyhow it's the last time he scratches anybody."

Someone laughed, but the laugh died away in silence. The prince, who had looked up with an impatient expression, once more bent over the child. Suddenly the boy seemed to sense the weight of his gaze. He turned his head and opened his eyes to encounter those of the prince.

Hamid found himself staring down at two uniformly gray irises bearing no trace of either green or blue — the color, as Butros had so poetically declared, of the sky when dawn first appears, or better, when a veil of clouds dims the winter sun. These were eyes that opened upon the soul and allowed the regard of another to look into their depths. Fixed upon the dark and impenetrable gaze of the man who stood above them those gray eyes lighted up with joy and relief, as if in long-awaited recognition. They had the expression of one who, left alone and helpless among enemies hopelessly incapable of understanding him, finally sees a member of his own kind, someone who, he feels, he can rightfully hope will help him. And in those eyes shone an offer of love so intense, so certain of being returned that the prince, unused to submitting to violent acts or sentiments, wrested his own gaze away from the child's and addressed the castrator who was standing respectfully waiting for a sign from him to begin his operation.

"How did you learn this trade?" he asked abruptly.

"My prince, this is a hereditary art in my family. When I was seven I was already practicing on roosters and then when I got a little older I followed my father into the countryside, learning to castrate colts and rams."

"And how did you pass from animals to men?"

" I was good at my work, Sire, and the *fellahin,* the farmers who want docile slaves to work in the fields, began to ask me now and then to castrate a boy. Then I was called to noble houses and I can say without false pride that the best-looking eunuchs in this area are the work of my hands. I'm not one of those barbers who wield the razor carelessly, just cutting any old way."

"It does not seem to me to be a difficult art."

"No, Sire, but it's not like mutilating defeated enemies on the battlefield when you don't care whether somebody lives or dies. Castration for domestic purposes," he continued, putting down his knife and bowing, gratified by the attention of such a prestigious listener, "is an operation requiring considerable skill, both to avoid infections, which leave ugly scars and can even be fatal, as well as to ensure everything is indeed cut away. Then there is the question of age."

"Is that important?"

"Certainly, my prince. Usually young men are castrated at eighteen to twenty because by then their bodies are already fully developed and you have good-looking individuals. Little by little the beard disappears along with other male characteristics. But the eunuch retains his intelligence and can even be aggressive, which makes for valuable harem servants, as your lordship knows. Slaves are almost always glad to be castrated because they are sure to be used for tasks that are more decorative and less tiring. Of course, nobody takes this kind of trouble for the poor wretches destined to turn millstones or chain pumps. Hard labor castrates them."

"I see you really know your job," approved the prince, who appreciated efficiency in all walks of life. "And why would anyone castrate a child?"

"My lord, precocious castration, practiced on boys the age of this one, for instance, is not very often in demand. The subject will not develop well, goes completely to fat, with thin arms and legs and an elongated head. The only desirable trait that remains, if he already has it, is the voice, which retains a special timbre. I have heard that in other countries the voices of these castrati are highly valued and noblemen often keep one with their musicians. But among us such a custom is rare."

"So then why do it?"

"It's a matter of convenience, Sire. Especially in harems there is always a need for docile and harmless youths to perform domestic services. But more often, as in this case, it's done to tame a rebellious nature. The effect upon character is definitive and sure. It's a lot better than constant use of the whip and to my way of thinking, much more humane. You see, my prince, by the time the wound heals this little rooster, all beak and claws now, will have turned into a pretty plump little capon so quiet you won't even recognize him."

As he spoke, the castrator had snapped apart the pieces of wood to which his little prisoner's ankles were tied, forcing him to bend and spread his legs. Held in that obscene position the child tried again to break free, arching his back and struggling against all the straps that held him, but then fell back exhausted. At that point he reopened his eyes, reclosed during the brief discussion, and sought the prince's gaze.

Butros was watching the scene in a cold sweat, holding his breath. What on earth did he want now, that devil of a prince? Did he like the boy? Would it make sense to offer him the child as he was, asking a high price? And what if, once he was freed, the boy went after him biting and scratching? What then? Prince Hamid was hardly the emir's overseer and would be quite capable of cutting off the head of Butros himself after killing the rebellious boy.

The child, panting softly, continued to stare at the prince's inscrutable face. And suddenly they heard his voice, still child-like but clear and firm.

"Take me away with you, my lord. Take me with you."

It was neither an entreaty nor a supplication and much less a command, but it contained something of all three. The tone belied a certainty that the request was legitimate, as well as the urgency of one who can't wait any longer. The prince continued to look at the boy but allowed his face to betray no reaction to his appeal. Until the castrator, tired of all the delays, broke the silence.

Annie Messina

"All right, that's enough," he said. "Let's not bother his lordship with your complaints. You brought this on yourself and it serves you right. But you'll find you'll feel better afterwards without these little testicles. And since you're a slave you wouldn't have much use for them anyhow." He turned, picked up the knife and with an almost affectionate gesture placed his big hand on the child's genitals. The boy started violently, writhing to escape the contact. At that instant the prince's voice broke in like the crack of a whip.

"Take that hand away! Don't you dare touch him, you worthless scoundrel!"

The big man jerked his one hand back as if it had been burned and the other hand, still holding the knife, fell to his side. No one in the room breathed.

In silence the prince bent over the boy and manipulated the pieces of wood so the child's body was again composed and stretched out. Then he looked him in the eye.

"Do you really want me to take you with me?" he asked in a low voice, and he seemed to be talking not to a helpless and humiliated child but to an equal, free to accept or refuse. "If you want me to take you, you must give yourself entirely to me. Do you understand? Are you capable of doing that?"

"Put me to the test, my lord," was the barely whispered reply.

The prince straightened up and moved a few steps away. "Untie him," he ordered. The servants hastened to obey, assisted by Butros, perplexed now, but hopeful. The castrator, having understood there was nothing more for him to do, retired resentfully into a corner. So much for that noble visitor's interest in his art!

"Get up," said the prince. Numerous hands helped the boy down from the table and steadied him on his legs, so wobbly he could scarcely stand. Now that he was on his feet his genteel nudity appeared in all its beauty.

"Come here," said the prince.

The child took several steps toward him.

"Kneel."

The boy slowly lowered himself first on one knee then the other, looking up at the man who dominated him from above. The prince, still staring at the child, pulled out a dagger tucked under his belt and removed it from its sheath. It was a stiletto so sharp the point looked like a needle. He studied it for a moment, then passed his index finger over it and a vermilion drop immediately squirted from the fingertip he had barely grazed. For an instant the boy lowered his eyes to the reddened point of the blade, then looked back up at the prince.

The man bent over him, "Boy," he said, "you are beautiful. Do you know that?"

"If you say so, my lord," was the submissive response.

"You are a beautiful boy and your beauty is the only wealth you possess. Will you give it to me?"

"My lord," said the child in a thin but steady voice. "It is yours. Take it."

At that, the prince placed two fingers under the boy's chin, tilting back his head, and rested the point of the dagger on his left cheekbone. He held it there for a second, and then with a decisive gesture drew it down across the cheek to the jawline. Then he straightened up and flung the dagger away.

The child had remained perfectly still, without the slightest hint of pulling back. A series of tiny red drops appeared on the long cut, grew larger and multiplied and blood ran down his throat to his bare chest. For another minute the two gazed at each other as if materially bound together by something others couldn't see. Then the boy swayed, tried to recover, but fell backward on the floor, his face dripping with blood.

Those in the room had watched in shock and the most horrified of all was Butros. Now that the prince had ruined the boy what was he supposed to do with him? Oh yes, he had hoped the child's courage would please Prince Hamid enough to induce him to buy him just to keep him from being mutilated. Instead he himself had mutilated him in a way that was much worse. Would there be anyone left who'd buy him now, in that state?

No one dared move. The prince studied the unconscious child at his feet, his dark skinned face still wearing the same inscrutable expression. Suddenly he took off his heavy cloak of gold and brown brocade, bent over, and waving off Hassan who had leaped forward to help, wrapped the inert body in the silken mantle, lifted the child in his arms, paused a moment to look at the beautiful face now completely covered with blood, and headed for the door.

"Ibrahim," he called back to his overseer from the threshold, "talk to the merchant and arrange a price for the boy. And give something to that butcher since we've spoiled his fun."

He went out into the open where his men were waiting, handed the child to Hassan to hold while he mounted his horse, but quickly leaned down to take him back. He settled the boy on the saddle in front of him, holding him against his chest with his left hand, caught up the reins with his right and set off at a gallop followed by his twenty horsemen.

AL-HAKIM

"Hakim! Hakim! The master wants you!"

In the doorway of the small pavilion a slender elderly man appeared, wearing a black tunic that could be said to represent a compromise between Middle- and Far-Eastern dress. On his head was an embroidered skullcap and his still-dark hair was pulled to the back of his neck and braided into a pigtail. His face was wrinkled and flat, his eyes lively under thick brows and his nose a bit too pushed in for a Chinese of pure race.

He was the prince's personal physician. When Hamid was three his father, an astute observer of human nature, had sent for a certain young slave who had been the object of his attention for some time, and said to him, "Chinese slave (he always called him that because his name was too hard to pronounce) from now on you will devote yourself exclusively to the care and development of Prince Hamid. He's my only son and certainly my last one. I'm old and no longer fit for vigorous procreation. Thus, I entrust him to you. He's a handsome child and I want him to grow up sound in mind and body. I know you are experienced in both Chinese and Arab medicine, two sciences unequalled in the world. Continue your studies on your own, take whatever texts you want from my library, test your remedies on my slaves, and perfect your methods for healing the wounds of war as well as the equally painful injuries that life deals us. The Imam will take care of instructing my son in the True Faith since this is now the state religion. In all other matters, I grant you a free hand. I have told the boy to obey you, but he is not by nature docile, as you will soon find out, and it's up to you to gain his trust and respect. You can get a lot out of him by persuasion, nothing by authority. I'll provide lodging for you next to his apartment and you will have free access to him at all hours of day and night. You will report to me about anything you think I ought to know. As for the rest, I don't wish to be distracted from my own studies." This said, he went back to his favorite occupation, observing the stars.

Thus the Chinese slave became known to all as al-Hakim, the doctor. It was he who had been Hamid's true father, because to the boy his natural father was a mysterious character who spent most of his time on the terrace of the royal palace watching the sky with odd looking instruments and deriving from it some strange kind of magical knowledge. The only occasion on which the child was brought to him, apart from from major religious solemnities, was the ritual of Friday prayer in the mosque of the capital. This canonical prayer, the *salah*, was followed by the *khutbah*, or sermon, and the whole ceremony lasted for hours, during which, despite his age, the boy remained motionless in that impassivity so typical of Orientals.

As far as his pupil's health was concerned, al-Hakim had had very little to do. Healthy child, then vigorous adolescent, Hamid reached manhood without illnesses or any kind of crises. While his father was still alive he had grown strong on the battlefields of the various wars of annexation, wars waged without mercy by the new caliphs, the Abbasids. When he took over the reins of the small coalition of tribes that formed his state, he won the title awarded to victorious commanders: al-Ghazi, the warrior. Al-Hakim's patient and discreet arts had played an important part in forming his character. Without resorting to confrontation he had inculcated in his pupil the moral code he himself felt was appropriate for a prince and had taught him to control the natural impetuousness of his temperament. Above all, he had sought to mitigate that flame of ferocity innate in the Arab, a flame that could never be completely extinguished. Perhaps indirectly he had contributed to making Hamid into the strong and gentle lover whom Butros the slave merchant had extolled as the delight of his harem.

Unfortunately when Hamid married, al-Hakim was unable to win the good will of his wife, a haughty and authoritarian woman. To avoid making things worse he kept his distance, devoting himself to the study of his herbs. Such a situation annoyed Hamid but the other sources of friction with his wife were so numerous and serious he couldn't risk a battle over this as well. He had hoped to follow his father's example and entrust to Hakim his own son, born when the marriage seemed destined to bear no fruit except miscarriages and female babies. However, the boy was spoiled by his mother, hostile to his father, cruel and violent by nature, and averse to any kind of discipline. When the prince finally closed the parentheses around that disagreeable cohabitation by assigning Shirin her own small personal court, she, supported by influential relatives, insisted on taking her son with her. When they both departed palace life returned to its former harmony.

Although Hamid lived a sumptuous life, took active and effective charge of his army, and demanded prompt obedience from his slaves, servants and concubines, he was a humane master and above all he had that rare capacity to inspire spontaneous devotion in those who served him. As far as his former tutor was concerned, he retained toward him that degree of filial respect compatible with his own sovereign authority, as well as an affection no less deeply felt by both, even though it remained unspoken. Further, he showed his gratitude by according the old man a privileged position. Hakim's lodgings inside the walls of the palace grounds and next to his own apartments had been gradually expanded and now included, besides his personal quarters, a laboratory for distillation, a dispensary and a place that might be called a rudimentary operating room.

Al-Hakim did not treat slaves; they had their own healers. But sometimes the prince asked him to care for a wounded soldier or a servant he held particularly dear. If he had no reason to need those healing arts himself, he often called upon his doctor for an hour of quiet conversation during which without seeming to, the master explained a current problem and the slave offered advice. Advice that was almost always heard and heeded.

"Hakim! Come at once!"

"What is it?" asked the old man standing in the doorway. "What does the master want me for?"

"He says to bring whatever you need to revive and treat a wounded patient."

Naturally it wouldn't be the master himself — in that case the call would have been far more urgent.

"Who will I be treating?" asked the old man again, as he alerted the servant who usually assisted him and selected whatever might be useful among the tools of his trade.

"I'm not sure. I think it's a young slave who's been injured. The master bought him from Butros al-Shami in the Bisah market. I don't know how he got hurt, but this slave must mean a lot to his lordship because Hassan's son Ahmed says his father told him the master brought him home on his own horse, holding him in his arms. Said he seemed really worried about him."

"All right, I'm coming," said the old man, without further comment. He was no gossip and the sole purpose of his questions was to find out what he would need to bring with him. It was indeed unusual for the prince to want a slave treated in his own rooms instead of handing him over to Hakim as he always had before, but this was not Hakim's affair. A few minutes later, followed by the soldier and by his servant, he was admitted to the prince's apartments.

After passing through the various doors, each one guarded by two armed members of Hamid's personal escort, he was conducted by Hassan into the prince's bedroom.

Precious rugs and hangings adorned the room and its two huge windows opened on the cool vista of an internal garden with flowers and pools. Against the back wall was the wide bed where the master habitually slept by himself, unwilling to admit to it even the most adored of his favorite concubines. To one side was a low divan, which could if needed serve as a bed for an occasional companion, but perhaps the only one who had used it now and then was the doctor. A few tables and chairs inlaid with mother of pearl completed a decor both sober and luxurious. Here and there braziers of highly polished and perforated brass added a brighter note.

There on the vast bed, lying on the prince's brown and gold cloak, was a young boy, naked except for that part of his body covered by the cloak's folded edge. The prince himself sat on the side of the bed holding the boy's hand in one of his own and stroking his hair with the other. The child was turned toward him, his eyes closed, his cheek buried in the pillow. But he wasn't completely unconscious because every once in a while old Hakim saw his fingers tighten around the man's big brown hand, as if he were afraid of losing that contact.

Annie Messina

Al-Hakim came forward and bowed silently. Because the prince then moved aside, he approached the bed and lifted the edge of the cloak, uncovering the child completely. A rapid glance was enough to determine the little fellow's exhaustion was due more to a suffering of the spirit than of the flesh. His body, a bit thin, though not seriously undernourished, showed no trace of wounds or blows, except for an ugly scar on one leg that might have resulted from a badly set fracture. The pubic area, marked only by the merest suggestion of downy hair, appeared to be intact.

The prince had stayed at the boy's side during Hakim's rapid examination. "A very beautiful child, my lord," said the old man softly. "How did you acquire him? And who is he?"

"I believe he was given to me by Allah the all-merciful," answered the prince, he too speaking in a low voice. "But in the material sense, I bought him from Butros the slave merchant. As for who he is, I don't know and neither does he. Look here." With a light touch he held back the chestnut curls over the boy's ear to reveal a deep scar along which the hair was just beginning to regrow. "He took a blow on the head, according to the merchant, and remembers nothing about his life before he was captured by bandits. But it's not for this that I've asked you for your services. He has a cut on his cheek. Can you take care of it so it doesn't leave a disfiguring scar on his face? Look."

He took the curly head gently in his hands and turned it to uncover the other cheek. It required some effort for the old man to stifle an exclamation. A single gash, black with clotted blood, crossed the whole side of the face from cheekbone to jawline. And it was not so much the injury itself that appalled — the wound was clean and not deep — what was horrifying was the offense to such perfect youthful beauty.

Sensing their gaze, the boy opened his eyes — huge and gray and edged with short dark lashes. Ignoring the old man bending over him, he sought out the prince, took his hand and with a tender and childish gesture drew it to his injured cheek. Then he closed his eyes again and sank once more into the pillow.

Meanwhile, in response to the old man's orders, his servant had brought a basin of warm water, while other servants hurried to bring pitchers and towels. After checking the temperature of the water, Hakim emptied the contents of one of his vials into it, soaked a cloth in the solution and then began to clean the wound with the most delicate care.

"It's not deep," he said after a bit. "And it's clean. But it's pretty long and I don't know whether it can be sutured."

He turned to the prince. "You did this, didn't you?" he said, more as an affirmation than a question.

Hamid nodded. "How could you tell?"

"You would never have let anyone else do this to him," answered the old man, continuing his work.

"Can you treat it so it will heal without a scar?" asked the prince once more.

"I don't know. But before we medicate the cut we have to help him regain some of his strength. He's got no resistance left."

"Hakim, do for him whatever you'd do for me if I'd been hurt."

The old man looked up at him for a moment with a shade of severity. "The first thing is to reassure him he's in friendly hands. Let's take him in there, to your bath."

The boy was lifted and carried with the utmost precaution into the adjacent room. It was a well-lighted space with beautiful tapestries on the walls and a large built-in tub in its center where a jet of water played like a fountain. There was also a cot covered with a heavy white cloth, various small cupboards, amphoras, basins of wrought silver and a large brass brazier filled with glowing coals. One servant already held a pitcher of hot water and another was helping the doctor's assistant to prepare pomades and potions.

Eased onto the cot, the boy was washed thoroughly with warm water, massaged at length with aromatic ointments to stimulate circulation in his chilled limbs and under such loving care he began to recover consciousness. He opened his eyes, no longer veiled and spent, and with a look of trust watched now one then another among those attending him, but his gaze always returned to the prince, who sat beside him.

"Now we've got to think about the wound," said the old doctor. "See, it has almost stopped bleeding. But I can't sew it closed. It would take too many stitches and this child is in no condition to stand any more pain."

"But what about the scar then? Will it be permanent?"

The old man would have liked to say, "You didn't know that, Sire?" But even he had to respect certain limits with Hamid and such a remark would have gone beyond those limits. Instead he replied, "I'm going to try another method."

He went over to the table where his medicines were lined up, used a spatula to take a wax-like material out of a small jar and then transferred it to a saucer, which he set on the edge of the brazier. He left it there for a while, working it with the spatula and touching the substance every now and then to see how hot it was. When it seemed to be softened to exactly the right degree he handed the saucer to his servant, instructing him to keep on stirring. Once again and with great care, he cleaned the cut on the boy's cheek. The patient had watched all the preparations with interest but no apparent fear.

"I won't hurt you, my child. All you'll feel is a slight burning."

"It's all right," said the boy, addressing the prince as if he had been the one who spoke. "I won't feel any pain if you stay here with me, my lord."

"Of course I'll stay. Don't be afraid. I won't leave you."

The old man had the boy lie on his side, adjusted his head so he could work on the injured cheek and began to apply the waxy material to the cut, being careful to keep its two edges together. "Does it hurt?"

"A little."

"It'll stop in a minute. You see, Sire," he explained while he soaked a strip of soft cloth and placed it over the whole length of the wound, pressing it down so it would stick, "this paste hardens as it dries and keeps the two sides together almost like stitches. Its advantage is it causes far less pain, even when it's removed. Now we'll wait until it dries."

For some time no one broke the silence. The servants remained motionless, the old man seated but getting up at intervals to see that things were progressing, the prince on a stool by the cot, still holding one of the boy's hands between his own.

Finally the old man touched the boy's cheek and ran his fingers delicately along the cloth strip now held fast by the paste, then washed his patient's face and chest with an infusion of cleansing herbs to remove all traces of blood and medicines. "It's finished, Sire. Now the child should rest."

They prepared a potion and the boy dutifully drank it. Then, after the servants had wrapped him in warmed woolen blankets, the prince picked him up again, returned to his bedroom and started to ease the child onto his own bed. But Hakim stopped him with a light touch on his arm.

"No, my lord, allow me — he'll be better off there on the divan."

The prince frowned at him, then gave an order and waited with the child still in his arms until a servant readied the divan for the night. When the boy, already asleep, was settled on the divan, the covers well tucked in and the uninjured cheek resting on a silk pillow, the prince motioned to the doctor and the two went out into the garden.

"Hakim, why didn't you want me to put the child in my bed?"

High above the wall enclosing the palace grounds the first quarter moon cast a pale light over the prince's dark scowling face.

The old doctor smiled. "Sire, you already know. Why do you ask?"

"Hakim, I have never had the depraved tastes of the Emir Husain."

"I know that very well, but the boy reaches out for you. He's beautiful and you are a hot-blooded man, Hamid, my son. What has not yet happened could happen."

"Yes, Hakim, you're right." The prince's voice was good-humored now. "But I am capable of restraining myself."

"I know this too, my son. But the child should have undisturbed rest tonight. Do you want your old doctor's advice? Go and pay a visit to the beautiful Lailah, who is pining because she hasn't seen you for forty-eight hours. Go on, you've had your share of emotions for one day, Sire, and these aren't the kind of emotions you're used to. If the child needs rest, you need something quite different. Better do as I say."

"You're probably right Hakim. I'll take your advice."

In the weak light of the crescent moon the old man could see his master smile. "May his God be praised," he thought. And as his slightly stooped figure made its way back inside to check on his little patient, the prince called for Hassan and set off toward the harem quarters.

A few hours later a calm and satisfied Prince Hamid left his favorite's rooms, stopped in the bath for his evening ablutions, repeated with a certain distraction the obligatory closing prayers of the day and dismissed all the servants, except for the two armed men remaining on guard in the corridor by his door, then entered his bedroom.

The first thing he did was direct his steps toward the divan. A night light made of perforated brass shown dimly on the motionless form of the child under the covers, but as he approached he saw the boy was not sleeping. Instead the gray eyes were open and followed the prince's every move through the semi-darkness.

"Go to sleep, little one. It's late. I'm going to bed too."

He touched the child's eyes lightly with his fingers and found them wet with tears.

"What's the matter, child? Why are you crying?"

No answer.

"Why? Does the wound hurt? Are you scared? What are you scared of?"

Still silence. The man bent down, placed his hand under the back of the boy's neck to raise him up enough to see his face more clearly. Suddenly the child wrapped his arms around the prince's neck, put his head on his chest and gave way to a fit of weeping.

"Why didn't you come, my lord?" he said between sobs. "Why did you leave me? I waited so long for you. I thought you'd never come back again!"

The prince picked him up, carried him over to his own bed, laid him down, then lay down himself beside him. To the devil with Hakim and all his wise counsel. The frail body was cold and trembling all over. The man held him close and the boy quickly curled up against his chest, pressing his face against the firm muscles, hugging him as if he still feared losing him. He was no longer the mysterious child who had stared at him from the castrator's table, calling upon him in the name of their common nature, no longer the unknown creature who offered himself to be loved and demanded acceptance, provoking in the man a tumult of sensations he still couldn't explain. He was only a frightened child weeping out the terrors, the solitude, the suffering of days and months — all he wanted was to be consoled.

The prince caressed him gently, murmuring words of comfort. As he felt the child's anguish gradually diminish, a never forgotten episode of his own childhood came to mind.

He was seven years old at the time and by his father's wish he was the guest of an uncle who cherished him as his favorite nephew. Unfortunately the uncle had two sons, big strapping fourteen- and fifteen-year-olds, aggressive and overbearing, rude to their peers and mean to their inferiors. The child, inimical to them because his family was richer and more powerful than theirs, had become the target of their heavy-handed pranks. The younger boy endured them without complaining to anyone, pondering impossible acts of revenge.

One day during an expedition whose purpose was to capture young raptors to train for the hunt, Hamid won permission to keep an immature falcon for himself. The bird, little more than a fledgling, had a badly injured wing and, according to the falconer, would always be somewhat hampered in flight. Hamid took the bird to his room, planning to care for it and then set it free, applying his Hakim's precept that the strong should always defend the weak.

But his cousins surprised him with the fledgling falcon in hand and partly because of their taste for cruelty, partly in sheer arrogance, they took it away from him, brought it to a grove of trees behind the house and set about torturing it, taking pleasure in the bird's screams as well as the child's desperate protests.

In the end, after pulling out the falcon's feathers and claws and in a frenzy of cruelty putting out its eyes with the point of a buckle, they grew tired of their game and tossed aside the ragged, bloody, still-palpitating remains of the bird and forced Hamid to follow them so he couldn't come to the aid of their victim.

The prince remembered how they had forcibly kept him with them for the entire day. He had suffered in silence, mad with rage at the violence done to himself and grief for the tortured bird. But he did not appeal to his uncle, who would certainly have taken his part. His pride rendered him mute.

When he was finally able to free himself and run back to the grove he found the poor martyred body of the falcon swarming with ants. Black lines of them moved over its bloody eye sockets and torn beak. And as he started to pick up the bird a weak cry told him the unhappy falcon was still alive.

At that point, trembling with grief and revulsion, he finished off the poor creature by hitting it with a stone. Then he rushed away to search for his cousins. Planting himself before them, his face gray with anger (such was his color when his dark skin went pale) he addressed the pair in measured syllables with extraordinary energy for one so young. One day, he declared, he would have his revenge. The two laughed at the childish threat. But they did not laugh when, twenty years later, finding themselves in an opposing military faction, they were taken prisoner by Hamid's soldiers and brought before him. Calmly certain they would be spared because of the family connection, they watched two warriors armed with swords come forward at a sign from the prince and heard the victor's implacable words: "Remember the falcon."

They barely had time to see Hamid turn his back on them before their heads fell under two simultaneous blows.

This episode came back to him now in a particularly vivid way. Perhaps that very memory had triggered his first impulse to rescue the child from the hands of the slave merchant and his acolytes. Never again would he be forced to stand helpless before cruelty and evil. But then another feeling had displaced that impulse, his mysterious response to the appeal of those eyes focused on his own. And now, finally, yet another emotion — never before had he felt such passionate tenderness, not even when he held a beloved woman in his arms.

"Falcon," said the prince softly, "my poor little falcon." And he himself didn't know whether he was speaking to the boy beside him or to the poor tortured bird of his childhood.

In answer a slight tightening of the arm wrapped around him, a soft sigh to end the long siege of weeping. And so the prince remained until dawn, listening to the quiet breathing of the child resting against his chest.

The next morning al-Hakim, ready and waiting, rushed to answer his master's call. He found him freshly emerged from the attentions of those servants who took care of his person — his hair and beard waved and shining, his skin lustrous as polished bronze over the sinuous muscles. He was sitting in the garden under the portico, breakfasting on milk, honey, foccaccia and various fruits.

"Did you sleep well, may Allah forever watch over your lordship?"

Of course both he and the prince knew he had been summoned to attend to the injured child. But it would be unseemly to inquire first after a child who, as far as al-Hakim knew, might be merely a young slave in whom his master had taken a passing interest.

"*Al-hamdulillah,* may God be praised, I slept well and so did the boy. Now, Hakim, listen to me. I have a lot to do. It's already time for audiences and I don't like to keep people waiting. Then I have some matters to settle with the overseer. I'm putting the boy in your care. See if you can get him to talk about his past. Try to find out a little something about him, whether he really has lost his memory or if it's a more or less conscious defense against the curiosity of that louse Butros. Anyhow even if we do find out who his father is, I'm certainly not going to give him back. The boy belongs to me. Come with me now because if I don't tell him he can trust you he might refuse to talk to you. If you have even the slightest concern about him, send Hassan to get me, no matter when. He'll know where I am."

Hamid went back into the bedroom and approached the bed, followed by the doctor. The child was still sleeping but he quickly sensed the prince's presence and opened his eyes, looking at him with a still uncertain smile. But it was obvious that he was rested and yesterday's terror had dissipated in his sleep.

Hamid, smiling in return, patted the child, so absorbed in him as to make the old man think that if there was any sign of bondage here it was a chain that bound them both.

"My little falcon, I have a lot of things to do. I'm leaving you with al-Hakim. He's my personal physician and he's going to take care of you. Don't tire yourself and may God keep you."

"But you'll come back, my lord?" asked the boy, a shadow of apprehension in his eyes.

"Of course, before evening if I can."

However, his duties as supreme judicial authority of his state, his need for a long horseback ride with Hassan, and a visit to his harem — fairness demanded that his attentions

should not be reserved only for his favorite — all this kept
Hamid away longer than he had anticipated. It was late at
night when he entered his apartments and found that al-
Hakim had persuaded the child to go to bed. A sleeping
potion had overcome the child's stubborn resolve to stay
awake and wait for his master and he now slept peacefully
on the divan. The prince gently touched the still red and
swollen cheek with one finger, patted him lightly so as not to
wake him and went back outside with the old man. A light
supper had been laid under the portico and Hamid invited
the doctor to share it with him, as he often did when they
were alone.

"So, Hakim, how did he spend the day?"

"Waiting for you, Sire," answered the old doctor with a
smile.

"Did the two of you talk?'

"Yes, but I don't know much more about him than you
do. He's twelve or thirteen — I'd say twelve — he's of mixed
race, mostly white. He's well-developed, healthy and of noble
origin. You can tell by the way he allows himself to be waited
on, as well as his whole general attitude. But I would guess
that he's been brought up without love. He's starved for
love, but he wants it only from you, Sire."

"Well that must be so. And the memory loss? Is it genuine?
Will his memory return with time?"

"Whether it will return or not, I can't say. The future is in
the hands of God. As far as the loss of memory being genuine, there's no doubt about that. He can't even remember
being captured. But without his realizing it, his desire to
blot out everything before he met you is contributing to his
amnesia. His life begins with you. He doesn't see anything
unusual in the fact that you saved him from his tormentors,
and I'd say he isn't particularly grateful to you for it. He was

yours — you came and you took him. His only fear was that you might get there too late."

"He doesn't even remember his name?"

"I asked him and he answered, 'The master calls me Falcon, so that's my name.'"

"Falcon," repeated Hamid to himself. "The name fits him. He's not always as docile as you've seen him. At the slave merchant's he fought the way a wild falcon does when an inept falconer tries to put the jesses on him." And the prince set about recounting what had happened the day before in Butros' emporium, from the noise of the struggle in the hallway to the gash inflicted upon the face of the kneeling boy.

"Hamid, tell me. Why did you do such a cruel thing?"

The prince did not answer right away. He felt as if he'd been carried backward in time to his childhood when, accused of some misbehavior, he used to hear those same words from his tutor: "Why did you do it?" And then from the ensuing examination of conscience a justification or an admission of guilt would emerge. Nothing obligated him to respond, not then or now. But there was a kind of honesty in him that would not refuse to be judged, even by an inferior.

"I don't know myself why I did it, Hakim. Maybe because the minute I saw him I wanted only to take him away, to keep him entirely for myself, to exist only for him, to take everything away from him in order to give him everything. Maybe I wanted to put myself to the test, more than him. I don't know. But I can tell you this: if I had it to do again, I'd do the same thing."

"You haven't changed, Hamid my son. But be careful. You came very close to killing him."

"I know."

And they both knew the old man was not referring to the wound, superficial in itself, but to the effort that supreme act of submission and devotion must have cost the child. And the man who had imposed it upon him had contracted a debt of love that would never be paid. The loser in that contest was not the injured party but the one who did the injury.

"Hamid, this you also know. If you subject him to such violence a second time, you will destroy him forever. Remember that."

"There will be no second time," the prince asserted crisply. "No one will ever harm my Falcon again — least of all myself."

THE CHILD

A few short weeks were enough to transform Falcon. The cut on his cheek had healed, leaving only a thin bluish scar, which would fade with time, and the clean contour of his pretty face was restored. His slender body was also growing stronger, but the muscles did not yet show on the still childish frame. Most important, he no longer displayed the excessive sensitivity of those first days, when the smallest twinge of joy or sorrow would set him painfully vibrating like a cord too tightly stretched. Happy in his own little world within the confines of the prince's apartments and enclosed garden, he let himself go and flourished like a plant an expert gardener has dug up from barren soil and transplanted to fertile ground.

He spent his time alone or with al-Hakim, lounging on cushions in the bedroom, or, more often, on the grass in a sunny corner of the garden, lazily watching birds in flight by day or following the movement of the stars at night. Only in the prince's presence did he show any animation. As for Hamid, he tried to spend as much time as possible with the boy. When he wasn't busy with his duties or engaged in the vigorous exercise his robust physique demanded, he would sit on the grass with the boy beside him resting his curly head on the prince's knees. Falcon would look up, and the prince's brown eyes, accustomed from childhood to betray no trace of either sentiment or emotion, would find themselves gazing into those clear gray ones so willing to reveal the depths of a soul overflowing with love.

They had also established a nightly ritual. Usually Hamid returned late to his apartments and found the child sleeping peacefully on the divan. He would pat him gently, eliciting a sleepy murmur in response and then get into his own bed and fall asleep at once. At first light he would awaken, joyfully aware of the sleeping child close by, like someone who has acquired a precious new possession and wakes up thinking about it, delighting in his good fortune. He would turn and call to the boy, softly, in case he might be still sleeping. But Falcon, already waiting for that signal, would bound off the divan and run to get into bed with the prince, then rest his head on his chest just as he had that very first night.

There they'd wait for the day to begin, sometimes talking — actually it was Hamid who talked, recounting selected events of the previous day, while the child listened, rarely intervening. When he did speak it would be to ask a question, always and only about the prince himself. More often they simply lay there together in peaceful and satisfied silence. Quite frequently the boy went back to sleep and the man listened to his light and regular breathing until he too fell asleep.

One day in that moment of predawn intimacy the child asked, "Why am I named Falcon?" and the prince, straying from the truth in certain details, told him how in his own childhood he had found a young falcon with a broken wing and taken it away from wicked people who wanted to harm it. "And you know, when I saw you that day, tied to the table and surrounded by evil men who wanted to hurt you, the falcon of my childhood seemed to come back to me. You were like him — a poor wounded bird held prisoner."

"What happened to that falcon, my lord?"

Hamid had been about to tell him about the sad fate of the bird but he was afraid he might cast an ominous shadow over his beautiful child. "The falcon got well," he replied instead. "And one day I set him free and he flew away."

"But I don't want to be set free, my lord. I don't want to fly away. I'll always be your Falcon," the boy answered passionately. The prince stroked the child's hair in silence.

Then one day al-Hakim had a serious talk with his master. "Sire, that boy isn't a weakling who has to be brought up indoors to keep him safe from the lightest breeze. He's a real male — he's got to have some action. He needs physical exercise and people around him."

"But that's not what he wants. He never asks for it."

"Sire, the boy will never ask you for anything. It's up to you to make the suggestion."

Thus, with a certain regret, for he hated to end that precious isolation, the prince asked Falcon if he would like to come with him, accompany him in his daily activities. He felt a bit guilty when he saw how quickly the child's face lighted up at his proposal.

First, however, they'd have to think about what sort of appearance he was going to make. The light tunics of their intimate hours wouldn't do now that he was going to be seen in public at the prince's side. Hamid called in his master of the wardrobe and ordered him to show the young gentleman his own best garments. He instructed him to invite Falcon to pick out three or four he liked and even if they were the most costly, the prince would have the court tailors make replicas in the right size as soon as possible.

But Falcon hardly looked at that fabulous apparel. "What are my lord's colors?" he asked al-Hakim, who had come along to help him choose.

"Brown and gold, my child. His banner is brown with a gold star above a verse from the Quran (the color brown had been Hamid's father's prudent compromise between the Umayyad white and the Abbasid black).

"Well then," said the boy to the master of the wardrobe, "have them make me a tunic out of brown cloth edged with a gold stripe."

"Nothing else?"

"No."

"No embroidery, no precious stones?"

"No."

"But you'll need a buckle for the belt. We'll make it out of gold and decorate it with jewels."

"All right, a buckle. But plain gold."

From that day on the child was frequently seen at the prince's side, a slender little figure in a brown tunic belted at the waist, the pretty curly head held proudly erect, the ivory-colored face serious and serene. On ceremonial occasions and during audiences he sat quietly behind the prince, attentive to all that was transpiring around him. At gala dinners, which were modeled after those in Baghdad, he remained apart from Hamid, seated with minor palace dignitaries on one of the divans placed against the wall. But every now and then he would get up to serve the prince, pouring wine into his cup or offering him the tastiest mango or the most perfectly ripened banana from the fruit bowls. He did so with such grace and gentle pride, the same manner in which he himself accepted the servants' attentions, that it warmed the heart of anyone who might be looking on.

From the moment of his first appearance at court this strange child had been the subject of a great deal of talk and gossip, not only among the servants but also those of higher rank. Everyone had a different theory. He was an ordinary slave bought in the market. No, he was the son of an aris-tocrat, a friend of the prince's, whom Hamid had promised to bring up in his own household. He was a child of noble origin kidnapped by nomads and given to the prince as a present because of his rare beauty. He slept in the prince's bedroom — a privilege never accorded to any concubine — thus he must be the favorite. But the prince treated him like a son — a son? Hardly a son! It was obvious he loved the boy as a man loves a woman. Still, the head eunuch maintained his master had never been more assiduous in his attentions to the beautiful Lailah, nor had he neglected the other beauties in his harem, conforming to the Quran's precept that a man should divide his favors equally among his women. And there were certainly enough of them, even for a man like Hamid.

Anyway the child was in the prince's graces, that was all that mattered. But how were they supposed to act toward him? For instance, what should they call him? By his first name as one does with inferiors or equals? The prince called him Falcon, but would they be allowed to use that name?

It was Hassan who unwittingly solved this problem. One day they heard his ringing voice give an order to a soldier: "Find Prince Falcon and tell him the master wants him in the audience hall."

Hassan's phrase spread quickly by word of mouth. That settled it. The boy was a prince and should be addressed as a prince. Besides, it was only natural — he was so handsome, so proud, so well-mannered — he had to be the son of a noble family. And a prince he remained.

But there was another difficulty. Now that Falcon was no longer confined to his little world of the prince's bedroom and enclosed garden, Hamid worried because he couldn't watch over him every minute. It was true that as far as his love was concerned, Falcon was steadfast and lucid of spirit far beyond his years, but when confronted with the harshness of daily life, he was lost — almost as if that love made him both stronger and more vulnerable. A companion must be found for him, someone not much older who would be both servant and friend, blindly devoted yet capable of opposing him if necessary, someone who would be able to remain obedient yet at the same time teach Falcon how to command. And above all it must be someone who would always be ready to defend the boy with his own life.

Hamid had not needed such guidance and protection during his own childhood. Leadership had come naturally to him. He himself had molded his soldiers, his servants and his loves. The only person he had not managed to control — his own son — he had sent away for good. He had always been master of himself and of others. But Falcon was something quite different.

Hamid discussed the problem with Hassan, who listened gravely.

"Sire, if you would agree to it, I think my son Ahmed is just the person you need. He is only seventeen but you have already given him battle experience and I can tell you he is as prudent as he is courageous. What's more, he's naturally devoted to our young prince."

Hamid had already noticed this. Ahmed behaved like an older brother to the child and Falcon readily turned to him when minor problems came up. In fact, Ahmed was exactly the choice of companion the prince had hoped for, but he knew that devotion is more profound to the degree it is spontaneous and not solicited. Therefore he had wanted the proposal to come from Hassan.

"If my memory serves me, your son Ahmed's wife presented him with his first son a few months ago, didn't she?"

Ahmed's bride had been a gift from the prince himself, a young slave girl who would have been a suitable wife for an administrator or an officer. Ahmed adored her.

"That's true, Sire, and I can tell you he's a good father and a good husband. But you can be sure if you assign him to our young prince, his first thought will always be for him."

"I know this, Hassan. Your son will be for Falcon what you are for me."

And so the child who came from nothing had his rank recognized at court, complete with title and squire, but not without some regret on the part of the man who in his secret heart would have liked to keep the sweetness of that love all for himself.

"Hakim, have you noticed how it distresses the child to limp that way? Can anything be done about his leg?"

"Well, there is something we could do, but it's a difficult and risky operation. We'd have to rebreak the leg and put it in traction so the two parts of the bone don't quite touch and the callus forms in the space between them. Then we would periodically increase the traction until the length is right and the callus is fully formed and strong. It's a long painful process."

"But the leg would return to normal?"

"Yes, quite probably, although there's always a risk. The callus might not form evenly for the desired length, the attachment might be defective. This is why the patient must be in perfect health and the trauma the child has suffered is too recent to subject him now to more pain."

"All right then, we'll wait. When you think the time is right, let's allow him to decide for himself. It doesn't bother me that he limps, but I've noticed he's ashamed of it when he has to walk in front of me."

"Sire, the boy is proud of his beauty for your sake. It's the only gift he can offer you and he sees his defect as an offense to you."

"I understand that, even though it isn't true. And I'm afraid talking to him would make things worse. But it pains me that I often have to deny him the pleasure of accompanying me."

"Then, Sire, why not teach him to ride? On horseback having one leg a bit shorter doesn't matter at all. Besides he could go out riding with you and build up his strength the way an adolescent should. I don't like the way he's living now."

"You're right Hakim, you're right, as always. We'll teach him to ride."

The next day Hamid, along with Hassan and his son Ahmed, took Falcon to the stable. The chief stablemaster went with them to the fenced pastures where the prince's best horses were grazing — all of them prized animals with pure bloodlines, from Mongols with dun coats, to tough strong Kurdish ponies, from purebred desert Arabians, agile and highstrung, to the more robust breeds from the coast. In a reserved paddock Hamid's roan stallion raised his beautiful head at his master's voice, then returned to cropping grass.

"Have you ever ridden a horse, Falcon?" asked the prince as the boy stood looking around, uncertain and seemingly perplexed.

"I…I don't remember, my lord."

"Are you afraid to try?"

"No."

"My lord prince," intervened the stablemaster, "if you want the young prince to learn to ride it would be well to start him on Negma, the gray mare — she's gentle as a lamb."

"Very well, Abdullah, have them saddle the gray mare."

When Negma was saddled Abdullah led her over to the boy. "Here, I'll put my hands together like this, you step up on them and I'll give you a boost into the saddle. All you have to do is sit straight and press your knees against the mare's flanks. You'll see, it's easy. Don't be afraid."

But before he could finish his sentence Falcon rose on tiptoe, placed his hands on the pommel of the saddle and sprang lightly onto Negma's back. Then he took the reins from the astonished Abdullah, touched the mare's sides lightly with his heels and guided her at a trot all the way around the inside of the fence.

"Well then, my lord prince, he already knows how to ride! Look how well he sits!"

"So it seems," agreed Hamid, delighted at the new prowess he had discovered in his child.

His circuit completed, Falcon stopped in front of them and dismounted before the servants could get to him. He was flushed and excited. The prince had never seen him like this. "My lord, if you don't mind, I'd like to try that pretty black one over there."

"But he's not well broken," protested Abdullah. "Even though the young gentleman seems to be a skilled rider, it wouldn't be wise to let him try a two year old colt, a purebred Arabian still not used to the saddle."

"That's not a boy's horse," said the prince. But seeing the enthusiasm fade from Falcon's eyes, he didn't have the heart to enforce his prohibition. "All right, go ahead and try him if you want to. But if he tosses you off on your head you'll have only yourself to blame. Abdullah, have the black saddled."

Delighted, Falcon approached the skittish horse standing nervously swishing his tail as the servants saddled him and pulled the girth tight under his belly. He went up to the animal with no fear, placed a hand on his neck and spoke softly. The horse turned his head far enough to fix the child with one great brown eye opened wide enough to show white. But he did not pull away and once saddled let the boy spring lightly onto his back. Falcon turned him and kept talking softly as he completed two circuits around the enclosure, barely guiding him with only the lightest pressure of his knees. Then he motioned to the servants to open the gate. They obeyed, but not before glancing at the prince to secure his consent, and the black horse exited the fenced area, still maintaining the pace set by his rider. However, once he sensed the open space before him, he broke into a gallop across the broad grassland with Falcon's diminutive figure sitting erect in the saddle.

Hamid experienced a moment of terror. The meadowland ended in a wood, half-timbered off, a treacherous terrain full of sharp stumps and twisted roots, and the colt was not yet trained to avoid hidden obstacles. Without hesitation he jumped on the nearest horse, not waiting for a saddle, and dashed off after the fugitive, followed at some distance by Hassan and his son. But no matter how hard he rode, the prince's mount was no match for the black and the distance between them lengthened while the distance between Falcon and the wood was rapidly shrinking.

But the boy, hearing the galloping hooves behind him, turned to look over his shoulder and saw his pursuers, the prince far in the lead. Without forcing his horse he brought it round in a wide turn and came up beside him.

Hamid intended to reprimand Falcon, but when he saw the boy's confident smile as he leaned forward to pat the colt's neck and then looked over at the prince with shining eyes, he couldn't bring himself to do it. Instead he exclaimed, "Well done, Falcon! Why didn't you tell me you could ride? I'd have taken you out with me long before this!"

"I didn't know I could, my lord. Not until I found myself in the saddle. That's when I remembered how. You were frightened for me, weren't you, my lord? Because you love me." Along with Hassan and Ahmed, who had now caught up with them, they returned to the stables at a trot.

From that day on Falcon went with the prince on his rides. It was a pleasure to see them pass by, the master tall and powerful on his roan, the child slender and elegant on the

Arabian colt. Usually they rode side by side in silence, but one look was enough for anyone to sense the strength of the feeling that bound them together.

A second surprise awaited the prince when he brought Falcon to the small lake that was one of the pleasantest spots on the outskirts of the palace grounds. Here the river that circled much of Hamid's domain emerged from a grove of larch and birch to widen into a mirror of clear deep water amid a landscape already picturesque but rendered even more so by the hand of man.

On the left the shore of the lake was formed of smooth rocks sloping gradually down to a narrow rounded landing that had been skillfully modeled to resemble the edge of a bathing pool. Nearby a rocky overhanging cliff, not really massive but big enough to dominate its surroundings, cast a deep violet shadow on the smooth surface of the water. The opposite shore was thick with vegetation except at one point. Here the bushes had been thinned out where a curious single whitish limestone formation protruded from the water, making a convenient goal for swimming races. The lake was several yards deep for its entire area and the bedrock at the bottom kept it clean and transparent.

Hamid wanted his soldiers well trained in all types of physical exercise and being a good swimmer himself, he demanded that they too should know how to swim. Hence he often visited the lake, sometimes with one group of men, sometimes with another, so the recruits might learn from their older comrades. One day he decided to bring Falcon with him.

After the servants had spread out rugs and cushions for Hamid and his retinue the soldiers took turns competing in swimming races amid the shouts and cheers of their companions. Meanwhile Falcon remained as usual at the prince's side, quietly interested in everything but excited about nothing. However when the prince undressed with his servants' help and stood poised on the bank, his supple muscular body magnificent to see, the boy took off his own clothes and as Hamid waded into the lake Falcon took his place at the edge of the water — a slender, clean-limbed adolescent figure.

"Come on in, Falcon," urged the prince, already immersed. "Come on, jump in. I'll hold you up."

But Falcon, who always obeyed the prince's every command, shook his curly ringlets, then turned and as fast as his lame leg would permit dashed off toward the rocky cliff.

"Where's he going?" wondered the prince, puzzled. Maybe he was afraid of being sucked under water and has run off to hide? But that was simply not in his character. He wasn't afraid of anything and if the prince asked him to he'd even throw himself into a fire with no hesitation.

For a moment all eyes remained fixed on the spot where Falcon had disappeared into the shrubbery. Then someone shouted, "There he is!" Many hands quickly pointed to the top of the cliff, where a slim silhouette now stood out against the sky.

Hamid felt a shudder of fear. The child couldn't be thinking of diving into deep water from that height, could he? He'd kill himself. "Falcon," he called. "Falcon, what are you trying to do?"

But the boy, standing with his arms spread wide as if about to take flight, leaped into the void, legs together and extended straight behind him, back arched in a perfect swan dive. Then the youthful body described a graceful arc into a head-first descent with arms coming forward and hands joining to break the water without a single splash. He swam a few lengths under water and then surfaced further out, shaking his wet hair away from his laughing face.

"Falcon, who taught you to dive like that?" shouted the prince, reaching him with a few strokes.

"I don't know, my lord. I don't know!" replied the boy in a lilting voice. "Did you like it, my lord? Tell me you liked it!"

The prince's response was to reach out his arms to hug him but Falcon wriggled free and headed off toward the opposite shore. Hamid tried to catch up, but couldn't. The boy was faster than he was and after waiting for Hamid at the white limestone point, he eluded him once more, laughing and slipping away. The prince, after a few more attempts to grab the lively agile body, finally gave up and shouting to the boy to go ahead and amuse himself, returned to the shore and stretched out on the grass.

He felt happy and sad at the same time. It pleased him to discover his beautiful child as skilled at swimming as he was on horseback — clear proof he'd had a proper aristocratic upbringing. And although the matter of birth or anything else was by now irrelevant to the older man's love for the boy, these things were always one more source of pride added to the joy of posssession. But he also realized that if the child had such a good time in the water it was partly because he could revert to the agile and harmonious movements natural to him, movements he couldn't achieve on land because of the defective leg. The broken wing was not completely healed, and his Falcon suffered from it.

A shadow blocked the sun and a shower of droplets touched his hot body. The child knelt beside him, watching him with a broad smile.

"My lord, my handsome lord!" And he ran his fingers through Hamid's thick beard now sprinkled with water drops. "Were you afraid your Falcon would fly away forever?"

Hamid put an arm around the boy's wet shoulders.

"Yes, my Falcon. I really was afraid you were spreading your wings to fly away. And maybe some day you really will."

But the child didn't hear. He had already broken free of the prince's embrace to run and dive into the water again.

A subtle change had come about in the relationship between Falcon and his lord. The boy's avid and anxious love had grown calm with the certainty of being loved in return, whereas the man's proud joy of possession was marred by worry. The only one who noticed was al-Hakim because of his vigilant paternal affection. If he had previously been apprehensive about the child, now he was concerned for Hamid, his spiritual son. The slave grown old alone without homeland or family knew that true love is always painful and he regretted that the prince, heretofore invulnerable in his superb indifference, should have to submit to love's yoke.

"Hakim, I'm worried about the child. What will become of him after I'm gone?"

"Sire, why worry over something so remote? You always say the future is in the mind of Allah. And you're still young."

"Yes, but I'm a soldier and I could die from one day to the next. What would happen to him then, so beautiful and so defenseless? I have to think about his future."

"If you really want to make a man of him Sire, send him away. For instance, you could arrange for him to spend some time with your cousin the Emir Abbas, a wise and good man. With him Falcon would be in no danger and he'd get used to not depending entirely upon you."

"No. Never." Hamid's tone was so definite, almost savage, that the old man didn't dare insist.

Two days later the impending visit of the Emir Husain ibn Ali was announced to the prince.

THE EMIR

The Emir Husain ibn Ali was a powerful man. He was related to the Grand Caliph of Baghdad through his mother, a cousin of the Prince of Believers' father-in-law. As chief of a strong coalition of tribes, he inspired both awe and fear, and he had at his disposal a formidable army and allies who were forced to be loyal. He was no soldier but his commander-in-chief was a eunuch whose fame was legendary. It was well known that this eunuch was a former enemy. Defeated in battle after strenuous resistance, he had been brought before the emir in chains. When told that his life would be spared if he submitted to mutilation and pledged absolute devotion he had accepted the offer and the emir had never had reason to complain of him.

Husain had married only once. His bride, beautiful and extremely young, was the daughter of a poor sheik. Less than a month after the wedding she had fled back to her father's house to die. Since Husain didn't care about the fugitive and his father-in-law didn't have sufficient power to avenge his daughter's death that was the end of it, and the emir returned to his natural inclinations. Inclinations that, as Butros the slave merchant well knew, were directed toward boys between the ages of eight and fifteen.

People said the poor things were kept in a state of constant terror because of the cruel caresses inflicted upon them by the emir in his frequent visits to what he called, somewhat inappropriately, his harem. Every now and then he would pick out a child and have the servants bring him to his bed, but nobody knew very much about what went on in that bed. The servants didn't talk. But after a period of time whose length was determined by the boy's physical stamina and by the major or minor satisfaction derived by the emir, the favorite — if you could call him that — would disappear without a trace and be replaced by another.

It was said that the docile and submissive ones were gradually exhausted by the exquisite sufferings prolonged by the emir's diligent affection until they were simply worn out. As for the more rebellious, some people whispered about iron rings the emir had had welded to the bedposts so the boys could be immobilized in the positions he wanted and nothing would interfere with his enjoyment of the agony he so amorously prolonged.

Otherwise the emir was a man of vast culture and refined tastes, a lover of good music and fine food. He could appreciate the smallest intervals in the chords of the four-stringed lute as they rose in a tremulous crescendo like a moan of pain, or the tenderness of a lamb kabab cooked exactly right, to rival the softness of a baby's cheek. He was an imposing figure, rather fat and always dressed with great affectation. Furthermore, although the Prophet had forbidden men to wear gold and jewelry, he was perennially bedecked with gems, his chubby fingers loaded with rings, his short neck adorned with necklaces and even his turban surmounted with a plume of fine pearls.

An expert in getting others to do what they didn't want to do, he himself was no lover of physical exertion and he liked to say the exercises he performed in bed were quite enough for him. He was also a master of deceit and intrigue, which he often practiced when there was no real need to for sheer love of such arts. And he was Hamid al-Ghazi's worst enemy.

Their two realms bordered each other, and inevitable boundary disputes had continually exacerbated their families over the course of generations. When the Umayyads were in power Husain's grandfather had had to swallow many a bitter pill and resign himself to watching his neighbor's power increase, this neighbor whose tiny realm was like a thorn in his side.

With the advent of the Abbasids Husain had gotten the best of Hamid's father, a peaceful studious man. A simple incursion had been enough to terrify him into giving up a hefty parcel of land in exchange for a precarious peace. Husain had not been able to repeat this tactic as he had intended because in the meantime Hamid had become a man and taken up arms. Thus the emir had preferred to make friends with him, especially now that the young prince was beginning to be appreciated at the court of Baghdad for his talents as a military commander. He had served the caliphs loyally in their ferocious suppression of the Shiite rebellions. Husain was now willing to wait for a more propitious moment to gain his ends.

Meanwhile he had fortified the territory seized from Hamid's father, a tract contained within the loop of a secondary branch of the river forming the natural boundary between the two states. Because of its shape and location, like a wedge driven into enemy territory, this land offered an excellent bridgehead in case of war.

Hamid went along with the game, he too waiting for the right moment to take back what was his, and in this interim both of them maintained the appearance of a cordial friendship. In this situation then, as soon as he knew Husain meant to visit him en route to pay his respects to the Grand Caliph of Baghdad, Hamid had been obliged, albeit reluctantly, to send a cortege of high ranking representatives to meet the emir, assure him that the prince was both honored and pleased at his visit and escort him with proper ceremony into the capital. The act of courtesy included a measure of prudence: the emir's spies were everywhere and it was wise to make certain he did not further widen his network of informers.

Knowing the emir, Hamid decided not to let him see Falcon. But when he told the boy an emir was coming to visit and during the entire time these guests remained he would have to stay in his apartments, Falcon was mortified. Believing he was to be excluded as unworthy to be seen by a man of such lofty rank, he was so upset that the prince, against his better judgment, gave in.

And thus it happened that as the emir descended from his palanquin, his foot in its jeweled slipper stepping carefully onto the rug spread out in his honor, the first thing to catch his practiced eye was a beautiful boy standing proud and smiling at the prince's side, in the midst of a group of prostrated dignitaries.

All day, until evening, the emir kept looking for that boy among the crowd of courtesans, but to no avail. Nor did he feel he could ask about him so soon, even though the child had aroused both his curiosity and his sensuality.

At last he spotted him during the grand ceremonial banquet. The tables had been sumptuously decorated and minor dignitaries who were not seated surrounded the diners in respectful attention. Emir Husain, enthroned in the place of honor on the prince's right, was savoring a delicious leg of mutton cooked to perfection in milk with just the right touch of seasoning and spices, when he noticed the mysterious boy standing behind them, not far from his master. He was dressed very simply in the same brown tunic he had worn in the morning, but his modest attire only accented his beauty. The light but warm coloring, the gray eyes, the shiny chestnut hair showed up clearly in the light of the torches.

The emir, who couldn't take his eyes off him, watched as the boy approached a servant, took from his hands an amphora of wine and then gracefully refilled the prince's cup. Hamid turned to thank him with a smile that seemed to the emir to clarify things and authorize a confidence that might have been offensive if the boy were a relative of the prince. He looked at the child with open admiration, protruding his thick dark lips, and reached out with one hand to take hold of Falcon's arm in a clearly insinuating grip — "My lovely cup bearer, would you mind pouring me some of your wine too? I'm already inebriated by your beauty and I wish to drink to your health."

Hamid's face darkened. But the boy had already freed himself tactfully from the unwelcome grip and was returning the amphora to the servant. "The most excellent emir would like to taste this wine. Pour him some." And he moved away.

"By Allah, Hamid, your cupbearer's manners aren't quite what they should be. But he's so beautiful we have to forgive him. Where did you find him?"

"Husain, do try this wine. It's a truly fine vintage," answered Hamid, impassive.

"What's this now? Have I asked an indiscreet question? I really didn't mean to offend either you or your pretty favorite."

"He's not my favorite."

"He's your son, perhaps? You had him by a white slave? Because he certainly has some white blood."

"He's not my son."

"Come now, Hamid. You've aroused my curiosity. Never mind all the mystery. I've seen perfectly clearly the way you look at him. Maybe now you'll begin to understand my situation and stop making those somewhat heavy-handed comments people keep reporting to me."

"Husain, shall we talk about something else?"

"As you wish. But just let me say that a boy his age, as you now know, gives far more enjoyment than a girl can offer. The woman's inferiority makes her naturally disposed to be submissive to the male. But there's a subtle pleasure to be derived from dominating a being who should be your equal. Because, you see...." And the emir launched into an erudite discussion on the different merits of the two sexes in passive love. The dignitaries listened respectfully but his host was barely able to conceal his aversion.

Fortunately at that point the dancing girls made their entrance. The tables were removed, the floors swept and the dignitaries and noble guests stretched out on divans to admire the dancers' skillful contortions to the sound of pipes and lutes. When previously selected beauties came and sat beside the men, often in groups of two or three, the music became more languid, new nectars were poured and the evening degenerated into an orgy. But if the emir had hoped to take advantage of the confusion to get his hands on the mysterious child, he was disappointed. Earlier in the evening, after a nod from the prince to Ahmed, Falcon had left the festivities.

The morning after, a grand parade was held. Hamid's finest troops filed past the guests and showed off in picturesque drills and maneuvers, along with the emir's personal guards. Falcon had prepared for the great day with such joyful impatience that once again Hamid didn't have the heart to disappoint him.

Sitting straight in the saddle on his purebred Arabian, wearing his simple brown tunic edged in gold, the boy rode beside the prince's banner and after the military drills he performed a solo number consisting of a series of elegant progressions in which rider and horse became as one. The emir, carried away in ecstatic appreciation, applauded at length and wanted to see the exercise repeated. Finally he asked Hamid if he might personally congratulate the boy. After the events of the night before the prince would have gladly dispensed with such an encounter, but he motioned to Falcon, who bounded off his horse, handed the reins to Ahmed and came up to bow down before the two rulers.

"Falcon, the most excellent Emir Husain ibn Ali al-Gilani has done you the honor of admiring your horsemanship."

"Falcon! " exclaimed the emir, graciously extending his hand to the boy to bid him to rise. "A pretty name and it suits you well. You are indeed proud as a falcon and I would wager sweet as a dove when you want to be. And you are uncommonly beautiful."

"My lord, the beauty is in your eyes, not in your humble servant."

It was the perfect response and Hamid smiled proudly to himself. But the smile gave way to a frown when he saw how the emir kept hold of both of Falcon's hands, fondling them greedily and moving his fingers past the slender wrists up the boy's arms, paying no mind to the discomfort he was causing.

"All right, Falcon, you can go now. You must be tired. Ahmed, take Prince Falcon to his apartments."

"Why send him away, Hamid?" protested the emir. "I'd prefer he sat here with us."

"I don't prefer it," answered the prince crisply.

"Oh come now, Hamid, don't be so quick to take things the wrong way. And stop being so mysterious about your pretty boy. You call him prince but I've found out all about him. He's a simple slave Butros unloaded on you for a bargain price because he was in such a sorry state. I admit you've got a good eye. On the other hand my imbecile of an overseer, who saw him before you did, told me he didn't like the boy."

"Maybe it was the other way around and the boy didn't like him. It seemed his finger was somewhat indigestible."

The emir laughed good naturedly. "I know about that too. I like you, Hamid, because you say what you mean without thinking twice. And I too will speak frankly. You have to maintain a strong army with all the enemies you've got, both here and in Baghdad." He paused to let the thinly veiled threat sink in. "And armies are expensive. I'm offering you a chance to make a killing. Whatever price you want for the boy — I'll pay it. Just name the figure."

"He's not for sale."

"Listen Hamid, be reasonable. It's not just a question of price. You don't mean you'd sacrifice a solid friendship just to hold on to a little slave boy who won't be worth anything in a few years? Of course he's a beauty now — this I grant you, but he'll never be a useful slave for hard work or warfare, and once his beard and mustache sprout you'll have no choice but to take him back to Butros for that little operation you so wanted to avoid."

"Husain, you are my guest and I would greatly regret having to escort you back to the border to measure the length of your sword against mine."

The emir, however, had decided not to take offense. "For goodness sake! I wouldn't think of it. I'm a man of peace. I'm no warrior. You'd run me through like a chicken on a spit. For Allah's sake, think it over! Today you refuse a good price for the boy and tomorrow you might be forced to part with him for nothing."

"That day will never come."

"Really Hamid, are you that sure?" said the emir. This time he was not smiling.

The next day, the last one of Husain's visit, the program included an outing at the lake. From the morning of the previous day contingents of servants had been busy setting up huge tents on the bank, putting down rugs and fashioning huts out of branches to shelter the soldiers of the two rulers' escorts. They had even planted blooming rosebushes interspersed among the vegetation to render the view yet more delightful. The cooks had prepared overflowing baskets of the most refined delicacies and the musicians were ready with their instruments. Dancing girls and jugglers would add to the spectacle and the finale would consist of swimming races between the soldiers.

This time Falcon, edgy and anxious as if he sensed the tension in the air, had asked the prince to leave him at home.

"My lord, I don't like the way that man looks at me. If you don't mind, I'd rather not come."

But the emir had specifically requested Falcon's presence and it would have been a serious breach of courtesy to ignore his desire.

"My child, I'd like nothing better than to leave you here. But the emir would be offended and I can't afford to make an enemy out of him. Try to stay well away from him and since I'll have to remain close to him, keep your distance from me as well."

"From you, my lord?"

"Yes. Make an effort to be patient — it's only for a few hours. Don't let yourself be separated from Ahmed for any reason. And try to stay in the midst of my guards. They're all boys you know well and they're devoted to you. As long as you stay with them no harm will come to you."

"What harm could come to me here with you in your court?"

Hamid didn't reply. The boy's faith in his invincibility and omnipotence was too sweet to lose. Thus he limited himself to repeating his admonitions and then left to conduct the emir to the designated place with the appropriate pomp and ceremony.

The first part of the morning went well. The emir, who seemed to be in excellent humor, admired the beauty of the rustic site, praised the mimes and dancing girls and then, upon Hamid's invitation, signaled the start of the swimming races. Among his guards Husain had a number of excellent swimmers, trained in the vast artificial lake on whose banks his fabulous palace was located. They bested Hamid's men with ease. One of them, a Parthian about thirty years old, a sinister brutal-looking heavily-muscled man, kept winning prize after prize. He swam with a powerful thrust of arms and torso that catapulted him forward while his legs doubled up to take their turn in driving him ahead. The emir gloated while Hamid hid his disappointment so as not to add to his men's humiliation. Falcon, obeying instructions, remained apart among the prince's guards with the vigilant Ahmed by his side and gave no sign of wanting to enter the water. The emir, who had been waiting for this very thing, finally decided to ask: "Hamid, doesn't your pretty boy know how to swim?"

"He can swim but you can see he doesn't feel like it today."

"Would you tell him to take a little dip for me? I'd like to see how he manages in the water."

"You'd like to see him in the nude," thought Hamid with rage. But the duties of courtesy and in part also the desire to show off his boy's other skill prompted him to give in to the emir's wishes.

"Falcon!"

The boy was there in an instant.

"Falcon, would you like to demonstrate a dive for our guests?"

"If you wish me to, my lord."

"All right, let's see a little of what you can do."

The emir was waiting, looking forward to the spectacle. But Falcon moved a few steps away, stretched lazily, then without even taking off his tunic headed toward the cliff, followed by Ahmed and two soldiers.

"Too bad he limps," observed the emir, watching him. "What's wrong with his leg?"

"A badly set fracture."

"And nothing can be done? This decreases his value."

"My doctor could get the leg back in shape at any time. But it doesn't matter to me."

"You're right Hamid. You're quite right. The leg has no importance. The boy wasn't made to walk but to lie between silk sheets on a golden bed."

"Husain, you're a filthy old goat."

"Ah my dear friend, nobody values you for your tact. But I'm not in the mood to quarrel — it's too hot. And where has the boy gone? He's nowhere in sight."

"You'll see him soon enough."

Everyone was waiting. The prince's men, anticipating the surprise, smiled happily now that someone was going to win a point for them. The emir's men assumed an attitude of insolent indifference.

"There he is — up there!" came a chorus of shouts.

The emir raised his eyes and saw the naked boy on the top of the rock, waving to the prince. "What's he doing? He's not going to dive from up there? He can't do that."

Hamid did not answer. And in the silence of the sun-drenched noontime Falcon leaped forward into his swan dive, coming down to enter the water directly in front of the prince and the emir. He surfaced and set off for the far bank where Ahmed had rushed to await him. The avid eyes of the emir hardly got a glimpse of the beautiful antique ivory-colored body before attentive hands quickly wrapped it in soft towels.

A few minutes later, ignoring the excited comments around him, Falcon, still wrapped in a towel, barefoot and with wet ringlets dripping onto his neck, was back on the sidelines among the soldiers. But his eyes gazed from afar with such melancholy that finally the prince could resist no longer and beckoned to him. He came quickly and sat down on the ground on the side of Hamid where the emir couldn't see him. Every once in a while he leaned his face against the prince's knee as if that contact reassured him.

"There's no doubt," said the emir, "that your boy is unbeatable as far as diving is concerned. I've never seen anyone dive like that. But as for swimming, you'll have to admit you haven't a single man who can even see my Mansur's heels in a race."

Hamid remained silent.

"You know, don't you Hamid, that among my vices I also have a passion for gambling. I'm ready to bet anything at all that not one of your men can outswim Mansur."

"I won't bet because you are quite right," said the prince. "I can recognize merit when I see it. Your Mansur is unbeatable."

He felt a light touch on his arm. It was Falcon.

"My lord, accept the emir's challenge. I'll race Mansur."

"Come, come my child. You're too young to compete against that man. You've seen what an excellent swimmer he is. And he's twice your size.'

"My lord, take the bet. I know I can beat him."

The emir had heard. He laughed: "Hamid, the challenge has been accepted. Our two champions are going to compete. And what shall we wager? I warn you I'm not one to bet unless the stakes are high."

Hamid was looking for a way out. He wouldn't contradict his boy for anything in the world, but he knew the bet was lost from the start. What could he possibly offer the Emir that wasn't too painful to lose?

"Hurry up, Hamid. Name your terms."

"Husain, why not let them race simply as a point of honor? Falcon is hardly more than a child. It's an unequal match."

"Why no, my dear friend. Your pretty Falcon is an arrogant little pup who needs to be taught a lesson. I'd like to teach him one myself — a most sweetly pleasant one. What do you say to betting your boy against my river lands?"

It was an unbelievable proposition but Hamid gave no sign of surprise. The lost lands were always in his thoughts — they were his life's primary goal. Only by winning back that territory could he assure the safety of his realm. But he did not hesitate for an instant, and he would not have hesitated if the odds had been in his favor.

"The boy cannot be the object of a bet."

And the young body, which had tensed at the emir's words, relaxed against his side.

"All right, all right, the boy is off limits. I won't insist. But I maintain my offer of the river lands. You could put up an equal extension of territory, measured out on both sides of my present parcel."

Hamid felt his blood run cold. Doubling his original loss of territory would be like inviting the enemy into his house. In case of war he'd be rendered defenseless. But he couldn't refuse a second time. With his usual astuteness the emir had trapped him.

"Now, now Hamid, don't be a poor sport. The boy is dearer to your heart than your lands are and this I understand. I'm willing to be satisfied with a lesser prize. But you must admit it's an even-handed bet."

"I accept the terms. Your river lands, or rather the lands you took away from my father, against an equal area of my territory." And he felt as if he were announcing by decree the official end of his own rule.

"As they are today," said the emir. "With all their fortifications and other existing structures."

"Certainly. And the same goes for you."

"Two weeks to evacuate you subjects."

"Agreed."

At that point Falcon touched his arm. "My lord," he whispered in the prince's ear, "I have to talk to you."

Falcon got up and went off toward the group of the prince's soldiers. Already informed about the terms of the bet, they were exchanging comments in dismay and disbelief. The child really thought he could beat a man who had proved himself stronger than all of them? And the prince was accepting a bet whose stakes were so high he'd be ruined if he lost?

Meanwhile Hamid had excused himself with the emir on the pretext of giving instructions about the race and had caught up with Falcon, followed by Hassan and Ahmed, each one more worried than the other.

But Falcon was calm. "Don't worry, my lord. I won't lose your lands. But listen carefully because this is important. I can win but only under certain conditions. First, it has to be a two-course race — from here to the white rock on the far bank, and back. We can both use whatever stroke we want. The winner must first touch the white rock with any part of his body — any part at all, this is very important —

then make it back here and be first to touch the edge of the point marked by the judges. Make sure you pick honest men you can trust."

The boy spoke with an assurance and authority the prince had not seen him demonstrate before.

"And then listen, my lord. That Mansur is a treacherous man. You'll see. He'll jump in the water before the starting signal and block my way. Our side will object but don't ask for a second start. And don't worry if he touches the white rock before I do. I'll pass him on the way back. The dangerous moment will be when the winner is proclaimed, if he isn't the winner. Then, if I'm right about him, he'll go after me and try to drown me or strangle me. I don't know which. So Ahmed has to be waiting at the finish line ready to dive in and help me if necessary, because that man is much stronger than I am and I couldn't hold out against him for very long. But here also my lord, absolutely nothing should be done before the winner is proclaimed, no matter what. We musn't give the emir a pretext for annulling the race. I couldn't beat Mansur twice."

His confidence was touching to see. All those precautions were useless because there was simply no way the boy could win. The only thing that mattered in all this was that some-one should be ready to rush to his aid, more likely because of a sudden weakness on Falcon's part than an attack by the Parthian.

"Sire," said Hassan, "if you approve, I'd like to be the one to come to Prince Falcon's aid if necessary. That man is very big and very strong and only someone of equal weight can best him in the water. Ahmed is too young."

"Very well, Hassan, you'll be the one to wait at the finish line. But keep your eyes open. If something should happen to the boy...."

Falcon took his hand, smiling. "Don't worry about me, my dearest lord. You'll see — you're going to get your lands back."

Hamid returned to the emir with a heavy heart, although his face betrayed no emotion. He was pained not only at the prospect of his own irreparable loss, but also at the thought of the boy's inevitable humiliation once he realized what a disaster his rashness had brought about.

Together he and the emir drew up meticulously detailed rules for the race, with the prince insisting upon all the points recommended by Falcon, even though he himself didn't think they mattered at all. The finish line was marked on the stone landing, and four officers were chosen as judges, men who could be trusted as both competent and objective. Two would take up their positions at the finish line, two on the opposite bank by the white rock. A wide band of the shore was cleared of spectators, but since Hamid wanted the captain of his guards at the finish line the same right was accorded to the captain of the emir's guards. Soldiers and dignitaries watched from a certain distance, the prince's men quiet and anxious, the emir's cheerful and insolent. At last the two contestants appeared, naked except for narrow strips of cloth wound low on their waists and passing between their legs to tie at one side. They took their places at the edge of the lake ready for the starter's signal.

If Falcon and his master seen together formed a complementary balance between the dark vigor of the one and the luminous grace of the other, the contrast between these two contestants was quite a different matter. Massive, powerful, broad-shouldered, muscled like a wrestler, Mansur, with his flat face, heavy mustache, and round hawk-like eyes, seemed to completely overwhelm his adversary, whose still-slender and smooth limbs barely suggested the delicate play of the muscles. The boy's head held high with its crown of chestnut ringlets and the tense and serious look on his handsome face further accented the difference between them.

Hamid, watching beside the emir, heard his voluptuous sigh and almost missed the starting signal. Just as Falcon had predicted, the judge had not yet lowered his hand before the Parthian was slicing through the water, veering decisively to his right where the boy, who had dived in at the signal, had to slow down in order not to be hit in the face. Shouts of protest rose from the prince's men — "False start! Cancel! Start over! Foul!" But Hamid raised his hand for silence and the race continued.

The two competitors headed straight for the white rock on the opposite bank. The child, constantly hampered by the water the Parthian kept splashing violently in his face, was struggling to find his pace and losing ground. If Hamid had allowed himself a moment's hope because of Falcon's confidence, he now felt his heart turn to stone as he helplessly watched the accomplishment of his own ruin.

Monitored by the two judges, Falcon and Mansur touched the rock, the Parthian ahead by a good many seconds. But already the turn brought the first surprise. As his adversary stretched forward to touch the stone with his hand and then reversed his course clumsily, losing his rhythm, the boy, still some distance away, dived completely under, reversing direction in one clean fluid somersault that brought his legs out of the water and then, pushing off with his feet against the rock, started back without losing a single stroke.

Little by little with an irresistible momentum Falcon was shortening Mansur's lead. The slight body was fully extended, the head under water, emerging only the instant necessary to breathe, the legs in a strong alternating kick, each arm in turn starting its stroke well back in a graceful dripping curve to reach forward and slice through the water in front, fingers together and slightly cupped. His light weight and the coordination of his movements worked to his advantage. By now the prince's men were on their feet cheering, while the emir's retainers watched in shocked silence.

Falcon touched the finish line with a comfortable lead over the Parthian. At that moment just as the judge proclaimed the winner and all eyes were on the boy, who was panting lightly and clutching the stone landing with one hand, Mansur came up behind him. Quickly diving back into the water, he grabbed Falcon's leg and pulled him under, forcing him toward the bottom with all his weight.

Sudden as it was, this was the move they had expected and the boy had barely disappeared before Hassan plunged into the lake with his dagger between his teeth. But neither he nor the others had foreseen that by sheer bad luck the Parthian had gotten hold of Falcon's lame leg. The pain was so acute the boy half fainted and sank like a stone, his mouth open in a cry that ended in a gurgle. With two strokes Hassan reached Mansur and planted the dagger in his back. Then he pushed him aside with all his strength, dived straight into the depths, grabbed the boy's hair — he was already at the bottom — and brought him to the surface.

Of all the hands reaching out to receive him, the quickest were those of the prince. Falcon, who gave no sign of life, was picked up by his feet and held upside down while Hassan slapped him on the back until he began to vomit the water he had swallowed. As soon as he began breathing again, they laid him on the grass and Hamid held him against his knee with his torso elevated. Every once in a while he struggled to vomit more water, then fell back against the sustaining arm. The prince was bending over him so intently he didn't notice the emir standing behind him avidly watching the boy.

His eyes feasted on every detail of Falcon's exposed nakedness, even sweeter in its helpless abandon: the limp arms and legs, the head thrown back, the throbbing throat, the bloodless face, the slightly parted lips, the eyes rolled inward to reveal a glimpse of white between lashes dripping with water and tears.

Suddenly conscious of that oppressive stare, Hamid turned his own eyes away from Falcon's face and said through clenched teeth: "Husain if the boy dies, not a single one of you will get out of here alive."

"But Hamid, I'm as grieved as anyone at what has happened. Would I wish for the death of such a beautiful creature? If you want my apologies, I offer them without reserve. And you," he bellowed to his soldiers, "fish that carcass out of the water!" He pointed to the Parthian's body floating with the dagger stuck in its back in the center of a spreading red stain. "Drag it out and throw it to the dogs!"

Meanwhile Falcon was beginning to revive. "My lord," he murmured as soon as he could speak, "my lord, you have your lands back."

"I should never have wanted them at this price."

The two of them gazed at each other so absorbed as to block out any awareness of the emir looking on, his dark tumid lips protruding.

"Yes indeed," Husain was thinking. "Yes, you've regained your territory and kept your pretty boy as well. But that's not the end of it, Hamid my friend. You haven't heard the last of all this."

Prince Harazad

The emir's departure was a relief for everyone, but he seemed to have left a long shadow behind him. Hamid knew he had made an enemy and a powerful one at that. Whereas the rivalry between them had once been concealed and undeveloped, it was now certain that Husain was actively plotting against him at the court of the Caliph. He would have to prepare for all eventualities: reinforce his frontiers, further improve his army, make sure his allies could be counted upon.

"Hakim, during the course of the coming year I intend to make an inspection tour of all my borders. I'd like to take Falcon with me. The boy rides very well. But we'll have to do some mountain climbing. It's unavoidable."

"He can't do it, Sire. His leg won't hold up."

"But if I leave him at home he'll be lonely and irritable. He's already badly shaken up by the emir's visit. He's having nightmares again and I often see him turn around suddenly and look over his shoulder as if he were afraid of an attack from behind."

"Sire, palace life is too easy for a boy going on fourteen."

"I understand that as well as you, but I don't know what to do about it, Hakim. We saw what happened at the lake — with that lame leg Falcon will always be an invalid. I feel for him. You told me once it might be possible to attempt an operation."

"Yes, but I also said it would be risky and painful. I'm not willing to take the responsibility."

"Very well. We'll let him decide."

When they discussed the possibility with Falcon he didn't hesitate for a moment. The mere idea of operating on his defective leg filled him with joy. The pain didn't matter, the risk didn't matter, even the long period of forced immobility didn't matter.

"Just so you don't go away and leave me, my lord. I'll be satisfied if you promise to spend at least an hour with me every day — no, make it two hours."

And so Hamid postponed his border inspection in order to keep Falcon company. The boy stood the operation well and there were no complications. The callus formed rapidly and as soon as the old doctor increased the traction to separate the two ends of the tibia another callus filled in the empty space.

Falcon, who never complained, spent his time listening to al-Hakim's stories about the prince's childhood or playing chess with dignitaries who came to visit or getting Ahmed, who was almost always at his side, to relate all the minor events at court. But it was only when Hamid appeared and sat down beside him and held his hand that Falcon really seemed to revive. The prince gave him far more than the promised two hours a day and between them there was no need even for words.

When, after two months, al-Hakim decided the leg had reached its desired length, he removed the complicated apparatus designed to hold it rigid and Falcon took his first steps. It was clear at once that the operation had succeeded. Mad with joy, the child stood before his master in his renewed physical integrity. Now Hamid finally understood how painful it had been for Falcon to be an invalid, and he felt a pang of remorse at the blindness of his own egoism. It took two more months of exercises, massage and gradual training in walking, running and jumping before al-Hakim declared the boy ready to accompany the prince on his trip.

But their departure was again postponed because of a disturbing event that might well have been even more serious. The Emir Husain maintained a network of spies, but Hamid also had informers, and through them he learned the emir was planning a raid to kidnap the child everyone believed to be the prince's favorite.

The raid was to be carried out by mercenaries who would not compromise the emir if they failed in their mission. The plan had been developed with great care and certainly with the complicity of local elements. It was known that the only place Falcon ever went without his master was the lake. He liked to swim and the doctor had prescribed swimming as a good way to develop the muscles of the mended leg. Thus he went often to the lake with a small escort, particularly now that the prince was busy getting things ready for the trip. Besides, since this place was so near the palace and so far from the frontier, it was considered secure.

It was also known the boy usually dived from the top of the cliff and habitually climbed up there accompanied by two or three soldiers. Thus the plan was for a first group of armed men to wait hidden in the bushes along the path, then jump out and seize Falcon as he passed, while a second group charged out of the woods and massacred his escort. No one would know about the raid for several hours and meanwhile the kidnappers would have fled by mountain trails and forced their way through the pass at the border. They were sure the surprise as well as the intervention of the emir's soldiers would render the crossing an easy one. The latter would justify their actions by claiming they'd been unable to distinguish friends from enemies before the marauders got away.

Hamid studied the situation at length with Hassan and his officers. They agreed it was best the raid should be attempted in order to expose the emir, and they tried to figure out the best way to thwart it. There was a white boy among the prince's lowest ranking slaves who was about Falcon's age and looked enough like him to fool the raiders from a certain distance. Since his hair was too blond they darkened it with a mixture of henna and walnut shells and then dressed him in one of Falcon's brown and gold tunics. They promised to exempt the slave boy from backbreaking labor in the fields and train him instead as a household servant and Ahmed swore he'd stay by his side just as he would with Falcon. The boy willingly agreed to play his part as well as he could.

Thus the marauders, thinking they were mounting a surprise attack, were themselves the victims of surprise. All were killed except for two who were captured alive and brought to the prince for questioning. Subject to the worst kind of torture, they admitted what was already known — that it was indeed the emir who had hired them but they refused to name their accomplices at court. There was nothing more to do but hang their horribly mutilated bodies in the main square of the capital in the hope of discouraging further treason.

The danger averted did not disturb Falcon, calmly sure as he was of his master's omnipotence. But for Hamid the event was cause for intense concern. Although he did not feel it was appropriate to accuse Husain openly, everyone knew he was the instigator of the failed kidnapping and thus the emir's original capricious desire had turned into a bitter grudge involving his personal prestige.

It was therefore necessary for the realm's defenses to be more alert and ready than ever before. As soon as possible Hamid left with Falcon and an ample escort for the lengthy tour of border inspections.

The journey enriched and completed the bond between them. The long horseback rides, the nights in a tent or in the open under the stars, the mountain climbing, the visits to isolated garrisons, all gave Falcon a clearer view of his master's real world — a man's world — and acquainted him with the principality itself.

The prince's tiny state was defended on the north by a mountain range completely impassable except for a single rough trail to the top. There it crossed the mountain pass at the border and continued down the other side through the aforementioned lands ruled by the Emir Husain. Of course the pass was well guarded by two opposing forts and their respective garrisons, who eyed each other with mutual distrust. Where the mountains sloped down to the west the river marked the frontier between the two states and it was there that the disputed land, now returned to its legitimate ruler, was located.

To the south in the arid and thinly populated plain lived a number of warlike tribes whose sheiks were loyal to the Abbasid sovereign. But since the Umayyads had never bothered them they had remained on good terms with Hamid, and therefore presented no danger.

To the east lay an area under the influence of the prince's cousin, the Emir Abbas, who was sincerely fond of Hamid and lived in peace with everyone, his strength reinforced by the Grand Caliph's protection.

Hamid and his escort scaled the most difficult peaks, followed the whimsical twists and turns of the meandering river, strengthening the fortifications along its banks, conversed amicably and at length with the sheiks of the plain and stayed for a while as guests of the prince's cousin Abbas. He welcomed them cordially and was quickly won over by Falcon's beauty and gentility — although in his own mind he interpreted the prince's evident love for the child in the most obvious way. On the last day of their trip before turning the horses toward the central plateau on which the capital was situated, Hamid took Falcon to see the precipice.

The bluff, called simply the precipice, was a wild and lonely place in the midst of the mountains, straddling the border between Hamid's and Abbas' lands. The side belonging to Hamid was a bare rock wall that plunged straight down into the ravine, whereas the opposite and lower side was covered with vegetation. A stream fed by mountain springs cascaded from the highest point in a series of waterfalls like a silver ribbon and disappeared into a chasm that no one had ever explored.

One bold adventurer had made an attempt to lower himself into it tied to a strong rope. His companions had seen him lose his balance and plummet headlong. His body, sucked into the waters of the abyss, had never been found and when they pulled the rope back up it was neatly severed at the end. Instead of attributing the tragic accident to friction between the rope and a jagged projecting rock, people began to whisper that the *djinns,* the genies of the place, had cut the rope to punish the daredevil for attempting to violate their domain. This gave rise to the legend that the precipice held a mystery beyond the reach of mortal understanding.

Actually the place itself justified the legend. The rocky summits towering above it from one side, the waterfall vanishing into dark depths that exhaled the cold breath of the abyss, the underground stream swallowed up by the ravine to reappear again only at great distance — and never known to give back any object that fell into it — all this added to its terrible fascination.

The precipice made an overwhelming impression on Falcon. The prince, who had led him right up to the edge, with an arm around his waist for fear of a false step, felt him shudder violently and when he looked into his eyes he saw the dizzying pull of the abyss and quickly drew the boy back and pressed his face against his own chest.

"Falcon, what are you scared of? Falling?"

"No, no, I wasn't scared. It was different, like somebody was calling me...."

"Who?"

"I don't know."

"But what did you hear?"

"Nothing. I don't know. I was thinking...thinking if anyone jumped off — they'd never find his body. It would be like he never even existed."

That night Falcon slept badly, thrashing about and talking in his sleep, as if answering a mysterious voice. In fact, although his physical strength was restored, the boy still had the peculiar sensitivity that made him react unpredictably to things he alone understood. It pained the prince because it seemed as if Falcon were withdrawing from him to a place where he had no right to follow. Then Hamid would wonder if perhaps the only thing keeping this child in a world so alien to him was his love for the prince, that love whose secret cause he himself would never know.

Once during the trip, in the intimacy of the tent, he had asked him: "Falcon, don't you remember anything about the past? I'd so like to know where you came from, where you're going."

"No, I don't remember anything at all, my lord. But what difference does it make where I come from? And as far as where I'm going, you'll be with me so that doesn't matter either. I told you I'd never fly away by myself, like your other falcon, the real one."

And as the boy settled down to sleep, the prince thought again about the poor little falcon who had not flown away. But this falcon, this one, he'd be able to defend.

As he looked at the boy, so trustfully sleeping there at his side, he felt a pang of joy tinged with melancholy. Because deep in his heart he had even hoped some day this love might give him the physical satisfaction all human love tends to bestow and now he knew such a thing would never be. The boy was his — he belonged to him as no other being had ever belonged to him, but the terms of ownership were not earthly ones. Thus it may happen that a bird comes down momentarily from its domain in the sky and lands beside us. And we watch it, happy to have it so close but wishing to touch it, hold it in our hands. Yet we know if we reach out for it a flutter of wings will carry it far away — and the only way to possess it is to kill it.

Someone had told Prince Harazad about Falcon.

Hamid's son had always been a problem for his father. Even as a little boy he rebelled against all authority and if he was forced to obey he did so with a show of hatred astonishing in a child. The prince had sought qualified preceptors for him but all had failed, one after another. He had sent him to stay with his cousin Abbas, hoping the tranquil atmosphere of the small court would have a benign influence on the boy, but Abbas had sent him home after a week, saying he was quite ready to do anything for the prince except take that little viper into his household.

The best solution would have been to have him brought up in the court of Baghdad, so as to assure him the good will of the caliph, but in that nest of intrigues no one could be trusted. Finally Hamid, having exhausted his own meager patience, and realizing his son was no longer a child, had simply left him to the mother who idolized him, providing generously for his support and giving him a numerous retinue of soldiers and servants. But Harazad soon dismissed all of these, preferring to surround himself with men of his own choosing. Hence the contact between father and son had been reduced to brief perfunctory visits and to religious observances during which the young prince participated at Hamid's side, in his role as heir to the throne.

It was an acceptable compromise. Harazad put up with it, dreaming of the day when everything would belong to him, and Hamid worried as little as possible about this single regrettable problem of his life. But then someone made a point of telling Prince Harazad about Falcon.

It was a beautiful morning and Falcon was practicing archery with a group of soldiers in a meadow behind the palace.

"Prince Falcon!" said Ahmed as he carried out an order to move the framework with the target further back and secure it to a tree. "Prince Falcon! I bet you can't hit the bull's eye from this distance."

"We'll see about that." Falcon picked up his bow, carefully tested the tension of the bowstring, chose an arrow and nocked it. The soldiers, all boys under twenty, drew back to watch the shot, when the sound of a racing gallop made them turn to look.

From the edge of the meadow a horseman dressed all in white and riding a white horse was approaching at full speed. A plume of white feathers adorned his turban and as he came closer they could see the sparkle of his silver-encrusted saddle. Even the riding crop, which delivered sporadic angry blows to the sides of his mount, had a jeweled handle that glittered in the sun. Although he was headed directly toward them, the young men watched with more curiosity than fear. The first to cry out in alarm was Ahmed, when he saw the horseman, now a mere fifty paces away, turn and aim straight for the slender figure of Falcon standing alone in the middle of the meadow. For an instant it seemed as if the boy would be trampled by the furiously galloping horse, but a few paces away the animal instinctively veered aside and the rider pulled him up and stopped him, scattering bits of earth and grass all around.

Falcon hadn't moved. His gray eyes encountered the rider's gaze and the the two stared at each other in silence.

"Prince Harazad!" called Ahmed, getting hold of himself as he recognized him. "We didn't know...."

"Shut up, dog!" snarled the rider, snapping his whip and turning to scowl at the group of soldiers who had hastened to prostrate themselves.

Prince Harazad was a youth of about twenty, different from his father but every bit as handsome. He had the frightening grace of a cat, the same agile and silent movements. Slender but broad-shouldered, he was much lighter-skinned than Hamid — he resembled his mother. His eyes were slightly oblique, his teeth sharp and white between his thin lips and his black hair was curled in the Persian style.

No one dared to speak. The young soldiers remained bowed down in servile reverence — Hamid would not have liked this but the young prince's reputation demanded it. Only Falcon — who hadn't moved, not even when the horse's hooves had thrown up the sod in front of him — only he remained standing and watched the newcomer with a slightly furrowed brow. The other backed up his mount a few steps so he could look Falcon up and down. The horse's mouth was bloody and he was covered with sweat.

"So — if I'm not mistaken you're the so-called Prince Falcon," he said in a loud and somewhat piercing voice. "My father's latest whim — as he's gotten older it seems his preferences have changed." He spun his horse, made him do a complete turn around Falcon so as to look him over from every angle and then returned to face him.

"I can see you are indeed a pretty fellow. My father has always had good taste in picking out slaves. When he gets tired of you, as is inevitable, you can always come to my court. You'll never lack for a piece of bread in recognition for past services." He laughed sarcastically. "And even if your charms are a bit faded you can always count on the good will of some kitchen boy who'll bring you leftovers from the table."

Slowly Falcon raised the already loaded bow he had been holding in a tense and spasmodic grip, straightened his left arm, pulled back the string with his right hand, and aimed directly at Harazad's chest. Harazad neither moved nor modified his contemptuous smile.

The soldiers were paralyzed with horror. Only Ahmed made as if to throw himself between the two antagonists, but then drew back. He was too far away and such a move might precipitate things. Prince Harazad's escort, left behind by their master's furious gallop, appeared at that moment on the far edge of the meadow.

Falcon kept his arrow firmly pointed at Harazad for a bit longer, then in one motion turned, aimed at the target affixed to the tree and let the arrow go. The shaft quivered as the point sank squarely into the bull's eye. Then he took his bow in both hands, broke it across his knee, flung the two pieces in Harazad's face, ran off to where his black was grazing nearby with the other horses, leaped into the saddle and raced off at a gallop.

"Harazad, I've repeatedly told you not to come here without letting us know and to wait for permission at the border."

"Sire," said the youth, bowing again, "I thought I was coming as a son, not an enemy."

The court dignitaries, who had hurried to gather in the audience hall when they heard of the young prince's unexpected arrival, were markedly ill at ease. The soldiers escorting Harazad had been detained outside and Hamid's men stood guard at the doors. This truly did not look like the meeting of a father with his only son and heir.

"Well, you're here now, and I hope you'll enjoy your stay. How is the Princess Shirin?"

Hassan had appeared at one of the entrances with young Ahmed beside him. The prince looked at him in a questioning way. He knew his man too well not to realize he would never interrupt an interview in the audience hall, especially in the presence of the hereditary prince, unless there were a compelling reason.

"Hassan, what is it?"

"Sire," answered Hassan, bowing, "something serious has happened. Do you give me permission to speak before the most illustrious prince, your son?"

"Speak."

"Ahmed, tell our master what has happened."

The young man stepped forward, urged by a paternal hand on his shoulder, and although he trembled with emotion, his voice was steady: "My lord, we were with Prince Falcon in the meadow by the woods, to get in some archery practice...."

"Quiet, you dog and son of dogs!" shouted Harazad.

The prince turned and frowned at him.

"You be quiet. I've told him to speak. Go on, Ahmed."

As the youth told his story, Hamid's face gradually went pale with rage. When Ahmed repeated word for word the insults Harazad had addressed to Falcon the prince turned to his son with clenched fists.

"Wretch," he hissed. "I won't touch you because if I did I know I wouldn't be able to keep from breaking your back like I'd crush a venomous snake. Get out and don't ever show your face here again!"

"But Father! You treat your son like this for the sake of a lowly slave?"

"You're not my son. If you're concerned about your inheritance, don't worry. When I die my lands are yours. You're still my heir but you're no longer my son. Get out while you still have time."

Prince Harazad started to say something more but then, pale with rage himself, he spun around and without a single gesture of farewell went out. They heard his imperious voice calling his escort.

"You don't know where he went, Hassan?"

They were in the middle of the meadow in front of the target with the arrow still stuck in its center. Hamid's cavalry waited with them, the horses stamping restlessly.

"Sire, my Ahmed immediately thought to send two riders after him but our horses are no match for his black and they came back a while ago. They lost his trail in the woods."

The forest paths were too well traveled to offer any kind of valid trail.

"Where do you think he might have gone?"

"I don't know, Sire. If he was thinking of taking refuge with the Emir Abbas, who was very kind to him, he should have taken the road for the plain."

"No, I don't think he'd have gone alone to another ruler. Where do they go…the slaves who try to escape?" said Hamid with a certain effort.

"Into the marshes. I can't believe Prince Falcon would go there. He's never been there before."

"Maybe to the city?"

"No, he doesn't like the city. He doesn't know anyone and he'd never go without your lordship. And besides what would he do in the city?"

Hamid was trying desperately to think with the mind of the mortally offended and humiliated boy. He wondered what he himself would have done in Falcon's place. Run away? No, he wouldn't have known where to go. But pick up a weapon, kill himself, this, yes, he might have done. Maybe Falcon had hidden in a forest cave to die of hunger.

"Was he armed?'

"No, Sire. He only had the bow, which he left here."

Hamid looked at the broken pieces of the bow lying on the ground. Falcon was indeed still the same child who had defended himself with all his strength, scratching and biting as well as he could when his dignity was offended. And who could say what violence he had had to do to himself in order to change the target of his arrow?

"Hassan we've got to search the entire forest. Take all the men you need, line them up side by side and search every bush and every cave. All the way up the mountain."

The mountain! He had a sudden intuition. "The precipice, Hassan, the precipice!"

In his mind he saw Falcon standing at the edge of the abyss. "If anyone jumped off they'd never find his body. It would be like he never even existed...."

Even before the thought was completely formed, Hamid touched the flanks of the roan with his heels and galloped off toward the heights. His cavalry followed, interspersed at wide intervals.

There where the trees thinned out just before the summit of the mountain trail, he saw him. The slight figure stood out against the sky. Nearby the horse, left to himself, was cropping the sparse grasses.

The prince dismounted cautiously, tied the roan to a tree, and started up the trail, careful to make no noise. The boy — he could see him clearly now — stood three or four steps back from the edge of the precipice, his head held high. That solitary figure gave off an air of irrevocable finality, of destiny already accomplished, as if he no longer belonged to this world. He was perfectly motionless, but no one could tell when that motionless state would cease and the body would plunge into the void.

Hamid stopped about ten paces back, not daring to advance any further. How would Falcon react when he saw him? Shame and grief might give him the final push into nothingness.

"Falcon," he called gently, keeping his voice low. "I've been looking for you for some time. Come here."

The boy seemed not to hear but the prince thought he saw him tense up momentarily.

"Falcon, do you hear me?"

At the sound of Hamid's voice the boy turned his head just a little, as if he had finally heard. The prince didn't dare move.

"Falcon, come here!"

Slowly the boy turned around and looked at him, his eyes so wide they seemed to reflect the depth of the abyss. Now he stood facing Hamid with the precipice behind him.

"Falcon, don't you know me? It's me. Come here to me!" And he held out his arms.

But the boy moved backward, staring blankly. He was close to the edge now and he almost staggered. One false move and he'd fall.

At that point the prince dropped his arms to his sides and his voice rang out loud and imperious. "Falcon, come here at once! Obey!"

Something like a flicker of consciousness lighted up the eyes staring at him. Falcon hesitated, started to turn around, then looked back toward the prince — and now he saw him.

"Falcon! You can't do this! Come here — obey!"

The boy took an uncertain step. Hamid waited, his heart in his throat. Could he risk lunging forward to grab him? And if the boy turned around and jumped? He'd never be able to get hold of him in time — they were too far apart.

Step by step the reluctant Falcon came away from the edge of the precipice toward the prince. Once he felt secure, Hamid leaped forward and firmly gripped both his arms.

"Falcon, my Falcon, why did you want to do it?"

But the boy didn't hear him. He slipped out of the prince's hands, dropping to his knees.

"My lord," he murmured, his voice barely audible. "My lord, punish me. I shouldn't have done it. My life is yours. I've disobeyed you. Punish me."

And he collapsed on the ground.

The boy thrashed about on the prince's vast bed, struggling against the hands that tried to hold him down. The immobility of those first hours, the almost corpse-like paralysis that had afflicted him until evening had given way to violent fever and delirium. He moaned and tried to throw himself off the bed with a strength hard to believe in a boy his size, banging his head from one side to the other, and crying out in disconnected phrases. Under al-Hakim's sensitive fingers, his pulse was tense, rapid and irregular and his chest heaved convulsively from his labored breathing.

This being who had always recognized and sought the prince's hand even in his sleep now pushed it away, refusing contact with anyone. Only when he fell back exhausted between one spasm and another could they sponge his sweaty forehead, bathe his parched lips and try to get him to swallow a little sweetened water. And he constantly murmured or shouted incomprehensible phrases, words in other languages, referring to places and things from his past, forgotten sorrows and terrors that now returned as monstrous nightmares.

"Hakim, what's wrong with him? What does this fever mean?"

"Sire, as a doctor I can tell you it's a fever brought on by a conflict, by a strong emotion — it's gone to the brain and inflamed it. As the old man that I am, I would say it's his heart that's affected."

"But, Hakim, how could all this happen, simply because of a stupid vicious verbal attack?"

The old man would have liked to answer, "Hamid my son, my spiritual son, haven't you yet learned that evil words hurt only when they contain some truth? He regarded himself as your prince and all of a sudden he understood how others saw him — as a slave, and not even a noble slave taken in war, just a servant bought in the marketplace who simply because of his physical charms has risen to the dubious honor of a ruler's bed but will be dismissed tomorrow and return to his rightful destiny of following some eunuch's orders and emptying chamber pots in a harem. This is the truth that's killing him." But he did not say these cruel words. Instead he replied, "Sire, the offense was aimed precisely at what he was so proud of — your love for him."

"But why didn't he come to me? Didn't he know I'd have defended him against anyone, no matter who he was?"

And the old man again would have liked to say, "He couldn't come to you because you are the last person he wanted to see him so poor and naked. He had nothing left, he was nothing himself. And wasn't this what you wanted? Didn't you deprive him of everything that didn't come from your love so that he'd live by that love alone. Isn't that why you marked him as yours from the first day with that scar? 'Take everything away from him in order to give him everything.' You said it yourself. And when they took your love away from him he had nothing more to live for. His heart was already dead when he wished to die."

"Sire, it's useless for you to torture yourself now. You have to understand that when you called him back from the abyss he was already in death's hands. He obeyed you, he tried to tear himself out of those hands, but death is still holding on to him and doesn't want to let him go."

"But you can overcome death. You can cure him."

"Nobody can do anything without God's help. God is the Merciful One. Let us then hope." But in his heart he was thinking, "God is also the Judge."

After three days the fever went down.

"Is it a good sign, Hakim?"

The old man said nothing. The child now lay in the prince's bed without moving. The liquids lovingly poured between his lips dribbled unswallowed from his half-open mouth. His warm ivory complexion was now bluish, his eyes dull. The prince held his hands, spoke to him, caressed him, stroked his hair, now dry and opaque. The boy no longer responded.

Toward evening al-Hakim, who kept taking Falcon's pulse at intervals, raised his eyes to the prince with a look of pity. "Sire, resign yourself. The boy is dying."

"No, I won't let him." It was the voice of the man used to commanding and being obeyed. The old doctor was moved to compassion.

"Hassan, get a blanket. Put it on the stone seat outside in the garden and bring me some pillows."

Hassan, who had been constantly present in a corner of the bedroom, attentive to his master's every gesture, hurried to obey.

"Hakim, help me wrap him up so he won't catch cold."

They helped him sit down so as to hold the boy on his lap, supported by the pillows. Al-Hakim squatted on the ground nearby. He watched the stars appear one by one in the soft summer sky and he knew that when the constellations began to decline toward the western horizon, and the forces of the day ending were exhausted but the forces of the day about to begin had not yet taken over — in that moment the child would die.

Hamid too raised his face to the stars, but without seeing them.

He neither saw nor heard anything, aware of nothing but his desperate desire to save Falcon. No, he mustn't end up like the other falcon, killed by men's cruelty — no, this the prince simply would not allow. He bent over the boy, rearranged the pillows, put an arm around his shoulders to raise him up further, the child's face against his own, and covered the boy's mouth with his own mouth. He concentrated on matching his own breathing to the barely perceptible breathing of the child, so that every feeble intake of the boy's breath was augmented by his own vigorous breath, so his own vitality would penetrate the boy, warming his cold and sluggish veins, and reaching his heart, would help it to beat. In that act he infused a greater force of love than he had ever put into any carnal penetration of a woman. Once in a while he paused and looked for some sign of life in the boy's face, silently calling him with his entire soul, begging him to stop on the dark threshold and come back to him. Then he returned to his mouth to mouth respiration.

The night wore on. Hassan had fallen asleep on his feet, leaning against a column. Al-Hakim sat with his arms wrapped around his own legs, his head resting on his knees. When the stars began to descend from the zenith the old man got up and took the boy's wrist between his fingers. The heartbeat was still weak but more sustained and regular.

"My lord, you've saved him. He's going to live."

Hamid raised reddened eyes, breaking his concentration with a certain effort and looked at Falcon's face. Now it seemed subtly different — the lips firmer, the nose less sharp, the skin not quite as pale.

"Come, Sire, let's take him back to bed."

This time it was Hassan who picked up the boy and settled him in bed, aided by al-Hakim. The prince followed them, stumbling from fatigue.

"Hakim, are you sure he's out of danger?"

"Yes, Sire. Your love saved him."

The same love that had almost destroyed him, thought the old man. And maybe you, Hamid, aren't even responsible for the strength of that love. God willed it for you, whether we call him Allah or by some other name. God willed it and He alone can judge you.

They covered the child carefully. He seemed to be asleep. Hamid took one last look at him, then stumbled heavily over to the other side of the bed, collapsed face down and fell sound asleep.

At dawn the old man, who had dozed off on a stool beside the bed, roused himself and saw that the boy was awake and looking at him.

"Hakim! What are you doing here? What was wrong with me?"

"You were very ill, my child."

Falcon closed his eyes, but after a while he opened them again.

"And my lord?"

"He's here beside you, don't you see him?"

The boy made an effort to turn his head on the pillows and saw Hamid sprawled across the bed.

"Was...was he sick too?"

"No, he's just tired. He's sleeping. He watched over you for four days and four nights. He's the one who saved you."

The boy stretched out his hand to touch him but couldn't reach far enough.

"Please, could you move me closer to him?"

Al-Hakim turned him gently and moved him next to the sleeping man, where he huddled up as close as he could. For the first time in Falcon's experience that robust body of a healthy and well-groomed man gave off a stench of sweat and fatigue. He passed his hand through the prince's hair and found it rough and tangled. Hamid sensed the caress, opened his swollen eyes to look anxiously at the boy and little by little a smile of relief lighted up his tired face.

"My lord, my poor master! You wore yourself out like this for me?"

"Falcon, why did you want to leave me? Don't ever do it again."

But the words came out muffled by sleep, his eyes closed again. He made one last effort to stretch out more comfortably and the boy snuggled still closer, resting his head on his shoulder.

Al-Hakim stood looking at them for a moment, then hobbled over to the divan. His bones hurt, his head was heavy. Now he too could sleep for a while. Those two were together again and their own merciful God was watching over them.

THE LITTLE OUTCAST

For Falcon that fever marked the end of childhood. He got up from his sickbed much thinner and taller and a short time later his adolescence burst into bloom like a rose. He looked older than his fourteen years. His delicate beauty had grown prouder, his features were losing their childish roundness and the cheek with the subtle white scar now had a sharper outline. His physique was growing more robust and solid without losing its slender elegance and his manner was becoming calm and quietly confident.

His relationship with the prince gained in depth what it lost in appearance. It was less often now that he'd move close to Hamid in that anxious desire for reassuring physical contact. The time when the childish hand reached out for the dark brown fingers to close it in their strong and manly grip was past. But the beautiful gray eyes still followed the prince wherever he went and Falcon's attention was always fixed on his master.

Even the intimacy between them had changed into something more virile. They shared long rides on horseback, swimming races, mountain climbing. Sometimes when they reached a summit at dawn the two of them would sit together and silently watch the sunrise while their guards kept watch nearby.

Al-Hakim, who would have preferred not to see their relationship interfere with the development of behavior normal for a boy his age, had repeatedly insisted Hamid take Falcon with him to the harem. Reluctantly the prince finally gave in. But the fears he had never admitted to anyone, not even himself, proved groundless. Falcon behaved with his usual gentility He thanked Lailah for the joy she gave his master and when the head eunuch brought him a young girl bursting with the desire to please he paid her compliments and politely concealed his increasing boredom until Hamid, in relief as well as amusement, gave him leave to withdraw.

Thus the circle that isolated them from the rest of the world closed ever more tightly around them. And sometimes Hamid, who had never given a thought to his own future, began to worry about it for Falcon's sake. He would watch him unobserved and enjoy the spectacle of that magnificent adolescence. He'd ask himself what kind of man his Falcon would be one day, what destiny awaited him once he became independent, for despite himself the prince knew this would have to be. But even in those moments something akin to a vague premonition told him his beautiful boy so overflowing with life would never cross the threshold of manhood.

"Falcon, I'm going to Bisah this morning to see Butros the slave merchant. Do you want to come?"

He watched the boy's face to discover whether he enjoyed the prospect of showing himself in his present guise to the man who had kept him in such barbaric captiivity or whether on the contrary revisiting those places might be unpleasant.

However, as usual, Falcon seemed indifferent — he didn't care where he went as long as he was with his master.

"Yes, of course if you like, I'll come, my lord."

Hamid smiled to himself, noting once more that Falcon never said, "Could I do this? Should I do that?" But always, "Would you mind if I did this? Would you like me to do that?" His total unconditional obedience was a free gift on equal terms, not the duty owed by an inferior to his superior. The prince liked this kind of pride; it confirmed the innate nobility he had seen from the first day when Falcon was only a poor mistreated child for sale to the highest bidder.

"You know, Falcon, our dear al-Hakim is getting older. He gets tired now looking for herbs in the mountains and watching over his alembics. The servant I gave him helps with physical chores but isn't capable of learning Hakim's art. I'd like to find him an intelligent, willing and well-brought-up youth he could educate in his own way. Let's go see if Butros has someone right for him."

When Hamid and Falcon, accompanied by their escort, dismounted before his emporium Butros, bowing deeply in obsequious reverence, could have bitten his hands as he recognized the handsome adolescent standing there proudly in his simple brown tunic beside the the magnificently dressed prince. This then was the little boy he had wanted to castrate two years before. What sort of magic had the prince resorted to to tame that little rebel? One had only to look at the boy (which Butros attempted to do surreptitiously) to read in his eyes the adoration he held for his master, a feeling clearly mutual. Oh well, of course. The two didn't have to be touching and making eyes at each other for anyone to see what held them together, quite simply a vigorous mature man's feeling for a pretty submissive boy. While it lasts! And Butros made a mental note to talk to the prince's overseer and let him know, should the occasion arise, that he'd be quite willing to buy back the merchandise at a good price.

As he mulled over these thoughts, Butros stood listening respectfully to his noble client's request. Meanwhile Falcon, a little bored, remained in the doorway, guarded by Ahmed and the escort and watched the activity of the marketplace with a certain curiosity.

Suddenly he noticed a small cart approaching. It was loaded with sacks of legumes and drawn not by a donkey, but by a skinny little half-naked boy about thirteen. He was completely covered with bruises and scars, some new, some old, and tied to the shafts with a sort of harness of leather and canvas straps. A dark bony man walked beside him, cracking a whip every now and then and urging the boy on with shouts and curses. Not far from where Falcon was standing the man called out an angry, *"And-ak!"* to stop the cart and since its downhill momentum made it impossible for the child to obey, the man himself, still bellowing and cursing, grabbed hold of the wheels. The cart finally came to a halt and the poor human beast of burden collapsed between the shafts, while the other unloaded some of the sacks and went in to negotiate with the shopkeeper to whom they were being delivered.

Falcon watched in horror. At that moment the little boy looked up and winked at him. The effect of such a sly expression in the little martyred face with its twisted stubby nose and half-toothless mouth was both pitiful and comic.

"Hey there, my pretty little gentleman, could you spare a crust of bread for a poor starving wretch, may Allah grant you good health?"

"I…I don't have any bread," said Falcon in dismay.

"But if you dig deep in your pockets, you'll surely find something."

"No, I really have nothing to give you."

"Oh come now, how could a gentleman like you not have any bread in his pocket? But maybe a little sugar for your horse? You might have some of that? Or a nice carrot?"

Falcon looked at him anxiously.

"Get along with you now, boy!" shouted one of the soldiers. "Don't bother the gentleman."

Another soldier, more kindly disposed, tossed a piece of bread to the child. Bound as he was to the shafts, the boy caught it on the fly with unexpected skill.

"But…but doesn't your master feed you?"

"Of course he does!" said the boy, chewing voraciously. "He gives me the water when he rinses out his cookpot, along with a handful of moldy beans. But he didn't even give me that this morning because he wants to sell me."

"Sell you? Who'd buy you?' laughed the soldiers. "Even a vulture couldn't find any meat to pick off your bones."

At that the boy winked and with a quick gesture collapsed head down between the shafts, hurriedly swallowing the last mouthful of bread. His master had reappeared in the doorway of the shop.

"Get up now, *homar!*" he yelled, grabbing the shaft to right the cart, "*Yalla,* let's go!" And the cart got under way, swaying under its load.

Just then Hamid came out into the street followed by Butros, who was trying to detain him, distressed at the thought of missing a good opportunity.

"No, Butros. Don't insist. I need a decent respectable youngster, a boy who'll make a good impression, who can be taught. Not one of those louts you've been showing me, good for nothing but turning millstones. Maybe next time. Come on, Falcon, let's go."

Hamid remounted, followed reluctantly by Falcon, who kept turning around to watch the cart.

"What's the matter, Falcon? You seem to be disturbed about something. And what are you looking at?"

"My lord, I saw a poor little boy near my age, tied to a cart like an animal, starving and covered with bruises. He asked me for a piece of bread and I had nothing to give him."

"I gave him some bread," said the soldier, laughing again at the thought. "By Allah, he gobbled it up in a second!"

"Don't worry about it, Prince Falcon," said Ahmed. "There are so many hopeless cases like his. Not many slaves are as lucky as ours."

Falcon, who had been riding along with drooping head, suddenly perked up.

"My lord, look! Look over that way!"

There at a crossroads in the skimpy shade of a tamarisk tree a dealer was displaying his human merchandise, the lowest class of slaves, filthy and chained together. The cart owner stood facing him, holding the boy by one arm. Unharnessed he was barely able to stand up.

"But I tell you, it's true!" the man was shouting. "This little scoundrel is strong, *w-allahi,* I swear to God. He's strong as a mule. He'll do the work of two men for you!"

"So why do you want to get rid of him?"

"By Allah who hears all, I'm giving him away only because I have ten children to feed and my wife is sick and my father-in-law died and I need money for the funeral. Otherwise I wouldn't take his weight in gold for him. I swear it!"

"Enough! Get out of here. You're driving away my customers."

"Give me twenty *dirahim* and I'll be satisfied. It's a steal. You can get at least twice as much for him."

"That's a laugh. He'll drop dead before the sun goes down."

"Fifteen *dirahim!* You'll never get another chance like this!"

"*Ya salam!* Are you going to get out of here?"

"Ten. Let's make it ten. It's a *balash,* a gift at that price! And you, stand up straight you miserable wretch. Never mind putting on the starving act after all you ate this morning. All right then, ten *dirahim* — is it a deal?"

"My lord!" said Falcon, squeezing the prince's arm. "He's the one."

"What one?"

"The boy who asked for bread. My lord, I beg you, buy him. We can give him to al-Hakim for an assistant."

"What? That pitiful specimen? He can't even stand up. Come on now, Falcon, let's go."

But Falcon didn't budge. "My lord, please buy him. Just ten *dirahim* — that's nothing for you!"

The prince turned around, read the pain in Falcon's eyes and remembered the day he had seen him in the castrator's hands. Maybe — even though it wasn't a valid comparison — the boy was feeling something of what he himself had felt then.

"All right, all right. Ibrahim, give that worthless dog ten *dirahim* and take the boy with you. We're leaving."

"Me, Sire? And how am I supposed to transport him?" protested the offended Ibrahim. "He's full of lice and he stinks. Who knows how many diseases he's carrying?"

"Ibrahim, just do what I say. Before you take him home get rid of his filthy rags, scrub him thoroughly under a fountain and have a barber shave him bald."

"But Sire, with all due respect to the honor of your lordship...."

"I've nothing more to say, Ibrahim. You can catch up with us as soon as you've finished. And try to lay your hands on some clean clothes for him."

Back at the palace Falcon waited anxiously for Ibrahim to arrive with the little boy. "Listen Falcon," the prince had told him, laughing. "I bought him for you to make you happy, but facing al-Hakim and telling him that piece of human rubbish is his new assistant would take a kind of courage I just haven't got. You'll have to do it."

Finally, his face sullen with resentment at the task that had befallen him, Ibrahim arrived with the boy in tow.

"Here he is, Prince Falcon. Do you need me for anything else?"

Falcon surmised it would be more prudent to dismiss him, along with his own escort. Only the faithful Ahmed remained at his side, but even he could not hide his disgust. In fact if the boy had first appeared poor and miserable, now that he was cleaned up he looked downright grotesque. His shaved head was bumpy and covered with scabs, bleeding from the energetic attempt to clean it. His skinny frame was lost inside a *gallabiya* made of coarse canvas and his feet, bandaged haphazardly, flopped about in a pair of sandals that were far too big. But the impudent little face was as cheerful as ever and Falcon found himself greeted with a jolly wink.

"Come with me. I'll introduce you to your new master. You're going to be his assistant. You must be available at all times to do whatever he says."

"What's this new master like? Very big and strong?"

"No, why?"

"Because," explained the boy, for whom certain words could have but one meaning, "because if he's got great big ones, he'll bust my...."

"Quiet!" bellowed Ahmed. "That kind of language isn't permitted!"

"Oh poor me. Sorry, please excuse me. I don't know how to talk to gentlemen."

Silence intervened, but not for long. Gazing around wide-eyed, the boy exclaimed, "What a beautiful place this is! What pretty gardens! And that grand tall gentleman with the fancy clothes, riding the great big horse — he's the master of all this?"

"Yes, he is our master, the most excellent Prince Hamid al-Ghazi, may Allah watch over him forever," said Ahmed.

"I heard him call you Falcon. Is that your name?"

"Yes."

"Are you his son?"

"No."

"Then you must be his grandson. The son of his son."

"No."

"All right now — enough of these questions!" Ahmed broke in again. "And listen carefully, when you address him, you must say 'Prince Falcon, sir.' Do you understand?"

Another silence followed. Falcon, annoyed by all that curiosity, had quickened his pace without realizing it. But when he looked back and saw the boy struggling to keep up with him, his mild ill-humor vanished.

"Now I should excuse myself. I'm walking too fast," and just for something to say he asked, "Your master was very cruel, wasn't he?"

"Oh most illustrious sir, Prince Falcon, you know how the saying goes: 'The potter made him and then broke the mold.' And I had to be the one to get him as a master."

"Did he work you very hard?"

"Night and day, my prince. All day long I had to work in the fields, hoeing and weeding or else he'd tie me to the noria to turn in circles round and round until I was so dizzy I didn't know what I was doing. And in the evening I had to clean that dungheap he calls his house and wash the pots and pans in the river and empty the…well anyhow I had to do everything."

"My God!" murmured Falcon, almost to himself. "What a life! Better to die than live like that."

The boy didn't have much going for him but his hearing was keen. "Oh well, my fine prince, sir, I knew I'd be better off dead. But that's not easy either. Once though I managed to lay my hand on a kitchen knife, but that scoundrel was quicker than me and took it away and then amused himself all night pricking me with it. He said if I liked the knife so much he'd give me a taste of it himself. Another time I thought I'd just starve myself to death, but when he realized what I was up to he forced me to eat his...well, anyway that stuff you do and when I spit it in his face he punched me so hard he knocked out two teeth, the missing front ones, see?" And he pulled down his lip using his index finger with the blackened and split nail to show his toothless gums. "So I had to swallow it along with my own blood for seasoning...."

"That's enough! A plague on you, you worthless wretch!" shouted Ahmed, who could see how such talk pained Falcon. "Shut up or I'll knock a few more of your teeth out!"

Fortunately they had arrived, but now even Falcon's courage failed at the thought of presenting the poor luckless creature to Hakim as the assistant he'd been promised.

"What's your name?" he asked the boy.

"My name is Omar but my master used to call me *homar* — jackass — because he said I was a work donkey."

"Omar is a fine name and that's what we'll call you. You wait here now. I'm going to talk to your new master."

But when he stood before the old doctor, Falcon didn't know what to say. He ended up taking his hand and leading him out to Omar, who was now sitting on the ground. "Hakim, this is your new assistant. I...I'm the one who picked him out and I'm...I'm sure he...."

The words died in his mouth. The boy had gotten to his feet and was trying to stand up straight in his oversized shirt. "Oh Sire, my most honored master, may Allah protect you, grant you long life, and bless you with sons. I'm your new servant and you will surely be pleased with me."

Al-Hakim stared at him, too dismayed to speak.

"Master sir, my most humble respects. Maybe I don't look it, but I'm a very good worker, very strong. I can do anything you want me to...."

Suddenly he fell silent, noting the shock and disapproval in the old man's eyes, and bowed his head in humiliation. "You're right," he said in a thin voice. "You're perfectly right not to want me. I'm good for nothing but to be thrown to the dogs. Sir Prince Falcon has been very generous to me, but I...I...."

At that the old man took pity on him.

"I'll be glad to take you into my service. Come." And with a certain effort he placed a hand on the child's shoulder. "If you are going to be my assistant we must be friends. But before you learn to be a doctor you'll need a bit of doctoring yourself. Come along now."

And he was rewarded by Falcon's radiant smile directed at him over the little boy's head.

"Falcon, you know I don't like to put restrictions on you, but I'd prefer you didn't get too friendly with that boy, that Omar."

"My lord, I only see him when I go to visit al-Hakim. He's pleased with Omar. He says he's intelligent and he's learning fast."

"I'm glad to hear it." The prince understood that Falcon had grown fond of the poor unhappy child because he represented the first good deed of his life — the only time Falcon had concerned himself with someone other than his master. His generic courtesy, which derived more from indifference than from an authentically cordial disposition, had suddenly changed into real human compassion for the unfortunate boy. "Indeed al-Hakim has reported to me that Omar is willing and obedient. But he is also impudent, a liar and above all, corrupt to his very bones."

"It's not his fault he's corrupt. It's because of the terrible way he's been treated, poor little fellow."

"I'm not saying it's his fault. But you don't leave a rotten banana in with a bunch of good ones. Al-Hakim is old and wise but you're still young. Anyhow I'd prefer you not get too familiar with the boy."

"If this is what you wish, my lord, I won't see him. But you shouldn't worry on my account. You're forgetting I spent more than two months in a slave emporium and those things he talks about — I've seen them happening."

"Yes," thought the prince, looking into those beautiful serene gray eyes, "Yes, but no ugliness or filth could ever corrupt you, my Falcon. That's not the point really. I'm always afraid for you, afraid of everything. I want to keep all harm away from you, may God help me." Aloud he said, "All the same, Falcon, try not to spend too much time with him for my sake."

Thus Falcon began to visit the old doctor less frequently. This disturbed Omar. He considered that, having acted as his benefactor, Falcon had contracted a debt toward him.

"How come Prince Falcon doesn't come to see us as often as he used to?"

"Prince Falcon is busy doing all those things a young gentleman has to do. But he hasn't forgotten you. He always asks me about you when I go to the palace."

"And you, Master, what do you say?"

"Oh well, I say you're in much better health than you were, and you've even grown a bit taller."

"You don't say what a good worker I am?"

"Yes, of course. I tell him you're learning to identify herbs and when you want to be you're a great help to me. Should I also tell him about your petty thievery in the kitchens?"

"Oh no, by Allah no. I beg you, don't tell him about that."

"Why do you do it then? You know you shouldn't. And you get all you want to eat."

"Yes, Master, I know. I have everything I need here. But I was hungry for so long that when I see all that good stuff to eat I can't control myself. Even if my belly is full I have to steal something."

"Careful, Omar. Sooner or later you'll regret it."

In fact, Omar was indeed caught in the act and brought before the servants' overseer, who scolded him harshly and assured him if they found him stealing from the kitchen stores again, he'd be in for a public whipping.

For two weeks Omar kept to the straight and narrow but then did something too serious to ignore.

This time the overseer went to the prince.

"Most excellent Sire, I know that such trifles are not proper matter for your lordship's attention, but they tell me that Prince Falcon is protecting this little boy and I thought I had better inform you. Until now I have closed an eye, in fact both eyes, but this time the offense is too grave. It would be the worst kind of example for all of the servants."

Falcon, who was at his chess board studying out a knight's gambit he had learned that morning, looked up in in concern.

"What's this all about? Let's hear it."

"Sire, that worthless little wretch undeserving of the benevolence he has received, got into al-Hakim's cupboards and took three crystal jars of rare herbs. He sold them in the city to an itinerant healer, then used the money to buy a turquoise necklace for Aziza, the daughter of the second cook's third helper."

For the overseer such a misdeed was rendered even more serious because for some time now he himself had had his eye on pretty little Aziza, and it was unthinkable an outcast like Omar should even dream of aiming so high.

"This is indeed serious."

"Extremely so, my lord prince. In the first place a robbery committed in the house of his master and teacher, aggravated by the fact that the crystal jars are, like everything else in the palace, your lordship's property. Then there is his running off to the city without asking permission and finally the unpardonable insolence of daring to set his sights on a young girl who is a member of your household staff and presenting her with a gift without my authorization."

Falcon's eyes were so clouded he could no longer see his chess board. What would they do to Omar now?

"My lord prince, we must make an example of him. Certainly I would have preferred to avoid bothering your lordship about the lowest of common servants, but...."

"Yes, I understand. What would you propose doing?"

"With your approval, Sire, I would suggest that he be given a whipping hard enough to tan his hide in front of an assemblage of all the other servants and then sent to the gristmills to turn the millstones."

"No!" Falcon cried out in such anguish that the prince turned to look at him. "No, no, don't whip him — no!" The thought of that poor little body being subjected to more torture was intolerable. "And don't send him to the gristmills! No! It would be better to kill him."

"Falcon, my boy, calm yourself. Nobody wants to be cruel to him. But you do understand he has to be punished? For his own good?"

"Yes."

"What then would you suggest?"

"My lord, it would be punishment enough if you banished him from your apartments, took away his privileged position with al-Hakim, and gave him a humbler task. I don't know what, maybe working in the kitchens...."

"With all due respect for your lordship, Sire, I really don't want him in the kitchens."

"Very well," the prince cut him off. "Send him to the stables. Give him a good dressing down in front of everybody and send him to the stables to work for the chief groom."

"Consider it done, Sire. But the young Aziza also needs to be punished. That insolent little wench should not have accepted the gift."

"Well, see to that yourself, then. That's your affair."

"Yes indeed, I'll see to her, I will," thought the overseer bowing and withdrawing. "Pretty Aziza deserves a little whipping and I myself will administer it. She's the apple of her father's eye and I'll tell him I don't want to dishonor her in public so I'll punish her in my own rooms. I won't use a heavy hand. It would be a pity to damage that silken skin, and she'll weep and beg for mercy. And I'll be generous and forgive her. And then she'll kiss my hands and I'll console her and everything will go the way it's supposed to. Come to think of it now that little scapegrace Omar has been useful to me."

Thus Omar's status was reduced to that of a stableboy.

The overseer had him called before the entire company of servants and reprimanded him severely.

"You know what punishment is reserved for a thief, liar and fornicator like you?"

"No sir, most illustrious overseer."

"I'll tell you what it is. You deserve to be turned upside down and tied to a tree by your feet and then whipped until you fall to the ground in pieces."

Omar lapsed into shocked silence. In six months of easy living he had gotten out of the habit of suffering and that terrible image made his flesh crawl.

"However, thanks to the personal intercession of the most excellent Prince Falcon, may Allah grant him long life, you will be spared. But from now on you will no longer live at the palace. There is no place here for malefactors of your kind. You will be a stableboy. And you must never again show your face anywhere near the quarters where honest and faithful servants reside. You are not worthy of their company. Get going now and don't come back."

Omar hoped he would at least be allowed to say good-bye to his kind-hearted master and pack up his belongings. He had managed to acquire a rather nice wardrobe — three cotton shirts and one silk one, a pretty brown wool cloak, some slippers made of fine red and yellow leather and some proper underwear — and he hoped also that he might get a glimpse of his benefactor. But the armed guard at the entrance to the prince's apartments refused to let him pass.

It was some consolation to see that the stables were quite pretty and well maintained and to discover he had been assigned to the part where the two princes' personal mounts were kept. Falcon had managed to communicate his recommendations to the chief groom, who showed himself to be reasonably humane. He outlined Omar's duties: washing the floors, changing the bedding, keeping the hayracks full of hay or other fodder. After a while, if he made a good impression, he might even be permitted to curry and brush the horses. At night he would have to sleep on a pallet right there in the stable and he would take his meals with the other stableboys and grooms.

Omar looked around with interest. *El-hamdu li-llah*, praise be to God, the devil isn't as ugly as he's been painted. Those beautiful animals pleased him very much. He recognized the prince's tall roan stabled apart in splendid isolation, standing there lazily pulling down a few stems of grass from a hayrack made of prized and polished wood. All he lacked was a rug on the floor. Then, observing the other horses, he seemed to recognize one more.

"Mr. chief groom, sir, whose is that pretty black over there?"

"That one? It's Prince Falcon's personal mount. Be careful, don't get too near him. He's pretty skittish."

But Omar, who wasn't listening, had rushed over to the purebred Arabian and thrown his arms around his neck. The chief groom expected to witness the demise of his new recruit before he even began his duties, finished off by kicks and bites. But instead the horse showed his gentler side. He didn't even move when Omar buried his pug-nosed little face in the shiny mane and wept hot tears.

Ramadan weighed heavily upon all the population of the faithful. During this month when the Prophet had experienced the Revelation every good Muslim had to observe the strictest fast from dawn to sunset, abjuring the smallest crumb of food and not taking a single drop of water. Even swallowing one's own saliva was forbidden. Children who had reached the age of required obedience to the rule might suffer the sharpest pangs of hunger, old folks might faint from weakness, vigorous youths have throats parched from thirst: there was no pity for anyone. When the voice of the muezzin at last called them to prayer, proclaiming the end of the day, they all rushed to eat and drink in excess, feasting together well into the night. Then they would fall into a torpid sleep, dulled by all the food they had gorged upon. After a short nap they'd wake up and hasten to eat and drink one last time before first light, as long as, to put it in the words of the Prophet, it was still not easy to distinguish a white thread from a black one.

The dusty back alleys of the capital were full of men lying on the ground asleep or merely dazed, with rags pulled down over their eyes, men who wouldn't even move out of the way of the rare horseman or wagon-driver who passed by. And if they were not trampled or run over, it was only because of the natural instinct of the beasts, not because of the rider's or driver's attention.

Hamid, tall and robust as he was, did not adapt well to abstinence. He hastily carried out whatever official duties he could not defer and then spent hours and hours stretched out on a rush mat in the shade of the garden, far from the tormenting and tempting sound of the bubbling splashing little fountain. Falcon, who adjusted easily to the fast as if in him the spirit counted much more than the flesh, stayed by him and tried to distract him by telling stories about faraway times and places, stories of knights and ladies and unknown cities. Hamid, listening more attentively to the clear sweet voice than to the story itself, finally asked, "But where did you learn all this, Falcon?"

"I don't know, my handsome lord, I just don't know!" said Falcon in his lilting accent, greatly amused by the question. "You're always asking me where I learned this or that, where I learned to swim or ride or something else, but I never know. I think I learned all such things just to please you."

"But if you didn't even know me!"

"Oh yes I did. I knew you. Didn't I recognize you as soon as I saw you?"

In the stables Omar also suffered as a result of fasting. His stomach, already shrunken from prolonged hunger, his liver, enlarged by the many blows he'd received, rendered the excessively heavy meals painful and worst of all he couldn't tolerate drinking copious quantities of water, then being thirsty for an entire day. He performed his tasks as quickly as he could and the chief groom overlooked his shortcomings. The only horse perfectly cared for was Falcon's black. Omar kept his coat shiny, his hooves polished, and his mane flawlessly groomed, woven first into multiple tiny braids, then moistened with lemon to preserve the wave. By now the purebred Arabian was used to his tough little hands and seemed to enjoy his attentions. At night the boy spread his pallet beside him and the restive black horse didn't even disturb his sleep.

Of course the horses didn't fast, and pouring cool water into their watering troughs was sheer torture for the thirsty child. Once, after looking around furtively, he dipped a finger in the water and sucked it avidly. Suddenly he was seized with a terrible fear — he had committed a serious sin even if no one had seen. Allah who sees all would surely punish him. For a while afterward he expected divine punishment to materialize in the form of an enraged chief groom, but when nothing happened he went back to dipping his finger in the water. Allah was kind, Allah was merciful — he wouldn't trouble himself over a poor little fellow dying of thirst.

Falcon frequently asked the overseer of the stables for news of his protege. He never got close to Omar because the honor of bringing his master's horse to him does not belong to a stableboy. But he could catch a glimpse from a certain distance and once Omar had even risked winking at him. The overseer reported the chief groom was pleased with the boy. The only objection he could make in his report to the prince was that when he took the horses to pasture if he thought no one was watching he'd jump on one of them and ride around the meadow.

"Bareback?"

"Bareback, Sire."

"Well, some day or other he'll break his neck, but that's his business. Just so he doesn't harm the horses."

"Oh no, there's no danger of that my lord prince. In fact, he has quite good hands. He could become an excellent horseman."

At that Falcon decided the moment had come to intervene in favor of the little outcast. And by sheer persistence he managed to get the life sentence reduced to a stated term.

"You see, my lord, although the palace overseer doesn't want him in the household anymore, he could remain in the stables to do less menial chores than the ones he does now. Maybe with time, if you don't mind, I could add him to my escort."

"A sorry looking type like that? Although it's true small stature is no great disadvantage for a rider. Well, all right, if the little scapegrace can go for six months without pulling off another of his tricks, he'll be pardoned."

Falcon saw to it that the good news reached the interested party. And Omar, completely happy, swore he would behave in an exemplary manner in anticipation of the pardon. He already saw himself mounted on a purebred steed and dressed in a flashy uniform, following the young prince and covering himself with glory by saving Falcon from some dreadful danger.

His wish would come true but — as almost always happens with human wishes — not in the form or the ways he had imagined. And it was also written in the Sacred Tables of Heaven that Omar would not see the end of his six-month sentence.

The Final Battle

Ramadan had ended and life was returning to its normal rhythm. With a sense of inner peace derived from observing the Prophet's law people went back to work with greater energy. In fact, anyone would have thought considerable time would pass before Prince Hamid would again be called upon to justify his epithet of al-Ghazi, the warrior.

Instead, one day near the end of summer an exhausted rider on a lathered horse arrived at the palace and asked to see the prince. He brought an urgent message: the tribes of the plain had taken up arms and were marching toward Hamid's southern frontier.

This was disturbing news. The tribes themselves did not constitute a real threat — their poorly organized bands couldn't put up much resistance against a well-trained army. But it was clear they wouldn't have gotten involved in such an adventure on their own. Considering the sheiks' recent declarations of friendship, the surprise attack could only mean one thing: the move had been planned ahead of time by a cleverer mind than theirs, the mind of the Emir Husain.

There was no time to lose. Fortunately Hamid always kept his army in a state of readiness for war. He summoned his officers and together they established a plan of action. Apparently the emir was waiting until Hamid's forces were engaged against the invader to launch his own attack on the western border. In fact, for some time observers had noted unusual movements along the river, activities ostensibly justified by the need to reinforce the dikes. It was certain, however, that the emir's men were constructing pontoon bridges since the water there was too deep for fording.

It seemed best to pretend to fall into the trap, to move against the sheiks with the entire army and at the last minute divert a part of the force toward the west so as to surprise the emir's men while they were busy crossing the river and drive them back. If that move didn't succeed they would confront them on the plain. Hamid knew he had far fewer troops than his opponent but he counted on his men's superior skills and the effect of his own presence on the battlefield.

There was still the problem of defending the palace and the capital. Location was a strategic factor. They were situated on a plateau bounded on the north by mountains that were impenetrable except for one well-guarded pass. On the east lay the domain of the Emir Abbas, whose loyalty to Hamid was beyond question.

In order not to divide his forces unnecessarily the prince entrusted the defense of his palace to a small contingent of his most faithful veterans under the command of a highly-skilled senior officer. Then he sent reinforcements to the garrison holding the small fort at the pass. Having done his best to provide for all eventualities, he prepared to depart with the serenity of a man who confronts danger knowing he has done everything humanly possible — the rest was in the hands of Allah.

Of course Falcon would come with him. It would be too humiliating to leave him at home with the old folks and the women. The boy would have liked to remain at his side during combat as well, but on that point Hamid was adamant.

"Now that you are a man it is only right that you get your first real battle experience. But not at my side."

"I can't stay away from you, knowing you're in danger, my lord."

"You'd only increase that danger by remaining close to me. You don't know what a cavalry charge is. You watched the drills during the emir's visit, didn't you? Those were nothing compared to what really happens. The horses don't turn aside at the last minute and the swords cut more than air. You have no experience of this type of combat and with you beside me, I'd be so worried about your safety I'd end up getting killed myself."

This last argument convinced Falcon.

"So what should I do?"

"You're an excellent archer. You'll join the archers and be subject to their commander. Their assignment is to try to prevent the enemy from crossing the river. You must obey this time, Falcon. This is war. You're a soldier just like all the rest."

But before he left for battle the prince sent for Ahmed. "Ahmed, I know you're burning with the desire to fight. But I want you to stay with Prince Falcon, to protect him and prevent him from committing some boyish act of bravado — he's still very young."

"Yes, Sire."

"And listen carefully now. If things go wrong for us or if despite the outcome of the battle I should be killed, you must kill Falcon with your own hands."

"My lord, what you are asking of me is terrible."

"But it is necessary. Swear you will do it."

"Yes my lord, *w-allahi*, I swear to God I will. You can count on me."

At dawn the day after the messenger had brought the news, Hamid was just mounting his horse at the head of his army when he was informed his son Prince Harazad had arrived.

Frowning with irritation, Hamid waited for his son to appear — Harazad had once again disobeyed by not requesting permission to cross the border. But as soon as he found himself in his father's presence the young man bowed in deep respect.

"My father, I have gone against your orders, but as soon as I learned of the danger threatening you I could not restrain myself from coming to your aid at once. I pray you to pardon my past offenses and to make use of me in any way you think best. At a time like this my place is at your side."

The prince studied the grave and serious young face and saw no trace of anything but a deferential solicitude. He was touched.

"Harazad, let's forget the past. You've come to me at a time of need and I will not forget it. If this war ends as I hope it will with Allah's help, I want you to take your rightful place at court in the future."

"My lord, that's more than I merit. Just tell me how to serve you best. I have with me fifty able-bodied men whose loyalty I can vouch for as I do my own."

"My son, your help comes at just the right moment. I was concerned about leaving the palace without adequate defenses. Your men combined with mine will be enough to fight off any kind of surprise attack."

He summoned the senior officer who commanded his veterans, presented him to the young prince and told him to submit to his command. Later, taking the older man aside, he told him to keep a watchful eye at all times because he was uneasy about his son's lack of experience. Then Harazad reviewed the small contingent, and they proclaimed their allegiance to him in a shout of acclamation.

Even the inevitable encounter with Falcon went well. When the two stood facing each other, one a prince by right of birth, the other a prince by right of love, Falcon bowed correctly to his superior in age and rank and Harazad graciously returned the salute.

Reassured on this matter as well, Hamid mounted his roan and gave the signal to depart. The huge brown and gold banner slowly unfurled in the early morning sun and the line of cavalry in helmet and cuirass on horses equipped for battle took the lead, followed by the livelier and less-encumbered archers, including Falcon, and finally by the long column of infantry.

Prince Harazad remained on the palace stairway watching the army move away until it disappeared from sight.

Twenty-four hours later in the early morning light the small platoon was making its way back to the palace. The great brown and gold banner still waved proudly in the sun but the arm that held it was tired, and the horsemen also seemed tired, their cuirasses broken and dented, their clothing torn. They numbered about two hundred — the surviving members of Hamid al-Ghazi's victorious army.

It had been a hard and bitter battle on two fronts. The bands led by the sheiks had fought ferociously and as soon as he had managed to put them to flight, Hamid had been obliged to rush to the aid of his other troops, hard-pressed by the onslaught of Husain's forces. Some of these had already crossed the river under the command of the eunuch Faragalla. Only the prince's presence and his constant encouragement transformed an apparent rout into a victorious counterattack. The invaders, encircled on the plain, tried to get back across the river on their unsteady pontoon bridges, but repeated cavalry charges and swarms of flying arrows left almost all of them either lying dead on the field or carried off by the surging river. But Hamid's side also sustained heavy losses and night descended over a scene of tragic desolation.

Obedient to his assignment, Falcon had fought with the archers and done himself honor. His infallible aim had dispatched many an enemy soldier to redden the whirling waters of the river. But if launching death against the invader from afar had brought him a kind of heroic exaltation, when it was over he was devastated by the sight of the battlefield covered with dead and the dying men, with crippled and disembowelled horses, and by the sound of the moans and pleas for help.

Now he too rode with head bowed at his master's side, thinking over and over about all those boys who had been his comrades in games and contests and who now lay unburied out there on the plain.

As for Hamid, his mind was on the most urgent matters still at hand. He had left a small number of uninjured men on the battlefield to provide first aid to the wounded. As soon as he reached the palace he would send out further help. His little army had emerged from its bloody victory considerably battered, but the enemy commander was now dead, the emir's troops were disbanded, and it would be a long time before his enemies could regroup against him even if they hadn't lost the desire for such an encounter. Meanwhile he was planning to make a journey to Baghdad in person to inform the Grand Caliph about what had really happened, counting on his own credibility as a faithful vassal to obtain justice. In this matter he could depend on the aid of Abbas, who was held in high esteem at court. All things considered, if he played his cards well, he might emerge in a position strengthened rather than weakened by that costly battle. Harazad's arrival had really been providential. At least he had nothing to worry about on that front. The young man had shown he wanted to mend his ways. Perhaps his violent character would grow more temperate with time and he could one day be taken into the government. *Inshallah*, thanks be to God, his son had been restored to him.

At that very moment Prince Harazad was coming down the palace stairs to greet the Emir Husain as he descended from his palanquin.

"So, my boy, we can be quite satisfied with the way things went."

"I hear your forces were totally wiped out at the river," said Harazad with a certain venom. But the emir showed no resentment.

"Yes, that is true, but I must confess I expected it. Your father was not nicknamed al-Ghazi for nothing. My eunuch was never a match for him, nor did I delude myself that he might beat him. I'm glad the stupid fool is dead. Otherwise I'd have had to have him decapitated. One less bothersome task."

"Were your losses heavy?"

"I lost a few hundred worthless idlers. But they served the purpose we had in mind for them, didn't they? Hamid's forces are greatly reduced. The trap is set and should be sprung any moment now. How did things go here?"

"As planned. The surprise attack was a complete success. That old imbecile of an officer tried to resist with his paltry group of followers, but my men surrounded them and cut them to pieces. As for the servants, a few tried to rebel but after I had ten or so hung and quartered the others saw the light and now they grovel at my feet like worms. Anyway I've decided either to sell them all or send them off to rot in the fields and replace them with my own people. It's always better not to trust slaves."

"And how about the harem?"

"Oh that couldn't have gone better. As soon as the head eunuch was killed and replaced by one of mine who has a very firm hand, those frightened little doves were waiting all atremble for me to judge them worthy of my favors. Only the beautiful Lailah is still sulking."

"It seems she really loved your father."

"We'll make her forget him. You may know how to dominate males, Husain, no offense intended, but I know how to handle females. Before long I'll have the beautiful Lailah licking my boots."

"Good for you, splendid my boy. I see you know what you're doing. And did you remember to send a garrison to guard the border with Abbas? He's not on our side."

"Of course, and the mountain pass is also well-guarded on both sides — yours and mine. Not a single soldier from the original garrison survived."

"Well, well, you've really thought of everything. But excuse me, what's that big cage for?"

The emir pointed at a cage about three yards square made of strong gilded bars and mounted on wheels. In the middle of its solid plank floor was a massive log circled by an iron band from which dangled heavy chains.

Harazad flashed a vicious smile. "That? That's for my father. You don't expect me to stain my hands with his blood do you? My father will live to a ripe and honorable old age and he'll attain that status right there inside his cage. I'll make sure no one can do him harm, least of all himself."

"My dear boy, you're extraordinary. But why the wheels?"

"Because I don't want to deprive myself of the dear paternal presence. This way I can take him with me wherever I go and have him participate in my government, just as he wanted me to share in his."

"Do you know you almost scare me, Harazad?"

"I intend to scare a lot of people around here. I'm going to teach this pack of dogs what it means to obey. They've got to understand their easy life is over. I only regret that I can't give a lesson in person to that insolent little insect, my father's faithful friend. Perhaps you'd like to take him off my hands, Husain? Would you be willing to do this for me?"

"My boy, do permit me to say I'm much better suited than you are to teach him a lesson. You lack finesse — no offense now."

"Perhaps you're right. But in return I shall ask that you show your talents in this direction at least once in front of the cage where I intend to put my father."

"Very well, just to please you. Besides I too would like to see my dear friend Hamid's face when that happens. I remember how he wouldn't let me lay a finger on his pretty little beauty. But afterwards I want to take the boy away with me. I've always preferred to savor my pleasure one to one."

"Sire," observed one of those present, "I've been told that boy is capable of letting himself die if he wants to. I wouldn't want you to end up with an empty plate, so to speak."

"Nonsense. No one dies as easily as that. I'll have all the time I need to enjoy him. And then if he's really set on dying, he'll die in my bed when and how I want him to."

"It seems you also know what you're doing, Husain," said Harazad. "We're a fine pair, the two of us. But where are they? Things should be over by now."

"It's still a bit early. We can wait."

Once they reached the last pass that led into the plateau, Hamid brought his troops to halt, more from habitual prudence than for fear of an ambush this close to the palace.

He sent out four scouts to search the slopes of the mountains on both sides of the pass. But the men were tired and believing such precautions completely unnecessary, they limited their efforts to a quick glance around, then returned to report everything was quiet.

The pass consisted of a long narrow valley. The troops moved into it in a single column and the first horsemen had not yet emerged when the last entered. As soon as all were inside the narrow passageway a band of nomads on light and agile mounts fell upon them from the mountains. They were desert Arabs with the edges of their white burnooses wrapped around their faces so that only their flashing eyes were visible.

The prince was the first to react. With a loud shout, instantly echoed by Hassan and the other officers, he managed to advance those in the lead while urging the rear guard to turn back. Their assailants, left facing a void in the middle of the column right where they had concentrated their attack, had to split their band in two.

The violence of impact was extreme. The narrow pass became an instant inferno — a single tangled mass of men and horses. Hamid, flailing about with his heavy sword and cutting down enemies with every stroke quickly realized the attackers had been ordered to capture him alive. More than once a weapon raised against him missed its mark and his major concern was to prevent them from killing his horse beneath him. Reinforced by this advantage he took bold risks, plunging constantly into the thick of the fray, his big stallion rearing and coming down on dead or wounded alike, trampling everything in his way.

As soon as he could he looked around for Falcon. The boy, totally innocent of hand to hand combat and horrified by the blood and violence, would have been overwhelmed and carried off if Ahmed and a handful of followers hadn't quickly surrounded him and fought off his would-be kidnappers.

It was all over in a little more than a quarter of an hour. Only a few of the attackers escaped, fleeing up into the mountains. But the cost of victory was heavy. When the prince and Hassan managed to assemble the survivors they counted no more than forty able-bodied men.

"I don't understand how they could have set up this ambush so close to the palace. How did they get through?" said Hassan, voicing the thoughts of all.

Hamid remained silent. He had dismounted and was sitting on a rock, his face contracted. A not-yet-clearly-defined suspicion was forming in his mind, too horrible to accept right away.

As long as he remained silent no one dared speak. And in that silence they heard the distant but distinct sound of a galloping horse. Someone was coming through the pass at top speed from the direction of the palace.

Hamid sprang to his feet and every man grabbed his sword. But they quickly realized it was only a single rider coming toward them. In fact, at first it looked like a horse with no rider at all. Only when it was quite close could they make out the minute figure bent over his mount's neck, holding on to its mane. It was Omar the stableboy.

He spotted the prince and headed directly for him. Reaching him, he slid off his horse, aided by many hands. He was panting and shaken and a thread of blood ran down his chin.

"My lord prince, for Allah's sake, turn back! Your son and the emir have taken over the palace and anybody who tried to resist was either decapitated or hung and quartered. Sire, by Allah, go back, go back!"

Hamid had listened without changing his expression.

"When did this happen, boy?"

"Soon after you left. So suddenly we had no chance to defend ourselves. Sire, your men got killed because they refused to betray you. And they're all dead. All of them."

"My son and the Emir Husain, you say?"

"Yes, and oh Sire, don't let them take you alive! Your son has prepared a huge cage for you, to lock you up in like an animal. And the emir wants Falcon taken alive. He wants you to see what he's going to do to him. I was hiding in a bush and I heard everything."

"But how did you escape?"

"I was in the stables when they came. They chased us all out, all the slaves, and then got us together in a courtyard. The overseer tried to defend us, but they tied him to a tree by his feet and whipped him to death, just what he wanted to do to me, poor man. But I'm small and I managed to crawl away on my belly without anybody noticing."

"Al-Hakim?" asked Falcon.

"Poor Hakim. He tried to object and scold your son, Sire, and that fellow, he just laid him out and beat his head in with the hilt of his sword. I heard the bones of his skull break."

"My wife, my son," said Ahmed. It wasn't even a question and Omar didn't answer.

"All the exits are guarded?"

"Yes, Sire, their soldiers are everywhere. In all the confusion I managed to get close to the stairway where your son and the emir were standing. And when I heard those horrible things I ran to the pasture, took the first horse I found and...."

He collapsed, his voice given out. Kindly hands laid him on a blanket and Falcon knelt beside him. "Omar, are you hurt?"

"Who'd want to hurt me? They kicked me some and I've got a bad pain here in my side...."

A stream of blood bubbled out of his mouth. Falcon wiped his lips with the edge of his own tunic.

"Falcon," the boy murmured. "Falcon, can I call you that now?"

"Yes, Omar, my brother."

"Falcon, you gave me six months of happiness, but I've repaid you with my whole life. Now you're in debt to me. Isn't that right?"

He started to wink at Falcon but the wink changed into a grimace of pain, and after one last spurt of blood he fell back dead.

Meanwhile Hamid had assembled his soldiers. "We have
to make a decision. We can't go back. It's clear now the field
we left behind has been attacked and overrun. Going back
would mean falling into another trap."

"Couldn't we surprise the palace and retake it?"

"There aren't enough of us. The emir certainly didn't
move without a sizeable escort and my son has his men with
him."

"Couldn't we head for the eastern frontier, go around the
palace, and take refuge with your cousin Abbas?"

"They're certain to be patrolling the border, even if we
did manage to reach it."

"The mountain route?"

"The pass will be in their hands and we'd have to conquer
two forts. But there's another way out. Hassan, do you know
what I'm talking about?"

"Yes, Sire, the secret pass."

"Does your son Ahmed know about it?"

"Following your orders, I showed it to him when he
reached his sixteenth birthday, and after that he's been there
with me a number of times."

"Brothers," said Hamid, looking around at his men. "You
have one chance to get to safety. Ahmed can guide you to
Abbas' lands by way of a mountain pass no one else knows
about."

"But aren't you going to take us yourself, Sire?"

"No, I'm not coming with you. Hassan and I will stay
behind. I have something to do first."

"May we ask what it is?" someone questioned.

"Kill my son."

A concerned silence fell over them. Not for the enormity
of the act, which all regarded as justified, or rather, as a duty,
but because of the impossibility of carrying it out. How could
Hamid hope to kill his son, now that Harazad was safely

established in the palace and guarded by his own as well as the emir's soldiers? It was a desperate undertaking.

"You'll risk being taken alive!" exclaimed Hassan for all of them.

"No, not if Allah helps me. Are you ready then to follow Ahmed to safety?"

No one answered. Then one of them spoke up. "My lord, if you've decided to make this attempt we're with you."

Hamid realized he wouldn't be able to change their minds and felt a pang of painful pride. They were his men, the flower of his strong and loyal army, and now even these last survivors would die.

He turned, seeking out Falcon, and saw him still bent over Omar. He approached, looked down from above at the pathetic little body, even more pitiful in death, and put a hand on Falcon's shoulder.

"Don't mourn for him, Falcon. He's with God now and Allah rewards the brave. Right now we've got to think about what's best to do. I have one more task to perform."

"Yes, my lord, I heard. Couldn't you....couldn't you let God be the one to punish that wicked man?"

"No, it's my duty. But it's going to be very dangerous. I want you to go with Ahmed to safety, to the court of Abbas. He'll gladly take you in."

"No my lord, I'm coming with you."

Hamid gazed into the clear steady gray eyes. "All right then. We don't have much time." He turned to his men. "Listen carefully. First does any one of you speak the desert dialect?"

"I do, Sire," answered a soldier. "My mother is a bedouin."

"Good. There are plenty of horses and burnooses here. Now then, listen to my plan."

The emir and Prince Harazad were starting to worry when several guards appeared, escorting two horsemen clad in white with only their gleaming eyes showing between their burnooses and turbans.

"Sire," said one of the two, making a brief gesture of greeting to the emir, and speaking with the unmistakable accent of the desert Arabs. "Sire, your orders have been carried out. The prisoners will be here very soon."

"They're both alive? The man and the boy?"

"Yes, Sire."

"They aren't wounded?"

"No, and this has cost us the lives of many men. It was a very hard fight."

"Things like this always cost a lot. When will they be here?"

"Any minute now."

"Very good. You two wait here with my men and once the mission is completed there will be rewards for all."

The two took their leave with a gesture. No one noticed that when they dismounted they placed themselves on both sides of the main gate to the park, now guarded by an armed picket.

The emir and Harazad remained waiting on the stairway. Before long they heard the rhythmic sound of trotting horses and a small troop entered the formal courtyard, followed by the emir's soldiers.

There were about forty of them, desert horsemen on swift mounts, wrapped in white cloaks and armed with long lances. In their midst, one on his roan, the other astride his black, both bound with chains, rode Prince Hamid and Falcon, their heads bowed. When they stopped in front of the stairway, Hamid looked up, saw the huge gilded cage and lowered his head again.

Prince Harazad descended the last few steps. "My lord father, I regret that this time you are not returning victorious. But I hasten to inform you, you need not fear for your life. I will take very good care of you."

Hamid said nothing, still keeping his head down. In his desire to see the shame on his father's face, Harazad came a step closer. At that instant Hamid suddenly let his chains drop, drew out the naked sword hidden in his clothes and holding it in both hands raised it high in the sunlight. "Wretch!" he shouted. And before the youth could open his mouth in surprise the sword had described a shining arc and Harazad's head was rolling between the roan's hooves.

The emir, who from entrenched habit had remained in the midst of his men, bounded backward. One glance told Hamid it would not be easy to reach him and he quickly raised his hand, still holding the bloody sword. "Let's go!"

The two fake bedouins at the gate had already leaped on the guards. Other horsemen, burnooses thrown aside, rushed to their aid and the heavy gates swung open barely in time for the fugitives to pass like a whirlwind through the opening and disappear into the plain.

But not all of them. Although Harazad's escort, terrified and horror stricken, had not moved, the emir's men after the first moment of surprise had galloped off in hot pursuit and Hamid's rear guard, turning to confront them and protect the prince's flight, was overtaken and massacred.

By now the entire courtyard was in an uproar — soldiers looking for their horses and repeatedly bumping into each other, wounded finished off by blows of lances or swords, orders confounded by counter orders.

Calm in the midst of the confusion, the emir summoned the captain of his guards. Don't be concerned, Sire," shouted the captain, arriving out of breath before his commander. "We'll get them. There's no way they can escape. The only way they can go is east, to the frontier, or else they might try to hide in the city or the forest. In any case we'll catch up with them. It's just a question of time."

"Do you have a plan?"

"Yes. I've divided my men into three groups. One has already left to pursue them along the road into the plain. Another will go around them and alert the border patrols, while a third will do a thorough house to house search in the city. If we don't find them before nightfall I'll organize a search party to comb the forest tomorrow. One way or another they'll be recaptured."

"I hope so. Whatever happens, kill them all except the boy."

"All of them? Even the prince?"

"Yes, I don't want to bother with him. All I want is the boy, alive and intact. Do you understand? No one is to touch a single hair of his head. Tell your men I'll give ten gold *dinanir* to whoever brings him to me safe and sound."

"Sire, your orders will be carried out."

"And this thing here? What are we supposed to do with it?" asked a soldier, poking Harazad's detached head with the tip of his boot.

The emir responded with a careless gesture and turned to enter the palace. After all, once the surprise was over, it was really all for the best. "Hamid," he thought to himself, "you've spared me a major nuisance by getting rid of that miserable little serpent. Otherwise I'd have had to take care of him myself. Tonight I'll sleep in your bed, and soon I'll also have your pretty boy to keep me company. *Makhtub!* So it was written, Hamid, my friend."

The fugitives were galloping across the plain, apparently heading toward the eastern border, the only way to safety, as represented by Abbas' zone of influence. They had thrown away the now useless burnooses. Riding lightly on fast horses they were already far from the palace when their pursuers were just beginning to get organized. The first scattered few who had caught up with them had been eliminated, but not without further losses. When Hamid, still maintaining his galloping pace, counted his men there were only fifteen left besides Hassan and Ahmed, who were riding on either side of Falcon.

At a turn in the road a group of archers resting lazily under some trees saw the riders from afar and without even knowing anything about what had happened sensed they were fleeing enemies.

At an order from their officer they hurriedly nocked their arrows and lined up along the road. Hamid had seen them and he knew there was nothing to do except trust that the horses were fast enough. No order was necessary for Hassan and his son to close in and cover Falcon, while the prince slowed to remain within the group.

The swarm of arrows hit them. Three men were unhorsed and left writhing in the dust. Falcon's mount collapsed with an arrow in his side and the boy barely had time to jump off and avoid being caught in the fall. Hamid, who had brusquely reined in his roan, bent down and seized Falcon, then quickly returned his horse to a full gallop. But Hassan, riding on the edge of the most exposed side, was losing ground and the prince could see with a backward look that he was bleeding profusely from one leg.

"My lord!" shouted Hassan in a strong voice. "By Allah, don't stop! Keep going and may the All-Powerful help you!" Then he slid to the ground.

Ahmed, riding behind him, leaped off his horse and raised his father's head, but it fell back inert. When he saw Hassan was dead he remounted and caught up with his waiting companions. From behind the arm holding him, Falcon turned a desperate face to look one last time at the lifeless man in the dust and his black horse kicking helplessly in the middle of the road. But Hamid did not slow down.

After about a half hour, when he was sure there were no more pursuers behind him, the prince turned into a secondary road and began to observe the forest on either side with great care. As soon as he saw a chance to enter it without leaving a trace, he raised a hand to signal to the others and turned in among the trees. The countryside was deserted. No one had seen them. For a while they rode along with bated breath for fear of an encounter, but little by little their fear diminished and they slowed their horses to a walk. Young Ahmed was stony faced, and all of them showed their tension and fatigue. But it was not yet time to stop. Cautiously, all his senses constantly on the alert, Hamid led them uphill. Only after two more hours, when the trees began to thin out and they came face to face with the steep slope that led to the solid rock mountain wall, only then did the prince order a halt.

Everyone slid off the saddle with a sigh of relief. A few, lightly wounded — the severely injured had been left behind on the road — could finally stanch their bleeding and bandage their wounds. Ahmed clenched his teeth and said nothing. He had lost his beloved father, left his young wife and first-born son in the hands of ruthless enemies. Hamid understood but there was nothing he could do for him except entrust him with the command that had been his father's. Responsibilities mature men. Ahmed was young. He would get over it.

Hamid sat down on a fallen trunk and called his men together.

"Ahmed, do you know where the secret pass is?"

"Yes, Sire."

"Do you see it from here?"

"Yes, it's behind that rock spur. The vegetation must have covered the opening since the last time I was there, but it should be easy to push aside."

"Good. Now I want all of you to listen to me. My plan has succeeded — my task is finished. I've settled accounts with my son. As far as Husain is concerned I regret that I couldn't also punish him with my own hands. But his fate is sealed. Husain is stupid, like all tricksters. He doesn't realize once he gets rid of me the Grand Caliph will take over my lands. And when the emir finds himself the only remaining vassal, the Caliph will get rid of him too. Allah will deal with him. He judges and rewards according to merit. But I must now think about you, who have been faithful to me unto death."

There was a murmur, weak protests of a devotion that needed no affirmation.

"This morning before the attack on the palace" — how long ago that all seemed now and yet the same sun that had shone at noon was now descending in the west — "I told you there was a way to safety. It's a passageway, a kind of tunnel in the rock barely big enough to permit a man on horseback to pass through. It comes out on the other side inside the territory of the Emir Abbas. This is a secret that has been handed down in my family for generations. I was supposed to transmit it to my son but, thanks to the grace of God, I did not. Instead I told Hassan, who was like a brother to me and on my orders he communicated it to his son.

You will therefore follow Ahmed, who will conduct you to safety. You will all present yourselves to Abbas and then Ahmed, it will be up to you to tell him what happened. My cousin is sure to welcome you warmly for your own sakes as well as for the love that exists between him and me. Those among you who have had enough of fighting and would prefer a quiet life from now on will certainly be able to find an honorable position at his court. But if I'm not wrong about you, Ahmed and certain others will want to continue as soldiers. In this case ask Abbas for a safe conduct and embark for Cordoba. The Emir Abd al-Rahman, the last of the Umayyads, will find a use for you. From this moment on, I absolve you of all obligations of personal fidelity to me."

"But, Sire, aren't you coming with us?"

"I'm going somewhere else."

"Then we'll go with you," protested a number of voices.

But Ahmed, who had understood, raised his hand to impose silence, demonstrating his new authority as leader.

"Now," Hamid continued, as if he hadn't heard them, "you'll remain here for a while before you set out for the last upward climb. The sun is still high and you might be spotted by a sentinel. Rest yourselves and rest your horses."

Falcon had remained seated apart, as if the discussion did not concern him. The prince came over, took him by the hand and led him a few paces away.

"Falcon, this is your last chance to make it to safety. You will go with Ahmed, who can protect you until you learn to protect yourself. If you want to remain at Abbas' court, my cousin will see that you have everything you need. And if, instead, you want to go to Cordoba to the Emir Abd al-Rahman perhaps you will even find your own people. You obviously aren't from this country, nor are you descended from these people."

"My lord, you are my country and my people. I won't leave you."

"Do you know where I want to go, Falcon?"

"Yes, my lord, and I'm coming with you."

For the first time Falcon's tone was almost brusque. It was as if the loss of all that was dear to him, the end of his happy little world, had left his love even stronger and more serene. But there were some things that had to be said, painful though they might be.

"Falcon, I can't come with you to the court of Abbas. I would compromise him in the eyes of the Caliph, who probably is not completely exempt from a certain complicity in the plot against me. Nor can I hope to make it to the coast with Ahmed, who will of course not stay on as a court servant to Abbas. Ahmed can get through unnoticed, but I'd be recognized at once and taken prisoner. Even if I did succeed in embarking for Cordoba, what would I do at the court of Abd al-Rahman? In the best possible case I might be a commander in the lower ranks. And that's a position I couldn't accept. There's only one way out for me. Anyhow I've lived a long time and I've lived well. But you are young Falcon. You have your whole life before you."

"You are my life, my lord. I won't leave you."

There was nothing more to say. Hamid had had to make an effort to offer this now-rejected freedom, and perhaps he offered it just because he knew it would never be accepted. There was only one thing he could not bear and that was to have Falcon leave him.

They returned to the group of soldiers. An hour passed, then another. When only the summits of the mountains were still tinged with the rose-colored rays of the setting sun and their slopes were cloaked with violet shadows, Hamid motioned with his hand. The men got up and untied their horses.

"Ahmed," said the prince, calling the young man over to him. "This is my seal." And he slid the large ring off his finger. "This will be your credential wherever you go, whether to Abbas or to Cordoba. Take this purse also. It's the only money I have with me. You should not have to present yourself as a beggar and there's enough here to keep you and your men for quite a while. In addition I want you to have this necklace as a memento of me and of the affection that bound me to your father." He took off the chain of gold and gems he always wore and as Ahmed knelt in front of him, he placed it around his neck. Then each man in turn knelt before him and kissed his hand. When Ahmed knelt in front of Falcon, Falcon raised him up and embraced him. "Ahmed, my brother, I have nothing to give you. Take this to remember me by — it's all I've got." And he tore the gold buckle from his belt and placed it in Ahmed's hands.

"All right now, on your way," ordered Hamid, not wanting them to get too emotional. "It'll be hard to find the entrance to the tunnel in the dark. Get going now, and God be with you!"

"God save you, Sire!"

And the little troop began their ascent.

"Let's wait here a while. I want to be be certain they're out of danger."

They sat down together on a fallen tree trunk.

"Are you tired, Falcon?"

"No, I'm not tired."

Hamid put his arm around the boy's shoulders, pulling him closer and Falcon laid his head on his shoulder. Hamid smoothed the boy's hair in silence, uncovering his neck.

"Falcon, how old are you?"

"According to al-Hakim's calculation — poor Hakim! — I should be fifteen."

The entire mountain slope was now in shadow and they could no longer see the horsemen. Certainly at that moment the resonant voice of the muezzin was descending over the bloodied streets of the tiny capital, imposing the eternal truth of Faith upon human contingencies and calling the people to pray in the words of the *shahadah: "La ilaha illa Allah....*There is no god but Allah...."

Slowly, very slowly, with his right hand, the prince took the dagger from his belt, drew it out of its case with no sound and gripped the handle tightly. It was the same dagger he had used on that long-ago day to make his mark on the face of the child kneeling before him. But he no longer felt the slightest glimmer of that savage impulse of love: he loved now as a defeated man loves.

He looked down at the boy's head, focusing on the point between the neck and shoulders, where the edge of his tunic touched the chestnut curls. Then, all at once, his fingers relaxed, his raised arm dropped and the dagger fell ringing against a stone. Falcon watched it roll away without looking up.

"I can't," said Hamid in a low and stifled voice. "I can't do it, Falcon."

The boy said nothing.

"For the first time in my life I know I ought to do something and I can't do it."

Falcon took hold of the abandoned hand, opened the palm and placed it on his own throat in his old gesture of childish tenderness. "Don't feel bad, my lord."

"I can't leave you alone. I must not leave you in the emir's hands. But I can't kill you. I can easily finish off myself. But not you, Falcon. I can't kill you with my own hands."

The last light lingered among the trees.

"And tomorrow it will be too late. Tomorrow they'll be sending out search parties into the forest and sooner or later they'll take us. They'll make you suffer in order to make me suffer, just the way it was with the poor falcon of my childhood. And this time too I won't be able to defend you."

"No, my lord!" Falcon had looked up suddenly, smiling, his eyes bright with hope. "No, they won't take us. We can still get away together — we can both save ourselves forever!"

The prince looked at him, perplexed.

"Yes, yes my lord, the precipice! I've always known my life would end there. I've always been drawn to it. I couldn't go by myself, but now we can both go — we'll vanish together and no one will ever find us!"

"The precipice!" Hamid felt a wave of relief. "You're right Falcon, you're right. Why didn't I think of it! The precipice will be our salvation. We'll simply disappear and they won't even be able to desecrate our bodies."

"My lord, is it far from here?"

"Maybe an hour or an hour and a half on horseback. We'll have to be careful they don't cut us off. We've still got a little light left, let's make the most of it. Then we'll stop somewhere for the night. It will be too dark for them to find us. And tomorrow at dawn...."

They mounted the roan and the prince guided him cautiously through the forest. As soon as he made out the distant sound he was listening for, he headed in that direction. It was the rippling of the stream that came down the mountainside and fed the waterfall at the precipice. He began to follow it. Every once in a while an impassable ditch or a rock outcrop forced him to detour further downhill, but as soon as he circumvented the obstacle he went back up. When it got too dark to continue he looked for a place to spend the night and chose a spot on the riverbank, a little glade closed in by trees.

Hamid took the saddle off the roan and let him graze nearby. Then he removed his dusty sweaty clothes and refreshed himself in the cold water, splashing it with open palms onto his chest and shoulders. Falcon also took off his tunic and washed his hands and face. Then they shared a handful of dates Hamid found in his saddlebag, spread out the blanket and lay down side by side, covering themselves with their cloaks. At that altitude the night was cool and calm.

Hamid awoke after a few hours of restless sleep. He looked up at the stars overhead: it seemed to be shortly after midnight. A fire stirred in his veins, an uneasy yearning. First there had been the excitement of combat, which exaggerates the sexual instinct in vigorous men and often leads them to violence and rape. Then came the storm of rage and grief at his son's treason, the final terrible anger that unleashed the blow of his sword and the bitter joy of seeing the head roll between his horse's hooves. All this had produced an intense excitement, controlled for the entire day, but now at last ready to explode.

Nor did the thought of his imminent death have any calming effect. His mind accepted death. It was the natural lifelong companion of a warrior prince, an ever-present reality that might be concealed in an assassin's dagger, the rearing of a maddened horse or the stabbing blow of a sword at his back during combat. He had lived with that thought for a long time and he was not afraid of it. But his flesh rebelled. It wanted to possess, to love, to destroy: to live again before the moment of annihilation.

"If only I had Lailah here, just for one last time!" thought the prince. But he knew too well it wasn't the soft body of his favorite he was longing for. It was the body of the boy lying beside him, the body he had desired from the beginning but had always respected because of a mysterious inhibition that now seemed as trivial as the rest of the moral imperatives he had obeyed throughout his life. Now in that supreme moment none of them mattered anymore.

"Falcon," he called in a hoarse voice. "Falcon." And he reached out to touch him. Falcon, already awake, should have been the one to draw close and huddle against his master during this final night, just as he had always done. But he didn't. He moved away instead, retreated. And whereas obvious trust on his part might perhaps have triggered the mature man's habitual protective response, this reluctance exacerbated the prince's urge to dominate and overpower.

He pulled the boy to him, bent over and took his face in his hands, caressing it roughly. In the dim light he could see the eyes dark with fear and he closed them with kisses feeling the eyelashes tremble, imprisoned between his lips. He didn't even hear the boy's moan of protest, but pressed his own mouth over his. That same mouth into which he had once poured all the strength of his soul now became the wellspring of acute sensual pleasure. The shirt of fine cloth fastened at Falcon's neck was in his way. In a single gesture he tore it off, then ripped away the silk sash at the boy's waist and undid the band that held up his trousers. The beautiful body was now unencumbered and at his mercy.

Perhaps if he had sensed the former child still present in the youth, respect for the vulnerability entrusted to his own strength would have held him back. But Falcon was now an adolescent — child, woman and man all in one body — and possessing that body meant satisfying all Hamid's instincts, the combined desires for tenderness, for love, for domination. It meant completing himself in the boy.

For an instant the joy of possession slowed his frenzy. He stroked the youth's throat, still soft with the curves of childhood, which would be so easy to squeeze until its pulsing ceased. He pressed even harder on the already developed pectoral muscles of the wide thorax, sought out the downy warmth of the armpits. Then his hands encircled the supple waist, following the outlines of the hip muscles, palpitated the smooth belly, lingering on the gentle dimpling of the umbilicus and finally, with a lighter and more delicate touch he ran his fingers through the silky public hair.

Suddenly he seized the boy by the waist and turned him over forcefully enough to counter all resistance if there had been any. But even in that impetus he was moved by a pity that increased with the hurt he was inflicting. He was panting with passion yet in a mixture of violence and tenderness he turned Falcon's head to the side so he could breathe, then lightly traced the line along the velvety cheek where the scar had sealed their love. He kissed the ringlets at the back of the neck, still redolent of childhood, ran his fingers along the indentation of the spine already strengthened by virile muscles, then down to the hollow at the base of the back and over the solid round buttocks. He persisted in his caresses, seeking a response in the beloved body that might bring them together in simultaneous fulfillment. But the boy remained inert, and his submissive and afflicted weeping finally reached the man's consciousness, awakening him to full awareness of what he was doing. A cold shudder ran through his entire being and put out the fire in his blood. The turgid thrust of desire collapsed, leaving him weak and empty. He moved away from the boy with an effort, rolled over on his side and lay there exhausted.

After a while he roused himself. But his first relief at thinking nothing irreparable had happened was overcome by shame and desperation. He struggled to his feet, not even daring to look at the denuded young body, took a few wavering steps, then ran into the depths of the wood without seeing where he was going until he stopped against a tree and stood there, his arm leaning on the rough bark and his forehead resting on his arm.

What had he done! True, a merciful God had prevented the ultimate offense but the trust and love of his boy were forever lost. This child, beloved but never fully known to him, who had entered into his life with the sole purpose of conferring upon him a gift of devotion the mystery of which he had never penetrated — this was the being he had debased to an object of pleasure. He had touched him brutally, obscenely. His hands had become the coarse hands of the castrator in Butros' slave emporium. They were the same as the perverted hands of the emir. Now the two of them would never be able to confront the final trial together, the death that would have united them for eternity. The boy who had regarded him as his protector through all those years, had found in him his refuge and his defense against the violence of an alien world, must now see him as his worst enemy.

What was left for him to do? He'd have liked to flee without ever seeing Falcon again, throw himself off the precipice, break his body against the rocks and end it all forever. But the boy, his boy, what would happen to him if he were left alone? Accustomed as he was to Hamid's supporting strength, could he find enough of his own to kill himself? If the emir's men took him alive what would be his fate? A fate for which he, Hamid, would be responsible right down to the last tears and the final drop of blood?

No, he couldn't permit himself the liberation of flight. He had never been a coward — he was not going to become one now. He had to go back and face Falcon, endure his revulsion, which he knew would be rendered even more painful by the absence of reproaches or accusations. He must guide his boy right up to the end and keep his own desperation to himself.

He stirred, retraced his steps, emerged from the darkness of the woods into the clearing under the stars. The boy was still lying down but he had composed himself, put his torn clothes back on. The prince went up to him, paused, hesitating, his heart so tormented with anguish that he would have wept if he had known how. But Falcon, who had seen him coming, lifted his head to look up at him, his face indistinct in the pale light. "Come and get some sleep my lord. It's still a long time until dawn."

The man knelt down in silence, bent over to scrutinize the gray eyes in the starlight and saw that they were calm and compassionate. He lay down beside Falcon under the cloak, being careful not to touch him. But the boy put an arm around his shoulders and pulled him close.

And so they remained in a markedly different embrace from the one that had bound them a short time before. Finally the prince asked softly, "Falcon why didn't you rebel? Why didn't you try to defend yourself from me?"

"I could never rebel against you, my lord. I belong to you. You can do what you want to with me. But that way you'd have lost me forever. We would never have been together, there where we are going."

"I was not myself, Falcon. There was a demon inside me."

"I know, but I couldn't help you. It was your battle. You had to fight it yourself — and you won. Go to sleep now, my lord. You'll need your strength tomorrow."

And this time it was the boy who gently took the man's head in his hands, drew it to his youthful chest and lightly caressed the thick brown hair, murmuring words of comfort. And it was the man who fell asleep consoled while the boy's wakeful eyes watched the slow march of the stars across the sky.

Hamid awoke before dawn. Falcon had finally fallen asleep and seeing him lying there peacefully at his side, he felt a surge of joy, the same joy he'd known that first day when he woke up with the child in his bed.

He got up quietly so as not to disturb Falcon, refreshed himself in the river and recited his morning prayers standing on the pure prayer rug of grass. Yesterday's oppressive feeling of defeat had disappeared. He felt light, freed of the weight of all earthly things except the only one that mattered. He had played his part in life, for good or ill, and it was up to others to continue. Such was God's will. And for the first time in the religion heretofore accepted only by his mind, he experienced that total surrender to God, which is the force of Islam: Allah is powerful. Allah is merciful.

Then he awakened the boy. "Time to get going, Falcon." They had nothing to eat but it didn't matter now. The prince mounted his roan, helped the boy into the saddle in front of him and set off, picking his way carefully among roots and stones. The sun had not yet risen when they reached the open terrain that sloped steeply up toward the precipice. And there, through the silence broken only by the twittering of birds, they first heard voices and the sound of armed men coming from the woods. Turning to look downstream they caught sight of a few scattered horsemen climbing slowly upward along the path. They themselves hadn't yet been seen, but at that very moment one soldier spied the two of them through the trees and let out a yell to alert his companions. Immediately the whole troop converged on the trail with loud and joyful shouts.

The prince took a quick look to see how far they were from the edge of the precipice, where Falcon had stood that day gazing into the abyss, and urged his horse upward. They were almost there when he spoke: "Falcon, are you afraid?"

"Not as long as I'm with you, my lord."

"Falcon, do you remember the day when you were a little boy tied down on the castrator's table and you looked up and saw me and said, 'Take me away with you?'"

"Yes."

"Well, Falcon, now I'm asking you to take me away with you — out there wherever you're going."

"Yes, my lord, you are coming with me and we will be together forever."

Quickly then the boy turned around in the saddle, placed his hands on the prince's shoulders and pulling himself up just far enough, kissed Hamid on the mouth.

They gazed at each other for a moment and for the last time the prince stared deep into those clear eyes where he'd never seen anything but love. Then the boy turned around and Hamid held him even more tightly. "Let's go, Falcon," and he touched the horse's flanks with his spurs.

The emir's men, now a mere hundred paces away, watched as the huge stallion broke into a full gallop toward the precipice, then tried to stop at the last second on the edge, planting his hooves and pulling back his head. For an instant the two riders were silhouetted against the dawn, then nothing.

When the first of the pursuers reached the edge and looked down, the echo of the disastrous plunge still resounded from one rock wall to the other while a veil of water droplets rose slowly from the depths of the abyss.

Thus ended the final battle fought and won by Prince Hamid al-Ghazi.

*This Book Was Completed on July 13, 1997 at
Italica Press, New York, New York &
Was Set in Galliard. It Was Printed
On 60-lb Natural Paper by
BookSurge,
U. S. A./
E. U.
* **

*

Made in the USA
Coppell, TX
19 October 2021